DUST TO DUST

"Darn it, Gleep!" Nunzio said, brushing the powder from his clothes. "Don't do that again, hear me? Next time you might d̶o̶ ̶m̶a̶y̶ ... dust loose ... and look

I had been aro̶ ... ect any thanks, but I ... led for saving his life. ... uld muster, which is c̶ ... and sat with my back to him.

"GLEEP! UP, BOY! GOOD DRAGON! GOOD DRAGON!"

That was more like it. I turned to face him again, only to find him hopping around holding his foot. Not lacking in mental faculties, I was able to deduce that, in making my indignant gesture, I had succeeded in sitting on his lower extremities. It was unintentional, I assure you, as human feet are rather small and my excellent sense of touch does not extend to my posterior, but it did occur to me in hindsight (no pun intended) that it served him right.

He limped over to one of the cartons and sat down, alternately rubbing his foot and brushing his clothes off.

The powder was, of course, the remains of the late intruder/assassin. Number 6 flame has that effect on humans. While human burial rites have always been a source of curiosity and puzzlement to me, I was fairly certain that they did not include having one's cremated remains brushed onto the floor or removed by a laundry service.

—from "Gleep's Tale"

BAEN BOOKS by ROBERT ASPRIN

Myth-Interpretations: The Worlds of Robert Asprin

The Time Scout series with Linda Evans:
Time Scout
Wagers of Sin
Ripping Time
The House That Jack Built

For King and Country (with Linda Evans)

License Invoked (with Jody Lynn Nye)

Myth-Interpretations
The Worlds of Robert Asprin

Robert Asprin
edited by Bill Fawcett

A Baen Books Original

Baen Publishing Enterprises
P.O. Box 1403
Riverdale, NY 10471
www.baen.com

ISBN: 978-1-4516-3753-3

Cover art by Bob Eggleton

Interior art by Phil Foglio

First Baen paperback printing, October 2011

Library of Congress Control Number: 2010029991

Distributed by Simon & Schuster
1230 Avenue of the Americas
New York, NY 10020

Pages by Joy Freeman (www.pagesbyjoy.com)
Printed in the United States of America

Contents

Introduction:
Robert Lynn Asprin's
Short Works

Robert Lynn Asprin mostly preferred to write novels, short ones on occasion, but novels. These let him have more fun with his unique characters and writing with Bob was fun. In his career of almost three decades, he produced just enough short stories to fill this one collection. That is in one way very surprising since he and Lynn Abbey basically changed the nature of short story anthologies forever by creating and editing the first shared world anthology, *Thieves World*.

We have collected here all he wrote, excepting a few of his Thieves World stories. We will leave it to you to go get all of the excellent TW anthologies if you missed them. Among those here are a few unpublished stories we literally found in boxes after we lost Bob. As an added treat we have included a few other treats that you may find fascinating.

The book begins with a copy of the proposal that Bob used to sell to Starblaze Publishing the Myth-Adventures book series. This is followed by several stories he wrote in that pun-filled universe and two Bob cowrote with his longtime friend and collaborator, Jody Lynn Nye. Next you will find an unpublished story, stories from other anthologies Bob wrote for, then the script from the fandom-notorious slide show *The Capture*, generously illustrated with four new cartoons from his longtime collaborator Phil Foglio, and then another fun script, *The Ultimate Weapon*.

"The Saga of the Dark Horde" will give you insight into Bob as one of the founders of the Society for Creative Anachronism's most infamous groups. If you can be any type from the Middle Ages, why be a knight, when you can be a Mongol? As Yang the Nauseating, Bob was the Dark Horde's Great Khan for many Tullamore Dew–filled years. It is hard to forget his smile as he led a swarm of highly armed members of the "loyal opposition" into a room full of elegantly garbed recreationists and bowed elegantly to the kings and queens of the SCA. He then loudly pronounced his infamous greeting of "With All Due Disrespect Your Majesties."

The book almost ends with Bob's first serious novella, written while he was being mentored by the great Gordon Dickson, *Cold Cash War*. This dark story featuring world corporations gone bad still rings amazingly true thirty-five years later. This is the novella as it originally appeared in the August 1977 *Analog* magazine. It was later expanded into a book, as was the formerly unpublished Tambu piece. The final stories are very Bob Asprin, being a romp full of space fleets and some serious double-dealing. As the amazingly eclectic table of contents shows, like Robert Lynn Asprin was himself, his stories are always fun, but never predictable.

—Bill Fawcett 2009

The Myth-Adventures: The Original Proposal

TO BE WRITTEN BY
ROBERT LYNN ASPRIN

An outrageously tongue-in-cheek series tracing the haps and mis-haps of a young sorcerer named Skeeve and his brusque demon-mentor, Aahz (no relation). In the course of their travels, they lampoon every done-to-death plot of action-adventure-fantasy literature and cinema.

Book 1: *Another Fine Myth* — Our heroes meet for the first time and pool their meager talents to stop a mad master magician who is out to rule the dimensions.

Book 2: *Myth Conceptions* — A battalion couldn't take that position, but a few, hand-picked, well-trained men ... At Aahz's insistence, Skeeve accepts a position as Court Magician at the down-at-the-heels kingdom of Posseltum. Too late, they discover that the job includes defending the kingdom—specifically against the oncoming might of a massive Roman legion-type army. At a McDonald's in another dimension, the pair recruit a force of their own, consisting of a Trollup assassin, an Imp who has lost his powers, an aging

3

Archer, a Gargoyle with his salamander sidekick, and a Gremlin. Of course, nobody warned them that the opposing army is funded by an organized crime syndicate.

Book 3: *Myth Direction* — A blend of the Master Heist, the Great Escape, and the Big Game. A shopping trip through the dimensions in search of a birthday present for Aahz goes awry, forcing our heroes to organize a team to compete in a three-way game which is best described as rugby played for keeps.

Book 4: *Hit or Myth* — A medieval War Against the Mafia. Remember the organized crime syndicate from Book 2? Well, they're looking for Skeeve with a vengeance, and this time he has to handle it on his own—Aahz is back visiting his home on Perv and completely incommunicado.

Hit or Myth

Troubles in Perv require that Aahz return to his home dimension, separating him from Skeeve for the first time since their initial meeting.

It couldn't have happened at a worse time.

The organized crime loan sharks arrive in Posseltum looking for a) their pet army, which has mysteriously disappeared, and b) the magician named Skeeve who was responsible for the disappearance—but not necessarily in that order.

Torn between his duty to protect king and kingdom and his more rational desire to hide until Aahz gets back, Skeeve settles on a compromise. He sends the king into hiding and masks his own identity behind royal robes to deal with the intruders. His charade is jeopardized, and eventually ruined, by the early arrival of the real king's bride-to-be.

His ruse discovered, Skeeve must solve the problems himself without the assistance or guidance of his mentor. In desperation, he strikes a bargain with the mob: an army for a world. To protect his friends in the mob's now-disbanded army, Skeeve trades their freedom for passage into another dimension—one ripe for the mob's brand of gentle plunder. Everybody's happy.

Then Aahz comes back.

Fast on his heels arrives a delegation from another dimension (guess which one) seeking the aid of the renowned magician Skeeve to save them from a criminal invasion. Of course, they offer a sizable fee for this service. Of course, Aahz accepts the commission. Of course, this puts Skeeve back in trouble up to his ears.

All he has to do is successfully move against the gangsters without a) endangering the friends he was protecting originally, b) breaking his promise to the gangsters, or c) letting his new employers know that *he* was the source of their newfound problem. That's all.

Under the best of circumstances, the assignment would be nearly impossible. Unfortunately, Skeeve is not working under the best of circumstances—Aahz has decided that his apprentice needs a helping hand.

Myth-Adventurers

ROBERT LYNN ASPRIN

"I'm sorry, Pookie. I just don't get it. Maybe I'm slow."

"Don't apologize, dear," her companion said. "It doesn't go with being a lady. And as far as being slow...well, little sister, trust me. You needn't have an worries on that score."

Even a casual observer would realize in an instant that the two women weren't really sisters. One was a human female, a Klahd, actually, with a short unruly head of hair framing her fierce expression. The female on the opposite side of the table had obviously emerged from an entirely different gene pool. Instead of pink skin, she was covered with the green scales, offset by pointed ears and yellow eyes, that marked her to any experienced dimension traveler as a Pervert...or Pervect if they knew what was good for them. Still, they both had that lithe, athletic, graceful look that put one in mind of a pair of lionesses discussing a kill. Different genotypes or not, it was clear they had more in common with each other than with many of their own species.

If their builds and manner weren't enough of a giveaway, their outfits completed the picture. The Pervect, Pookie, was wearing one of her favorite action leather jumpsuits with multiple zippers which both insured a skin tight fit and held the tools of her trade. The Klahd, Spyder, was still working on her look, but today had settled for calf-high boots with fishnet stockings, a dark plaid mini-skirt, and a sleeveless black leather halter top which left considerable portions of her midriff bare. All in all, she looked like a parochial schoolgirl gone Goth gone biker slut. What united their outfits were the accessories, which was to say the weapons. Throwing stars and knife hilts jutted from their sleeves and belts, along with various mysterious instruments a viewer hoped they would never see close enough to examine carefully.

The fact that this mismatched duo and their weaponry went practically unnoticed was an indication of the normal atmosphere and clientele of the tavern they were ensconced in.

"If I'm not slow, then why is it taking me so long to figure out this whole adventurer thing?" Spyder countered.

"Well, not to make too big a thing of it," Pookie said, "for one thing you're still young. I've been at this game for a couple centuries . . . we'll not dwell on exactly how many . . . and you've only been at it for a few months. It takes a while to get the hang of anything new. Just be patient and listen to your big sister."

"I guess it's just not what I was expecting is all," Spyder said, almost to herself.

"Really?" her green companion said. "Maybe we've been going at this backwards. This time, why don't you explain to me what it was you thought adventuring involved."

"I don't know. I was thinking we'd be doing body-guard work or something."

Pookie heaved a sigh.

"We've gone over this before, little sister. First of all, we don't have the manpower to do real bodyguard work. To do the job right, it takes at least a six person team to guard someone around the clock. You keep forgetting that we'd have to sleep sometime."

"But Guido and Nunzio guard Skeeve as a two man team," Spyder insisted stubbornly.

"From what I understand, They were assigned to Skeeve by Don Bruce primarily as an honor guard," Pookie said. "Besides, there are a lot more people on the team watching over Skeeve than just Guido and Nunzio."

"But..."

"...And even if we were to hire on as a token show force, believe me, you wouldn't like it," Pookie continued. "Remember, we're female, and like it or not that influences the people who hire us. Believe me, the kind of swell headed, self-centered celebrity types who hire female body guards are primarily looking for arm candy. The pay might look good, but they're not really people you want to hang around for any length of time. Usually, by the end of the job, you're ready to kill them yourself."

"So what is it exactly that adventurers do?" Spyder said.

Her green companion took a long swallow from the flagon.

"If you scrape away the bardic lyrics and all the escapist literature romantics, what it all boils down to is that basically adventurers are either thieves or killers...or both."

Spyder leaned back and blinked.

"How's that again?"

"Look at it close." Pookie shrugged. "If you're going after a treasure or artifact, it means you're taking it away from someone who think's it's theirs . . . even if they stole it themselves originally. That's stealing. Even if you're unearthing or re-discovering a long lost item, by law it belongs to whoever's property it is that you're on at the time. If you don't hand it over and maybe settle for a reward, if you try to smuggle it out without admitting you've found anything, that's still stealing."

"On the other hand, there's the 'slay the monster/bandit who is terrorizing the neighborhood,' or the traditional 'rescue the princess/damsel for the evil whoever.' Both of those bluntly involve killing."

"Um . . . Pookie?" Spyder said slowly. "If those are really the choices, I think I'd rather do thieving assignments if we can manage it. I mean, I try to be tough and put on a good front, but I really don't think of myself as a killer."

"If you say so." Pookie shrugged. "I'll keep it in mind. Personally, I lean toward the killing side, myself. There's usually less risk involved."

"Now, I'm not saying you're wrong," Spyder said, "but Skeeve and his M.Y.T.H. Inc. crew don't seem to fit with what you're saying."

"Don't forget that crew is pretty much top of the heap right now," Pookie said. "As near as I can tell, it's taken them over ten years to work their way up into the position they're in, where people come to them with work. I'll bet you, though, if you look closely at some of their early work, it involved things that wouldn't stand up to close scrutiny. For example, I know for a fact that Tananda was primarily an assassin before she hooked up with Skeeve. And as for Aahz... I probably shouldn't speak ill of my own cousin, but he's always been one of the family's black sheep. If anything, I was surprised to find out he was involved in something that was even vaguely legitimate."

"I guess you're right," Spyder sighed. "Even Skeeve had to start somewhere. Of course, he had a Pervect for a trainer."

"Don't forget, little sister," Pookie said, winking, "so do you. I'm not one to brag, but if I can't teach you as well or better than Aahz taught Skeeve, I'll hang it up. If nothing else, I think I've got better material to work with from the get go."

"Thanks, Pookie." Spyder smiled. "That means a lot to me."

"Don't mention it," Pookie said, holding up her flagon for her companion to clink with. "If nothing else, it beats the military gig you just got clear of."

"No question there." Spyder nodded.

She took a long pull of her own drink, then set it on the table with a decisive thump.

"So, how do we go about looking for work?"

Pookie cocked her head in surprise.

"Why, exactly what we're doing now. What did you think we were doing?"

"The same thing we've been doing for the last month." Spyder shrugged. "Sitting around a tavern and drinking. Frankly, I've been wondering when we were going to get started adventuring."

Pookie held her hand over her eyes for a few long moments before responding.

"Look, dear," she said finally, "remember what I was saying about us being pretty much criminals? Well, the old adage that 'Crime does not pay' is actually a shortened form of 'Crime does not pay well.' Well, in our line of work, that means that either you do a lot of little jobs . . . which ups the odds of something going wrong . . . or a few big jobs and live on the proceeds between."

"So what does that have to do with us sitting around a tavern?" Spyder frowned.

"I'm coming to that. Now, there's primarily two ways of finding work. Either we roam around and try to pick up a rumor or situation that takes our fancy, or we sit in one place and let the information come to us. Taverns in general are gold mines of information, and ones like this that cater to dimension travelers of all types are prime places to hear about a specific caper."

She glanced toward the door.

"Speaking of which, here comes a likely prospect now. Let me take the lead here. Little sister."

Spyder turned to follow Pookie's gaze.

Just inside the door, steadying himself on the back of a chair, was a warrior. His chain mail, helmet, and sword marked him as such, even though the body that was wearing it was rotund and hairy, topped with a head that sported a pig snout and tusks. Also noticeable was the fact that his left arm was in a sling and he moved with a noticeable limp.

"Care to join us, friend?" Pookie said, raising her voice. "You look like you could use a drink and some sympathetic company."

The newcomer studied them for a moment, then shrugged and lurched his way over to their table.

"Thank's for the invite," he said, dropping heavily into a seat. "It's more than I expected. Whoever said 'No one likes a loser' sure knew what they were talking about."

"First things first," Pookie said and waved the barmaid over.

After another round had been ordered and delivered, including a large flagon of ale for the guest, the three settled into conversation.

"Thanks again," the warrior said, taking a long draught from his flagon. "Truth to tell, I was trying to decide between having a drink or getting a room. The war chest is about tapped out after paying the healers. By the way, the name's Trog."

"Pookie and Spyder here," Pookie said, indicating who was who with a wave of her hand. "Looks like you're coming off a rough job."

"Darn near got my head handed to me." Trog said, taking another drink. "Sounded easy going in, but they all do until you're up against it."

"What was the job, anyway?" Pookie said. "You look to me like someone who could handle most anything and anybody."

"It was one of those 'Kill or scare off the beast that's terrorizing the countryside' deals," Trog explained. "This time around, it was a Hefalump. Never tangled with one before, but like you say, I can handle most things without much problem."

"Don't tell me, let me guess," Pookie said. "No money up front. Just a reward if you're successful. Right?"

"Got it in one," The warrior confirmed. "That's where the 'It always looks easy going in' part caught up with me."

"Where was this anyway? Around here or another dimension?"

Trog leaned back in his seat and studied them with narrowed eyes.

"Not to sound ungrateful," he said carefully, "but you're asking a lot of questions. More than one might expect from casual curiosity. What's you're interest in all this?"

"It's no big secret." Pookie shrugged. "We're in the same line of work as you and looking for a job. Since it sounds like your last find is still open and from the looks of things you won't be up to trying it again for a while, we might just look into it ourselves if the pay's right."

Trog set his flagon down with a loud think.

"And what makes you think two females could pull it off when I couldn't?" he demanded.

"For one thing, as you pointed out, there are two of us." Pookie smiled. "And don't down check us because we're female. We've been around for a while and are still here. A lot who went up against us aren't."

Trog started to say something, the stopped and cocked his head.

"Wait a minute," he said. "A Klahd and a Pervect working together? Are you two Aahz and Skeeve?"

Spyder choked on her drink.

"Right lineage, wrong gender," Pookie said. "Like I said, we're Spyder and Pookie. We know Aahz and Skeeve, though."

"You do?" Trog said, visibly impressed.

"Yeah. We worked with them on our last job," Spyder put in, wiping her chin.

"Let me handle this, little sister," Pookie said with a warning glance. "Since you seem to have heard of them, Trog, you should know that if we can hold our own free-lancing with the M.Y.T.H. Inc. crew, we might stand a chance with your Hefalump."

"Got to agree with you there," Trog said. "That gang has be tough rep."

"So where is the job you were talking about?"

"It's on a backwater dimension. Rinky-dink."

"That bad, huh?"

"No. That's the name of the dimension. Rinky-dink. I'll give you directions if you'll spot me another round."

"Really, Spyder, dear," Pookie said, "You have to be more careful about what you say and who you say it to."

"But I didn't say anything!" Spyder protested. "I did what you told me. I kept my mouth shut and let you take the lead."

"... Except when you mentioned that we had done out last job with Aahz and Skeeve," her companion pointed out.

"What's wrong with that?" Spyder said. "He seemed really impressed. Besides, you were the one who mentioned that we knew them."

"That we knew them. Not that we had just worked with them," Pookie pointed out. "Think about it. The reason he was impressed is that Skeeve's crew has a rep for drawing the high end, high pay jobs."

"So?"

"... So if we just worked with them, then it's not too big of a logic step to figure that we've got more than a bit of money on us. Not exactly the wisest thing to mention in front of an adventurer who just botched a job and is admittedly short of cash."

Spyder stopped short.

"You mean he might have tried to take it away from us?"

"There's always that chance," Pookie said with a shrug. "I believe I mentioned that most adventurers are some form of thief. Not to worry, though. I kept an eye behind us when we left the tavern. He doesn't seem to be following us."

Spyder threw a quick glance behind them. Obviously, the possibility of them being followed hadn't occurred to her until just now. Pookie pretended not to notice.

"Well . . . we probably could have taken him if he tried anything," she said with firm confidence.

"Probably," Pookie agreed. "Still, there's no need to stir up trouble unnecessarily. Remember we're professionals, dear. We're not supposed to fight for free. Ah! This should be the place just ahead."

Spyder hung back, slowing her pace.

"Explain to me again, Pookie. Why is it we're going to talk to the sheriff?"

"Since we're pretty much legit this time around, it doesn't hurt to check in with the local law," her partner said.

"Never did like talking to the law." Spyder scowled. "It doesn't ever seem to work out to my advantage. In fact, I usually end up in trouble."

"That might be because you were usually in trouble before you talked to them," Pookie said, sweetly. "Look at it this way, little sister. From what we've heard this job is going to involve us working the countryside. That's never been my favorite setting, since it's invariably full of things that go squish when you step on them and bite you when you're trying to sleep.

If at all possible, I'd like to know what or who else will be out there with us. All we need is a bunch of trigger happy bounty hunters that let fly at anything that moves. The sheriff here should be able to supply us with that information if we ask him nice. So smile pretty and let me take the lead again."

The office they entered was small and cluttered, with empty wineskins and half-eaten plates of food scattered here and there. It was dominated, though, by the sheriff.

He was stocky with a noticeable bulge around his waist line, and outfitted in a wrinkled ranger uniform that looked like he slept in it. That suspicion was easily confirmed by the fact that he was currently sitting behind his desk with his head down on his arms, snoring nasally.

Spyder looked at Pookie with her eyebrows raised. Her partner responded with a shrug and a roll of her eyes before clearing her throat.

"Um...Excuse me. Sheriff? Are you the sheriff?"

The man lurched upright, blinking dazedly. He did a slight double-take when he realized the nature of his company and wiped a grubby hand over his face and beard, forcing a smile.

"Sorry," he mumbled. "Long night and a slow day. So...What can I do to help you...ladies?"

"We've heard that you've been having some problems with a Hefalump," Pookie said. "Thought we might give a shot at going after it...if the price is right."

"You have to take that up with the Duc," the sheriff yawned. "He's the one putting up the reward. I can tell you the money's good, though. Enough to draw a small troop of sell-swords trying to collect it."

"The Duc?"

"He's the one who runs the territory around here. Actually, his name is Duke Rybred, but most folks call him the Duc on account of the way he's built. He pretty much stays on his estate just north of the town and leaves the tax collecting and keeping of order to me and my deputies."

"If you don't mind my asking," Pookie said carefully, "why isn't he having you and your deputies take care of this Hefalump instead of advertising for outside help?"

"What me? Go traipsing around the woods chasing some huge critter that's only bothering the farmers?" the sheriff seemed actually surprised at the thought. "That wasn't what we were hired for. I'm more than happy to leave it to the young bloods who are out to make a name for themselves."

"Anyone out there ahead of us right now?"

"Naw," the sheriff said, scratching his beard. "Last one came back and left a couple days ago. There were a fair number parading through here for a while, but it's kind of petered out lately. Guess the word has gotten out that the Hefalump is tougher than anyone thought and doesn't take kindly to anyone trying to shoo it away."

Pookie looked at Spyder who shrugged in return.

"Well, I guess we'll go talk to the Duc ... Duke now," the Pervect said. "Any tips you can give us on handling the Hefalump?"

The sheriff thought for a moment.

"Take extra bandages," he said finally. "And be sure your insurance is paid up."

❖   ❖   ❖

If the sheriff was unimpressive, the Duke of Rybred was positively underwhelming.

Whereas the sheriff had been stocky with a bit of a pot belly, the Duc was short and pudgy. He also walked with a rolling waddle that made him look... well, like a duck. Though he dressed well, he had a habit of rubbing his hands together and licking his lips like a miser with an unexpected tax refund. It left one with a feeling one should count one's fingers after shaking hands... if one cared to shake hands at all.

"Well, well, well," he said, licking his lips and rubbing his hands together. "If nothing else, you two are the most attractive adventurers to try our little quest. Tell you what. Instead of going after the Hefalump and maybe getting your sweet selves dinged up or killed, what would you say to hiring on as my personal bodyguards? It would only be for public appearances... though I'm sure we would work out some kind of a bonus program for overtime."

"I think we'll take our chances with the Hefalump," Pookie said. "That was for five hundred in gold. Right?"

"That's right," the Duc said, apparently unaffected by the rejection. "Five hundred once the beast is killed or scared off. Now you two girls be careful when you go after it."

"You have no idea how careful we can be." Pookie smiled. "For example, how do we know we'll get out money after we've killed the critter?"

The Duc's smile wavered a little.

"Why because I've told you I'll pay you. Surely you don't doubt my word?"

"Not yours specifically," Pookie said. "Still, it isn't entirely unheard of that an adventurer has taken on some dangerous assignment only to find that when it was over, whoever hired him had a sudden memory lapse as to the exact amount promised. Some have even forgotten that payment was promised at all. On the off chance that something like that happened to us, we don't have much recourse. I mean, what can we do? Sue you? As I understand it you're the one who sits in judgement around here. We couldn't forcibly take it from you without having to face your household guards who, of course, would be on the alert at that time. Even if we got mad and just killed you, that still wouldn't get us our money. See what I mean?"

"Yes. I can see where that would be a problem," the Duc said, avoiding their eyes.

"Now, we don't mind risking our necks for money," Pookie said. "That's our business. It's just that we'd like some kind of assurance that we'll actually get our money at the end of it."

"What do you suggest?"

"Put it in escrow," Pookie said with a shrug. "Send the money to... say, the sheriff to hold until the job's over. We check with him, make sure the money's there and waiting for us, then we go after your Hefalump."

"That's fine by me," the Duc said, licking his lips. "I'll be glad when this situation is handled, believe me. As far as I'm concerned, the beast could go on doing its thing. It didn't bother anybody until they expanded their fields into his territory. If the farmers hadn't threatened to withhold their taxes until I did something about it, I would have just ignored the whole thing."

"Part of the price of ruling, I guess," Pookie said. "So, if we're in agreement, we'll drop by the sheriff's...

say, tomorrow to check on the reward. Then we'll be on our way."

"...496...497...498...499...500! It's all here."

Pookie waved at her junior partner as she poured yet another flagon of wine for the sheriff.

"I gotta hand it to you two," the sheriff said, raising the flagon in a mock toast. "I always thought the Duc was clever, but you've got him beat. 'Put the money in escrow.' I tell you with all the sell-swords and adventurers that have come through here, no one else has come up with that move."

"We've just had a little more experience with money grubbers than most." Pookie smiled, sipping at her own drink.

"Umm...can I ask a question?" Spyder said.

"You not only can, you may," her companion said.

"Huh?"

"Never mind." Pookie waved. "What's the question?"

"Well, you keep talking about how clever the Duc is." Spyder frowned. "I wasn't all that impressed with him."

"Bit of a scum bag, isn't he," Pookie said with a grimace. "Do you see what I mean about the offers female bodyguards get?"

"So what makes him so clever?"

"You have to learn to listen closer, dear," Pookie said. "The Duc had no intention of paying us...or anyone else regardless of the failure or success."

"He didn't?"

"Add up the pieces," Pookie said, counting off the points on her fingers. "First, the farmers try to expand their holdings and run into a local critter, the Hefalump, that takes offense at their trespassing. Second, by his own admission, the Duc would have ignored it, but the farmers threatened to withhold their tax monies unless he did something. His response was to offer a reward to anyone who would kill or scare off the beast."

Spyder frowned thoughtfully, then shook her head.

"So what's wrong with that?"

"Nothing's wrong with it," Pookie said. "It's actually very clever. He had to do something, so what he did was make an offer. A move that cost him no money or effort. Simply by making the offer, he kept the farmers paying taxes."

". . . And if anyone were actually successful going up against the Hefalump, he could renege on the payment and it still cost him nothing," Spyder finished. "That is kind of clever. But we outfoxed him with this escrow thing. Huh."

"Not really." Pookie shrugged. "Remember the sheriff here answers to the Duc. That's why the Duc agreed so readily. Tell me, sheriff, were your instructions to send the money back as soon as we went after the Hefalump, or were you supposed to wait until tomorrow?"

Silence answered her.

"Hey! He's asleep!" Spyder said.

"Yes," Pookie said without looking. "And with what I put in his drink, he should be out until well after midnight."

She rose to her feet and stretched.

"So, little sister, gather up that lovely gold and we'll be on our way."

"What?" Spyder exclaimed. "You mean we're just

going to take the gold without going after the Hefalump at all? But that's..."

"...Stealing," Pookie said. "If you want to pretty it up, the Duc was ready to swindle adventurers by taking advantage of their short sightedness. We're just returning the favor. Remember I told you that adventurers are thieves or killers...and you specifically said that, if possible, you'd rather be a thief?"

She paused and considered the sleeping sheriff.

"Of course, if you've changed your mind, we could slit his throat on the way out."

"But won't they come after us?"

"And admit that they've been flim-flamed? By a couple females?" Pookie smiled. "I doubt it. Even if they do, they don't even have our names when it comes to tracking us down. Looking for a Klahd and a Pervect, they'd be lucky if they didn't run smack into Aahz and Skeeve."

Gleep's Tale

Robert Lynn Asprin

Inevitably, when conversing with my colleagues of the dragon set, and the subject of pets was raised, an argument would ensue as to the relative advantages and disadvantages of humans as pets. Traditionally, I have maintained a respectful silence during such sessions, being the youngest member in attendance and therefore obligated to learn from my elders. This should not, however, be taken as an indication that I lack opinions on the subject. I have numerous well-developed theories, which is the main reason I welcomed the chance to test them by acquiring a subject as young and yet as well-traveled as Skeeve was when I first encountered him. As my oration unfolds, you will note . . . but I'm getting ahead of myself. First things first is the order of business for organized and well-mannered organisms. I am the entity you have come to know in these volumes as . . .

"Gleep! C'mere, fella."

That is Nunzio. He is neither organized nor well-mannered. Consequently, as is so often the case when dealing with Skeeve and his rather dubious collection of associates, I chose to ignore him. Still, an interesting point has been raised, so I had probably best address it now before proceeding.

As was so rudely pointed out, I am known to this particular batch of humans, as well as to the readers of these volumes, simply as Gleep. For the sake of convenience, I will continue to identify myself to you by that name, thereby eliminating the frustrating task of attempting to instruct you in the pronunciation of my *real* name. Not only am I unsure you are physically able to reproduce the necessary sounds, but there is the fact that I have limited patience when it comes to dealing with humans. Then, too, it is customary for dragons to adopt aliases for these cross-phylum escapades. It saves embarrassment when the human chroniclers distort the facts when recording the incidents...which they invariably do.

If I seem noticeably more coherent than you would expect from my reputed one-word vocabulary, the reason is both simple and logical. First, I am still quite young for a dragon, and the vocal cords are one of the last things to develop in regard to our bodies. While I am quite able to converse and communicate with others of my species, I have another two hundred years before my voice is ready to attempt the particular combination of sounds and pitches necessary to converse extensively with humans in their own tongue.

As to my mental development, one must take into consideration the vast differences in our expected lifespan. A human is considered exceptional to survive for a hundred years, whereas dragons can live for thousands of years without being regarded as old by their friends and relations. The implications of this are too numerous to count, but the one which concerns us here is that, while I am perhaps young for a dragon, I am easily the oldest of those who affiliate themselves with Skeeve. Of course, humans tend to lack the breeding and upbringing of my kind, so they are far less inclined to heed the older and wiser heads in their midst, much less learn from them.

"Hey, Gleep! Can you hear me? Over here, boy."

I made a big show of nibbling on my foot as if troubled by an itch. Humans as a whole seem unable to grasp the subtleties of communication which would allow them to ascertain when they are being deliberately ignored, much less what it implies. Consequently, I have devised the technique of visibly demonstrating I am preoccupied when confronted with a particularly rude or ignorant statement or request. This not only serves to silence their yammerings, it slows the steady erosion of my nerves. To date, the technique yields about a twenty percent success ratio, which is significantly better than most tactics I have attempted. Unfortunately, this did not prove to be one of those twenty percenters.

"I'm talkin' ta *you*, Gleep. Now are ya gonna go where I tell ya or not?"

While I am waiting for my physical development to enable me to attempt the language of another species, I have serious doubts that Nunzio or Guido will master their *native* tongue, no matter how much time they are allowed. Somehow it reminds me of a tale one of my aunts used to tell about how she encountered a human in a faraway land and inquired if he were a native. "I ain't no native!" she was told. "I was born right here!" I quite agree with her that the only proper response when confronted by such logic was to eat him.

Nunzio was still carrying on in that squeaky little-boy voice of his which is so surprising when one first hears it, except now he had circled around behind me and was trying to push me in the direction he had indicated earlier. While he is impressively strong for a human, I outweighed him sufficiently that I was confident that there was no chance he could move me until I decided to cooperate. Still, his antics were annoying, and I briefly debated whether it was worth trying to improve his manners by belting him with my tail. I decided against it, of course. Even the strongest humans are dangerously frail and vulnerable, and I did not wish to distress Skeeve by damaging one of his playmates. A trauma like that could set my pet's training program back years.

Right about then, I observed that Nunzio's breathing had become labored. Since he had already demonstrated his mental inflexibility, I grew concerned that he might suffer a heart attack before giving up his impossible task. Having just reminded myself of the undesirability of his untimely demise, I decided I would have to humor him.

Delaying just long enough for a leisurely yawn, I rose and ambled in the indicated direction...first sliding sideways a bit so that he fell on his face the next time he threw his weight against me. I reasoned that if he wasn't sturdy enough to survive a simple fall, then my pet was better off without his company.

Fortunately or un-, depending on your point of view, he scrambled rapidly to his feet and fell in step beside me as I walked.

"I want youse to familiarize yourself with the shipment which we are to be protectin'," he said, still breathing hard, "then wander around the place a little so's yer familiar with the layout."

This struck me as a particularly silly thing to do. I had sized up the shipment and the layout within moments of our arrival, and I had assumed that Nunzio had done the same. There simply wasn't all that much to analyze.

The warehouse was nothing more than a large room...four walls and a ceiling with rafters from which a scattered collection of lights poured down sufficiently inadequate light as to leave large pockets of shadows through the place. There was a small doorway in one wall, and a large sliding door in another, presumably leading to a loading dock. Except for the shipment piled in the center of the room, the place was empty.

The shipment itself consisted of a couple dozen boxes stacked on a wooden skid. From what my nose could ascertain, whatever was inside the boxes consisted of paper and ink. Why paper and ink should be valuable enough to warrant a guard I neither knew nor cared. Dragons do not have much use for paper...particularly paper money. Flammable currency is not our idea of a sound investment for a society. Still, someone must have felt the shipment to be of some worth, if not the human who had commissioned our services, then definitely the one dressed head to foot in black who was creeping around in the rafters.

All of this had become apparent to me as soon as we had entered the warehouse, so there was no reason to busy oneself with make-work additional checks. Nunzio, however, seemed bound and determined to prod me into rediscovering what I already knew. Even allowing for the fact that the human senses of sight, hearing, taste, touch, and smell are far below those of dragons, I was nonetheless appalled at how little he was able to detect on his own. Perhaps if he focused less of his attention on me and more on what was going on around us, he would have fared better. As it was, he was hopeless. If Skeeve was hoping that Nunzio would learn something from me, which was the only reason I could imagine for including him on the assignment, my pet was going to be sorely disappointed. Other than the fact that he seemed to try harder than most humans to interact positively with dragons, however crude and ignorant his attempts might be, I couldn't imagine why I was as tolerant of him as I was.

Whoever it was in the rafters was moving closer now. He might have been stealthy for a human, but my ears tracked him as easily as if he were banging two pots together as he came. While I was aware of his presence two steps through the door, I had been uncertain as to his intentions and therefore had been willing to be patient until sure whether he were simply an innocent bystander, or if he indeed entertained thoughts of larceny. His attempts to sneak up on us confirmed to me he was one of the latter ilk, however incompetent he might be at it.

Trying to let Nunzio benefit from my abilities, I swiveled my head around and pointed at the intruder with my nose.

"Pay attention, Gleep!" my idiot charge said, jerking my muzzle down toward the boxes again. "This is what we're supposed to be guardin'. Understand?"

I understood that either humans were even slower to learn than the most critical dragons gave them credit for, which I was beginning to believe, or this particular specimen was brain-damaged, which was also a possibility. Rolling my eyes, I check on the intruder again.

He was nearly above us now, his legs spread wide supporting his weight on two of the rafters. With careful deliberation, he removed something from within his sleeve, raised it to his mouth, and pointed it at us.

Part of the early training of any dragon is a series of lessons designed to impart a detailed knowledge of human weapons. This may sound strange for what is basically a peace-loving folk, but we consider it to be simple survival ... such as humans instructing their young that bees sting or fire is hot. Regardless of our motivations, let it suffice to say that I was as cognizant of human weapons as any human, and considerably more so than any not in the military or other heroic vocations, and as such had no difficulty at identifying the implement being directed at us as a blowgun.

Now, in addition to having better sense, dragons have armor which provides substantially more protection than humans enjoy from their skin. Consequently, I was relatively certain that whatever was set to emerge from the business end of the blowgun would not pose a threat to my well-being. It occurred to me, however, that the same could not be said for Nunzio and, as I have said before, I have qualms about going to some lengths to ensure my pet's peace of mind by protecting his associates.

Jerking my head free from Nunzio's grasp, I took quick aim and loosed a burst of #6 flame. Oh, yes. Dragons have various degrees of flame at their disposal, ranging from "toast a marshmallow" to "make a hole

in rock." You might keep that in mind the next time
you consider arguing with a dragon.

Within seconds of my extinguishing the pyrotechnics,
a brief shower of black powder drifted down on us.

"Darn it, Gleep!" Nunzio said, brushing the powder from his clothes. "Don't do that again, hear me?
Next time you might do more than knock some dust
loose . . . and look at my clothes! Bad dragon!"

I had been around humans enough not to expect
any thanks, but I found it annoying to be scolded
for saving his life. With as much dignity as I could
muster, which is considerable, I turned and sat with
my back to him.

"GLEEP! UP, BOY! GOOD DRAGON! GOOD
DRAGON!"

That was more like it. I turned to face him again,
only to find him hopping around holding his foot. Not
lacking in mental faculties, I was able to deduce that,
in making my indignant gesture, I had succeeded in
sitting on his lower extremities. It was unintentional,
I assure you, as human feet are rather small and my
excellent sense of touch does not extend to my posterior, but it did occur to me in hindsight (no pun
intended) that it served him right.

"Look, you just sit there and I'll sit over here and
we'll get along fine. Okay?"

He limped over to one of the cartons and sat down,
alternately rubbing his foot and brushing his clothes off.

The powder was, of course, the remains of the late
intruder/assassin. #6 flame has a tendency to have that
effect on humans, which is why I used it. While human
burial rights have always been a source of curiosity
and puzzlement to me, I was fairly certain that they

did not include having one's cremated remains brushed onto the floor or removed by a laundry service. Still, considering my difficulty in communicating a simple "look out" to Nunzio, I decided it would be too much effort to convey to him exactly what he was doing.

If my attitude toward killing a human seems a bit shocking in its casualness, remember that to dragons humans are an inferior species. You do not flinch from killing fleas to ensure the comfort of your dog or cat, regardless of what the surviving fleas might think of your callous actions, and I do not hesitate to remove a bothersome human who might cause my pet distress by his actions. At least we dragons generally focus on individuals as opposed to the wholesale slaughter of species humans seem to accept as part of their daily life.

"You know, Gleep," Nunzio said, regarding me carefully, "after a while in your company, even Guido's braggin' sounds good...but don't tell him I said that."

"Gleep?"

That last sort of slipped out. As you may have noticed, I am sufficiently self-conscious about my one-word human vocabulary that I try to rely on it as little as possible. The concept of my telling Guido anything, however, startled me into the utterance.

"Now, don't take it so hard," Nunzio scowled, as always interpreting my word wrong. "I didn't mean it. I'm just a little sore, is all."

I assumed he was referring to his foot. The human was feeling chatty, however, and I soon learned otherwise.

"I just don't know what's goin' on lately, Gleep. Know what I mean? On the paperwork things couldn't be goin' better, except lately everybody's been actin' crazy. First the Boss buys a casino we built for somebody else, then overnight he wants to sell it. Bunny and Tananda are goin' at each other for a while, then all of a sudden Bunny's actin' quiet and depressed and Tananda...did you know she wanted to borrow money from me the other day? Right after she gets done with that collection job? I don't know what she did with her commission or why she doesn't ask the Boss for an advance or even what she needs the money for. Just 'Can you spot me some cash, Nunzio? No questions asked?', and when I try to offer my services as a confidential type, she sez 'In that case, forget it. I'll ask someone else!' and leaves all huffy-like. I'll tell ya, Gleep, there's sumpin' afoot, and I'm not sure I like it."

He was raising some fascinating points, points which I'll freely admit had escaped my notice. While I had devoted a certain portion of my intellect to deciphering the intricacies of human conduct, there was much in the subtleties of their intra-species relationships which elude me...particularly when it came to individuals other than Skeeve. Reflecting on Nunzio's words, I realized that my pet had not been to see me much lately, which was in itself a break in pattern. Usually he would make time to visit, talking to me about the problems he had been facing and the self-doubts he felt. I wondered if his increased absences were an offshoot of the phenomenon Nunzio was describing. It was food for thought, and something I promised myself I would consider carefully at a later point. Right now, there were more immediate matters demanding my attention...like the people burrowing in under the floor.

It seemed that, in the final analysis, Nunzio was as inept as most humans when it came to guard duty.

They make a big show of alertness and caution when they come on duty, but within a matter of hours they are working harder at dealing with their boredom than watching whatever it is they're supposed to be guarding. To be honest, the fact that dragons have longer lives may explain part of why we are so much better at staving off boredom. After a few hundred years, days, even weeks shrink to where they have no real time value at all. Even our very young have an attention span that lasts for months...sometimes years.

Whatever the reason, Nunzio continued to ramble on about his concerns with the status quo, apparently oblivious to the scratching and digging sounds that were making their way closer to our position. This time it wasn't simply my better hearing, for the noise was easily within the human range, though admittedly soft. By using *my* hearing, I could listen in on the conversations of the diggers.

"How much farther?"

"Sshhh! About ten feet more."

"Don't 'sshhh' me! Nobody can hear us."

"*I* can hear you! This tunnel isn't that big, ya know."

"What are you going to do with your share of the money after we steal the stuff?"

"First we gotta steal it. *Then* I'll worry about what to do with my share."

That was the part I had been waiting to hear. There had always been the chance they were simply sewer diggers or escaping convicts or something equally non-threatening to our situation. As it was, though, they were fair game.

Rising from where I had been sitting, I moved quietly to where they were digging.

". . . unless Don Bruce wants to . . . Hey! Where are you goin'? Get back here!"

I ignored Nunzio's shouting and listened again. On target. I estimated about four feet down. With a mental smirk, I began jumping up and down, landing as heavily as I could.

"What are you doin'? Stop that! Hey, Gleep!"

The noise Nunzio was making was trivial compared to what was being said four feet down. When I mentioned earlier that I was too heavy for Nunzio to move unassisted, I was not meaning to imply that he was weak. The simple poundage of a dragon is a factor to be reckoned with even if it's dead, and if it's alive and thinking, you have real problems. I felt the floor giving way and hopped clear, relishing the sounds of muffled screams below.

"Jeez. Now look what you've done! You broke the floor!"

Again I had expected no thanks and received none. This did not concern me, as at the moment I was more interested in assessing the damage, or lack of damage, I had inflicted on this latest round of potential thieves.

The floor, or a portion of it, now sagged about a foot lower, leading me to conclude that either the tunnel below had not been very high, or that it had only partially collapsed. Either way, there were no more sounds emanating from that direction, which meant the thieves were either dead or had retreated empty-handed. Having accomplished my objective of removing yet another threat to the shipment, I set my mind once again on more important things. Turning a deaf ear to Nunzio's ravings, I flopped down ad pretended to sleep while I indulged in a bit of leisurely analysis.

Perhaps Nunzio was right. It was possible that my pet was reacting adversely to the change in his status from free-lance operator to the head of a corporation, much the same as tropical fish will suffer if the pH of the water in their aquarium is changed too suddenly. I was very much aware that an organism's environment consisted of much more than their physical surroundings...social atmosphere, for example, often influenced a human's well-being. If that were the case, then it behooved me to do something about it.

Exactly how I was to make the necessary adjustments would be a problem. Whenever possible, I tried to allow my pet free will. That is, I liked to give him the illusion of choosing his own course and associates without interference from me. Occasionally I would stray from this stance, such as when they brought that horrible Markie creature into our home, but for the most part it was an unshakeable policy. This meant that if I indeed decided that it was time to winnow out or remove any or all of Skeeve's current associates for his own good, it would have to be done in a manner which could not be traced to me. This would not only preserve the illusion that I was not interfering in his life, but also save him the angst which would be generated if he realized I was responsible for the elimination of one or more of his friends. Yes, this would require considerable thought and consideration.

"Here, fella. Want a treat?"

This last was uttered by a sleazy-looking Deveel as he held out a hand with a lump of some unidentifiable substance in it.

I realized with a guilty start that I had overindulged, sinking too far into my thoughts to maintain awareness of my surroundings. After the unkind thoughts I had entertained about Nunzio's attention span, this was an inexcusable lapse on my part. Ignoring the offered gift, I raised my head and cast about desperately to reassess the situation.

There were three of them: the one currently addressing me, and two others who were talking to Nunzio.

"I dunno," the latter was saying. "I didn't get any instructions about anyone pickin' up the shipment early."

Something was definitely amiss. From his words and manner, even Nunzio was suspicious...which meant the plot had to be pretty transparent.

"C'mon boy. Take the treat."

The Deveel facing me was starting to sound a little desperate, but I continued ignoring him and his offering. It was drugged, of course. Just because humans can't smell a wide range of chemicals, they assume that no one else can either. This one was no problem. I was more concerned as to whether or not Nunzio would require assistance.

"I can't help it if your paperwork is fouled up," the smaller Deveel with Nunzio snarled, with a good imitation of impatience. "I've got a schedule to keep. Look. Here's a copy of my authorization."

As Nunzio bent to look at the paper the Deveel was holding, the one standing behind him produced a club and swung it at his head. There was a sharp "CRACK"...but it was from the club breaking, not from Nunzio's head, that latter being, as I have noted, exceptionally dense.

"I'm sorry, I can't let you have the shipment," Nunzio said, handing the paper back to the short Deveel who took it without losing the astounded expression from his face. "This authorization is nothin' but a blank piece of paper."

He glanced over his shoulder at the larger Deveel who was standing there staring at his broken club.

"Be with you in a second, fella. Just as soon as we get this authorization thing cleared up."

I decided that he would be able to handle things in his own peculiar way and turned my attention to the Deveel with the drugged treat.

He was looking at the conversation across the room, his mouth hanging open in amazement. I noticed, however, that he had neglected to withdraw his hand.

There are those who hypothesize that dragons do not have a sense of humor. To prove that that is not the case, I offer this as a counterexample.

Unhinging my jaw slightly, I stretched out my neck and took the treat in my mouth. Actually, I took his hand in my mouth . . . all the way to the shoulder. This was not as hazardous as it sounds. I simply took care not to swallow and therefore avoided any dangerous effects which might be generated by the drugged treat.

The Deveel glanced back when he heard my jaws crash together, and we looked into each others' eyes from a considerably closer range than he had anticipated. For effect, I waggled my eyebrows at him. The eyebrows did it, and is eyes rolled up into his head as he slumped to the floor in a dead faint.

Funny, huh? So much for not having a sense of humor.

Relaxing my jaws, I withdrew my head, leaving the treat and his arm intact, and checked Nunzio's situation again.

The larger Deveel was stretched out on the floor

unconscious while Nunzio was holding the other by the lapels with one hand, leisurely slapping him forehand and backhand as he spoke.

"I oughtta turn youse over to da authorities! A clumsy hijack like this could give our profession a bad name. Know what I mean? Are you listenin' ta me? Now take your buddies and get outta here before I change my mind! And don't come back until you find some decent help!"

I had to admit that Nunzio had a certain degree of style... for a human. If he had been fortunate enough to be born with a brain, he might have been a dragon.

While he was busy throwing the latest batch of attackers out the door, I decided to do a little investigating. After three attempts to relieve us of our prize, though Nunzio was only aware of one of them, I was beginning to grow a bit suspicious. Even for as crime-prone a lot as humans tend to be, three attempts in that close succession was unusual, and I wanted to know more about what it was we were guarding.

The cases still smelled of paper and ink, but that seemed an inadequate reason for the attention they had been drawing. As casually as I could, I swatted one of the cases with my tail, caving it in. Apparently I had not been casual enough, for the sound brought Nunzio sprinting to my side.

"Now what are you doin'? Look! You ruined... Hey! Wait a minute!"

He stooped and picked up one of the objects that had spilled from the case and examined it closely. I snaked my head around so I could look over his shoulder.

"Do you know what dis is, Gleep?"

As a matter of fact, I didn't. From what I could

see, all it was was some kind of picture book...and a shoddily made one at that. What it *didn't* look like was anything valuable. Certainly nothing that would warrant the kind of attention we had been getting.

Nunzio tossed the book back onto the floor and glanced around nervously.

"This is over my head," he murmured. "I can't... Gleep, you keep an eye on this stuff. I'll be right back. I've gotta get the Boss...and Guido! Yeah. He knows about this stuff."

Admittedly perplexed, I watched him go, then studied the book again.

Very strange. There was clearly something in this situation that was escaping my scrutiny.

I rubbed my nose a few times in a vain effort to clear it of the smell of ink, then hunkered down to await my pet's arrival.

"Comic books?"

Skeeve was clearly as perplexed as I had been.

"The 'valuable shipment' we're guarding is comic books?"

"That's what I thought, Boss," Nunzio said. "Screwy, huh? What do you think, Guido?"

Guido was busy prying open another case. He scanned the books on top, then dug a few out from the bottom to confirm they were the same. Studying two of them intently, he gave out with a low whistle.

"You know what these are worth, Boss?"

Skeeve shrugged.

"I don't know how many of them are here, but I've seen them on sale around the Bazaar at three or four for a silver, so they can't be worth much."

"Excuse me for interruptin'," Guido said, "but I am not referrin' to yer everyday, run-of-the-mill comic. I am lookin' at these, which are a horse from a different stable."

"They are?" My pet frowned. "I mean...it is? I mean...these all look the same to me. What makes them special?"

"It's not easy to explain, but if you will lend me your ears I will attempt to further your education, Boss. You too, Nunzio."

Guido gathered up a handful of the books and sat on one of the cases.

"If you will examine the evidence before you, you will note that while all these comics are the same, which is to say they are copies of the same issue, they each have the number 'one' in a box on their cover. This indicates that it is the first issue of this particular title."

I refrained from peering at one of the books. If Guido said the indicator was there, it was probably there, and looking at it wouldn't change anything.

"Immediately that 'one' makes the comic more valuable, both to someone who is tryin' to obtain a complete set, and especially to a collector. Now, certain titles is more popular than others, which makes them particularly valuable, but more important are titles which have indeed grown in popularity since they made their first debutante. In that situational, there are more readers of the title currently than there were when it began, and the laws of supply and demand drive the price of a first-issue copy through the roof."

He gestured dramatically with one of the books.

"This particular title premiered several years ago and is currently hotter than the guy what swiped the crown jewels. What is more, the print run on the first issue was very small, makin' a first-issue copy exceedingly valuable . . . with the accent on 'exceedingly.' I have with my own eyes seen a beat-up copy of the comic you are currently holding on a dealer's table with an askin' price of a hundert-fifty gold on it. Mind you, I'm not sayin' he got it, but that's what he was askin'.'"

Now it was Skeeve's turn to whistle. I might have been tempted myself, but whistling is difficult with a forked tongue.

"If that's true, this shipment is worth a fortune. He's got enough of them here."

"That is indeed the puzzlement, Boss," Guido said, looking at the cases. "If my memory is not seriously in error, there were only two thousand copies of this issue printed . . . yet if all these cases are full of the same merchandise, there are considerably more copies than that in this shipment to which we are referrin'. How this could be I am uncertain, but the explanation which occurs to me is less than favorable to the owner."

"Forgeries!" Nunzio squeaked. "The guy's a multi-colored paper hanger!"

"A multi . . . never mind!" Skeeve waved. "What good would a forged comic be?"

"The same as any other forgery," Guido shrugged. "You pass 'em off as originals and split with the money before anyone's the wiser. In some ways, it's better'n phony money, since it isn't as hard to duplicate comics and, as youse can see, they're worth more per pound. The paper's cheaper, too."

My pet surveyed the shipment.

"So we've been mad unwitting accomplices to a comic-forging deal, eh?"

". . . And without even gettin' a piece of the action," Nunzio snarled.

"That wasn't what I was thinking about," Skeeve said, shaking his head. "I was thinking of all the collectors who are going to plunk down their money to get a genuine collector's item, only to have the bottom drop out of the market when it's discovered that it's been flooded with forgeries."

He rubbed his lower lip thoughtfully.

"I wonder how much my lunch buddy has insured this shipment for?"

"Probably not much, if at all," Guido supplied. "To do so would necessitate the fillin' out of the documents declarin' the contents of said shipment, and any insurance type knowledgeable enough to give him full value would also know the discrepancy between the shipment count and what was originally printed. You see, Boss, the trouble with runnin' a fraud is that it requires runnin' additional frauds to cover for it, and eventually someone is bound to catch on."

Skeeve wasn't even listening by the time Guido finished his oration. He was busy rubbing the spot between my ears, a strange smile on his face.

"Well, I guess nobody wins all the time."

"What was that, Boss?"

My pet turned to face them.

"I said that M.Y.T.H. Inc. fumbled the ball this time. Sorry, Nunzio, but this one is going into the records as a botched assignment. I can only assure you that it will *not* be reflected on your next performance review."

"I don't get it," Nunzio frowned. "What went wrong?"

"Why, the fire of course. You know, the fire that

destroyed the entire shipment due to our inattentive-
ness and neglect? Terribly careless of us, wasn't it?"

"Fire? What fire?"

Skeeve stepped to one side and bowed to me,
sweeping one hand toward the cases.

"Gleep? I believe this is your specialty?"

I waffled briefly between using a #4 or a #6, then
said "to heck with it" and cut loose with a #9. It was
a bit show-offy, I'll admit, but with Guido and Nunzio
watching, not to mention my pet, it was pointless to
spare the firepower.

They were impressed, which was not surprising, as
#9 is quite impressive. There wasn't even any afterburn
to put out, since by the time I shut down the old
flame-thrower, there was nothing left to burn.

For several moments we all stood staring at the
charred spot on the warehouse floor.

"Wow!" Guido breathed at last.

"You can say that double for me," Nunzio nodded,
slipping an arm around my neck. "Good dragon, Gleep.
Good dragon."

"Well, gentlemen," Skeeve said, rubbing his hands
together, "now that that's over I guess we can head...
What's that?"

He pointed to the collapsed portion of the floor,
noticing it for the first time.

"That?" Nunzio squeaked innocently. "Beats me,
Boss. It was like that when we got here."

I didn't bother to return his wink, for I was already
starting to retreat heavily into thought. I only hoped
that in the final analysis I wouldn't decide that either
Guido or Nunzio was an unsettling influence on my
pet. Time would tell.

M.Y.T.H. Inc. Instructions

ROBERT LYNN ASPRIN AND JODY LYNN NYE

First down the long white aisle came the flower girls, ten of them dressed in green organza tossing handfuls of petals into the air. I got a faceful of their perfume and sneezed. That expression caused me to bare my teeth involuntarily, causing an equally involuntary back step by the six people standing nearest to me in the great hall of Possiltum Palace. I never expect Klahds to really appreciate Pervect teeth like mine.

I tugged at the tight collar of the formal tunic I'd let Massha talk me into wearing. If she hadn't become such a valued associate of mine and Skeeve's, I would tactfully have arranged to be elsewhere on this, her special day of days. But if you are smart you will never say 'no' to a woman about to get married, unless you're planning on finishing the sentence with "of course I don't mind you dressing me up like an organ-grinder's monkey." Which, naturally, leads your former apprentice and present partner to ask what an organ grinder is. When I explained, he said it sounds like a devious torture device which, now that I come to think of it, isn't all that far from being accurate, if you consider your inner ear an organ.

47

The horde of little girls was succeeded by a host of little boys dressed up like pages. Every one of them looked like I felt. I know Massha has a somewhat garish color sense, but I'd have done a little better for these kids than coral and pink striped satin breeches and caps, and bright aqua tunics. All around me I could see optic nerves shorting out, and the bridal attendants hadn't started down the aisle yet.

Before I'd finished the thought, here they came in a bevy. A lot of the bridesmaids were of Massha's globular body type, though none of them matched her in sheer magnificence. (This is her wedding day. It behooves me to be more than my usual tactful self.) Her confidence and warmth brought out the best in fellow large ladies of the Possiltum court, who sought her out as a friend and role model, helping them to like themselves as they were. She had plenty of friends there. Even Queen Hemlock, whom I would have voted "Girl Least Likely to Have Friends of Her Own Species," had gotten onto cordial, even warm terms with her.

In an unusual display of insecurity, Massha had run color choices for the ladies' gowns past Bunny, who has a good eye for fashion. Instead of a wallow of wild hues, which is what I would have expected, the bridesmaids were all dressed in pale pink silk. In spite of the vast difference in complexions and sizes, the pink served to flatter rather than draw attention. Bunny herself looked glorious and demure in her gown. The pink even looked good against the green of Tananda's hair. She resembled some species of orchid, shapely and exotic. I'd never before seen bridesmaids' dresses that didn't look like bedspreads or horror costumes. Mentally, I awarded points to Bunny for skill and Massha for knowing when to ask for help. It just showed what kind of trust the team inspired.

Subtlety ended with the arrival of an entire marching band. Two women in pink and aqua skirts shorter than anything Tanda had ever worn on a job catapulted into the room and began to turn flips down the white carpet. Behind them, a drum major in bright orange and blue came to a halt at the door and blew a sharp blast on a whistle. He hoisted his baton on high and marched forward, leading the Possiltum army's music corps in full dress uniform, playing Honywagen's Wedding March. This was a discordant dirge that had become traditional for weddings across the dimensions, to the everlasting regret of real music lovers. Since the band was a little heavy on bagpipes and horns, the effect was as hard on the ears as their outfits were on the eye. Since we Pervects have more sensitive ears than Klahds, I was ready to kill someone by the time they finished mauling Honywagen and struck up "A Pretty Girl is Like A Melody."

A full color guard strode in time to the tune. The eight soldiers took positions at intervals along the white carpet, holding the Possiltum flag high. Ten more soldiers, Klahds in the peak of physical perfection, such as it is, marched in past the flag bearers, sabers drawn and held erect in front of their noses. At a cue, they formed an arch with their swords. The band halted in the middle of its song, and struck up the Possiltum marching song. Enter Big Julie, in his best armor, clanking with weapons.

There'd been a lot of discussion about who would be the General's best man, but the former strongman turned out to be the perfect choice. After all, the traditional role of best man was to hold the door and keep unwanted visitors from intruding on the ceremony. Except for me, Guido, Chumley and a few of Don Bruce's enforcers who were present as invited guests, Big Julie was the only person who was big enough and mean enough to prevent any potential interruptions. As soon as he reached the front of the room Hugh Badaxe appeared at the door.

If there was ever a groom who wasn't nervous at his wedding I never met him. The big man had beads of sweat on his forehead under the crest of his helmet. He ought to be nervous; he was getting a terrific wife who had a lot of dangerous friends who'd still be looking out for her well-being even after she married him. The people around me backed further away. I realized I was smiling again. Still, he bore himself with military pride. Pretty good under the circumstances.

Badaxe wasn't a young man, but neither was Massha a spring chicken. I hated wallowing in sentimentality, but it was kind of nice that they'd found each other at a comfortable time of life. I admired him for his honesty. He ran a good army. She was a terrific woman, and a decent magician, even if her power did come from gizmos. It was a good match.

As if he suddenly remembered where he was and what he was supposed to be doing, Badaxe lurched forward, then regained his composure. He walked forward with his head high, smiling at faces he recognized in the audience. I caught his eye, and he nodded to me. I nodded back, warrior to warrior, businessman to businessman. Once at the front of the room, he removed his helmet and handed it off to Big Julie.

A team of acrobats came hurtling into the room, followed by jugglers and fire-eaters. Dancers, accompanied by musicians playing zithers, harps and flutes, undulated down the white strip, flirting with guests and flicking colored scarves around like filmy rainbows. In their midst, eight pink and purple-dyed ponies drew a flatbed cart down the aisle. On it sat a tall, slender, bearded man in black leather pants and a silver tunic playing arpeggios on a tall, slender silver harp.

"Quite some thing, eh?" Chumley whispered. Behind me, he was leaning against a pillar so he wouldn't block anyone else's view. I nodded. Neither one of us wanted or needed to be part of the ceremony. It was busy enough without us.

There wasn't a hint of magik anywhere. Massha wanted things to go well, but she wasn't going to force them that way artificially. I thought it was pretty brave of her.

The dancers and jugglers surrounded the altar at the front of the room where a green-robed priestess was waiting with the bridesmaids and the groom.

The harp struck up the Honywagen fanfare, and all eyes turned to the door.

In my wildest dreams I could never have pictured Massha looking lovely. Radiant, perhaps, but something about the look of joy on her face transformed her from plain to fancy. The unspoken rule that crossed dimensions held good here: all brides are beautiful.

The bodice of the white silk gown could have gone around Tananda or Bunny five or six times. It was sewn with crystals, pearls and, if my eye was still good, genuine gemstones. Massha probably had a bundle left over her income from M.Y.T.H. Inc., and here was where she'd chosen to spend it. The skirt, which extended behind her into a train five yards long, was picked out in crystals that flashed on and off as she walked, and embroidered with little scenes in white silk thread. I'd have to get a close look at them later and find out what she thought was important enough to memorialize on her wedding dress. Never one to wear shoes just for looks, she'd broken her own rule and splashed out on crystal sandals with five-inch spike heels. Her orange hair was gathered into a loose knot underneath a wreath of pink and orange lilies and a white veil that flowed down around her shoulders. I wondered about the symbolism of all the white and thought it was quite possible she was entitled to it. Even if the color was purely for the ceremony, it looked great on her. She was like a glistening pearl as she entered on Skeeve's arm.

My partner, who often looked like a kid in spite of his years, looked grave and thoughtful, which went well with his full magician's robes. I thought it was a nice touch: since Badaxe was wearing his uniform, Skeeve, who was giving away the bride, wore his. I knew Massha and the seamstresses had been working on the outfit while Skeeve was away. The plum velvet was picked out in silver and gold constellations, magik sigils and mystic symbols which, on closer scrutiny proved to be phrases in languages from other dimensions. I particularly liked the one in Deveel near his knee that read "This space for rent." Massha squeezed his arm and he smiled up at her.

I watched them go up the aisle, master and apprentice together. It was hard to know which one was which sometimes. Skeeve seemed to be everybody's apprentice, as well as mine. He learned from everybody he met, including Massha, but sometimes, like now, he was an adult guiding someone who trusted him. He was the only person who was surprised when Massha asked him to give her away. I felt my eyes burn suspiciously.

"I'm not crying," I muttered, my teeth gritted. "This doesn't move me at all." I heard Chumley sniffle audibly behind me.

The general stepped into the aisle. Skeeve met him, shook hands, and transferred Massha's hand from his arm to the groom's. Massha kissed him. Skeeve blushed as he sat down beside the Queen with the other honored guests in the front row. Gazing at one another, the bride and groom went to stand before the altar.

"Dearly beloved," the priestess began, smiling. "We are all here to stand witness to the love of this man and this woman, who wish to become husband and wife. Marriage is a wonderful institution, but should not be entered into lightly let those who understand it stay quiet and let this couple learn it for themselves yet let us allow one or both of them to unburden his or her heart to you but always remembering that it's usually the husband who doesn't understand what the wife is saying and the wife who claims the husband isn't listening to her anyhow and though you may wish to side with one or the other of them you shouldn't do that because they are both blessed under Heaven and nobody's perfect let the chips fall where they may and they will form a more perfect union in tolerance so they'll both live to a happy old age together and love is rare enough in this world that you should give them the benefit of the doubt and should this union be blessed with children their names will live on into infinity as honored ancestors and anyhow it's much more fun to spoil grandchildren than children your mileage may vary you can remind them of this day on anniversaries for years to come even if they don't remember which present you gave them. Do you Hugh Badaxe take this woman to be your wife? You do? Repeat after me: with this ring I thee wed. Do you, Massha, take this man to be your husband? You do? Repeat after me: with this ring I thee wed. By the power vested in me by the great gods all around us and the government of Possiltum I now pronounce this couple to be husband and wife for ever and ever under heaven onward into joyful eternity and beyond letanyonewhohasanyobjectionslethimspeaknoworforeverholdhispeace amen!"

"I need a drink," I told Chumley as soon as the wedding party marched out. "Several."

"Unless I'm greatly mistaken," the troll said, "there's Poconos punch in the courtyard."

"Good. If there's any left the guests can have some." I strode through the crowd, which parted like a curtain before me. The Klahds were used to our outworldly appearance by now, but it didn't mean they wanted to be close to us. That suited me just fine.

The first gulp of Poconos exploded behind my sinuses and burned down my throat like lava. I drank down two more cups of the fire-red liquid before sensation returned. I emitted a healthy belch, spitting a stream of fire three feet long.

"That's more like it," I said.

"I say!" Chumley exclaimed, his eyes watering. "I suspect Little Sister had something to do with the mixing of this."

"Tanda always could mix a good drink," I said.

There must have been three hundred people in the palace courtyard. Dancing had already started near one wall. I could tell where the jugglers were by the gouts of fire shooting up into the sky. Deveels and other transdimension travellers were doing small spells to the astonishment and delight of the Klahds (and no doubt to their own profit.). Music and laughter rose over the din of people shouting happily at one another. I took my cup and went to stand in the reception line.

Massha and Badaxe accepted congratulations, handshakes and hugs from everybody.

"Dear, I expecially loved the birds singing while you recited your vows."

"The jugglers made me remember my wedding day."

"Hey, what legs! What style! And you looked pretty, too, babe."

Massha showed off the gaudy ring on her left hand, and Badaxe beamed with pleasure. Don Bruce and his enforcers were just ahead of me in line. The Fairy Godfather, dressed in a formal lilac tux that went well with his usual violet fedora, fluttered high enough to kiss Massha on the cheek.

"You take care of her," he warned Badaxe. "Oh. I brought a little something for you." He snapped his fingers. Two of his largest henchmen staggered toward him with a giftwrapped box the size of a young dragon. "You should enjoy it. If it doesn't fit, tell Skeeve. He'll let me know." He turned to introduce the others in his retinue, a slim, sharp-eyed man with bushy black eyebrows, and a stocky, short man with no neck and short, wide hands suitable for making a point without using a weapon. "These are new associates of mine, Don Don deDondon and Don Surleone."

"A pleasure," Don Don said, bowing over Massha's hand. Don Surleone's huge hands folded around Badaxe's. I noticed the general's face contort at the pressure. The burly man must be incredibly strong.

The dancing and singing continued long into the night. I kept an eye on things to make sure nobody got out of line. I maintained eye contact with Big Julie, who was across the courtyard from me. He had the same idea, especially as so many people from the Bazaar kept turning up to give the happy couple their good wishes. So long as they stuck to that intention, I didn't mind.

"Hey, short, green and scaly, how about cutting a rug?" The cuddly presence that draped itself across my chest could only be Tananda. The pink dress was cut low enough on her shapely decolletage to cause traffic jams. I'd seen a few already.

"I appreciate the invitation, but I'm watching," I said.

"Who'd dare to cause trouble here and now?" she asked, but she was a professional. She understood my concerns. Enough of our old clientele and our present neighbors were around to spread the word across the Bazaar if something blew up and we couldn't handle it. We'd be going back there in a day or two. Fresh rumors would make it tougher than it had to be. "I'll get Chumley to watch things, too."

Noticing our tete-a-tete, Guido and Nunzio stopped by for a chat, and got my take on the situation. Skeeve was hanging out by himself. None of us wanted to bother him. He'd had enough stresses the last couple of weeks, between the near-fatal accident to Gleep and acting as best man. Keeping an eye on his back was only what one partner would do for another. He needed some time to himself.

"Aahz, can I talk to you?"

I turned. The bride was there in neon and white. Her face looked worried in the torchlight. "Massha! How come you and Hugh aren't dancing?"

"I've got a little problem," she said, edging close and putting her hand through my arm. Any time someone looked at us she beamed at them, but not convincingly. "We started opening the wedding presents, and one of them kind of blew up on us."

"What?" I bellowed. The whole crowd turned to look. I grabbed Massha and planted a kiss on her cheek. "Congratulations! You'll make a great court magician." Skeeve had let me know about Queen Hemlock's decision. I concurred that it was the best solution for both of them. That way she and Badaxe would have equal status at court. I knew I was trumping Hemlock's own announcement, but it was the most legitimate way I could think of to cover my outburst.

"Thanks, Aahz," Massha said, beaming from the teeth out. The crowd lost interest and went back to their drinks and conversation. She looked like she might burst into tears.

"Which gift?" I murmured.

"Don Bruce's."

My eyes must have started glowing, because she grabbed my arm. "Hold on, hot stuff. It's not his fault. If anything, it's ours. When we peeled off the paper there was this big box with a red button on one side. No instructions. My detector," she showed me the gaudy bracelet studded with orange stones on one arm, "didn't show any harmful magik inside, so we went ahead and pushed the button."

I sighed. "What happened? What was it?"

She giggled, torn between worry and amusement. "A house. A cottage, really. It's lovely. The carpets are deep enough to hide your feet, the walls are draped with silk hangings embroidered with all of Hugh's victories, and the windows are sixteen colors of leaded glass. The trouble is it's in the middle of the throne room."

It was. An otherwise good-looking, split-level cottage with a two-stall stable and a white picket fence had appeared practically on the steps of Queen Hemlock's throne. The room had been designated as the repository for wedding gifts, since security there was always tight, and no one was likely to wander in without an invitation, no matter how curious they were about Massha's china pattern. Tananda and Chumley were on guard in the room. Tanda had taken off her elaborate headpiece. Chumley, a bow tie now undone under his furry chin, sat with his back against the doorpost. Nunzio and Guido, dapper yet businesslike in tuxedos, had arrived. They'd donned their fedoras in a sign to anyone who knew the trade that they were working. Massha's bridesmaids were clustered around a table full of presents. One of them was making a bouquet out of the ribbons. Another had a big bag full of discarded wrappings. Another had a quill and a bottle of ink, writing down who had given what.

"Has anyone told Skeeve yet?" I asked, taking the members of M.Y.T.H. Inc. to one side.

"No," said Massha.

"Don't," I said flatly.

"The Boss has a right to know," Guido said automatically, then looked guilty. "You got it. Mum."

"Have you tried to get it back in the box?"

"Of course," Massha said. "But the button has disappeared. So has the box."

I peered at the house. Fairytale honeymoon cottages didn't come cheap. This couldn't be construed as an insult from Don Bruce. Besides as far as I knew, based upon updates from Tanda and Bunny, that we were in good books with the Fairy Godfather. He was a careful man. He would have furnished instructions. So where were they?

"Has anyone else been in here that shouldn't have been?" I asked.

"No one," the bridesmaid with the quill said. Her name was Fulsa. She had round hazel eyes in a round, pink face. "A few people peeked in. Oh! There was a blue dragon in here for a while. I think he belongs to the Court Magician."

Gleep? I glanced at Massha.

"He just came in to sniff around the presents," she explained. "I think he felt left out, but I didn't really think he was well enough to be in the ceremony." She studied my face. "Any reason I should be worried about him?"

"I don't know," I said. But the two of us went out to the stable to make sure.

I'd never been thrilled that Skeeve had acquired a baby dragon. They live for hundreds of years, so their infancy and youth is correspondingly long. Gleep was still considered to be a very young dragon. He had a playful streak that sometimes wreaked havoc on our habitations. Skeeve believed he was a lot smarter than I did. But other times, I was reconciled to his presence, even grateful. He was still recovering from having stopped an arrow. The foot-wide trail through the straw on the way to his stall showed that something long and heavy had passed through there at least once.

A scaly blue mass in the corner began to snore as I entered. I went to stand by its head.

"Come on, Gleep," I said. "I know you're only pretending to be asleep. If you're as intelligent as Skeeve thinks, I'm sure you understand me."

The long neck uncoiled, and the head levered up until it was eye to eye with me. "Gleep!" the dragon said brightly. I jumped back, gagging. That reptile's breath could peel paint off a wall.

"Did you take a piece of parchment from the throne room?" I asked.

Gleep cocked his head. "Gleep?"

Massha came to nestle close to the dragon. "I know you were there," she crooned, running a finger around Gleep's jowls. The dragon almost purred, enjoying the chin-rub. "Did you take something you shouldn't?"

The dragon shook his head. "Gleep!"

"Are you sure?"

"Gleep!" He nodded energetically.

Massha turned to me and shrugged. At that moment, I spotted the corner of a parchment hidden under a pile of straw. I lunged for it. Gleep got in between me and it. I dodged to one side. He swung his long neck to intercept me.

"All right, lizard-breath, you asked for it. Partner's pet or no partner." I grabbed him around the neck just underneath his chin and held on. He writhed and struggled to get loose. I let go when Massha retrieved the paper. It was torn at one corner, where it had obviously been ripped away from a tack. Gleep tried to grab it back, but I stiff-armed him. He retired to the corner of his stall.

"It's the instructions," she said, scanning the page. "'Choose the location you wish to site your Handy Dandy Forever After Honeymoon Cottage, then push the button.' Then below is an incantation." Massha's worried eyes met mine. "We didn't chant this! What if something terrible happens because we missed out on the verbal part of the spell? It might fall down!" She hurried out of the stable. Gleep let out a honk of alarm and scooted out after her.

"Come back here!" I said, setting off in pursuit. I was not going to let that goofy dragon upset the festivities. It was bad enough one of Massha's wedding presents had misfired.

Gleep was quicker than both of us. To the alarm of the bridesmaids, Gleep blocked the doorway of the throne room and was whipping back and forth, preventing Massha from entering. Guido and Nunzio ran over, their right hands automatically reaching into their coats.

"Grab him," I said.

"Be careful," Nunzio warned. "He's still healing. What's upset him?"

"He doesn't want Massha to read the spell that came with Don Bruce's present," I said. I stopped for a moment to think. That was how the situation appeared, now that I considered it. But that was ridiculous. "He can't read. How could he know something like that?"

Nunzio came up to lay a gentle hand on Gleep's neck. "Maybe he smelled a bad scent on the parchment," he said. "Dragons have a remarkable sense of smell."

Massha held out the paper in alarm. "Do you think it's booby trapped?"

"I don't know," I said, grabbing it from her. I started to read. My eyebrows rose until I thought they'd fly off the top of my head. "I see. Good boy, Gleep!"

"Gleep!" the dragon said, relaxing. He stuck his head under my hand and fluttered hopeful eyelids at me. I scratched behind his ears.

"What is it, hot stuff?"

I snorted. "I don't know how that dumb dragon knew, but his instincts were good. This isn't a barn-raising spell, it's a barn-razing spell. If you'd recited it, it would have blown up the building and everyone inside!"

Massha's eyes went wide. "But why would Don Bruce want to do that?"

I scanned the page again. "I don't think he did. Look, the spell is printed in a different hand than the instructions." The swirling handwriting above was Don Bruce's. The message below, though also in lavender ink, was written by a stranger.

"How do we find out who did it?"

"With a little subterfuge," I said. "And a little dragon."

The boom that shook the castle was barely audible above the noise of the crowd and the musicians. I staggered out, supporting Massha. Her dress was torn and patched with black burns, and her hair was askew. Guido threaded his way ahead of us, making sure that Skeeve was nowhere in sight. We all agreed he shouldn't be bothered. I was pretty certain we could handle this by ourselves. He spotted Don Bruce and his two associates boozing it up at one of the tables near the harpist. Don Bruce set down his goblet and kissed his fingers at the musician.

"Beautiful! That boy plays beautifully." Then he turned, and spotted us. "Aahz! Massha! What has happened to you?"

"The house," Massha said, playing her part. She let go of me and threw her meaty arms around the Fairy Godfather. "My husband! Oh, I can't say."

"What happened?" the don demanded.

Massha sobbed into a handkerchief. "We only just got married!"

"Are you saying that my present killed your husband?" Don Bruce demanded, drawing himself up four feet into the air.

"If the Prada pump fits," I growled, "wear it. The news will be all over the Bazaar in an hour: Don Bruce ices associates at a wedding!"

But I wasn't watching Don Bruce. I had my eye on his two associates. Surleone's heavy brows drew down over his stubby nose, but he looked concerned. Don deDondon couldn't keep the glee off his weaselly face.

"I'm good with casualties," he said, starting to rise from the bench. "I'd better go and see if I can help." Suddenly, a blue, scaly face was nose to nose with his. Gleep hissed. "Help?"

The dragon bared his teeth and flicked his tail from

side to side. It was all the proof I needed that Don deDondon had his hands on the parchment I'd had Gleep sniff, but I thrust it in front of his skinny nose.

"This your handwriting?" I asked.

"Gimme dat," said Don Surleone. He looked over the page. "Yeah, dat's his."

DeDondon threw up his hands. "No! I have nothing to do with any explosion! Call off your dragon!"

I did, but Guido and Nunzio were there flanking him, hand crossbows drawn but held low against the don's sides so they wouldn't disturb the other wedding guests. "You can clean up again, Massha. We have a confession."

"Confession?" Don Bruce demanded, fluttering madly, as Massha's bruises faded and her dress and coiffure regained their gaudy glory. "What's the deal?"

"I don't know the whole story," I said, sitting down and grabbing the pitcher of ale from the center of the table. I took a swig. Subterfuge was thirsty work. "But I can guess. New people in any organization tend to be ambitious. They want to get ahead right away. Either they find a niche to fill, or they move on. When you introduced these dons to Massha and Badaxe their names didn't ring any bells with me. At first. Then you said they were new.

"The present you gave Massha was princely, but it also provided a heck of an opportunity to take you down, and at least a few of us with you. The box containing the house had a sheet of instructions attached to it. How easy would it be to add a booby-trap that Massha would innocently set off when she went to open your present? We trust you; she'd follow the instructions as they were written. Your reputation for doing business in an honorable fashion would be ruined. But your enemy didn't take into account you have a host of intelligent beings working for you from a number of species."

"Gleep!" the dragon interjected. He'd withdrawn to a safe distance, with his head against Nunzio's knee.

"Something with so easy a trigger mechanism wouldn't need extra incantations to operate. The additional verbiage aroused our suspicions, enabling us to figure the puzzle out in time to stave off disaster."

"Then why the costume drama?" Don Bruce asked, snatching the pitcher out of my hand and pouring himself a drink.

I grinned. "To draw out the culprit," I said. "If you and your associates were innocent you'd be concerned about the loss of life. And Don deDondon here knew about an explosion even though Massha never used the word. He was thinking about it, because he'd rigged one to go off."

"But it did!" the scrawny don protested. "I felt it."

"A little subsonic vibration, courtesy of Massha's magik," I said, with a bow to her. "Nothing too difficult for a member of M.Y.T.H. Inc., which is why Don Bruce employs us to watch out for his interests in the Bazaar at Deva."

The Fairy Godfather turned as purple as his suit. He spun in the air to face the cowering don. "You wanted me to lose face in front of my valued associates? Surleone, Guido, Nunzio, please escort our former employee back to the Bazaar. I'll be along shortly." The meaty mafioso took deDondon by the arm and flicked a D-hopper out of his pocket. In a twinkling, they were gone.

Don Bruce hovered over to take Massha's hand. "I offer my sincere apologies if anything that I or my people have done to mar your wedding day in even the slightest way. I'll send someone with the counterspell to pack the house up again. I hope you and your husband have a long and happy life together. You made a beautiful bride." In a flutter of violet wings, he was gone, too.

"I'm glad that's over," I said, draining the rest of the ale. "Take that silly dragon back to the stables, and let's keep the party rolling."

Gleep's ears drooped.

"Now, Aahz," Massha said, "you owe him an apology. If it wasn't for Gleep, the palace would have been blown sky high."

The dragon rolled huge blue eyes at me. I fought with my inner self, but at last I had to admit she was right.

"I'm sorry, Gleep," I told him. "You were a hero."

"Gleep!" the dragon exclaimed happily. His long tongue darted out and slimed my face. I jumped back, swearing.

"And no one tells Skeeve what happened here tonight!" I insisted. "None of it! Not a word!"

"Who, me?" Massha asked, innocently, as Badaxe wandered in out of the shadows, in search of his wife. She sauntered over and attached herself to his arm with a fluid langour that would have been a credit to Tanda. "In a few minutes, I'll be on my honeymoon. Nighty-night, Aahz."

Mything in Dreamland

ROBERT LYNN ASPRIN AND JODY LYNN NYE

The dark green roof of the forest stretched out endlessly in every direction. To most, it would look like an idyllic paradise. To me, it was a major problem.

I gazed out over the massed pine trees, wondering what kind of wilderness we'd gotten stuck in. A few bare crests, like the one I was sitting on, protruded above the treeline, but they were miles away. None of it looked familiar, but no reason why it should. There were thousands of dimensions in existence, and I'd only been to a few.

At the very least, it was an embarassment. Here I was, considered publicly to be a hotshot magician, the great Skeeve, utterly lost because I'd tripped and fallen through a magic mirror.

I went through my belt pouch for the D-hopper. I was sure it was there somewhere. I wasn't alone, of course. Behind me, my partner and teacher Aahz paced up and down impatiently.

"I told you not to touch anything in Bezel's shop," the Pervect snarled. When a native of the dimension called Perv snarls, other species blanch. The expression shows off a mouth full of 4-inch razor-honed fangs set in a scaly green face that even dragons considered terrifying. I was used to it, and besides, I was pretty much to blame for his bad mood.

"Who'd have thought anybody could fall through a looking glass?" I tried to defend myself, but my partner wasn't listening.

"If you had paid attention to a single thing I've said over the last however many years it's been..." Aahz held up a scaly palm in my direction. "No, don't tell me. I don't want to know. Garkin at least should have warned you."

"I know," I said. "It's my fault."

"It's just basic common sense when it comes to magik. Don't eat anything that says 'Eat me.' Don't drink anything that says 'Drink me.' And don't touch Klahdforsaken magik mirrors with barriers around them that say 'Don't touch!'...what did you say?" Aahz spun around on his heel.

"I said I know it's my fault. I was just trying to keep Gleep from eating the frame," I explained, sheepishly.

"Gleep!" the dragon added brightly, beside me.

"So why didn't you tie him up before we went in?" Aahz said.

"I did tie him up!" I protested. "You know I did. You saw me knot the leash around a post." But we could both make an educated guess as to what had happened.

My dragon was not allowed in most reputable places—or what passed for reputable at the Bazaar at Deva, the largest trading area anywhere in the multitude of dimensions. It often happened that unscrupulous Deveel shop proprietors ridded themselves of unwanted merchandise at a profit, by arranging for accidents to occur. Such as having a convenient fire during which time the owners have an unshakeable alibi. Such as leaving the door ajar while they just run next door to borrow a cup of sugar. Such as loosening the tether on a baby dragon whose reputation for clumsiness was almost as impressive as its masters' reputation for magical skill and deep pockets. Said dragon would go charging after its beloved owner. Merchandise would start to hit the tent floor as soon as it entered. More goods, not even close to being in range of said rampaging dragon, would shatter into pieces. Outraged shopkeeper would appear demanding reimbursement at rates inflated four or five times the true worth. Unlucky customer would be forced to shell out or risk expulsion (or worse) from the bazaar. All genuine valuables would have been removed from the shop ahead of time, of course.

"Maybe one of Bezel's rivals let him loose," I suggested hopefully, not liking my skills at tying knots to be called into question.

"What were you doing looking at that mirror anyhow?"

I felt a little silly admitting the truth, but it had been my curiosity that had gotten us stranded out here. "Massha told me about it. She said this was a really great item. It shows the looker his fondest dream. . . . Naturally, I wanted to see if it was anything we could use in our business. You know, to scope out our clients, find out what it is they really want . . ."

"And what did you see?" Aahz asked quickly.

"Only my own dreams," I said, wondering why Aahz was so touchy. "Daydreams, really. Me, surrounded by our friends, rich, happy, with a beautiful girl . . ."

Although the mirror had been a little sketchy about the actual physical details, I remembered vivid impressions of pulchritude and sex appeal.

A slow smile spread over Aahz's scaly features. "You know those dream girls, partner. They never turn out like you hope they will."

I frowned. "Yes, but if it's your own dream, wouldn't she be exactly what you want? How about yours? What did you see?"

"Nothing," Aahz said flatly. "I didn't look."

"But you did," I insisted, grabbing onto a fleeting memory of Aahz with an astonished expression on his face. "What did you see?"

"Forget it, apprentice! It was a big fake. Bezel probably had a self-delusion spell put on the mirror to spur someone stupid like you into buying it. When you got home you'd have seen nothing reflected in it but Bezel's fantasy of a genuine sucker."

"No, I'm sure the mirror was real," I said thoughtfully. I knew what I'd daydreamed over the years, but those wishes had been piecemeal, little things now and again. I'd never had such a coherent and complete vision of my fantasies. "Come on, Aahz, what did you see?"

"None of your business!"

But I wasn't going to be put off that easily.

"C'mon. I told you mine," I wheedled. Aahz's wishes were bound to be interesting. He had seen dozens of dimensions, and been around a lot more than I had. "You probably have some sophisticated plan about an empire with you at the top of the heap, in charge. Hundreds of people begging for your services. Wine! Women! Song!"

"Shut up!" Aahz commanded. But by now, my curiosity was an unignorable itch.

"There's no one around here for miles," I said, and it was the truth. "Nobody could get up here in hearing range. They'd have to build a bridge to that next peak, and it's miles away. There's no one here but us. I'm your best friend, right?"

"I doubt that!"

"Hey!" I exclaimed, hurt.

Aahz relented, looking around. "Sorry. You didn't deserve that, even if you did make a boneheaded move by touching that mirror. Well, since it's just us... Yeah, I saw something. That's why I think it's a delusion spell. I saw things the way they used to be, me doing magik—big magik—impressing the heck out of thousands—No, millions! I got respect. I miss that."

I was astonished. "You have respect. We respect you. And people in the Bazaar, they definitely respect you. The Great Aahz! You're feared in a hundred dimensions. You know that."

"It's not like in the old days," Aahz insisted, his gaze fixed on the distance, and I knew he wasn't seeing the endless trees. "Time was we'd never have been stuck up here on a bare mountaintop like two cats on a refrigerator..."

I opened my mouth to ask what a refrigerator was, then decided I didn't want to interrupt the flow. Aahz seldom opened up his private thoughts to me. If he felt like he wanted to unload, I considered it a privilege to listen.

"...I mean, it ain't nothing showy, but time was I could have just flicked my wrist, and a bridge would've appeared, like that!"

He flicked his wrist.

I gawked. A suspension bridge stretched out from the peak on which we were standing all the way to the next mountain. It was made completely out of playing cards, from its high arches down the cables to the spans and pylons that disappeared down into the trees. We stared at each other and gulped.

"That wasn't there before," I ventured. But Aahz was no longer looking at the bridge or at me. He was staring at his finger as if it had gone off, which in a sense it had.

"After all these years," he said softly. "It's impossible." He raised his head, feeling around for force lines. I did the same.

The place was full of them. I don't mean full, I mean FULL. Running through the ground like powerful subterranean rivers, and overhead like highly charged rainbows, lines of force were everywhere. Whatever dimension we'd stepped into was chockablock with magik. Aahz threw back his head and laughed. A pretty little yellow songbird flew overhead, twittering. He pointed a finger at it. The bird, now the size of a mature dragon, emitted a basso profundo chirp. It looked surprised.

It had nothing on me. For years, I had thought only my late magik teacher Garkin could have removed the spell that robbed Aahz of his abilities. I didn't know a dimension existed where the laws of magik as I had learned them didn't apply. It seems I was wrong.

Aahz took off running toward the bridge.

"Hey, Skeeve, watch this!" he shouted. His hands darted out. Thick, fragrant snow began to fall, melting into a perfumed mist before it touched me. Rainbows darted through the sky. Rivers of jewels sprang up, rolling between hills of gold. I tripped over one and ended up in a pool of rubies.

"Aahz, wait!" I cried, galloping after him as fast as I could. Gleep lolloped along with me, but we couldn't catch him. As soon as Aahz's foot hit the bridge, it began to shrink away from the mountainside, carrying him with it. He was so excited he didn't notice. Once when I hadn't really been listening he had told me about contract bridge. This must be what he meant. This bridge was contracting before my eyes.

"Aahz! Come back!" I called. There was nothing I could do. Gleep and I would have to jump for it. I grabbed his collar, and we leaped into space.

I was pushing with every lick of magik in my body, but we missed the end of the bridge by a hand's length. A card peeled itself up off the rear of the span. It was a joker. The motley figure put its thumbs in its ears and stuck out its tongue at me, just before the bridge receded out of sight. I didn't have time to be offended by its audacity, since I was too busy falling.

"Gleeeeeeeep!" my dragon wailed, as he thudded onto the steep slope beside me. "Gle-ee-ee-eep!"

"Gr-ra-ab so-ome-thi-ing," I stuttered, as we rolled helplessly down the hill. Where had all those force lines gone? I should have been able to anchor myself to the earth with a bolt of magik. We tumbled a good long way until my pet, showing the resourcefulness I knew was in him, snaked his long neck around a passing tree-stump, and his tail around my leg. We jerked to an abrupt halt. I hung upside down with my head resting on a shallow ledge that overlooked a deep ravine. We'd only just missed falling into it. As soon as I caught my breath, I crawled up the slope to praise Gleep. He shot out his long tongue and affectionately planted a line of slime across my face. I didn't flinch as I usually did. I figured he deserved to lick me if he wanted to. He'd saved both of us.

I studied my surroundings. If there was a middle to Nowhere, I had unerringly managed to locate it. The remote scraps of blue visible through the forest roof were all that was left of the sky. Once my heart had slowed from its frantic "That's it, we're all going to die now" pounding to its normal, "Well, maybe not yet" pace, I realized that the ledge we almost fell off was wide enough to walk on. I had no idea where it led, but sitting there wasn't going to help me find Aahz or the jokers who had carried him off.

"You lost, friend?" a male voice asked.

I jumped up, looking around for its source. I could see nothing but underbrush around me. Out of reflex, I threw a disguise spell on me and Gleep, covering my strawberry-blond hair with sleeked-back black and throwing my normally round and innocent-looking blue eyes into slanted, sinister pits. Gleep became a gigantic red dragon, flames licking out from underneath every scale.

"No! I'm just . . . getting my bearings."

A clump of trees stood up and turned around. I couldn't help but stare. On the other side of the mobile copse was the form of a man.

"Well, you sure look lost to me," said the man, squinting at me in a friendly fashion. He was dressed in a fringed jacket and trousers, with a striped fur cap perched on his head and matching boots on his feet. His skin was as rough as bark, and his small, dark eyes peered at me out of crevices. Hair and eyebrows alike were twiglike thickets. The eyebrows climbed high on his craggy forehead. "Say, that's pretty good illusion-making, friend! You an artist?"

"Huh?" I goggled, taken aback. How could he have spotted it so readily? "No. I'm a master magician. I am . . . the Great Skeeve."

The man stuck out a huge hand and clenched my fingers. I withdrew them and counted them carefully to make sure none had broken off in his solid grip. "Pleased to meet you. Name's Alder. I'm a backwoodsman. I live around these parts. I only ask because illusion's a major art form around here. You're pretty good."

"Thanks," I said dejectedly. An illusion was no good if it was obvious, I let it drop. "I only use it because I don't look very impressive in person."

Alder tutted and waved a hand. "It don't matter what you look like. It's only your personality anybody pays attention to. Things change around here so often." He lifted his old face, sniffed and squinted one eye. He raised a crooked finger. "Like now, for example."

Alder was right. While I watched, his leathery skin smoothed out a little and grew paler. Instead of resembling a gnarled old oak he looked like a silver-haired birch instead. I was alarmed to discover the transformation was happening to me, too. Some force curled around my legs, winding its way up my body. The sensation wasn't unpleasant, but I couldn't escape from it. I didn't struggle, but something was happening to my body, my face.

"Gleep!" exclaimed my dragon. I glanced over at him. Instead of a green dragon with vestigal wings, a large, brown fluffy dog sat looking at me with huge blue eyes. Once I got past the shock I realized the transformation really rather suited him. I pulled a knife out of my pocket and looked at my reflection in the shiny blade. The face looking back at me was tawny skinned with topaz-yellow eyes like a snake and a crest of bright red hair. I shuddered.

"What if I don't like the changes?" I asked Alder.

Meditatively, he peeled a strip of bark off the back of one arm and began to shred it between his fingers. "Well, there are those who can't do anything about it, but I'm betting you can, friend. Seeing as how you have a lot of influence."

"Who with?" I demanded. "What's the name of this dimension? I've never been here before."

"It ain't a dimension. This is the Dreamland. It's common to all people in all dimensions. Every mind in the Waking World comes here, every time they go to sleep. You don't recognize it consciously, but you already know how to behave here. It's instinctive for you. You're bending dreamstuff, exerting influence, just as if you lived here all the time. You must have pretty vivid dreams."

"This is a dream? But it all seems so real."

"It don't mean it ain't real, sonny," Alder whistled through his teeth. "Look, there's rules. The smarter you are, the more focused, the better you get on in this world. Lots of people are subject to the whims of others, particularly of the Sleepers themselves, but the better you know your own mind, the more control over your own destiny you've got. Me, I know what I like and what I don't. I like it out in the wilderness. Whenever the space I'm in turns into a city, I just move on until I find me a space where there ain't no people. Pretty soon it quiets down and I have things my own way again. Now, if I didn't know what I wanted, I'd be stuck in a big Frustration Dream all the time."

"I just had a Frustration Dream," I said, staring off in the general direction in which Aahz had disappeared. "How is it that if I have so much power here I couldn't catch up with my friend?"

"He's gone off on a toot," Alder said, knowingly. "It happens a lot to you Waking Worlders. You get here and you go a little crazy. He got a taste of what he wants, and he's gone after more of it."

"He doesn't need anything," I insisted. "He's got everything back at home." But I paused.

"There's got to be something," Alder smiled. "Everyone wants one thing they can't get at home. So what does your friend want?"

That was easy: Aahz had told me himself. "Respect."

Alder shook his head. "Respect, eh? Well, I don't have a lot of respect for someone who abandons his partner like he did."

I leaped immediately to Aahz's defense. "He didn't abandon me on purpose."

"You call a fifty-mile bridge an accident?"

I tried to explain. "He was excited. I mean, who wouldn't be? He had his powers back. It was like . . . magik."

"Been without influence a long time, has he?" Alder asked, with squint-eyed sympathy.

"Well, not exactly. He's very powerful where we come from," I insisted, wondering why I was unburdening myself to a strange old coot in the wilderness, but it was either that or talk to myself. "But he hasn't been able to do magik in years. Not since my old mentor, er, put a curse on him. But I guess that doesn't apply here."

"It wouldn't," Alder assured me, grinning. "Your friend seems to have a strong personality, and that's what matters. So we're likely to find your friend in a place he'd get what he wanted. Come on. We'll find him."

"Thanks," I said dubiously. "I'm sure I'll be able to find him. I know him pretty well. Thanks."

"Don't you want me to come along?"

I didn't want him to know how helpless I felt. Aahz and I had been in worse situations than this. Besides, I had Gleep, my trusty...dog...with me. "No, thanks," I said, brightly. "I'm such a powerful wizard I don't really need your help."

"Okay, friend, whatever you want," Alder said. He stood up and turned around. Suddenly, I was alone, completely surrounded by trees. I couldn't even see the sky.

"Hey!" I yelled. I sought about vainly. Not only couldn't I see the backwoodsman, but I'd lost sight of the cliffside path, the hillside, and even what remained of the sky. I gave in. "Well, maybe I need a little help," I admitted sheepishly. A clearing appeared around me, and Alder stood beside me with a big grin on his face. "Come on, then, youngster. We've got a trail to pick up."

Alder talked all the way through the woods. Normally the hum of sound would have helped me to focus my mind on the problem at hand, but I just could not concentrate. I'm happiest in the middle of a town, not out in the wilderness. Back when I was an apprentice magician and an opportunistic but largely unsuccessful thief, the bigger the population into which I could disappear after grabbing the valuables out of someone's bedroom, the better to escape detection. Alder's rural accent reminded me of my parents' farm that I had run away from to work for Garkin. I hated it. I forced myself to remember he was a nice guy who was helping us find Aahz.

"Now, looky-look here," he said, glancing down as we came to a place where six or seven paths crossed in a knot of confusion. I couldn't tell which one Aahz and his moving bridge had taken, but I was about to bolt down the nearest turning, just out of sheer frustration. "Isn't this the most interesting thing?... What's the matter?" he asked, noticing the dumb suffering on my face. "I'm talking too much, am I?"

"Sorry," I said, hiding my expression too late. "I'm worrying about my partner. He was so excited about getting his powers back that he didn't notice he was getting carried away—literally. I'm concerned that when he notices he's going to try to come back and find me."

"If what you say is true, it's going to take him a little time to get used to wielding influence again," Alder said. I started to correct him, but if this was the way the locals referred to magik, I wouldn't argue. "Right now we're on the trail of that bridge. Something that big doesn't pass through without leaving its marks, and it didn't." He lifted a handful of chocolate colored pebbles from the convergence, and went on lecturing me.

"Now, this here trail mix is a clear blind. Those jokers must have strewn it to try and confuse us, but

I'm too old a hand for that. I'm guessing that bridge is on its way to the capital, but I'd rather trust following the signs than my guesses. We have to hurry to see them before the winds of change blow through and mess up the tracks. I don't have enough strength myself to keep them back."

"Can I help?" I asked. "I'm pretty good at ma—I mean influence. And if my partner packs a kick here, I should, too."

Alder's branchlike eyebrows rose. "Maybe you could, at that. Let's give it a try!"

Let's just say I wasn't an unqualified success to start. Dreamish influence behaved like magik in that one concentrated hard picturing what one wanted to achieve, used the force lines to shape it, then hoped the committee running the place let one's plans pass. Like any committee they made some changes, the eventual result resembling but not being completely like my original intention, but close enough. Over the several days it took us to walk out of the forest, I attained a certain amount of mastery over my surroundings, but never enough to pop us to the capital city of Celestia or locate Aahz. I did learn to tell when the winds of change were coming through. They felt like the gentle alteration that had hit me and Gleep the first day, but far stronger. They were difficult to resist, and I had to protect the entire path we were following. This I did by picturing it, even the parts we couldn't see, as a long rope stretched out in front of us. It could have knots in it, but we didn't want it breaking off unexpectedly. I might never find Aahz if we lost this trail. I did other little tasks around the campground, just to learn the skill of doing two things at once. Alder was a great help. He was a gentler teacher than either Garkin or Aahz. For someone who had little influence of his own, he sure knew how to bring out the best in other magicians.

"Control's the most important thing," he said, as I struggled to contain a thicket fire I had started by accident when I tried to make a campfire one night. "Consider yourself at a distance from the action, and think smaller. What you can do with just a suggestion is more than most people can with their best whole efforts. Pull back and concentrate on getting the job done. A little effort sometimes pays off better than a whole parade with a brass band."

I chuckled. "You sound like Aahz."

"What?" Alder shouted.

"I said . . ." but my words were drowned out by deafening noise. The trees around us were suddenly thrust apart by hordes of men in colorful uniforms. I shouldn't say 'horde,' though they were dressed in red, black and gold, because they marched in orderly ranks, shoving me and Alder a dozen yards apart. Each of them carried a musical instrument from which blared music the likes of which I hadn't heard since halftime at the Big Game on the world of Jahk.

I picked myself up off the ground. "What," I asked as soon as my hearing returned, "was that?"

"That was a nuisance," Alder said, getting to his feet and brushing confetti off his clothes.

"No kidding," I agreed, "but what was it?"

"A nuisance," Alder repeated. "That's what it's called. It's one of the perils of the Dreamland. Oh, they're not really dangerous. They're mostly harmless, but they waste your time. They're a big pain in the sitter. Sometimes I think the Sleepers send them to get us to let go of ourselves so they can change us the way they want. Other people just plain attract them, especially those they most irk."

I frowned. "I don't want to run into any more of them myself," I said. "They could slow us down finding Aahz."

Alder pointed a finger directly at my nose. "That's exactly what they might do. Stick with me, friend, and I'll see you around the worst of them, or I won't call myself the finest backwoodsman in the Dreamland."

Using the virtually infinite reservoir of power available to me, I concentrated on keeping the trail intact so that Alder could find it. I found that the less influence I used, the fewer nuisances troubled us. So long as I kept my power consumption low, we had pretty easy going. It would have been a pleasant journey if I hadn't been concerned.

It was taking so long to locate Aahz that I began to worry about him. What if the contracted bridge had trapped him somewhere? What if he had the same problems I did with influence? He might have trouble finding enough food, or even enough air! He wasn't as fortunate as I had been, to locate a friendly native guide like Alder. Visions of Aahz in dire straits began to haunt my dreams, and drew my attention away from admiring the handsome though sometimes bizarre landscape. Gleep, knowing my moods, tried to cheer me up by romping along and cutting foolish capers, but I could tell that even he was worried.

One day Alder stopped short in the middle of a

huge forest glade, causing me and Gleep to pile up against the trees growing out of his back.

"Ow!" I said, rubbing my bruises.

"Gleep!" declared my dragon.

"We're here," Alder said. He plucked a handful of grass from the ground and held it out to me. It didn't look any different from the grass we'd been trudging over for the last three days. "We're in Celestia."

"Are you sure?" I demanded.

"Sure as the sun coming up in the morning, sonny," Alder said.

"All this forest in the midst of the capital city?"

"This is the Dreamland. Things change a lot. Why not a capital made of trees?"

I glanced around. I had to admit the trees themselves were more magnificent than I'd seen anywhere else, and more densely placed. The paths were regular in shape, meeting at square intersections. Elegant, slender trees with light coming out of the top must be the streetlights. Alder was right: it looked like a city, but all made of trees!

"Now, this is my kind of place," Alder said, pleased, rubbing his hands together. "Can't wait to see the palace. I bet the whole thing's one big treehouse."

Within a few hundred paces he pointed it out to me. What a structure! At least a thousand paces long, it was put together out of boards and balanced like a top on the single stem of one enormous oak tree. The vast door was accessible only by way of a rope ladder hung from the gate. A crudely painted sign on the door was readable from the path: "Klubhse. Everywun welcm. The King." In spite of its rough-hewn appearance, there was still something regal about it.

"No matter what shape it takes, it's still a palace," Alder said. "You ought to meet the king. Nice guy, they tell me. He'd like to know an influential man like you. Your friend has to be close by. I can feel it."

A powerful gale of changes prickled at the edge of my magikal sense. I fought with all my might to hold it back as Alder knelt and sniffed at the path.

"This way," he said, not troubling to rise. Unable to help himself, he became an enormous, rangy, blood-red dog that kept its nose to the path. Overjoyed to have a new friend, Gleep romped around Alder, then helped him followed the tracks. The scent led them directly to two vast tree-trunks in the middle of a very crowded copse. Alder rose to his feet, transforming back into a man as he did.

"We're here," he said.

"But these are a couple of trees!" I exclaimed. Then I began to examine them more closely. The bark, though arrayed in long vertical folds, was smooth, almost as smooth as cloth. Then I spotted the roots peeking out from the ground. They were green. Scaly green. Like Aahz's feet. I looked up.

"Yup," said Alder with satisfaction. "We've found your buddy, all right."

A vast statue of Aahz scratched the sky. Standing with hands on its hips, the statue had a huge smile that beamed out over the landscape, Aahz's array of knife-sharp teeth looking more terrifying than ever in twenty-times scale. I was so surprised I let go of the control I was holding over the winds of change. A whirlwind, more a state of mind than an actual wind, came rushing through. Trees melted away, leaving a smooth black road under my feet. White pathways appeared on each side of the pavement. People rushing back and forth on foot and in vehicles. Across the way the palace was now undisputedly a white marble building of exquisite beauty. But the statue of Aahz remained, looming over the landscape, grinning. I realized to my surprise that it was an office building. The eyes were windows.

With Alder's help I located a door in the leg and entered. People bustled busily around. Unlike the rest of the Dreamland where I had seen mostly Klahds, here there were also Deveels, Imps, Gremlins and others, burdened down with file folders and boxes or worried expressions. Just as I had thought, given infinite resources Aahz would have a sophisticated setup with half of everybody working for him, and the other half bringing him problems to solve. And as for riches, the walls were polished mahogany and ivory, inlaid with gold and precious stones. Not flashy—definitely stylish and screaming very loudly of money. I'd always wondered what Aahz could do with infinite resources, and now I was seeing it. A small cubicle at one end of the foot corridor swept me up all the way to the floor marked "Headquarters."

A shapely woman who could have been Tananda's twin with pink skin sat at a curved wooden desk near the cubicle door. She spoke into a curved black stick poking out of her ear. She poked buttons as buzzers sounded. "Aahz Unlimited. May I help you? I'm sorry. Can you hold? Aahz Unlimited. May I help you? I'm sorry. Can you hold?"

I gazed into the room, at the fanciest office suite I could imagine. I knew Aahz was a snazzy dresser, but I never realized what good taste he had in furniture.

Every item was meant to impress. The beautifully paneled walls were full of framed letters and testimonials, and every object looked as though it cost a very quiet fortune. All kinds of people hurried back and forth among the small rooms. I found a woman in a trim suit-dress who looked like she knew what she was doing and asked to see Aahz.

"Ah, yes, Mr. Skeeve," she said, peering at me over her pince-nez eyeglasses. "You are expected."

"Gleep?" added my dragon, interrogatively.

"Yes, Mr. Gleep," the woman smiled. "You, too."

"Partner!" Aahz called as I entered. He swung his feet off the black marble-topped desk and came to slap me on the back. "Glad to see you're okay. No one I sent out has been able to locate you."

"I had a guide . . ." I said, looking around for Alder. He must have turned his back and blended in with the paneling. I brought my attention back to Aahz. After all the worrying I had done over the last many days, I was relieved to see that Aahz seemed to be in the very best of health and spirits. "I was worried about you, too."

"Sorry about that," Aahz said, looking concerned and a little sheepish. "I figured it was no good for both of us to wander blindly around a new dimension searching for one another. I decided to sit tight and wait for you to find me. I made it as easy as I possibly could. I knew once you spotted the building you'd find me. How do you like it?"

"It's great," I said firmly. "A good resemblance. Almost uncanny. It doesn't . . . put people off, does it?" I asked, thinking of the seven-foot fangs.

"No," Aahz said, puzzled. "Why should it?"

"Oh, Mr. Aahz!"

A small thin man hurried into the office with the efficient-looking woman behind him with a clipboard. "Please, Mr. Aahz, you have to help me," the man said. "I'm being stalked by nightmares."

Aahz threw himself into the big chair behind the desk and gestured me to sit down. The little man poured out a pathetic story of being haunted by the most horrible monsters that came to him at night.

"I'm so terrified I haven't been able to sleep for weeks. I heard about your marvelous talent for getting rid of problems, I thought..."

"What?" Aahz roared, sitting up and showing his teeth. "I've never heard such bunkum in my life," Aahz said, his voice filling the room. The little man looked apprehensive. "Pal, you've got to come to me when you really need me, not for something minor like this."

"What? What?" the little man sputtered.

"Miss Teddybear," Aahz gestured to the efficient woman, who hustled closer. "Get this guy set up with Fazil the Mirrormaster. Have him surround this guy's bed with reflectors that reflect out. That'll scotch the nightmares. If they see themselves the way you've been seeing them they'll scare the heck out of themselves. You'll never see them again. Guaranteed. And I'll only take a...thirty percent commission on the job. Got that?"

"Of course, Mr. Aahz." The efficient woman bowed herself out.

"Oh, thank you, Mr. Aahz!" the little man said. "I'm sorry. You're just like everyone said. You are absolutely amazing! Thank you, thank you!"

Aahz grinned, showing an acre or so of sharp teeth. "You're welcome. Stop by the receptionist's desk on the way out. She'll give you the bill."

The little man scurried out, still spouting thanks. As soon as the door closed another testimonial popped into existence on the already crowded wall. Aahz threw himself back into his chair and lit a cigar.

"This is the life, eh, partner?"

"What was that about?" I asked, outraged. "The guy was frightened out of his life. You gave him a solution without leaving your office. You could have gone to see what was really going on. He could have someone stalking him, someone with a contract out on him..."

Aahz waved the cigar and smoke wove itself into a complicated knot. "Psychology, partner, I keep telling you! Let him worry that he's wasting my time. He'll spread the word, so only people with real troubles will come looking for me. In the meantime, Fazil's an operative of mine. He'll check out the scene. If the guy just has some closet monsters that are getting above themselves, the mirrors will do the trick. If it's something worse, Fazil will take care of it." He pounded a hand down on a brown box on the desktop. "Miss Teddybear, would you send in some refreshments?" Aahz gestured at the wall. "Your invisible friend can have some, too. I owe him for getting you here safely."

"It's nothing, friend," the backwoodsman said. He had been disguised as a section of ornamental veneer. He turned around and waddled over to shake hands. "You've made yourself right at home here."

"You bet I have," Aahz said, looking around him with satisfaction. "I've been busy nonstop since I got here, making connections and doing jobs for people."

The efficient aide returned pushing a tray of dishes. She set before Gleep a bowl of something that looked disgusting but was evidently what every dragon wishes he was served every day. My pet lolloped over and began to slurp his way through the wriggling contents. My stomach lurched, but it was soon soothed by the fantastic food that Aahz's assistant served me.

"This is absolutely terrific," I said. "With all the information you've gathered, have you figured out a way to get us back to Deva?"

Aahz shook his head.

"I'm not going back."

"We'll tell everyone about this place, and ... what?" I stopped short to stare at him. "What do you mean you're not going back?"

"For what?" Aahz asked, sneering. "So I can be the magic-free Pervert again?"

"You've always been Pervect without them," I said, hopefully trying to raise his spirits with a bad joke.

It didn't work. Aahz's expression was grim. "You don't have a clue how humiliating it is when I can't do the smallest thing. I relied on those abilities for centuries. It's been like having my arm cut off to be without them. I don't blame Garkin. I'd have done the same thing to him for a joke. It was just my bad luck that Isstvan's assassin happened to have picked that day to put in the hit. But now I've found a place I can do everything I used to."

"Except D-hop," I pointed out, slyly, I hoped. "You're stuck in one dimension for good."

"So what?" Aahz demanded. "Most people live out their whole lives in one dimension."

"... Or hang out with your old buddies."

Aahz made a sour face. "They know me the way I was before I went through the mirror. Powerless." He straightened his back. "I won't miss 'em."

I could tell he was lying. I pushed. "You won't? What about Tanda and Chumley? And Massha? What about the other people who'll miss you? Like me?"

"You can visit me in here," Aahz said. "Get the mirror from Bezel, and don't let anyone else know you've got it."

"You'll get bored."

"Maybe. Maybe not. I've got a long time to get over being powerless. I can't do anything out there without magikal devices or help from apprentices. I'm tired of having people feel sorry for me. Here no one pities me. They respect what I can do."

"But you don't belong here. This is the world of dreams."

"My dream, as you pointed out, apprentice!"

"Partner," I said stiffly. "Unless you're breaking up the partnership."

Aahz looked a little hurt for the moment. "This can be a new branch office," he suggested. "You can run the one on Deva. You already do, for all practical purposes."

"Well, sure, we can do that, but you won't get much outside business," I said. "Only customers with access to Bezel's mirror will ever come looking for you, and you already said not to let anyone know we've got it."

"I can stand it," Aahz assured me. "I'm pretty busy already. I'm important here. I like it. The king and I—we're buddies," Aahz grinned, tipping me a wink. "He said I was an asset to the community. I solve a few little problems for him now and then." The efficient aide leaned in the door. "'Scuse me, partner."

He picked up a curved horn made of metal and held it to his ear. "Hey, your majesty! How's it going?"

If there was ever a Frustration Dream, I was living it. For every reason I presented as to why Aahz should return to Deva, Aahz had a counterargument. I didn't believe for a moment he didn't care about the people he would be leaving behind, but I did understand how he felt about having his powers restored to him. He'd get over the novelty in time.

Or would he? He'd been a powerful magician for centuries before Garkin's unluckily timed gag. Would I be able to stand the thought of losing my talents twice? He did seem so happy here. He was talking with the local royalty like an old friend. Could I pull him away from that? But I had to. This was wrong.

"I'd better leave, sonny," Alder said, standing up. "This sounds like an argument between friends."

"No, don't go," I pleaded, following him out into the hallway. "This isn't the Aahz I know. I have got to get him through the portal again, but I don't know how to find it."

Alder cocked his shaggy head at me. "If he's half the investigator he seems to be, he already knows where it is, friend. The problem you're going to have is not getting him to the water, but making him drink. Right now, things are too cushy for him. He's got no reason to leave."

I felt as though a light had come on. "You mean, he hasn't had enough nuisances?"

Alder's rough-skinned face creased a million times in a sly grin. "I think that's just what I do mean, youngster. Best of luck to you." He turned his back and vanished.

"Thanks!" I called out. Using every bit of influence that was in me, I sent roots down into the deepest wells of magikal force I could find, spreading them out all over the Dreamland. I didn't try to dampen Aahz's light. I brightened it. I made every scale on the building gleam with power, both actual and perceived. Anyone with a problem to solve would know that this was the guy to come to. Aahz would be inundated with cases, important, unimportant and trivially banal. There would be people looking for lost keychains. There'd be little girls with kittens up trees. There'd be old ladies coming to Aahz to help them find the eye of a needle they were trying to thread.

Most important, unless I had missed something on my journey here, with that much influence flying around, every nuisance in the kingdom would converge on the building. If there was one thing my partner hated, and had lectured me on over and over again, it was wasting time. If I couldn't persuade Aahz to leave the Dreamland, maybe nuisances could.

My gigantic injection of magik took effect almost immediately. While I watched, things started to go wrong with the running of Aahz Unlimited. The files the efficient employees were carrying to and fro grew so top-heavy that they collapsed on the floor, growing into haystacks of paper. Some of the employees got buried in the mass. Others ran for shovels to get them out, and ended up tangled with dozens of other people who came in to help. Framed letters began to pop off the wall, falling to the floor in a crash of glass.

Then the entire building seemed to sway slightly to the right.

"What's going on here?" I could hear Aahz bellow.

He emerged from his office, and clutched the door frame as the building took a mighty lurch to the left. I grabbed for the nearest support, which happened to be Gleep. He had become a giant green bird with a striped head and a flat beak and curved talons which he drove deep into the wooden parquet floor. "Why is everything swaying?"

Miss Teddybear flew to the eye-windows and looked down.

"Sir, giant beavers are eating the leg of the building!"

"What?" Aahz ran to join her, with Gleep and me in close pursuit. We stared down out of the huge yellow oval.

Sure enough, enormous brown-black creatures with flat tails and huge square front teeth were gnawing away at the left leg of Aahz Unlimited. As each support in the pylon snapped, the building teetered further.

Aahz leaned out of the window. "SCRAM!" he shouted. The attackers ignored him.

"Everyone get down there and stop them!" Aahz commanded. Miss Teddybear hurried away, following the flood of employees into the moving-box chamber.

As Aahz and I watched, his people poured out of the building. They climbed the leg, clinging to it in an effort to keep the monsters from burrowing any further. The beavers turned, and swatted them off with flips of their flat tails. Wailing, the employees whirled out of sight like playing cards on the wind. The monsters went on chewing. I felt bad about the people, though Alder has assured me that Dreamlanders were not easily hurt or killed.

"Call for reinforcements!" Aahz bellowed. I stared in amazement as white circles whirled out of the air, plastering themselves all over the leg, but the beavers chewed right through them. In no time they'd whittled the leg down to a green stick. The building was going to fall. Aahz's empire was crumbling before our eyes. Gleep seized each of us in one mighty claw and flew with us to the elevator. The floor split under us as we crowded into the small cabinet.

The ride down seemed to take forever and ever. Aahz paced up and back in irritation, dying to get out there and do something to stop the destruction. I could tell he was trying to focus his magik on driving the monsters away and keeping his newfounded empire intact. I concentrated all my magik on keeping us from getting hurt. The forces I had stirred up scared me. I didn't know if I'd get us killed trying to bring Aahz home.

"Come on," he snarled, leaping out of the chamber as it ground to a stop. "We've got to hurry."

It was too late. Just as we emerged from the front door, the enormous Aahz-shaped structure wobbled back and forth, and crashed to lie flat in the park. I gulped. One second sooner, and we'd have been inside when it fell. Aahz stared at the wreckage in dismay.

"Oh, well," I said, trying to look innocent. "Easy come, easy go."

"Yeah," Aahz said, with a heavy sigh. "It was just a dream. There's always more where that came from."

A boy in a tight-fitting uniform with a pillbox hat strapped to his head came rushing up. He handed Aahz a small package the size of his hand. Aahz gave the boy a coin and tore open the paper. Inside was a small mirror. I recognized the frame. "It's the portal back to Deva," I said in surprise. "You were looking for it after all."

"This was supposed to be for you," Aahz mumbled, not meeting my eyes. "If you had wanted to use it. If you had wanted to stay, I wouldn't be upset about it."

The change of tense made me hopeful. "But now you want to go back?" I asked encouragingly.

"I don't need to be bashed over the head with it," Aahz said, then looked at the fallen building, which was already beginning to be overgrown with vines. "But I almost was. I can take a hint. Come on." He took hold of the edges of the mirror. With a grunt of effort, he stretched the frame until the mirror was big enough for all of us.

Through it, instead of the reflection of our dreams, I could see Massha, my apprentice, my bodyguards Nunzio and Guido, and Tananda, our friends all surrounding the hapless Bezel. The Deveel, scared pale pink instead of his usual deep red, held his hands up to his shoulders, and his face was the picture of denial. Terrified denial. He might not be guilty for setting us off on this little adventure after all.

Aahz grinned, fearsomely.

"C'mon. Let's let him off the hook." He took a deep breath and stepped through the mirror.

"Hey, what's all this?" Aahz asked, very casually. "You trying to raise the roof?" He lifted a hand. In the Dreamland the gesture would have sent the tent flying. In this case, it was merely a dramatic flourish. Aahz looked disappointed for less than a second before recovering his composure. I experienced the loss he must have felt, and I was upset on his behalf, but relieved to have gotten him home. He didn't belong in the world of dreams. Some day we'd find a way to undo Garkin's spell.

"Aahz!" Tananda squealed, throwing herself into his arms. "You've been gone for days! We were worried about you."

"You, too, big-timer," Massha said, putting a meaty arm around me and squeezing just as hard. The embrace was a lot more thorough coming from her.

"Thanks," I gasped out.

"Gleep!" my pet exclaimed, wiggling through behind us. The trip through the mirror restored him to dragon-shape. In his joy he slimed all of us, including the trembling Bezel, who was being prevented from decamping by the firm grip Nunzio had on the back of his neck.

"Honest, I swear, Aahz," Bezel stammered. "It wasn't my fault. I didn't do anything."

"Altabarak across the way let the dragon loose, Boss," Guido said, peering at me from under his fedora brim.

"Okay, Bezel," I said, nodding to my bodyguard. If he was positive I was positive. "I believe you. No hard feelings. Ready to go get a drink, partner?" I said. "Everyone want to join me for a strawberry milkshake?"

"Now you're talking," Aahz said, rubbing his hands together. "A guy can have too much dream food." Bezel tottered after us toward the door flap.

"I don't suppose, honored persons," the Deveel said hopefully, the pale pink coloring slightly as he dared to bring business back to usual, "that you would like to purchase the mirror. Seeing as you have already used it once?"

"What?" I demanded, turning on my heel.

"They ought to get a discount," Massha said.

"Throw him through it," Guido advised. Bezel paled to shell-pink and almost passed out.

"Smash the mirror," Aahz barked, showing every tooth. Then he paused. "No. On second thought, buy it. A guy can dream a little, can't he?"

He stalked out of the tent. My friends looked puzzled. I smiled at Bezel and reached for my belt pouch.

Myth-Trained

Robert Lynn Asprin

I focused on the candle's flame. Forcing myself to remain relaxed, I reached out and gently wrapped my mind around it.

The flame didn't flicker. If anything, it seemed to steady and grow. Moving slowly, I extended a finger, pointing casually at the object of my attention. Then, as I released a quick burst of mental energy, I made a small flicking motion with my hand to speed the spell along its way. There was a tiny burst of power, and the flame flared and went out. Neat!

I leaned back in my chair and treated myself to a bit of smug self-congratulation.

"Have you got a minute, Skeeve?"

I glanced toward the doorway. It was my curvaceous assistant. At least, the theory was that she was my assistant. Since she tagged along when I retired from M.Y.T.H. Inc., however, she had taken over not only running the household and the business side of things, but also my life in general. Some assistant.

"Bunny!" I said with a smile. "Just the person I wanted to see. Com'on in. There's something I want to show you."

With a casual wave of my hand, I relit the candle.

"So?" Bunny said, unimpressed. "I've seen you light a candle before. If I remember right, it was one of the first spells you learned."

"Not that," I said. "Watch this!"

I wrapped my mind around the flame, pointed my finger, and released the spell again.

The candle exploded, scattering droplets of hot wax across the table and onto the wall behind it.

"I see," Bunny said, drily. "You've learned a new way to make a mess. Some day you'll learn a spell that helps with cleaning up. Then I'll be impressed."

"That's not how it's supposed to work," I protested. "I did it perfectly just before you came in."

"What is it, anyway?" she said.

"Oh, it's a new spell that was in my latest correspondence lesson for the Magikal Institute of Perv," I said. "It's a magikal way to extinguish a flame. It didn't seem very difficult, so I've been puttering around with it as a break when I'm working on the other lessons."

"A magikal way to extinguish a flame," she repeated slowly. "Is it really a vast improvement on simply blowing the candle out?"

"It's an exercise," I said, defensively. "Besides, if I get good enough at it . . . I don't know, maybe I could put out a whole burning building."

"Hmpf," she said, and I realized I was losing an argument when we weren't even arguing.

"Anyway, what was it you wanted?"

It's an old ploy. When in doubt or in trouble, change the subject. Sometimes it works.

"I just wanted to say that I think you should take a look at Buttercup."

"Buttercup? What's he done now?"

Buttercup was a war unicorn I sort of inherited early in my career. While he isn't as inclined to get into mischief or break things as Gleep, my dragon, that still leaves him a lot of room for minor disasters.

"Nothing I know of," Bunny said. "He just doesn't seem as perky as he usually is. I'm wondering if he's coming down with something."

"Maybe he's just getting old." I realized that I know even less about the longevity of unicorns than I did about their ailments. "I'll take a look at him."

We were currently based in what used to be an old inn. Actually, I had a bit of my history tied up in the inn even before my current relocation. When I first teamed with Aahz, this very inn was the headquarters for our adversary of the moment, one Isstvan. After successfully vanquishing him and sending him off to roam the dimensions, Aahz and I used it as our own base until our subsequent move to Possiltum, and eventually to the Bazaar at Deva. It seemed only natural to return to it when I retired and was looking for a quiet place to pursue my studies.

Buttercup shared the stable area of the inn with Gleep, though more often or not they only used it to sleep. The rest of the time they roamed the grounds playing with each other and getting into the aforementioned mischief. To say the least, this insured that our neighbors and folks from the nearby village gave the place wide berth as a general rule.

I wasn't wild about running him down if they were out terrorizing the countryside, as they were both fleeter of foot and in better condition than I was.

Fortunately he was in residence when I reached the stables.

"Hey, Buttercup! How's it going?"

The unicorn raised his head and glanced at me, then let it sag once more.

Bunny was right. Buttercup did seem very droopy, not at all his normal manner. What was more, his coat seemed dull and dry.

"Are you okay, fella? What's wrong?"

That inquiry didn't even earn me a second glance.

Normally, I'd be at a loss for what to do. This time around, however, I had an idea. Glancing out the stable door to be sure Bunny wasn't within hearing, I turned to Gleep who was watching the proceedings with interest.

"Gleep? Do you know what's wrong with Buttercup?"

I had discovered that my dragon could actually talk, though only in halting sentences. At his request, I had withheld that particular bit of information from my colleagues.

Gleep craned his neck to look out the door himself, then brought his head close to mine.

"Buttercup . . . sad," he said.

My pet's breath was foul enough that it usually drove me back a step or two. My concern was such, however, that I held my ground.

"Sad?" I said. "About what?"

Gleep seemed to struggle to find the words.

"You . . . not . . . use . . . him."

"Not use him?" I echoed, trying to understand. "You mean he wants me to play with him more?"

The dragon moved his head slowly from side to side in ponderous negation.

"No. Not...play. You...not...use...him...to... fight."

Slowly it began to sink in what the problem was.

Buttercup had been working with a demon hunter when we first met. The hunter, Quigley, had moved on to a career in magik, leaving the unicorn with me. While there had been many and varied adventures since then, I had never called on Buttercup to assist in any of them, preferring to deal with the problems by magical means. Well, magik combined with a fair amount of underhanded double talk. Whatever the reason, though, what was once a proud fighting animal had been reduced to the status of a house pet...and he didn't like it.

That seemed to be the problem. The trouble was, I had no idea what to do about it.

For a change, this lack of knowledge or a specific plan did not distress me. If nothing else, in my varied career prior to my retirement, I had amassed an impressive array of specialists, most of whom were usually all too happy to advise me in areas where my own experience was lacking. In this case, I thought I had a pretty good idea of who to turn to.

Big Julie had been commanding the largest army this dimension had ever seen when we first met. I can refer to its impressive size with some authority as, at the time, I was on the other side.

Shortly thereafter, he had retired and was living in a villa near the Royal Palace of Possiltum. We had gotten to be pretty good friends, however, and he had helped me and my colleague out several times on an advisory basis. Not surprising, with his background his advice was unswervingly helpful and insightful. As such, his was the first name that sprang to my mind to consult with regarding my current dilemma with Buttercup.

As always, he was happy to see me when I dropped in, and we immediately fell to reminiscing about old times like old war comrades...which we sort of were. The wine and lies flowed in roughly equal quantities, making for a very pleasant, relaxed conversation.

[author's note: Yes, that was an abrupt shift of time and location. Short stories don't give you much space for lengthy travel sequences. Besides, if they can get away with it in STAR WARS, why can't I?]

As he was refilling our goblets with yet another sample from his extensive wine cellar, he cocked an eye at me and winked.

"So! Enough small talk. What's the problem?"

"Problem?" I said, taken a bit aback. I had figured to ease into the subject slowly.

Big Julie leaned over and clapped me on the knee with his hand.

"You're a good boy, Skeeve," he said. "I'm always glad when you take time to visit. Still, you're busy enough I figure you don't come all this way just to chit chat with an old soldier. To me, that means you've got some kind of a problem you think I might help you with."

A little irked at being found out so easily, I filled him in on my perception of the problem. For all his self-depreciating comments about being an 'old soldier,' as I mentioned before Big Julie had the finest mind regarding things military that this dimension had ever seen.

"A war unicorn, eh?" he said, raising his eyebrows. "Don't see many of those anymore. Still, you could be right. Do you know much about war unicorns?"

"Practically nothing," I admitted easily. "I sort of inherited this one."

"Well, you can forget about that poetic stuff with unicorns and virgins," the retired general said. "Unicorns are fighters, bred specifically for their ferocity and loyalty. They're particularly popular in certain circles because they're all but immune to magik."

"Really? I didn't know that."

"I don't think I've ever heard of one retiring, though," Julie continued. "Usually they die in combat. Once they're trained, it's pretty much all they know. I've had men in my command like that. Been soldiers all their lives and can't imagine being civilians."

I nodded my head thoughtfully. I had thought my problem with Buttercup to be fairly unique. I had never really stopped to think about what soldiers do once they leave the service.

"A lot of the boys go into police work or some other kind of security in the private sector. If you look at it close, though, that's just another form of wearing a uniform and being ready for a fight if the situation calls for it. That's why that plan you came up with to use some of the boys for tax collectors was such a good idea. It took care of our problem of what to do with our excess personnel once Queen Hemlock put her expansion policy on hold. It let us give them an option of a new assignment instead of just cutting them loose after a lifetime of service."

It seemed I had done something intelligent for a change, though I'll admit that at the time I had not been aware of the full ramifications of my action.

"So how does that help me figure out what to do with Buttercup?" I said, frowning.

"Well, it seems to me you need to find Buttercup some action, even if it's just a dummied up training exercise," Big Julie said. "Between the two of us we should be able to come up with something."

"A training exercise?"

"Sure. We do it all the time in the service. Schedule a war game to keep the troops on their toes," he dropped his voice to a conspirator level. "We don't ever admit it, but sometimes we even deliberately position our forces a bit too close to an opposing force... like over their border accidentally on purpose. Of course, they respond, and by the time things are sorted out and apologies have been made, the boys have had a little action to clear away the cobwebs. We could rig something like that for your unicorn."

I got up and did the honors of refilling our goblets. I didn't really want more wine, but it gave me a few minutes to mull over what Big Julie had said. Something about it wasn't sitting right with me.

"Actually, I don't think so," I said finally, shaking my head. "I appreciate the advice, Big Julie, and it's given me something to think about, but I think I'll try a different kind of solution."

"What do you have in mind?"

"Well, instead of hunting down or making up some kind of conflict to make Buttercup feel useful," I said, carefully, "I'm thinking what I need to do is spend some time re-training him."

Big Julie cocked his head.

"Re-training him to do what?"

"I don't really know just yet." I sighed. "As you were talking, though, it occurred to me how sad it was that all Buttercup knows how to do is to fight. More specifically, that, in his opinion, his only value is as a fighter. Instead of trying to re-enforce that problem, I think I want to spend the effort to try to change his self-image."

The general stared at me for several moments.

"I've never asked you, Skeeve," he said at last. "Why did you retire?"

"Me?" I said, caught off guard by the subject change. "I wanted to spend more time studying magik. I'm supposed to be this hot shot magician, but I really can't do all that much. Why?"

Julie made a derisive noise.

"Like the world needs more magicians," he said. "As I understand it, there's barely enough work for the ones we already have."

That stung a little.

"Now I know you military types don't think much of magik or magicians, Big Julie," I said a bit stiffly, "but it's what I do."

"Uh-huh," he said. "Like fighting is what Buttercup does."

"How's that again?" I frowned.

"You should listen to yourself, Skeeve," the general said, shaking his head. "You're saying that your only value to anyone is as a magik user. You still think that even though you admit that you don't really know all that much. Do you really think that's why your old team gave you their respect and followed your lead?

You think I ended up running the army because I'm a rough, tough, invincible fighter?"

That really gave me pause for thought. I had never really considered it, but looking at his frail body, even allowing for age, it was doubtful that Big Julie could go toe to toe with any of the heavyweights I knew like Guido or Hugh Badaxe.

He leaned toward me.

"No, Skeeve. What you did just now, thinking through what's best for other people . . . in this case, your unicorn . . . that's a rare talent. To me, that's more valuable than any new magik tricks you might pick up. The world needs more of that kind of thinking."

Someone, sometime, might have said something nicer than that to me, but if so, it didn't spring readily to mind.

"So what is it exactly that you're suggesting that I do? Come out of retirement?"

"Exactly?" he smiled and winked at me. "I haven't got a clue. You're the thinker. So think about it. Maybe while you're working on Buttercup's self-image you can do a little tinkering with your own."

From the Files of Tambu: The Incident at Zarn

ROBERT LYNN ASPRIN

As the airlock door hissed shut behind him, the reporter took advantage of the moment of privacy to rub his palms on his trouser legs. He wished that he had a bit more faith in his Newsman's Immunity.

He had never really expected to be granted this interview. The request had been the prelude to a joke, a small bit of humor to casually drop into the conversation with other reporters at bars. He anticipated making lofty reference to having been refused an interview with the dread Tambu himself, then as the skeptics voiced their doubts, he could silence them by producing the letter of refusal. These plans had come to a jarring halt when word arrived that his request had been granted.

He had half expected, half hoped that when he completed Phase-Shift he would be greeted by empty space. The ship had been there. Now, here he was aboard Tambu's own flagship about to meet face to face with the most feared individual in the settled Universe. He had only a moment to reflect upon these thoughts when a soft chime sounded and the inner door opened to receive him. Taking a deep breath, he entered.

The first thing that struck him about the quarters was the physical warmth of the room. Since man first invaded space, engineers had been struggling unsuccessfully to combat the chill inherent in dwelling in a metal-alloy ship cruising the cold voids. Even after the problem was supposedly solved with insulations and heated walls, the chill remained, though many claimed it was purely psychological, a subconscious human reaction to the nagging knowledge of the icy emptiness waiting just outside the thin metal walls. But, here it was warm, a heavy, enveloping warmth unlike any he had ever experienced in space.

He instinctively wanted to examine the room more closely and, just as instinctively, suppressed the desire. Instead, he contented himself with a brief visual scan of the room and it's contents. The walls were of a texture unfamiliar to him, which might contribute to the warmth. Or perhaps it was their dark gold color, which was a dramatic contrast to the customary white found in all other ships, and in this one as well, outside the airlocks he had just traversed.

Then, too, there were the trappings of the room making quiet contribution to the atmosphere. There were paintings on the wall and books lined the shelves, honest-to-God books, instead of the sterile tape-scanners usually found in libraries and studies. Facing the far wall was a large desk, clean but well stocked and obviously accustomed to use. The reporter made special note of the fact the desk was set against the wall and faced away from the door, in direct contrast to any other office he had ever been in. Apparently,

Tambu was not accustomed to receiving visitors in these quarters.

The overall effect of the room was quite different from what the reporter had expected. It had the lived-in, personal air of a home, rather than the cold efficiency of a command post. Anywhere else it would have had the effect of being incredibly relaxing. Here, it gave the room the feeling of a lair. The reporter glanced about him again. Where was Tambu?

"Please be seated, Mr. Erickson."

The reporter started at the voice. Glancing around again, he saw a small speaker on the desk he had observed earlier. He crossed the room and seated himself at the desk, facing the speaker.

"I see you brought a Tri°D A/V Recorder with you."

The reporter stiffened in his chair. As he replied, he closely scrutinized the room, particularly the desk in front of him, but was unable to locate the camera which was obviously watching him.

"Yes, sir. I was promised a personal interview."

"Personal, in that you will be dealing with me directly, rather than with one of my subordinates. Unfortunately, a face-to-face meeting is out of the question. In fact, I am not even on the same ship with you. I maintain several flagships identical to the one you are now on. Part of the problem confronting any Defense Alliance ship seeking to capture me is discovering which ship I'm on, and when. Frankly, I was a little dubious about this meeting with you. No offense, but reporters have been known to stray from their oaths of neutrality. If there had been a fleet waiting for us when we completed Phase-Shift, or if you had attempted to sabotage the ship in any way, the crew was under orders to blow the craft up. It is loaded with sufficient explosives to destroy or damage any ships in firing range at the time of detonation. It would have been a costly, but necessary, example to any who might entertain similar thoughts of entrapment."

No wonder the crew had been so glad to see him when he arrived. The calm voice which so casually informed him that the ship he was currently aboard was in actuality a huge bomb did little to ease his frame of mind.

"If you would care for a drink, Mr. Erickson, you will find a bottle of your preferred liquor in the top right-hand drawer. Please, feel free."

More out of curiosity than need, the reporter opened the drawer. In the drawer was a bottle of a particular brand he was extremely fond of, but whose limited production kept the price well beyond his reach, save on special occasions.

"There is a case of that particular brand being loaded onto your ship right now. Please accept it as a personal gift from me."

"You seem to know a great deal about me."

"Probably more than you do about yourself and definitely more than you'd like me to know. Family history, health records, psychological reports, as well as copies of everything you've ever written, including that rather dubious series of articles you wrote in school under an assumed name. That is to say, you were very closely checked before permission for this interview was granted. I don't talk with just any maniac who drops me a note. In my line of work, my whole future, and that of my forces, hinges on my ability to gather and analyze data. If I didn't think you were safe, you wouldn't be here."

"Yet you refuse to meet me face to face and rigged the ship to blow in event of betrayal?"

There was a moment of silence before the reply came.

"I've made mistakes before. Often enough that I long since abandoned any ideas of infallibility. In lieu of that, I guard against all possibilities to the best of my abilities. Now, if you don't mind, could we start the interview? Even though I have tried to set aside time for this meeting, there are many demands on my time and I can't be sure how long we'll have before other priorities pull me away."

"Certainly. I guess the first question would be to ask why someone of your intelligence and abilities turned to the ways of War and world conquering as a way of life, rather than seeking a place in the established order?"

"Purely a matter of convenience. If you think for a moment, I'm sure you could think of several men both as intelligent and as ruthless as I in your so-called established order. As you pointed out, they have successfully risen to positions of power, wealth, and influence. I am not that much different than them, only I chose to move into a field where there was little or no competition. Why fight my way up a chain of command when, by taking one step sideways, I could form my own chain of command with me at the top, running things the way I felt they should be run from the start, instead of adapting someone else's system until I was high enough to make my presence felt."

"But why resort to terrorism and violence as a way

of life? It seems a rather harsh way to extract a living from the universe."

"First tell me how you differentiate between what I and my forces do and the methodology of the Defense Alliance. As near as I can tell, we both make a living from violence and threats. I tell a planet they have to pay me a certain percentage of their resources as tribute, or I'll burn them to a crisp. The Defense Alliance tells them to pay a certain percentage of their resources in taxes to support the fleets or I'll burn them to a crisp. We're both exacting protection money on the threat of violence if they don't pay. Only when they do it, it's an accepted 'police action within the established order.' When I do it, it's a 'reign of terror.' Perhaps I am oversimplifying the situation, but I don't see that much difference between the two."

"Then you don't see anything wrong with what you're doing?"

"Please, Mr. Erickson. None of your journalistic tricks of putting words into my mouth. I did not say I don't see anything wrong in what I do, simply that I don't see that much difference between my own forces and tactics, and those of the Defense Alliance."

"Are you then asserting that in the current conflict that it is you who are the hero and the Defense Alliance the villains?"

"Mr. Erickson, I have asked you once. I will now warn you. Do not attempt to twist my words into quotes I have not said. If I make a statement or express an opinion you take exception to, you are, of course, welcome to comment to that effect, either in this meeting or in your article. However, do not attempt to condemn me with opinions which are not my own. I have shown my respect for you and your intelligence by granting this interview. Kindly return the compliment by remembering that in this interview you are not dealing with a dull-witted planetary sub-official and conducting yourself accordingly."

"Yes, sir. I'll remember that."

"See that you do. You did raise a curious point, however. The rather romantic concept of heroes and villains, good guys and bad guys. That's another reason I granted this interview. It stands out all over your writing, and I wanted to meet someone who really believes in heroes. In exchange, I offered you a chance to meet a villain."

"Well, actually . . ."

"There are no heroes, Mr. Erickson, just as there are no villains." The Death Lord's voice was suddenly cold. "There are only humans. Men and women who alternately succeed and fail. If they are on your side and succeed, they're Heroes. If they're on the other side, they're Villains. It's as simple as that. Concepts such as Good and Evil exist only as rationalizations, an artificial logic to mask the true reasons for our feelings. There is no Evil. No one wakes up in the morning and says 'I think I'll go out and do something rotten.' At the time, their actions are logical and beneficial to them. It's only after the fact, when things go awry, that they are credited with being Evil."

"Frankly, sir, I find that a little hard to accept."

"Of course. That's why you're here. So I could take this opportunity to show you another viewpoint than that which you are accustomed to. As a journalist, you are no doubt aware that in the course of my career I have been compared with Genghis Khan, Caesar, Napoleon, and Hitler, depending upon who was doing the comparing. Yet I believe that, if you could have interviewed any one of these men, he would tell you the same thing I am today, that there is no difference between the two sides of a battle, except the 'Them and Us' concept. There may be racial, religious, cultural, or armament differences, but the only determination of who is the Hero and who is the Villain is the side he's on. That and who wins."

"Then what you are claiming is that this equality of opponents also applies to today's situation?"

"Especially today. Now that mankind has moved away from the bloodbath concept of war, it is easier than ever to observe. Despite the blood-curdling renditions of Space Warfare which adorn the news tapes and literature, actual combat is a rarity. It's far too costly in men and equipment, and there is no need. Each fleet has approximately four hundred ships of varying sizes and there are over two thousand inhabited solar systems. Even at the rate of one ship per solar system, there is always going to be over one half of the systems unoccupied. For either force to move on a new system means temporarily abandoning another system. As such, there is little or no combat between the fleets. The objective is to either move into unoccupied systems and divert their tribute into our coffers, or move into an occupied system with sufficient force to where the opposing ships will abandon the system rather than enter into a lopsided battle. It's a massive game of move and counter-move with little, if any, difference between the gamesmen."

"What about the inhabitants of the planets?"

"The civilians? What about them? Oh, you mean are they an important factor in the game? Not really. That's not so much cold-blooded as fact. With the current armament of the ships, one ship could easily wipe out an entire system planet by planet, if that was our aim. The planets themselves have little effective defense against a ship in orbit and no means of counterattack. However, that is not our aim, any more than it its that of the Defense Alliance. We both make a living by demanding a percentage of each planet's resources. If we burn them, we're only hurting ourselves. Even if we have to abandon a system, there is always the possibility of having a chance to win it back, so it's left as intact as possible. Again, both we and the Defense Alliance encourage non-resistance. We'd like nothing better than to have no resistance at all from the planets, no matter who they're fighting."

"Yet you do encounter resistance."

"Yes, both sides do occasionally, when there is a change of control. I've always found that puzzling. The rate of tribute doesn't change that much. Some feel it's because the civilians take the propaganda about loyalty more seriously than the fleets do. My own theory is that they may have already paid the month's tribute to one side and are resisting having to pay twice in one period."

"Yet you claim it is a bloodless war."

"Compared to the Old Wars, yes. The waste of men and machinery in those days was unbelievable. While we have our casualties, they can, usually, be counted on one hand. In today's war, the only time someone dies is by mistake, either his own or someone else's."

"Without counting civilians, of course. What about the times there is a battle? What about things like the incident at Zarn?"

There was a prolonged silence. Finally the reporter

cleared his throat in preparation to speak, though whether to apologize for the question or to restate it, he had not completely made up his mind. But before he could organize his thoughts, much less put them into words, the voice of Tambu hailed him again from the speaker.

"Very well. You have given me a blunt question. I could give you an equally blunt answer. However, if I did, it would only be my word, which you seem reluctant to accept. Instead, I will allow you to judge for yourself. Open the second drawer from the top on your left."

The reporter did so, and found himself looking at a Tri°D headset and keyboard, similar to one he would find in the editing office for a major news service.

"Usually, the Ship Log of any combat ship is considered classified and only edited portions are published, if that. In this case, however, I will allow you to view the uncensored tapes of the incident you questioned, which were salvaged from the wreckage of the battleship. They are from my personal files and have, to date, been viewed by none but myself. The action you are about to watch begins as the ship was preparing to launch its attack on Xoltan, the third smallest outpost in the system under dispute. In my opinion, it is here that all the pertinent action leading up to the incident at Zarn begins. If, after viewing it, you wish to see any earlier tapes, feel free to ask. When you're ready, key in the following tape reference..."

The reporter donned the headset and keyed the code into the Tape Retrieval Unit. There was a momentary pause, and he was there! The Tri°D illusion was frighteningly realistic. He was in the Command

Station of the Battleship, sitting behind a uniformed figure seated in a swivel Captain's Chair. As the figure turned to flip the switches activating the triple bank of viewscreens, the reporter recognized him as Podan, the soon-to-be infamous villain of intergalactic infamy. His appearance was startling, quite unlike the photos currently in circulation of him. All newsfile pictures either showed a uniformed figure braced in typical military arrogance or a flat, unemotional personnel picture which gave him the appearance of a convict. In contrast to this, the figure, or rather, the projection before the reporter was nervously animated. The features of his face were lined with worry, or possible fatigue, and he was constantly running his hands through his sparse hair, a habit apparently lingering from the days when the hair was more plentiful

"Weapons. Report!"

"Here, sir!" a young girl's face winked onto one of the viewscreens.

"I said, report!"

"Yes, sir! All weapons on standby, as per your instructions." There was a hurt admonishment in the girl's voice.

"Good! Navigation!"

Another screen winked to life, revealing a male figure, older, with a startling shock of white hair.

"Yes, Po?"

"Is the position for attack on Xoltan entered in the computer?"

"Yes, Po."

"And the secondary unit?"

"Set with our current position for immediate retreat,

as per your instructions. Come on, Po...." The patient reproach was far more apparent in the Navigator's voice.

"Can it Phil. Communications!"

"Yes, sir!" The face of a smiling young man appeared on the third screen.

"Anything on the detectors?"

"No, sir." The smile faded to a look of mild annoyance. "If I might point out to the Captain, if anything *was* on the detectors, then by the Captain's *own* orders..."

"All right, all right!" Podan interrupted. He heaved a great sigh and ran his fingers through his hair once more. "Okay, crew, listen up! I know I've been a bit jumpy lately and I've probably leaned on you more than was necessary. As you know, we've encountered rather unusual resistance in this system. We've already burned two of their outposts without the slightest sign of surrender from the system. Well, there is a strong chance that there is more involved here than stubbornness."

He paused, more out of reluctance to continue than for effect. The crew waited attentively. "Intelligence reports that there are three Defense Alliance scout ships currently stationed in this system. The captains are Elkhart, Set, and Yahnos, respectively."

The crew suddenly stiffened to attention in the viewscreens.

"That's right. The famous 'Three Musketeers.' The pride of the Defense Alliance. Each of these captains is individually credited with blocking over a dozen efforts of Tambu's, either by combat or by trickery, and we are now faced with all three of them working as a team. It is my belief the system under attack has refrained from surrender primarily because these three have given their assurances that we can be stopped."

"Let 'em try!" the brash voice of the Communications man interjected. "Anyone fool enough to try to stop a battleship with three scouts is going to which he hadn't."

"Don't bet on it, Benji. Theoretically, you're right. It's impossible. But bigger ships than ours have been stopped by these three, theories or not. They're quick to take advantage of overconfidence, and that's one edge we're not going to give them. Get me?"

"Yes, sir," replied the Junior Officer, properly mollified.

"Okay. Now patch me through to Tambu for final confirmation."

"Can I have a word with you while he establishes contact, Captain? Privately?" It was the Navigator.

"Sure, Phil. Benji, buzz me when you're ready."

With that, the Captain flipped two switches, and the Weapons and Communications screens went blank, leaving him "alone" with his navigator.

"Okay, Phil. What's up?"

"Po, I'd like to ask you to back away from this one."

"That's more than a bit out of line, Lieutenant! A junior officer can't—"

"I'm asking as your friend, Po. Back away from it."

The Captain sighed. For a moment, he seemed to almost shrink in stature and, when he spoke, his voice was tired.

"I can't, Phil. You know what happened before..."

"Yes, I do. And that's exactly why I'm asking you to back off."

"But the orders clearly state—"

"Any Captain can halt a campaign at any point at his own discretion if, in his opinion, the situation warrants it! That's in the book, too."

"At my own discretion! On what basis? Because I've tangled with them before and got walked on? For all we know, that's why we were assigned this campaign. Maybe that's why I was chosen to hit this system, instead of another captain who's only heard about those three by legend. Oh, don't worry. I'm not entertaining any delusions about my own skills. But I can't back out just because of their name before they've openly opposed us. I can't and I won't!"

"But dammit, Po..."

A quiet buzz interrupted the argument. Immediately, Podan pivoted around and flipped a switch.

"Okay, Benji. Patch him through. I'm ready."

"Uh, Captain, we've got problems. I can't get through."

There was a frozen moment, then the Captain hit another switch, allowing the Navigator to hear and see the Communications man.

"Report, please."

"I said I can't get through to Tambu. Communications are blocked."

"Have you checked your Trans-gear?"

"Yes, sir. Twice! I've never seen anything like it. All equipment checks out perfectly, but I can't raise anyone."

"Settle down, Benji. Okay, now you're supposed to be some kind of genius with a squawk box. You tell me. If you wanted to jinx our Communications from outside the ship, completely shut us down, how would you do it?"

The youth gnawed his lip thoughtfully.

"Well, sir, the only way I see it could be done would be with a jamming buoy, maybe a series of them, between the ship and our relay station, but—"

"Then that's what they've done!"

"But, sir," insisted the youth, "to do that, they'd have to know our exact, well, at least our approximate location in the system, and that's impossible."

"Benji, the first thing you learn when dealing with opponents the caliber of these three we're up against is to forget the word 'impossible,' because *they* do!"

"But why? I mean, what could they hope to accomplish by shutting down our Communications?"

The Captain sighed.

"If you can't figure it out, Benji, I don't have the time to explain it. Stand by for further instructions."

He smashed a switch down with his fist and the Communication screen went blank.

"Well, that's that!" contributed the Navigator.

"Shut up, Phil!"

"C'mon, Po. It's over! If final attack orders are not confirmed with Tambu, a ship is to break off the campaign and return to rendezvous. You know the standing orders as well as I do. For all we know, the system has surrendered."

The Captain slumped in his chair.

"You're right, Phil. But, damn, it galls me. You and I both know it's their countermove. They're using our own regulations to knock us out of the campaign."

"As neat a checkmate as I've ever seen," agreed the Navigator, "but unless you see an out, I don't. We're stuck! Shall I calculate the Phase-Shifts to rendezvous?"

"First, let me see the charts showing our position."

"C'mon Po, you're stalling."

"Lieutenant! I want to see those charts."

"Okay, Po, we'll do it your way."

In the viewscreen, the Navigator turned to a Retrieval Keyboard. He lazily punched a series of keys and his image was replaced by a highly detailed star chart criss-crossed with luminous lines and speckled with military symbols. The Captain glowered at it for many long moments, then suddenly his body stiffened. Half rising from his seat, he craned his neck forward to examine the chart more closely.

"Phil!"

"Yes, Po."

"What's the dotted red line?"

There was a brief pause.

"Uh . . . the blue line is our course to dated in this system . . . and the green is the rendezvous zone."

"I know how to read a star chart! I asked you a question! What is the dotted red line?"

"That's, um, that's our anticipated course if the mission continues."

"But I haven't issued orders yet on our future course! When did you plot this line?"

"As soon as were assigned to this system."

"But how did you know our course in advance?"

"C'mon, Po. Recommended procedure is no big secret. We start with the smallest uninhabited planet with a manned outpost and work our way up to the largest. Then, if they haven't surrendered, we start on the inhabited planets in the same pattern of smallest to largest. I just applied recommended procedure to the data on this system and *presto!* I've got our course."

"But the actual attack pattern is left up to the

individual commander. At his discretion, he can vary the pattern to fit the situation."

"True enough, Po. But in all the years I've served with you, you haven't deviated from recommended procedure once. It's just a little shortcut I use to get a little leisure time."

"Phil, do you realize what you're saying? For God's sake! It's textbook tactics! Once you allow yourself to become predictable, the enemy can move against you at leisure! That's how they knew where we'd be! If you can do it, they can do it!"

"Now, settle down, Po—"

"Settle down, hell! We've got them. I've finally figured out how those bastards do it! The more we follow rules and procedures, the more we're playing into their hands!"

"But the rule states—"

"The rule states that a commander can continue on a mission if, in his opinion, there is an immediate advantage to be seized upon and, by God, we've got an advantage! What's the nearest inhabited planet?"

"Um, that would be Zarn."

"Good. I want you to give me two courses. First, plot a shift directly to Zarn, then enter a course from Zarn to Xoltan into the secondary unit."

"Okay, Po. But—"

The Captain ignored the reply as he switched on the other two viewscreens.

"Attention all stations! There is a change in procedures. Prepare for immediate combat! Suz, I want one bank ready for a planet and all other banks prepped for ship-to-ship combat!"

"Yes, sir. But—"

"No 'buts'! Do it! Phil! Have you got those shifts computed yet?"

"Ready, Po. But would you mind telling us what we're doing?"

"Not at all, but first we shift. Suz, stand by weapons, just in case. All stations, ready. Shift!"

If there was any question as to whether a ship actually vibrated during a Phase-Shift, or if it merely was a biological impact from the high speed transfer, the log tapes clearly settled the dispute once and for all. The furniture and equipment remained stoically immobile, while the Captain flinched and writhed in the agonies of unseen pressures. Finally, he straightened, shook his head as if to clear it, and turned to the viewscreens once more.

"Shift complete! Communications! Detector report of craft in the vicinity!"

"Negative, sir!"

"Good. Standby for screen change to full 360/360 exterior. All communications on audio only!"

Again his hands darted across the switches, and the viewscreens changed to display a tri-screen view of the space surrounding the ship. There, stretched out below them, was the bluish-green terrain of the target planet.

"Hold at present position! Now, where are we? Oh, yes! Phil, you were asking what we're doing. Well, we're going to break the sterling record of Captains Elkhart, Set and Yahnos by taking this damn system right out from under their noses. They've been having a grand old time at our fleet's expense because they've found our rules have made us predictable. Well, I've got a hot flash for them. Now that we know how they're doing it, they are just as predictable as we are.

"Take, for example, our current situation. They correctly guessed where we were going to be in the system and set up a communications blockade. Knowing our regulations, they expect that this maneuver will make us abort the mission. But, where will they be? It is my guess that they are currently holding position around Xoltan on the off chance we might ignore their gambit and push on to our next target. At least, that's what they *think* our next target would be. Suz! Is that planet-side bank ready?"

"Yes, sir!"

"Okay, Benji! How long do you think it will take the civilians downstairs to realize we're here?"

"Their detectors should be reading us right now, Captain. I imagine it's causing quite a bit of fuss."

"Right! Suz! Stand by to fire. Phil! I want you to shift us out of here immediately after we fire—and I mean immediately. I don't even want to see the strike land."

"Okay, Po, if you say so."

"I say so! Now then, the civilians are going to start screaming for help, and who have they got to turn to but our three heroes? We are giving our Captains a problem. All of a sudden they get an emergency call from a planet threatened by a ship they thought was on its way home. The question is, will they abandon their picket on the word of some panicky civilian to go chase space bogies?

"Incidentally, Benji, do you think those clowns will get caught in their own communications blockade?"

"Not a chance, Captain. They're well within the radius. The block's primarily intended to stop communication from outside the system. They should be screaming right now, if my guess is right."

"Perfect. Well, gang, let's shut that message down in mid-transmission. It should lend a certain air of urgency to a distress call. All systems, stand by! Ready to fire and Phase-Shift. Ready...Fire!...Shift!"

Again, the Captain jerked and twisted as though tortured by unseen hands. The stars in the viewscreen suddenly reeled and jerked as the ship plunged off to its new destination. By sheer physical effort Podan kept erect in his command seat, his eyes riveted on the screens. Suddenly, the shift was complete. This time, instead of the bleak face of a planet, the screens steadfastly displayed the image of a Defense Alliance Scout Ship laying almost directly alongside their vessel.

For several long moments, the Captain stared at it without comprehending. Then he reacted.

"Suz! Get him! Damn it! Burn him! Quick, before—"

Almost at the same moment as he shouted, a dozen beams and tracers leaped to life on the screen. Hungrily, they closed on the vessel on the screen. Suddenly, there was a blinding flash of light and the ship had disappeared. The screens showed only the stars, the planet beneath them, and a few lingering tracers racing out into the blackness.

For several heartbeats, there was a hush, tension hanging heavy in the air. At last the communicator broke the silence.

"Detectors show no other vessels in immediate vicinity, Captain."

Body still tense, eyes still locked on the screen, the Captain leaned slightly forward toward the panel mike. As he spoke, his voice was hushed and tight.

"As I was saying, presented with such a problem, the probable action is to dispatch two of the three ships to investigate the distress call, leaving one ship to maintain the picket. There is a gamble in this move of dividing their strength, since a battleship has over three times the shift range of a scout ship. They just lost their gamble, crew. The vessel we have just destroyed was their picket."

"Weapons here, sir. Do we hit Xoltan?"

"What's that? No. We've hit our planet for today. That bit was to prove my theory the only way it could be proved. Phil! Shift us out of here."

"Where to, Po?"

"Anywhere. Just make it maximum distance from here. And make it quick! The other two will be back soon and I'm not up to another fight today!"

"Okay, Po. On my command. Stand by to shift. Ready . . . Shift."

For the third time the battleship moved on. This time, the Captain sat hunched over the console, eyes downcast, the reflexive twitching almost unnoticed. When the shift was completed, he remained in this position, seemingly lost in his own thoughts.

"Communications here! Captain, we've reestablished contact! Tambu's on the squawk box and wants to talk to you!"

Podan snapped out of his reverie with a start. "Right, Benji! And patch this through to the other stations. I want the whole crew to hear it!"

"Right, Captain! Here he is!"

"Captain Podan?" Tambu's voice was chilly and abrupt.

"Yes, sir!"

"Do you know what you've done?"

"Well, we—"

"I'll tell you what you've done! You've just burned a planet in a system that had already surrendered!"

The words crackled and hung in the air.

"But, sir! Our communications—"

"Don't give me that 'sir' crap! You have set procedures to follow in the event of a communications failure!"

Podan drew himself up angrily. "And I was exercising my prerogative as Ship's Commander to countermand any standing order if I felt the situation warranted it. I had reason to believe the enemy was using our Standing Orders to maneuver us into abandoning the mission!"

There was a long silence. When Tambu spoke again, his voice was weary.

"All right, Captain. I can understand your position and, to a certain degree, sympathize with it. However, I hope you can also understand mine. I cannot sanction your action. If I did, we'd never have another planet surrender to us without a pitched battle.

"As such, I have been forced to disclaim any knowledge of your attack on Zarn, and join with the Defense Alliance in decrying you as a maniac. Captain, you and your crew are now full-fledged War Criminals, and in the future you can expect to be fired upon by any ship which comes into contact with you, no matter which fleet she's from. The most I can do for you is delay reporting your position for eight hours to allow you a head start. That, and wish you luck. And believe me, you're going to need it!"

There was an air of grim determination to the Captain as he bent towards the panel-mike.

"Sir! In this mission we have gained vital information

about the methods of certain key captains in the Defense Alliance fleet. We are willing to exchange this information for refuge in your sphere of protection!"

"Captain, that information if of no value to us. I regret to inform you that Captains Set and Yahnos have resigned from the Defense Alliance. If our information is correct, they have pledged themselves to the job of hunting you down. Again, I wish you luck, but there's nothing else I can do."

The reporter slowly removed the headset and replaced it in the drawer. The events he had just witnessed had had a great impact on him and he made no effort to hide it.

"Is that your arch-villain, Mr. Erickson? That dullard of a Captain who tried to be brilliant, only to see it fall apart before his very eyes?"

"Then, if I understand you correctly, sir, you are setting for the hypothesis that if Podan had not made a mistake, if he had not attacked without confirmation, the entire incident at Zarn would never have occurred?"

Tambu's voice was weary, almost as if he was talking to himself.

"Mr. Erickson, I'm afraid you miss the point entirely. The error was mine in assigning Podan to that system. I knew about his personal involvement with the Musketeers. I also knew his earlier failure was haunting him, gnawing at the self-confidence so necessary in a battleship commander. I knew the system would surrender, despite the Musketeers assurances—it's that kind of system. I wanted to hand him a victory on a platter, something to build him up. I underestimated his self-confidence, I underestimated the Musketeers, and I underestimated his emotional involvement. The mistake was mine, and it cost me a planet, a battleship, and one of my captains.

"People die today from mistakes, not by plan."

The Ex-Khan

ROBERT LYNN ASPRIN

My first day in Hell was the worst. I mean, I hadn't thought it would be a picnic, but my wildest imagining still left me unprepared for the reality of my afterlife existence.

Actually, I hadn't expected to find myself here at all. On the rare occasions during my former life that my thoughts had drifted toward death, my logical twentieth-century mind had calmly concluded that when I died, that would be the end of things as far as I was concerned. No angels with harps, no devils with pitchforks. Just...nothing. Pull the plug. End game.

If I had allowed myself to seriously consider an afterlife, I probably would have figured that I'd end up with the good guys. While I had always kidded around a lot about what a perverted, wicked person I was, most of it was just hooey. Villains are more interesting people than heroes, as a rule, and neither I nor my cronies wanted to be thought of as the "goody two-shoes" type, so we made a big deal of our coarse humor and imagined coups, both business and social. Underneath it all, though, we really thought we were good people. Evil people were killers or rapists or child molesters or something. Heck, I had never even gotten a traffic ticket, just a couple parking fines. My few attempts at sowing wild oats were pleasant and amicably terminated by mutual consent. Surely little things like that couldn't count against you in the grand scales of life.

So what was I doing in Hell?

This question was foremost in my mind upon my arrival in my new home. The horrible Welcome Woman was no help at all, continually insisting that "Everybody feels the same way when they first arrive," and "It will all come clear to you after a while," and generally being a pain in the butt without providing one whit of information in response to my questions. I finally grew frustrated with my unrewarded efforts, and while she was prattling on about the politics of Hell (which did not interest me any more than earthly politics had), wandered off to try to find the answer on my own.

My first impression of Hell was that it was surprisingly ordinary...well, sort of. No devils, no pitchforks, no pools of molten lava with tortured souls shrieking in agony. There were, however, a fair number of people moving purposefully about in an amazing array of costumes. It reminded me a bit of the time I took a guided tour of a West Coast movie studio... so much so it took me a while to realize that these weren't actors in costume, but individuals wearing what to them were normal clothes from their native eras of history. Aside from the strange wardrobes and mottled red sky, there was little to distinguish the panorama of Hell from any busy business section or college campus. I didn't know whether to be relieved or disappointed.

The feeling of familiarity continued when I tried to stop people to ask questions. Just like the streets of home, my efforts were rebuffed with comments of "No time now," and "Ask someone else." All in all, the people here were a rather self-centered lot, each caught up in his or her own affairs and not really caring about the problems of a stranger. Of course, that's what I was doing myself . . . expecting everyone to drop everything until my curiosity was satisfied. This gave me food for thought. Was it a sin to be self-centered? If so, then Hell must be a bigger place than I imagined. Even the most saintly people I knew back in the '80s still kept an eye out for the old Number One.

I was still pondering this hypothesis when I noticed him for the first time. If he hadn't been outside the mainstream of normal foot traffic in a small park, and sitting, which placed him well below eye level, I would have seen him at once. Though unimposing physically, he still would have stood out in the crowd.

While most of the people I had seen or tried to talk to were civilians of one sort or another, this one was a warrior. What's more, his armor and weapons marked him as being from the Far East, while most of the crowd seemed to be of Western European origins.

Intrigued, I drifted closer for a better look.

The man raised his head as I approached and regarded me with eyes as hard and dark as obsidian. His face was round and weathered brown, with expression lines as deep as if they had been carved into wood with a chisel. His manner was neither hostile nor friendly, but rather held the detached watchfulness of a reptile contemplating whether I were small enough to eat. I was briefly reminded of an old photograph of Geronimo I had once seen.

I halted my advance and smiled in what I hoped was a friendly and, above all, harmless way. After a moment, he gave a silent grunt and returned his attention to his work.

My distress at not knowing why I had been condemned to Hell was upstaged by my fascination with the man and the chore he was addressing. His weapons were laid out before him on a blanket and he was checking them with the unhurried certainty of one who has performed the same task hundreds, if not thousands of times. With deft precision he checked the edge of the sword and knife, then began working his way through his quiver of arrows one by one, checking each for straightness, like a hustler checking a pool cue. Finally, I could contain my curiosity no longer.

"You're a Mongol, aren't you?"

That earned me a longer look.

I wondered briefly if he understood English, but then I noted that his carriage had shifted slightly. While still appearing relaxed, the man was now poised and ready to move fast, and his eyes were warier and more analytical than they had been a few moments before. He understood me all right, and for some reason, my words had raised his guard.

"What makes you ask that?"

His voice was resonant bass with a bit of a flat accent I couldn't identify.

"Your weapons," I answered with a casual shrug. "Your armor is Chinese, but your weapons are those of the Great Horde. Double-recurve laminated bow, the hooked sword, thrusting lance . . . that's standard gear for a Mongol horseman, isn't it? The arrows are a dead giveaway. As far as I know, the Mongols were the only ones to use two different caliber arrows: light for flight, or heavier for close, armor-piercing work."

His head dipped slightly in the briefest of nods.

"You are knowledgeable in our ways," he said. "I am not familiar with your manner of dress. Are all men of your era so well versed on the weapons of their enemies?"

"No. Military history just happens to be a hobby of mine . . . and we don't consider Mongols to be our enemies. No offense, but your descendants are no longer the world power they were in your time."

His eyes were distant for a few heartbeats, then his face split in a sudden grin, showing surprisingly white teeth. "So they tell me. Still, one can always hope for a rebirth of the old times, can't one?"

I returned his smile, but shook my head.

"Not much chance of that happening, I'm afraid. Everything today is firearms and missiles. Masses of men and machines are settling today's wars, not the skill of the individual warrior."

"It was much the same in our day," the Mongol shrugged carelessly. "Large numbers of troops won the day for the Horde often enough."

"Really?" I frowned. "I was under the impression that more often than not you were outnumbered. The Mongols I studied relied more on tactics based on psychological warfare and incredible mobility to take advantage of the myth of vast mobs of horsemen."

The dark eyes studied me again, all hint of laughter gone.

"Once more you are correct," the man acknowledged. "I would know the name of the man who is not easily deceived in this land of deceptions."

It took me a moment to realize what he meant.

"Who, me? My name is Will Hawker."

The man nodded, then turned his attention to his weapons once more, picking up his sword to test its edge again.

It seemed that he felt our conversation was at an end. I, however, was eager to prolong the discussion and cast about desperately for something to say.

"Does your sword have a name?"

That at least earned me another glance.

"Does your right thumb have a name?"

I had been expecting a yes-or-no answer, so his question caught me off guard.

"My...No. It doesn't."

"Neither does my sword. My weapons are to me as your thumb is to you...a part of my body. They require no more thought to use than does your thumb. The custom of naming a weapon as if it were an independent being has always been a puzzle to me."

His level, matter-of-fact tone made me feel chastised to a point where I felt it necessary to defend my question.

"I always felt it was a way of expressing respect for one's weapons. The people I knew who named their weapons usually claimed to love a named weapon with the same passion they did a brother or a lover."

"That is what I've been told," the Mongol said with a shrug. "I have simply never agreed with it. To me a weapon is a tool to be used, not loved. If one becomes emotionally attached to a weapon..."

He broke off suddenly, his attention captured by something nearby in the park.

I followed his gaze, and saw a bush that moved... first with a tentative tremor, then flipping back along with a portion of the ground it was rooted in to reveal a dark hole beneath. Before I could speak, a small figure in dark, loose-fitting pajamas popped out carrying a rifle. He scanned the park and the passers-by on the street, his eyes pausing briefly on me, then moving on to my companion. His head dipped in a brief nod of acknowledgement or recognition, then he turned and gestured at someone in the hole.

Four more men, dressed and armed like their point man, emerged from the hole. The last two had their weapons slung and were carrying a sixth man on a litter between them. The borne man was still, though whether dead or unconscious I couldn't tell. The point man replaced the bush to hide the hole once more, and the band moved off silently in single file, carrying their fallen comrade with them.

"Those look like Viet Cong!" I exclaimed, finding my voice at last.

"That's right," the Mongol said calmly, turning his attention to his weapons once more. "Some of them have been included in our honored ranks here in Hell. You'll get used to seeing them. Hell is riddled with their tunnels and spider holes, so there's no telling where they'll pop up next."

He seemed unimpressed by their unexpected intrusion into our area, so I decided to try to match his manner and return to our conversation. "Tell me, we've been discussing weapons here. Why is it that you still have sword, lance, and bow when they have more modern weapons? Those are AR-15s they were carrying, weren't they?"

"I am used to these weapons," he said. "Besides, you would be surprised at how well these old tools work against more modern devices. The sword is still one of the best close-combat weapons ever devised, if one has the time to train with it . . . and I've had lots of time."

"I notice the Cong didn't seem particularly anxious to fight with you."

The Mongol's lips twisted into a flat smile. "There is an unspoken truce between us. While they respect my weapons, sometimes a name is more power than the keenest sword. They know me . . . or at least their ancestors did."

Something in his voice sent a chill down my spine, though I couldn't put a finger on it.

"Speaking of names," I said as casually as I could, "I've shared mine with you, but you haven't yet told me yours."

He seemed to hesitate for a moment before answering.

"I am called Temujin by some."

The name struck me like a blow. As I said earlier, military history is a hobby of mine. While the name might be unknown to many of my age and era, it was more than familiar to me. The person I was talking to was none other than . . .

"Genghis Khan."

I was almost unaware of saying the name aloud, my awestruck words matching my thoughts. I would have been glad for the opportunity to chat with any member of the Mongol hordes, but it had never occurred to me that I would ever have the chance to talk to the Great Khan himself! Maybe Hell wouldn't be such a bad place after all.

"You know the name . . . and the title," the man said in a flat tone that was as much an accusation as a statement. "I would know your thoughts regarding your discovery."

I realized with a start that his sword was now between us, held in a loose guard position. I had seen experienced fencers in similar stances so I was not fooled by the apparent casualness of his position. The Mongol could attack me without even a split-second delay to prepare . . . only his sword was real and there was more at stake here than tournament points! Taking care not to move my hands, I groped for the proper words.

"Um, amazement . . . curiosity, admiration . . ."

"No anger?" the Mongol interrupted. "No desire to attack me or at least raise an alarm?"

"Why should I want to do that?"

The Khan's lips flattened into a humorless grin.

"Forgive me if I'm wrong, but you seem to be of European stock. My people were the scourge of your ancestors, and as their leader, I am one of your greatest folk villains. You would not be the first in these lands who felt it meet to attempt to make Hell a little less pleasant for an old enemy."

"I can't speak for the others here," I said, raising my hands to shoulder height, palms forward, "but you have nothing to fear from me. Even if I could attack you successfully, which I doubt, I wouldn't. You see, I've never really thought of you as a villain. While it is true that you and your troops were ferocious and brutal, your culture and era required a certain amount of viciousness for survival. What's more, even in my era it was difficult to distinguish how much of the documented brutality of the Mongol hordes was accurate, and how much was exaggeration on the part of either your enemies' chroniclers or your own propaganda machine. No, I have been more fascinated by the more admirable side of your reported personality."

"And exactly what is it about me that you feel is admirable?" he pressed.

"Well, first of all, there's the basic success story that would be the envy of any businessman of my time: a boy without family or village in his early teens being actively hunted by his enemies, and in less than three decades building an empire that ruled over a third of the known world. Your abilities as a military leader and tactician are acknowledged by even your staunchest critics, but most of them choose to overlook your other contributions. You not only united the tribes into a massive army, the horde, but you also gave them a written language and a governing set of laws on the Yassa. Your arrowriders formed a communications network far ahead of its time . . . in fact, it lasted longer and performed better than the Pony Express of a much later period. As far as I have been able to discover, you were the one who introduced the concept of paper money to the world, and you insisted on religious tolerance to a degree that makes the European and Middle East indulgence in holy wars look like ignorant barbarism. No, I have no difficulty admiring you, and I am frankly grateful for the chance to speak with you in person."

Apparently my sincerity was convincing, for the Khan sheathed his sword with a dry laugh.

"It is comforting to know that my efforts have not gone totally unnoticed in your lands," he said, "but beware, Will Hawker. Beware of being as blind with your admiration as others are with their hate and fear. While some of the things I did may have had a beneficial long-term effect on mankind, many of them were instituted from motives as base and greedy as the worst in history."

"Could you give me an example?" I said. "I have often wished I could learn the motives and thoughts behind some of your policies...good or bad."

"Well...you mentioned our Mongolian scrip—paper money, I think you called it. That was nothing more than bloodless, systematized looting. When we were occupying a new area, we would insist that taxes and tributes be paid in gold, jewels, or other valuables. For our own debts, we would pay with paper notes. The trick was that when it was time to collect taxes again, we would not accept our own paper in return, but instead insisted on another round of valuables. Within a few years, all the hard wealth, such as gold, was in our coffers and all the people had to exchange was paper."

I found myself smiling. "Actually, your concept has been followed with frightening accuracy. In my era, all nations have their citizens exchanging paper while the government holds the actual wealth—be it in gold, silver, or crown jewels. I just never thought of it as organized looting before."

The Khan joined me in my laughter.

"So I've been told. If nothing else, I fear that particular contribution of mine to civilization has guaranteed me a place in your Hell."

A random thought brought my laughter to a slow halt.

"That raises an interesting point," I said. "What are you doing in Hell?"

Though he also stopped laughing, the Khan's eyes still smiled at me with mischievous humor.

"You have to ask? Me? The bloodiest butcher of history? If anyone, surely I've earned a place here."

"No, I meant . . . well, Hell is primarily a Christian concept. How is it that you have been drawn to an afterlife outside your own religion?"

That earned me a shrug. "There have been several theories posed by the various philosophers here to explain my presence. Some feel that the religious tolerance of mine you referred to earned me a place in the eyes of the Christian God, and subsequently resulted in my assignment here. Others feel that my presence is actually a stage prop for the Europeans here . . . that their Hell would not be complete without their arch-enemy lurking in the background. The presence of the Viet Cong here seems to support their theory. Then again, it may be that part of my own afterlife punishment is to exist surrounded by Europeans rather than my own countrymen."

"But what do you think?"

The amusement vanished from the Mongol's manner, and he turned his attention once more to his weapons. "I think that it is pointless to think of such things. I am here. Why I am here is unimportant. The time to plan and ponder a battle is before the conflict is joined, not while actively engaged with the enemy. Then hindsight is a dangerous indulgence, for it draws our concentration away from the task at hand. One must condition oneself to reject such thoughts in favor of studying the terrain and the changing face of the battle in progress. I do not care why I am here. I am, however, interested in the nature of my punishment and how best to endure it."

For a few moments, I watched him examine the tools of his trade.

"That reminds me of a question I meant to ask when I saw the Cong," I said at last. "You speak of battle. Is there fighting here? War? Can people die in Hell?"

"My words were figurative," he grunted. "In my mind, life itself, or afterlife, is a battle...a constant confrontation of opposition in an effort to exert one's own will on others. To answer your question, however, yes, people can die in Hell. I have experienced it myself. As I said earlier, not all the people here share your admiration of me or my kind. The revival process is unpleasant enough that I do not wish to repeat the experience any more than is absolutely necessary. In regard to war and fighting..."

He paused and looked around us with the tight-lipped, humorless grin I had noticed before.

"...There are people here. Anywhere there are people there will be war and fighting...sometime, on some level. As a student of military history, I'm surprised you didn't know that."

"Is this the punishment you spoke of, then?" I said after a few minutes' thought. "Are you paying for a life-long series of battles with eternal battle in the afterlife?"

The hard, dark eyes fixed on me again.

"You know very little of Hell, Will Hawker."

With those words he began to gather his weapons, securing them one by one upon his body. It occurred to me that I had somehow offended the Khan with my last question.

"You're right. I don't know about Hell. That shouldn't

be surprising, as I've just arrived today. What you said earlier about not wasting time wondering why you're here... I didn't even know that. Since I got here I've been doing nothing but bothering people about why I'm here. I didn't know the protocol or customs, so if I insulted you somehow by asking about your punishment, it was unintentional. You mentioned it yourself earlier is all. I thought it was all right to discuss it."

The man's movements slowed, then ceased completely.

"You owe me no apology, Will Hawker," he said with a sigh, his eyes never leaving the ground. "It is simply that my true punishment is distasteful enough to me that I do not like to dwell upon it, much less discuss it. If anything, our talk has provided me with momentary divergence from my thoughts. For that I owe you thanks, and will answer your questions."

He raised his gaze to meet my own.

"I did fight my entire life, but because of that, battle would not be a punishment to me... simply a continuation of my normal existence. No, my punishment is far more subtle than that. You have correctly perceived that I am preparing for battle. Look around you and tell me what you see... or more important, what you don't see."

Puzzled, I swept my eyes around in a full circle.

"I... I'm afraid I don't understand."

"What you don't see," the Khan supplied, "is followers. I have no army, no horde. Unlike any previous life, any battle I encounter here I must fight alone."

It took a moment for the irony of the Khan's situation to sink in. One of the greatest leaders the world has known—a ruler of nations, commander of troops numbering in the hundreds of thousands—reduced to single combat with nothing to organize other than his personal weapons.

"I'm sorry," I said, and meant it. "It must be very difficult for you."

The Khan was on his feet in an angry surge.

"Do not pity me, Will Hawker," he hissed. "Hate me, fear me, for those reactions I am accustomed to dealing with. But spare me your sympathy. In my entire life I never imposed my burdens or sorrows on another, and I will not have that happen now. I have been stripped of everything I worked to build. Leave me my pride."

Snatching up his bow, he turned to leave.

"Wait!" I called. "Take me with you!"

He faced me again, the dark eyes studying me intently.

"I will be your army . . . or aide. I'm not much, but it will double your force."

"It may not be wise to interfere with the fate planned for me," the Khan said carefully. "Perhaps you should wait until you know more of Hell before making such a rash commitment."

Now it was my turn to laugh.

"To follow Genghis Khan into battle would be the dream of a lifetime for me. I'd face the Devil himself for the chance."

"You may not be speaking figuratively," the Mongol warned. "But come, walk beside me and tell me of yourself. It is clear you have a warrior's interest and heart. What is your background?"

A small chill flitted across my heart.

"Well, as I told you, I've studied military history. I'm familiar with the writings of Clausewitz, Sun Tsu, Hart . . ."

The Khan waved his hand impatiently.

"No, I mean, what is your firsthand experience."

"I . . . um . . . studied the martial arts for over twenty years—you know, karate and kung fu. I did a little fencing and riflery, but never had a chance to get into archery . . ."

I stopped talking, for the Khan had halted in his steps and was studying me carefully.

"Am I not making myself clear, Will Hawker?" he said. "I am not asking about your studies. I wish to know what your actual combat experience is."

I licked my lips, unable to meet his gaze.

"None," I admitted. "My country had only one war while I was of age to serve, against the Viet Cong we saw earlier. When I tried to volunteer for combat duty, I was rejected. Medically unfit for active service, they said."

"And so you studied war as a hobby."

"That's right. I had always wanted to be a soldier. Not getting into the army was one of the biggest disappointments of my life. It made me feel I had somehow failed as a man, so I kept up my studies as best I could on my own."

"You had friends? You would talk to them of strategies and battle plans?"

"That's right."

"And whenever possible, you would talk to other noncombatants—children and women—explaining to them the mind of a soldier and his necessary role in society?"

"Well, sometimes. Most of them didn't want to listen, but I did what I could."

In the silence that followed, I sneaked a glance at the Khan. He was staring at the horizon, his face expressionless. Finally, he heaved a great sigh.

"You may not fight beside me, Will Hawker. Better that I fight alone."

"But I'm fit enough to fight. Those doctors only..."

"I didn't say that you *can* not. I said that you *may* not. I do not wish you for a follower."

"But...I...Why..."

Words failed me in my confusion. The Khan shook his head minutely and turned to face me.

"I told you before, all I have left is my pride and I guard it jealously. It will not allow me to accept a follower such as you. Still, your offer of loyalty was both generous and sincere, so courtesy demands that I at least try to explain my position to you."

He paused for a moment and his gaze drifted into distant focus as he organized his thoughts.

"I mention earlier that I tried not to waste time wondering why I was here in Hell, but the most disciplined minds wander, and I have formed a theory as to the reason for my punishment. My fatal weakness is not that for killing and bloodshed, but rather of vanity. You see, I liked being Khan. Liked it far too much for the good of my followers or the world. When I was elected Khan of the united tribes, the Horde, I perceived that we were too strong to be attacked. Whatever defense I organized would eventually stagnate from disuse, until the tribes fell to bickering among themselves from boredom. Then the Horde would dissolve, taking with it my position and title. To avoid this, I instituted an expansionist policy and put the Horde on the attack. We were constantly pushing our borders outward, which guaranteed the Horde would be fighting, and I kept them fighting, and therefore united in purpose, until my death. Vanity made me a warmonger, so here I am paying the price that I never accounted for during my life."

His eyes focused on me again.

"But I got something for it. It is my guess that you are in Hell because you got nothing for your war efforts. War is a terrible thing, Will Hawker. It is not a game or a hobby, but a horrible means to an end. Wars are fought for land or wealth, or as in my case, a title and power. Noncombatant warriors such as you and your friends cling to romantic ideas of honor and ideals that any combat soldier loses in his first encounter. You never fight the wars yourself, so you have no idea of what is involved. Still, you encourage others to war, or even worse, argue to make battle an acceptable part of life. Blind ignorance makes you a warmonger, and ignorance is uncontrollable because, unlike greed, it can never be satisfied. I may be condemned by history for my part in war, and justly so . . . but you, Will Hawker, and all your friends, are a hundred times worse than I and my kind, and I will not sully my name and banner by having you stand beside me in battle."

With a final curt nod, he left me standing there as he stomped away to his unnamed battle alone.

Watching him go, I had pause to consider the bitter irony of Hell. The legendary leader of men was now forced to fight alone, while I, who yearned for battle all my life, would be denied the chance even in afterlife. It occurred to me that, unlike the Khan, my afterlife was going to be simply an extension of my previous life, for I had succeeded in building and living in Hell even before I died.

Bowing my head, I wept.

Two Gentlemen of the Trade

Robert Lynn Asprin

House Gregori and House Hannon were not particularly noteworthy in Merovingian hierarchy. There was old money behind each to be sure, but not enough to rate them as exceptionally rich. They had not specialized in commerce as so many other houses had, and therefore were not a controlling or even influential force in any given commodity or market. They were not old enough or large enough to impact the convoluted politics of either the town or the local religions. In fact, it is doubtful they would have been any better known than a fashionable shop or tavern, were it not for one thing: the Feud.

No one in town knew for sure how the feud between House Gregori and House Hannon began. Questions brought widely varying answers, not only from the two houses, but from different members of the same house as well. Some said it had something to do with a broken marriage contract, others that it was somehow related to a blatant criminal act involving either a business deal or a gaming wager. There were even those who maintained that the feud pre-existed the settlement of the town and had merely been renewed.

In short, almost every reason for a feud to exist had at one time or another been touted as the truth, but in reality no one in Merovingen really knew or cared. What mattered was that the feud existed.

Violence was common enough in Merovingen-above. While differences were not always settled by physical confrontation or reprisal, the option was always there and never overlooked in either planning or defense. Feuds were also fairly commonplace, but they were generally short lived and nearly always limited in their scope by unspoken gentlemen's agreements. In direct contrast, the Gregori-Hannon Feud was carried on at levels of viciousness that made even the most hardened citizen uneasy. There were no safe-zones, no truces. Women, even infants were as fair targets as the menfolk. It was said that both houses retained assassins to stalk the other, as well as offering open contracts for the death of any rival house member. Whether it was true or not, it made each member of either house a walking target for any local bravo who believed the rumors.

If anything, the feud doubtlessly saved many lives in the overall scheme of things—by example alone. Many a dispute in Merovingen cooled at the last moment with the simple advisement of "Let's not make a Gregori-Hannon thing out of this." And while the more sane edged away from the Gregoris and Hannons, the feud raged as the two houses mechanically acted out their obsessive hatred.

Festival time was usually Gregori-Hannon open season, each house stalking the other through the celebrations, each never pausing to think that they themselves were the bait that lured the other side out. This year, however, House Gregori remained barricaded in its holding. The elder Gregroi was ill, perhaps dying. So for the moment, at least, natural death took precedence.

"It's the Hannons! It has to be!"

The doctor paused in his ministerings and scowled up at the pacing man.

"Pietor Gregori!" he intoned in a stern voice. "Again I must ask you to keep still! Your father needs his rest, and I cannot concentrate with your constant prattle."

"Sorry, Terrosi," Pietor said, dropping heavily onto a chair. "It just doesn't make any sense. You've said yourself that Father's never been sick a day in his life. The only time he's spent abed is recovering from wounds. He was fine when you gave him his yearly check-up last week. It has to be poison . . . and the Hannons must be behind it. The question is how did they do it?"

"Of course it's the Hannons." The elder Gregori was struggling to rise on one elbow, waving aside the hovering doctor. "You know it, and I know it, Pietor. Never mind what this doddering fool says. It's poison. I can feel it eating at my insides. Now quit fretting at what we already know. The question isn't how they did it, it's what you're going to do about it! You're the eldest since your uncle was killed. The house will look to you for leadership. I want you out hunting Hannon blood, not sitting around here trying to hold my hand."

Pietor looked around the room uneasily, as if looking for allies in the furniture, then, as was his habit, ran a hand nervously through his unruly hair.

"Father . . . I don't want to argue with you. You know I fear for what this feud is doing to our house.

We can't afford to lose you, much less anyone else if the Hannons see them first in the crowds. As for me, I've never killed anyone, and..."

"Then it's time you did!" the elder Gregori broke in. "I've pampered you in the past, Pietor, but it's time you woke up to the facts of life. Get it through your head that this feud will only end when either the Hannons or we Gregoris are all dead. You owe it to the House to be sure it's them and not us who face extinction. Kill them, Pietor. Kill them all, or they will certainly kill you as they have killed me!"

Exhausted by the effort, he sank back in his pillows as Terrosi leapt to his side.

"That's enough... both of you!" the doctor snapped. "Now listen to me. I don't want to have to say this again... though I'll probably have to. It isn't poison. Believe me, in this town I know the symptoms. More likely one of the marketfolk sold you some overaged fish. You'll be up and around in a few days, *if* you get your rest and *if* certain parties can refrain from airing old arguments and getting *you* so upset my medicines get negated. Am I speaking clearly?"

Pietor shrank before the physician's glare.

"Terrosi's right," he said, rising. "I should be going."

Reaching the door, he hesitated with one hand on the knob.

"You're sure it's not poison?"

"OUT!" the doctor ordered, not looking up from his work.

Terrosi was genuinely annoyed by the time Pietor had closed the door behind him. It was obvious that the son loved his father, but his concerns didn't make the physician's work any easier. Most annoying of all was the reluctance on everyone's part to believe the diagnosis.

The doctor had served the Gregoris his entire career. In fact, the Gregoris had financed his training and education to insure his loyalty to their house. His retainer was sufficient to guarantee him a comfortable life without seeking other patients. Everything possible had been done to see to his needs, and the Gregoris' strategy was successful. His loyalty was total and unquestioned. Terrosi would never dream of accepting a commission from anyone outside the house, whether or not it was potentially harmful to the Gregoris. His skills (and they were considerable) were solely at the disposal of the house. Over the years his treatments were accurate and effective, so that now it was unthinkable to have his diagnosis challenged. Unthinkable and annoying, for Terrosi knew that the elder Gregori had *indeed* been poisoned. Terrosi knew this for a fact, as he had been the one who had done it.

It had been easy enough to effect during the old man's check-up; just a drop or two of poison on the tongue depressor was all that was necessary. The only tricky part had been to keep the dosage low enough to cause illness, but not death, for immediate death would have cast suspicion on him. The fatal dosage would be reached through his continued treatment of the elder Gregori's "illness."

Of course, Terrosi did not see this as a betrayal of the Gregoris' trust in him. After all, it had been a Gregori who had paid him to do the murder, and while he was sworn to help no one outside the house, he felt that

this was merely an extension of the services he offered
to his retainers. What surprised him was that it was
not Pietor who had made the request, but one of his
younger brothers. Had the commission come from the
eldest, Terrosi would have understood it as a bid for
the inheritance and control of the house. As it was...

The doctor sighed and turned once more to his
task of administering yet another dose of poison to
his patient. His job was to see to the "how," not the
"why." It would have been easier if Pietor had been a
party to the plot. It was hard enough to work under
the watchful eyes of the elder Gregori without having
his eldest son fluttering about as well. Still, Terrosi
was a professional and used to doing his job under
adverse conditions.

With a reassuring smile, he held out the spoonful
of death.

Torches blazing on a score of boats lit the assemblage
and served as a beacon for latecomers as the boat people
of Merovingen pranced and capered in one of their
rare parties. It was late, well after most of the Festival
activity had finally staggered to a halt, but flushed with
the energy of the day's frenzy and buoyed by the lavish
earnings and tips from drunken Uptown revelers, the
canalers were disinclined to rest, even realizing the
chaos would start anew on the morrow.

A dozen boats had lashed themselves together in
the middle of the canal, and planks had been scav-
enged and laid across the gunwales to form a large,
if unstable platform, as the crowd beat on anything
wooden with hands or sticks to provide a steady rhythm
for those who eased or fed their tensions by dancing.

Wine and occasional bottles of liquor, usually closely hoarded, passed around freely in acknowledgement of friendship or generosity. It was Festival time, and purses were too fat for the canalers to be miserly.

The man known only as Chud perched on a low cabin roof, beating time against the wall with his heels as he leisurely drank in the spectacle with his eyes. He thoroughly enjoyed the canalers with their earthy speech and robust zest for life. Clapping his hands and whistling at a particularly outrageous bit of capering, he reflectively smiled at the contrast between this emotional outpouring and the more restrained, formal gatherings that were the pattern Uptown. There one had to watch every word, every gesture for fear of inadvertently offending the powerful, as well as tracking everything that transpired within hearing in hopes of gleaning a clue of the shifting favors and trends. While his work often required it, it was not a particularly relaxing pastime.

That was why he had chosen to establish himself with the canalers, buying his own boat and donning the worn garb of the working class to labor among them for days at a time. Acceptance had been slow, but eventually he learned enough to be acknowledged as a fellow, if poorly skilled, boatman. He never asserted himself in competing for the small hauling contracts, meekly taking whatever fell his way by chance. His few acquaintances were annoyed by this, and harangued him to stand up to the boat bullies who crowded him out of fares in mid-negotiation, but he just smiled and shook his head until they gave up in disgust, vowing never again to give advice to someone not man enough to fight for himself.

In truth, Chud did not need the money and enjoyed the luxury of being gracious. His normal work was profitable enough to make his venture into boating more of a vacation than a vocation, and much of what made it relaxing was that he could accept second place without losing more than an unearned handful of small coins.

Someone lurched up to him offering a wineskin, but Chud refused with a smile and a wave of his hand. This, too, was part of his character on the canal: the quiet one who never drank or chased women. Combined with his tendency to disappear for long periods of time, this habit led people to believe that there was another part of his life which kept him from becoming truly one of them. There was idle speculation as to his reasons ranging from an ailing parent to a demanding mistress, but no one was interested enough to follow him or even ask directly to confirm or deny suspicions. The canalers were inclined to respect each other's personal privacy, and whatever it was that had unmanned Chud and kept him from being more open and assertive was generally deemed to be nobody's business but his own.

As caught up as he was with the celebration, Chud was never completely unwary, and he suddenly sensed a new presence in the crowd. There was nothing which specifically alerted him to it, yet he knew it with the same instinctive certainty that lets a bug know when it's going to rain.

Without changing expression or breaking the rhythm of his heel drumming, he casually scanned the growing crowd for the source of his subconscious alarm. Despite the fact that he was already alerted, it took three passes with his eyes before he identified what he was looking for.

She was standing well back toward the edge of the raft having just stepped aboard but yet unwilling to push her way forward as did the other new arrivals. What finally drew Chud's eyes to her was this lack of forward motion, that and her tendency, like his own, to watch the crowd around her rather than the dancers. Dark of hair and slight of build, she was wrapped in an old blanket which both protected her from the night chill and hid her garments at the same time. Though unremarkable in appearance, once Chud's attention was focused on her she seemed to stand out in the crowd like a pure-bred in a pack of mongrels. Of course, his knowledge of who she was sharpened his perceptions.

For the barest moment he thought of ignoring her. She was no threat to him, and this was his chosen retreat from her world. Then the reality of the situation rose to dominate his mind; a chance meeting like this was rarity, unlikely to be repeated. It was not wise to ignore what fate had so conveniently dropped in his lap.

Once resolved, he had to fight back an impulse to rush to her side before someone else noticed her or she retreated. Instead, he made his way across the raft in leisurely stages, zigzagging his way through the crowd as he paused to exchange greetings with acquaintances or to listen to a heated conversation. Watching her obliquely all the while, his heart leaped each time someone glanced her way or brushed past her, but maintained his pace.

Finally he reached her, or rather the position he

had targeted; squatting a few feet away, facing away from the dancers, staring out over the water.

"You shouldn't be here, m'sera," he said loud enough for her to hear. "It's dangerous."

The girl started and looked at him as if he were a venomous snake.

"What did you say?"

He shook his head without shifting his gaze.

"Don't stare at me. It'll draw attention," he instructed. "I said it's dangerous for you here."

"Why do you say that? And who are you? You don't talk like a canaler."

"Neither do you," he said pointedly. "I'm just doing a little slumming, myself. These folks will usually leave a man alone if he's fit and seems to have his wits about him. There are people on this raft, though, who would love nothing better than to have an Uptown lady for a plaything . . . when they spot what you are."

Chud felt her relax as he spoke and congratulated himself on his word choice. He had been rehearsing his approach as he made his way across the raft, and it seemed he had been correct. His expressed concern was for "what" she was, not "who" she was, and this confirmation of her anonymity eased her fears.

"I thought if I dressed . . ."

"The first time you open your mouth, it won't matter what you're wearing. They'll know. What are you doing here, anyway? Does your family know you're here?"

"I . . . I slipped out of the house after they were asleep," she said. "I've heard . . . I'm looking for a woman named Zilfi. The boatman said I would find her here."

"Old Gran Zilfi?" Chud frowned. "The boatman cheated you, or was too lazy to pole with his pockets full. She's not here. Her tie-up place is up in the Spur Loop."

"It is? Then how...?"

"Don't worry. I'll take you there myself. Come on."

He rose and started to move away, then realized she wasn't following him. Had his eagerness betrayed him?

"How do I know you aren't as crooked as the last boatman? Maybe you're lying to me to make a few extra coins yourself."

Chud smiled at her, though his expression was prompted as much out of relief as for reassurance.

"It's Festival time, m'sera. A few coins one way or the other doesn't make much difference. I was more thinking to help you out of a bad spot."

She nodded, but still hesitated.

"Tell you what," he said, "I'll take you where you want to go. On the way, you mark the buildings and docks to be sure I'm not poling in circles. When we get there, you pay me what you think the trip's worth. Fair enough?"

A rare smile escaped her then as she nodded again, more firmly this time.

"Fair enough. Forgive me for being suspicious. I was raised...I haven't had much experience dealing with people. I hope my clumsiness doesn't offend you."

He made the proper reassuring noises, but guided her to his skip as he did. Now that she had agreed to accompany him, his major concern was that they get underway without drawing too much attention. There seemed little chance of that, though. The canalers were too preoccupied with the festivities at the center of the raft to pay much mind to anything happening at the edges.

After seating her securely, Chud cast off, then moved to the stern of the craft with his pole to back them out of the tangle of gathered boats.

"Ware, hey!"

The call came out of the darkness behind them, and he desperately dug in with his pole as he echoed the warning.

"Hey, ware!"

The regular boatmen were far more adept at handling their vessels, and he usually found the safest course in potential collision situations was to hold steady while they maneuvered around him.

"That you, Chud?"

A weathered skip eased into the torchlight with a white-haired crone wielding the pole as she peered at the craft blocking her path. Chud groaned inside.

"'S me, Mintaka. Got a fare."

"This late? Good, good. You young 'uns kin keep the canal open 'round the clock. Good fer the town."

He felt her eyes studying them as the boats passed.

Damn! That arthritic old lady was one of the biggest gossips on the canal. It was unthinkable that she'd be able to resist spreading the news that Quiet Chud had left the party with a young girl. Anyone who didn't hear it tonight would know before noon tomorrow.

"You handle the boat very well."

The girl's words dragged Chud's thoughts back to the task at hand. If any of the other canalers had heard her, they would have laughed aloud. While he was not the poorest boatman on the canal, his skills had a ways to go before they would even be considered mediocre.

"Thank you, m'sera. It's really easier than it looks once you get the hand of it."

They were picking up a bit of speed now as Chud got the rhythm of the poling going, the sounds and lights of the party slipping away behind them.

"You said you were slumming. How is it that someone who can, and apparently does, move freely Uptown choose to spend time with the canalers—even to the point of having his own boat and learning to pole it?"

"One tires of intrigues and politics," he said in a rare display of honesty. "However frugal their existence, the canalers control their own lives. In their company, I can at least enjoy the temporary illusion that I'm in control of my own life, instead of dancing to the tune of factions and houses."

The girl was silent for a while, watching the piers and bridges slide by in the darkness, and Chud wondered if he had offended her with his candidness, or if she were simply bored with the conversation.

"I envy you," she said suddenly, proving her thoughts were still with him. "I, too, tire of being controlled by the politics and feuds of this town's hierarchy, but I am never offered the chance you have to escape... even temporarily."

"Never?"

He smiled, confident that the dark would hide his expression.

"Well, rarely. So rarely that my one venture into independence only served to show me the extent to which my life is normally controlled by rules and traditions of my family. Even worse, it made me admit to myself that I was not strong enough to stand alone against them."

"Is that why you decided not to have the baby?"

His words hung in the night air as if they were sketched in fiery paint.

The girl was still for a moment, then he saw her turn, staring at him in the dark.

"What did you say?"

"Come now, m'sera. It is not so hard to deduce. Your sneaking out alone tonight is in itself evidence of a degree of desperation. And looking for Gran Zilfi... there are only two medicines she offers that can't be had easier and cheaper Uptown. One renews the potency of elderly men, and I somehow doubt you require that; the other rids a woman of an unwanted pregnancy. Do you see my logic?"

He thought she might argue or at least deny his assertion, but instead she simply shrugged half-heartedly.

"It's true. As I said, there some things I'm not strong enough to face alone."

"Alone? What of the father?"

"The father? He's part of the problem... most of it, really. My house would never accept him, nor his me. He says he'll find a way to take care of things, but it's been more than a week since I told him and he hasn't been in touch. Whether or not he has abandoned me becomes inconsequential. I know now that I'll have to deal with this problem myself."

"Perhaps the matter will be resolved for you."

"What do you...?"

His pole caught her on the side of the head, sending her over the side into the inky waters.

She floundered weakly, too stunned to even cry for help, and Chud debated for a moment whether she stood a chance for survival, weighted down as she was with clothes and blanket.

Better safe than sorry, he decided finally. Reaching out again with his pole, he anchored it between her shoulder blades and pushed with all his strength until he felt her pinned against the bottom, then held her there until the water was smooth.

Several of the menfolk were present as the assassin was ushered into the elder Gregori's presence. This had been the custom ever since they had lost a member to a killer supposedly seeking a private pay-off.

Pietor Gregori was uncomfortable with the interview, but as the next in line to head the House it was his duty to be present, both as part of his training and to ease the strain on his ailing father.

"This man claims to have killed one of the Hannons last night, Father," he said, "but he has no evidence..."

"It was Teryl Hannon, the youngest daughter," the assassin interrupted, clearly annoyed. "I drowned her in the canal, and her body should be discovered shortly if it didn't get hung up in the silt at the bottom. I'll wager nobody else even knows she's dead, much less the method. There's a possibility that witnesses may associate me with her disappearance, so I'll have to lay low for a while and would just as soon not have to wait around for my payment."

The elder Gregori waved aside the hovering family physician.

"This man has killed Hannons for us before, Pietor. Do you have any reason to suspect he's lying to us now?"

"Even if he's telling the truth about the girl's death, it may have just been an accident that he's trying to claim credit for."

"An accident?" the killer hissed. "I may have ruined one of my favorite identities for that death, and if you think..."

"Pay him," the elder Gregori ordered. "Even if it was an accident, there's one less Hannon, and that's worth something to us. If you want to be sure of how they die, Pietor, you'll have to kill them yourself instead of waiting for assassins to do your work for you. It's good to see that *someone* is hunting Hannons this Festival."

Pietor flushed at the reminder of his negligence, but fumbled in his purse for the required sum.

"Thank you, sir," the assassin said stiffly, still irritated at the haggling. "You're lucky I don't charge you for two deaths."

"How's that?"

The elder Gregori was alert now.

"The girl, Teryl, was with child. That's what got her out from behind the Hannons' defenses so that I could get a crack at her. By rights, that's another Hannon that won't be around, even though the death was a little premature. I should probably try to find the lover who abandoned her and get payment from him. He's the one who's interests I really served."

"Pay him half again for the child, Pietor," the old man cackled, sinking back into his pillows. "He's served us well, and if he's going into hiding, he won't be able to scour the town for some rake."

"Father, you shouldn't excite yourself."

"Pay him! This kind of excitement is the best medicine for me."

Despite his patient's agitated state, Terrosi was covertly studying the reactions of Demitri, Pietor's middle brother.

The lad had gone pale, his eyes almost sightless with his apparent shock.

It was becoming clearer why Demitri had commissioned his father's death. With the elder Gregori out of the way, Pietor would be in charge of the house, and that son's sentiments on the feud were well known. Yes. If little brother Demitri *had* wanted to bring a Hannon bastard into the house, Pietor would be far easier for Demitri to deal with as Househead than his father would have been. If anything, Pietor might have seized on the idea of legitimizing the Demitri-Teryl Hannon pairing as his chance to try to make peace between the houses. It was thoroughly logical on Demitri's part, but all for naught now, of course.

Terrosi wondered if Demitri would try to cancel his commission now. If he did, would he still be willing to pay the full fee, or would he try to haggle for half? There was only one way to be sure. The final dosage would have to be administered today, before Demitri had a chance to speak with him alone.

Fumbling in his bag, the physician happened to glance up, and met the eyes of the assassin. The man was watching Terrosi with the same calculating gaze that the doctor had directed at the killer when he first entered the room. Bottle in hand, the doctor gave a small nod of recognition which was mirrored by his colleague. Then the assassin excused himself as Terrosi turned to his ministerings ... two killers returning to their work.

A Harmless Excursion

ROBERT LYNN ASPRIN

Pietor Gregori did not like being the head of the House, but the death of his father had left him no choice in the matter. For the better part of a year he had done nothing, or as little as possible, while House Gregori languished from neglect. The minor details of maintaining a functional Household went untended, while major decisions . . .

Had it not been for Terrosi stepping into the void as family doctor when winter's fever penetrated their holdings, House Gregori might have been wiped out completely. Pietor for his part, had done nothing to take command or make even the smallest gesture of leadership during the crisis—while Demitri seemed bent on destroying himself with alcohol since the elder Gregori's death—though in truth Pietor had never considered his brother and father to be that close. Still, he hesitated to dictate behavior, so Demitri's drinking continued unchecked.

Meanwhile the census was grinding toward its end, in the slow way of Merovingian affairs, and the family still argued the best course to follow: did they exaggerate their headcount to keep their mortal enemies the Hannons at bay, or report accurate or even reduced figures to keep their tax burden with the government in bounds? In lieu of agreement, someone would have to decide, yet a few hoped that Pietor would rise to the occasion.

Sharrh-inspired fireworks terrified the city, and strange plants multiplied in the canals—unprecedented occurrence. Things changed in Merovingen, and there were stirrings of ambition in various Houses high and low—but Pietor did nothing to advance House Gregori.

And worst of all, Pietor did absolutely nothing at all about the Feud. The entire city had braced itself for the bloody vengeance of House Gregori on House Hannon when their rivals succeeded in poisoning the head of the Gregori household (for no one really believed the old man's death to be natural)—yet fall passed to winter and winter wore on to spring without any sign of counterattack. In fact, the famous Feud not only failed to escalate, there were no signs that it was even being maintained at its earlier levels.

Now, while nearly all of Merovingen traditionally deplored the Gregori-Hannon feud as an obsessive waste of money and personnel, there were many in the city nonetheless disquieted by its absence—in somewhat the same way as a cat is upset by rear-ranged furniture. The Feud was a constant, a part of native Merovingen, and the prolonged lack of activity seemed to leave a void in the ordinary goings-on and gossip of the city—while certain people whispered dire rumors of extremist activity and speculated that fear had driven the Feud to subtler measures; and while the foreign Sword of God acted unchecked and impious, Nev Hettek folk walked unmolested in broad daylight in Merovingen of the Thousand Bridges.

In short, there was *no* one who was pleased with
Pietor's performance as head of House Gregori...
including Pietor himself. He knew his hopes that
family affairs would take care of themselves were in
vain. Sooner or later he was going to have to take
an active hand in running the House, which meant
accepting the responsibilities of his actions as well, and
that day was something he would avoid indefinitely,
given a choice. Unfortunately, one might not always
have a choice....

"It's not that I expect you to *do* anything, Pietor...
God knows you've done little enough since father
died. Stephan insisted I should tell you, that's all.
Everyone loves little Nikki so, though for the life of
me I can't see why. He's a mediocre artist for all his
claimed devotion, and no use at all in the Feud...."

Pietor avoided meeting his sister's eyes as she prat-
tled on. Sister Anna was one of his greatest personal
decriers...certainly she was his loudest. Anna Gregori
had had a caustic tongue for as long as Pietor could
remember, and he had been secretly glad when she
had married out of her House on a five-year contract,
thinking they were free of her at last—or at least free
until the contract expired—but instead of taking her
from the House, her new husband, Stephan, had simply
moved himself into their holdings—since it turned out
he seemed less fond of Anna as a partner than as a
passport into the Gregori fortunes.

Needless to say, this discovery had done little to
improve Anna's disposition, but strangely Pietor felt
more sympathetic toward her since that unfortunate
discovery. He had always envied Anna the inner fire

which he had always seemed to lack, and now that that fire was sputtering with frustration he was willing to make the extra effort to make her five years of suffering minimal.

"Could you tell me about it again, from the beginning?" Pietor said, interrupting her in mid-grumble.

"Really, Pietor. I've already..."

"Yes, yes. But you yourself have commented on how slow I am. Please, Anna?"

She grimaced and rolled her eyes melodramatically, but she complied.

"Baby brother Nikki...you *do* remember Nikki, don't you?—Well, he's decided that he's tired of being sheltered from the slings and arrows of the real world...not to mention the swords and knives of the Hannons. Some drivel about how artists have to experience life, not watch it through a window. Anyway, he's decided to slip out for his appointment with the College this afternoon without a bodyguard or escort, says he's *tired* of bodyguards in his life— says *other* folk go out unescorted, and he's *tired* of living with guards."

Pietor pursed his lips.

"...And you heard this scheme from one of the servants?"

"Old Michael," she nodded. "He claims to be afraid for the boy, but it's more likely he's afraid of what would happen to *him* if anything happened to Nikki and we found out he'd known about it all along."

"Well, for whatever reason he's alerted us. Now just what is it you want me to do about it?"

"Do? Why, I want you to stop him! Just because you haven't the stomach to kill Hannons doesn't mean they return the feeling! If Nikki goes out alone, in a place like the midtown, he's a sitting target for the first Hannon or Hannon retainer that sees him. He's got to be confronted and kept behind our defenses! I know I've said a thousand times I don't like the little twit, but still he's..."

"No," Pietor said, shaking his head. "I won't do it."

"But he's our own brother! Think of our reputation! You can't just—"

"...Because if I do, he'll just sneak out again some other time!"

They locked gazes in stony silence. Anna's dark eyes still held the wildness of her sudden anger, but her lack of argument told Pietor louder than words that this was one of his rare victories.

"Think about it, Anna," he urged her, "if brother Nikki has taken it into his mind to go outside on his own and we stop him, he'll simply try excursions like this again and again until he succeeds. This time we were warned because he confided in a servant. Next time, he might not be so open."

His sister turned and dropped heavily into a chair.

"So what do *you* propose?" Anna said sullenly. "If we let Nikki try his little venture, the Hannons will eat him alive."

"Maybe not," Pietor muttered, then added hastily, "still, it's a risk we can't take."

Secretly, he was rejoicing. This was the first time since their father's death that Anna had asked his opinion rather than immediately chiding him for being too foolish to follow her recommended path. He suddenly realized with no small surprise that preserving that small spark of respect in Anna meant as much to him as saving his brother, and for the first time Pietor Gregori actually started to *feel* like the head of the household.

"What we've got to do," he said in that heady moment, "is convince him that traveling alone is dangerous for him, and the best way to do that is to let him go on and try his little venture."

"But you said..."

"Oh, he won't *really* be alone. He'll just think he is. Hurry along now and pass the word to the rest of the family. We have a lot of planning to do before little Nikki makes his escape! What time's his appointment?"

Demitri Gregori was in a foul mood, or, to be accurate, fouler mood than normal, which these days took some doing.

Ensconced at a sheltered table in the small open-air café across from the Gregori apartments, he watched the kitchen delivery entrance via the walkways that led up from the water-stairs—Pietor's instructions—while vainly trying to offset the aftereffects of yesterday's drinking with a fresh onslaught of wine.

Pietor was obviously going daft from the weight of his new responsibilities. His little scheme to trick their little brother was far too elaborate to be practical. If nothing else, Demitri was aware of the peculiar dangers of being overly subtle in one's planning.

At which thought a sudden wave of guilt broke over Demitri Gregori, and he hurriedly fought it off by tossing down what was left in his goblet and refilling it, as he forced all thoughts of his father's death from his mind.

On the surface, Pietor's hastily improvised plan

seemed simple enough: let Nikki wander a few isles
along the walkways toward the College and his appointment, apparently unescorted but actually covered by
available Gregoris and Gregori retainers from hiding,
then scare him back to the House with the appearance
of several hired "Hannons" in his path.

Simple in concept, perhaps, but execution was
another thing entirely.

It wasn't until the Family had hastily tried to figure
how to position people along the anticipated route that
dear Pietor had begun to count just how many routes
and shortcuts there were in the three tiers between
the Gregori apartments and the College. In the end,
by whatever calculations, it had proved impossible to
cover them all, so Pietor had had to settle for trying
to establish a "floating" circle of spotters around feck-
less Nikki that would advance before him and cover
his back as he moved.

Of course, this also meant trying to devise a system
of signals to let the others in the guard party know
which way dear fool Nikki was heading, which of course
increased the chances of Nikki spotting his shadows
and thereby negating the point of the whole exercise.
There was also a shortage of good hiding and lurking places along the most likely route, that lay along
Archangel, forcing them to "cover both ends of the
tunnel" in some stretches and ignore some stairways
and passages as unlikely. All in all, Pietor's crackpot
idea of trying to shadow the fool was proving more
difficult than anticipated, and it was altogether so cum-
bersome as to introduce the possibility of the escorts
tripping over each other in their own maneuverings.

Then again, there were the Hannons they had

hired... or rather the bully boys they were paying to play the role of Hannons. Could they be trusted? What if they took advantage of the situation to collect the Hannon-offered bounty on a Gregori themselves?

No. *Not* likely. The whole plan was far too complicated and too hastily conceived for comfort, but Pietor had insisted and the Family had gone along with him, if for no other reason than to encourage slack-handed Pietor to take an active hand in running the household: among themselves, they had admitted a fear that if they had refused to aid Pietor in this, his first effort at involvement, he might retreat back into the lethargy he had been showing to date—a laissez-faire Demitri privately reckoned more dangerous to House Gregori than Nikki's fecklessness.

Better to get him moving by cooperating today, then, the consensus in the House was, and once Pietor had a bit of momentum and confidence behind him, they could try to guide their Househead's steps into wiser courses of action.

That was, of course, providing House Gregori survived the day.

Demitri grimaced wryly at the thought. He had disagreed with Pietor's plan from the start, and still remained skeptical even after younger House members had teamed up to vote him down. He felt that Anna had been right in the first place, and Pietor should have simply confronted Nikki and acquainted him with the facts of life. As head of the household, Pietor should have met the challenge of the established procedures squarely and dominated their younger brother with the sheer force of his personality and his anger. That was certainly what their father would have done....

Demitri groped for the wine again, only to find the pitcher empty.

Damn! Why couldn't he keep his thoughts away from his father? He had made a conscious choice between the old man and his pregnant Hannon lover before arranging for the elder Gregori's assassination. Was his current guilt a matter of second thoughts, or was it merely anger that Teryl Hannon's death—and, unknown to either House, Demitri's own unborn child's—had made his father's demise both unnecessary and pointless?

If the latter were true...

A furtive movement at the delivery entrance caught his eye.

Nikki.

Demitri had to smile to himself as he leaned back into the shadows and averted his face. If he had not been forewarned and watching, he probably wouldn't have recognized his little brother in that getup. The youngest Gregori was decked out in the garb of a common laborer several sizes too large for him, creating the illusion of underfed poverty in scrounged clothes. With the added touches of a few artfully placed streaks of soot on his face and a slouch cap pulled low over his eyes, Nikki bore little resemblance to the dapper young artist who was prone to spending such considerable time in front of a mirror polishing his appearance and manner.

Demitri waited a few more moments to insure he would not be spotted, then rose casually to follow his brother. Fumbling for a few coins to leave as a tip, he glanced down the walkway...and froze. Nikki was nowhere in sight!

In a flash Demitri was up and well along the walkway, casting about in all directions for a glimpse of the disguised artist, but it was as if the walkways had dropped him abruptly elsewhere, into the nether tiers of the city. There were a few people strolling along the boards, but none bore the slightest resemblance to Nikki!

Demitri waffled for a few more precious moments between trying to find his little brother himself and alerting the waiting net of the watchers. Finally, he swallowed his pride and sprinted off to find Pietor—who would curse him for a careless drunk perhaps, not without justification—but Nikki might now be wandering Lord knew what tier of the walkways and bridges without anyone protecting him, and that took priority over any personal affront Pietor might deal him.

As he ran, Demitri prayed that one of the other watchers had spotted his little brother's course somewhere across the bridges and taken up guard duty. If not, if Nikki came to harm...

He forced the thought from his mind and plunged on.

"I don't like it. I should've thought it out more before takin' this job. No sir! I don't like this one bit."

Gordo nodded at his companion's growled complaint. He had been experiencing similar reservations himself.

"I know what ye mean," he said. "I was just thinking the same thing. It sounded easy enough at first, but what if one of the *real* Hannons comes along and finds us wearing their House colors? It's not going to endear us to them any, I tell ye that much."

He found himself nervously fingering the bits of gold and orange ribbon pinned to his sleeve, the traditional mark of the Hannon household and their retainers. They had been given these badges by the Gregoris when they were hired for what had seemed like a harmless masquerade. The more Gordo thought about it, however, the less comfortable he was with the arrangement.

"Ye got a point there, Gordo," the original speaker grunted, "but that weren't what I was thinkin'."

"Oh?"

"I was more worried about us bein' set up."

"Set up?" Victor, the third man in their group said, joining the discussion. "How d'ye figure that?"

"Well, it occurs to me that if I was the Gregoris and I planned to do some mischief, it wouldn't hurt none to have a couple Hannons around to pin the rap on . . . and here we are, standin' around when and where they done told us, wearin' ribbons to mark us as Hannons."

Gordo felt a quick lance of fear shoot through him, but he tried to laugh it off.

"Come now, Curt. You don't really believe they'd do *that* to us, do ye?"

"Well I, for one, don't," Victor stated emphatically. "I've worked for the Gregoris afore, and they've always dealt me fair."

"That was *old* Gregori," Curt shot back. "How about Pietor, this new head of the House? Either of ye dealt whatsoever with *him*? I haven't. What's more, I'm wonderin' how smart it is to be wearin' Hannon colors out on the walks on nothin' more than his say-so that it's all right. Not that I'm sayin' he'd *be* up to no good, mind you. Just that we should look sharp if we want to be sure to come outta this in one piece, is all."

They had been stationed at the foot of the last bridge on the direct route between the Gregori apartment and Kass Isle, a point young Nikki would be certain to pass on his self-engineered adventure. Though warned to keep their faces toward Kass so that he would only see their Hannon colors, the three men found themselves glancing around nervously as they continued their debate. What had seemed like easy money now looked increasingly hazardous, and their feeling of vulnerability was growing by the moment.

"It's a possibility," Gordo conceded. "Still, we can't walk off a job because a' some *possible* danger. We should've thought of all this 'fore we went and took their money. All we can do now is..."

"Hullo there!"

Three heads snapped around and fixed on the figure approaching them.

A figure wearing Hannon colors.

"*Now* what do we do?—Lord, if he recognizes us—"

"That's Lonnie Hannon. Don't worry, he's blind as a bat. So far he only sees our ribbons."

"He'll see well enough to tell we ain't Hannons if he joins us."

"Let him," Curt growled softly, slipping his belt dagger from his sheath.

"Lord, what are ye doing?"

"Can't ye see? This is our chance to be away and free from here. Ain't nobody expects us to hang around after we was jumped by one o' the Hannons, can they? And he ain't tellin' nothin' t' anybody."

Without waiting for a reply from the others, he turned and waved a welcome to the oncoming Hannon...hiding his dagger behind his leg as he did.

Helwein Hannon was surprised to find himself regretting, in such bewildering times as this, not having attended the funeral of old Gregori. It was true that old enemies could be as dear as old friends... especially when they were known quantities that were reliably consistent.

Of course, his presence would have been interpreted as gloating, though the Hannons had had no part in that notable's demise...a fact no one in Merovingen was inclined to believe, especially the Gregoris. With a sigh, Helwein returned his attention to the subject at hand.

"How many are there, again?"

Zahn, who had been haranguing the other family members assembled, broke off his oration to frown at his Househead.

"But Uncle...I already told you..."

"So tell me again!" Helwein snapped, then softened his tone. "Have patience with an old man. My ears aren't as good as they were...or my mind as quick."

This, of course, fooled no one, as Helwein held his position by the strength and speed of his judgment and could wield a sword with an agility that denied his years—but it did cause Zahn to swallow his impatience and repeat some of the highlights of his report.

"At least a dozen, maybe two," Zahn said. "It's hard to tell for sure, since they're scattered singly or in small groups on the walkways and bridges around the Pile and Kass and Borg. More important is..."

"...But so far, they're mostly around their old holding?" Helwein interrupted. "They're not near *our* House?"

"Yes...but I think it's important that they aren't wearing House Gregori colors, any of them. If anything, they seem to be trying to avoid being seen, staying mostly in shops and in shadowed walks and cut-throughs on the middle tier. To me, that means they're up to something."

A low growl from the others assembled showed their assent, an opinion that was noted by the head of the House as he tried to collect his thoughts.

"It's important, yes," he said. "But so is the fact they aren't making any direct moves on us or our holdings. It's also important to know how many of them there are...exactly...as well as where each is stationed. Once we have that information, we can decide..."

The door burst open before he could complete his thought.

"They're killing us! PAPA!"

Instantly, the room was filled with exclamations and babble.

"I knew it!"

"Who was it...?"

"But what about...?"

"We've got to..."

"Quiet! ALL of you!"

Helwein's voice, seldom raised, now roared, shocking the assemblage to silence.

"Now, you tell *me*," he demanded, fixing the interloper with a steely gaze, "who's been killed."

"I...don't know, Papa," the youth faltered. "It was just reported downstairs by a deliveryman. He said that one of our House had just been killed...stabbed in broad daylight and dumped off a bridge by three men who ran. He didn't know..."

The head of the House was suddenly on his feet, towering in his anger.

"Who's outside right now?" Helwein Hannon asked, not waiting to hear the balance of the report.

"Five, I think," someone volunteered. "William . . . and Uncle Lonnie . . . and—"

"Six. Tellon went out early."

"Tellon can take care of himself. There isn't a Gregori who can match sword with him."

"One on one, maybe. But there dozens of them on the walkways."

"*Enough talk!*" Helwein bellowed. "Zahn, assemble everyone in the House who can carry a weapon and follow as soon as you can. The rest of you, come with me, *now!*"

Despite his earlier impatience, Zahn was taken aback by the sudden flurry of action.

"But Uncle, shouldn't we wait . . ."

"There's no more time if the Gregoris have already started their move," was the snarled response. "we've a chance, though, if we can make our countermove in force while they're still scattered. Aye, catch them in their small groups before they can unite or scuttle back to their hole. All of you now . . . *with me!*"

The assemblage followed Helwein out of the room, caught up in his urgency and excitement, though more than a few were chilled by the bloodlust that shone in his eyes.

Damn Demitri . . . and damn Nikki!

Anger and worry warred within Pietor Gregori as he half walked, half ran toward Kass Middle Bridge.

If harm came to his youngest brother because Demitri had been too busy drinking to keep proper watch . . .

He prayed that Nikki was already at the College. If so, then he would fetch him home if he had to drag him kicking and screaming every step of the way. Safety was more important now than teaching a lesson.

He was nearly at the Pile West Bridge now, but his path was blocked by a shopper speaking with a walkway vendor. Beside himself with impatience, Pietor started to edge past just as the shopper turned... revealing a bright gold and yellow sweater beneath his cloak.

Tellon Hannon! Said to be the best swordsman in his House!

The two men stared at each other in shocked recognition.

"Tellon... Have you seen my brother Nikki?" Pietor blurted suddenly, voicing the first thing that came to his mind.

The Hannon blinked in surprise and bewilderment.

"The artist? No, I haven't... You're asking *me*?"

The absurdity of the situation began to creep into Pietor's mind. Here he was, seeking assistance from a Hannon, the very ones he feared were threatening Nikki. Still, he had blundered into a conversation with one of the Gregori's arch rivals, and he set himself to make the most of it.

"That's right. The young fool is out here some-where... Say, Tellon, while we're talking... I wanted to tell you how sorry I was about your sister's death."

"Teryl?" Tellon's bewilderment changed to a scowl. "Why should you be sorry? I heard the Gregoris paid for her murder."

"My father did," Pietor admitted, "but even he didn't order it. I'm the head of the House now, and... Look, my father was killed by your family, but I'm still willing to talk. Can't we...?"

"We had nothing to do with your father's death,"

Tellon said. "I won't try to tell you we wouldn't have killed him if we had the chance, but no one from my House is laying claim to that death."

"Really? See what I mean? No . . . I'm saying this badly. Look, Tellon, can you tell Helwein that I'd like to meet with him? If we can't stop this feud, maybe we can at least modify . . ."

"*Pietor*! There's no sign of Nikki at the . . ."

Demitri Gregori halted his approach and his news in mid-step as he realized who his brother was speaking to. His hand flew to his sword hilt as Tellon drew back, mirroring the move with his own weapon.

"Stop it! Both of you!" Pietor ordered sharply, stepping between them. "Demitri. Take your hand off your sword! We were just talking. I was telling Tellon here how sorry I was about Teryl's death."

"Teryl?"

Demitri blanched at the name, his shoulders tightening as if expecting a physical blow.

"That's right," Pietor continued hurriedly, wondering what was ailing his brother. "You remember Teryl. She was . . ."

"*Tellon! 'Ware!*"

They all started, then turned toward the hail. No less than eight Hannons were hurrying toward them across the bridge.

"'Ware the Gregoris! *It's an ambush!*"

"What?" Pietor gaped. "No! Wait!"

Tellon's sword leaped from its scabbard as he backed away from the Gregoris, his head turning back and forth between the two groups in confusion.

Demitri stepped forward, shoving Pietor toward the upstairs of the pile as he fumbled for his own weapon.

"Run for it, Pietor!" he hissed. "I'll try to hold them here!"

"Stop, Demitri!" Pietor cried desperately, seizing his brother's arm in an attempt to keep him from drawing his weapon. "We've got to..."

"Let go, dammit! I can't..."

That was how they died when the Hannons swept over them...Demitri trying to do something right, even if it meant sacrificing his life to save his brother— and Pietor struggling to keep a Gregori sword in its scabbard.

"It were terrible," Old Michael returned to the House to report—

Which report stopped cold midway, at the sight of Nikki Gregori on the stairs, paint-smeared and smelling of turpentine.

Everyone stopped...of those servants who were there to hear. And Anna Gregori, who came from the parlor to hear the account.

Nearly a dozen had been killed, mostly Gregoris... though a few Hannons as well as innocent bystanders had been cut down in the fighting that had ebbed and swirled through the walkways near the College for nearly an hour.

Pietor lost, his brother Demitri—both killed. The servants, realizing the status of things—gave new deference to Anna, who cast a look of amazement and outrage in Nikki's direction.

"Where did *you* come from?" Anna asked; and Nikki, puzzled, answered his new Househead:

"Upstairs...."

—It being that he had left the House only briefly,

to turn back when he realized the afternoon light was perfect, falling on the fact of the upper tiers opposite his studio window—and his study arrangements with Rhajmurti in the College had been informal at best.

Damn you, Anna might have said. But Anna said nothing at all. Anna only stared at him.

And Nikki Gregori, who had a houseful of such stares to face, instead went upstairs and methodically put away his paints, folded down his easel, and threw his latest work down from the topmost tier into the dark of the canals.

He took his disused sword from the armoire then— his middle brother had given him the blade—and sat down on the bed, taking up a discarded canvas-knife to scratch a name patiently and deep in to the shining metal.

Tellon Hannon, it said.

Wanted: Guardian

Robert Lynn Asprin

"Baaaaa!"

Even if dragons did not have exceptional hearing, the sound would have been sufficient to rouse Schmirnov from his slumber.

Without opening his eyes or raising his head, the massive reptile reached out with his senses to confirm the noise.

"Baaa-aaa."

No. There could be no doubt about it. There was a sheep . . . no, *several* sheep in his cavern.

Sheep!

What in the blazes were those idiot villagers up to now?

"Baaaa." *Clink.*

The second noise, almost obliterated by the sheep's bleating, caught Schmirnov's total attention. His eyes opened and his head came up, searching for the source of the sound.

Sheep don't wear armor. Whether four legs with fleece, or two-legged with huts, sheep don't wear armor.

"Show yourself!" the dragon demanded.

"Baaaa."

He could now see the sheep, at least half a dozen of them, milling around the entrance to his cavern. As suspected, however, none of them were wearing armor.

"*Show yourself!*" Schmirnov called again. "State your intent, or I shall assume the worst and act accordingly!"

A short, chunky figure emerged from behind a boulder and stood silhouetted in the light from the entrance.

A dwarf! First sheep, and now a dwarf! Well, now. And he had thought this was going to be just another boring day.

"I am Ibble!" the figure said. "I come in peace!"

"In peace?" the dragon growled. "That would be a pleasant change."

Still, the dwarf had no visible weapons...unless he had some secreted behind his boulder. Then too...

"And what about the others?" Schmirnov sneered.

Ibble started visibly, and shot a glance back over his shoulder.

"Others?" he said.

"Don't play games with me, little man! There are at least a dozen more of you waiting outside. Warriors, from the sound of them."

Now that he was more awake, Schmirnov could clearly hear the creak of leather scabbards and other small noises that bespoke a group of armed men. What's more, the very sparseness of the sounds indicated not only warriors, but seasoned veterans.

This was a bit more like what the dragon had learned to expect from humans.

The old sneak attack, eh? If he were a bit less sporting, he would pretend that he didn't know they were there and let them try it.

"There are others, yes," the dwarf said hastily. "But we all mean you no harm. We seek only to talk to you. That and, perhaps, to request a favor."

"A favor?"

This was getting interesting indeed. Searching his memory, Schmirnov could not recall the last time, if ever, that a human had requested a favor of him. Whether he granted it or not, simply the asking could be amusing. Still, one could not be too careful. The treachery and deceit of humans was their trademark.

"How do I know this isn't a trick?" he said, letting a suspicion creep into his tone.

It had the desired effect, and the dwarf began to glance nervously at the cavern entrance. If Schmirnov became angry, there was no way Ibble could reach safety before suffering the consequences . . . and they both knew it.

"I . . . we've brought you presents as a sign of our good intentions."

"Presents?"

Though much of what is said or known about dragons is exaggeration or flat-out falsehood, the reports of their avarice are accurate.

Schmirnov raised his head to the greatest extent his neck and the cavern's ceiling would allow and peered about for his promised gifts like an eager child . . . a very *large* eager child.

There was nothing readily apparent in sight.

"Baaaa."

The dragon stared at the sheep for a moment, then swiveled his head around to gaze down on the dwarf.

"When you mention 'presents,' you didn't, by any chance, mean these miserable creatures, did you?"

"Well...yes, actually," Ibble said, edging a bit closer to his boulder. "I...we thought you might be hungry."

Schmirnov lowered his head until it was nearly resting on the ground, confronting his visitor nearly face to face.

"And in return for this, you expect me to grant you a favor?" he said. "You. Personally?"

"We're emissaries from Prince Rango," the dwarf explained hastily. "The favor we seek is in his name... for the good of the kingdom."

"A Prince, is it?" the dragon said. "But, of course, he isn't with your party himself. Right?"

"Well...no."

"In fact," Schmirnov continued, "I'd be willing to wager that you aren't even the leader of the group. Is that correct?"

Ibble drew himself up to his full, diminutive height and puffed out his chest proudly.

"I am the closest friend and confidant of the leader," he declared. "What's more, I've been his right-hand man and companion at arms for many harrowing campaigns and quests, and..."

The dragon cut him short by throwing back his head and giving off a short bark, which was the closest Schmirnov had come to laughing in decades.

"Let me see if I have this straight," the reptile said. "Your leader wasn't sure of the reception I'd give him if he just walked into my home...if I'd listen or simply fry him where he stood on general principles...so he sent you in ahead to test the water. You, in turn, decided to try to maximize your chances of survival by herding a bunch of sheep in to see if I was hungry before trying to approach me yourself. Am I right so far?"

"Well...in a manner of speaking," Ibble admitted.

"Just for the record, where did you get those sheep?"

"The sheep? Umm..."

"From that meadow in the valley below. Right?" Schmirnov supplied.

"As a matter of fact..."

"Quite a lot of them, aren't there?"

"Well..."

"Ever stop to wonder where they came from, or why they were there untended?"

"That *did* puzzle me a bit," the dwarf said. "Still, there were so may we didn't think the ones we took would be missed."

"Really?" The dragon smiled. "Well, try this one on for size. What would you say if I told you that the villagers maintain that flock specifically to keep me fed...at least, fed well enough that I leave their village alone."

"That...would make sense."

"More sense than trying to curry my favor with sheep from what could be called my own flock. Wouldn't you say?"

"I see your point." Ibble flushed. "Still, our intent was good."

"Ah, yes. Your intent." Schmirnov was genuinely enjoying himself now. "As I recall, we've established that your intent was to test my appetite...and possibly glut it if I were hungry...before venturing forth yourself. Tell me, do you have any idea how tired I can get of eating nothing but sheep?"

"I...can see where that could be a problem."

The dwarf was looking uncomfortable again.

"What I'm saying is that I have to be *really* hungry before I can bear to even *think* of indulging in another of those bleating creatures. On the other hand, I'm always up for something new to nibble on...especially a *small* something. Am I making myself clear?"

Ibble wavered for a moment, then squared his shoulders bravely.

"If we have offended you with our ignorance, Lord Dragon, you have our deepest regrets. If more than an apology is necessary...well, as you have noted, I am expendable."

Now, dragons in general, and Schmirnov specifically, have little regard for humans...which, in their minds, includes dwarves and elves. Still, being intelligent creatures, they respect and admire courage...if for no other reason than the fact that particular trait might well become extinct unless actively encouraged and protected.

"Well said, Ibble." Schmirnov smiled. "You do your master proud. What's more, you can ease your mind. I have no intention of eating or otherwise harming you or any of your party."

"Thank you, Lord Dragon," the dwarf said with a bow. "I could ask no greater guarantee than your word."

"Well, don't count *too* heavily upon it," the dragon cautioned. "I reserve the right to reverse my position if anyone tries to abuse my hospitality by using it as an opportunity for an attack. Is that understood?"

"Of course," Ibble said. "I assure you, however, that my lord is an honorable warrior who would not stoop to such a low trick."

"Really?" Schmirnov's voice took on a tone of sarcasm. "You'd be surprised how many so-called 'honorable warriors' feel that their normal rules of conduct and combat do not apply when facing dragons."

"Believe me, my lord is not one such as they. I have been at his side when he has faced numerous foes, many of them nonhuman and some not living, and never have I seen him sway from his code."

"That's good enough to get him an interview," the dragon said. "But you'll forgive me if I retain my caution nonetheless. The reason there are so few of us left is that far too many trusted the words and promises of humans. Now, who is this lord of yours?"

"He is Stiller Gulick, personal friend and comrade of Prince Rango."

"Gulick?" Schmirnov frowned. "You mean Spotty Gulick? The one with the complexion problem?"

"You know him?"

"I know *of* him," the dragon. "I didn't reach my current ripe old age by ignoring who or what might be coming up the hill at me. It pays to keep track of the current crop of heroes and bravos who are building their reputations."

"I see."

"What's he doing chumming around with a Prince? Last thing I heard he was a mercenary."

"That was before the war," Ibble exclaimed. "We aligned ourselves with the Prince to help throw down Kalaran."

"War? Kalaran?" Schmirnov shook his head. "It never ends, does it? I swear sometimes I think you humans have as much trouble living in peace with each other as you do living with my kind."

"If you'd like me to explain," the dwarf said, "I'm sure you'll agree our cause was just. Kalaran truly *was* a figure of evil."

"Of course." The reptile smiled. "He lost, didn't he?"

"I don't understand."

"The losing side is always wrong," Schmirnov said. "Especially since it's the winners who have the privilege of defining good and evil."

"But Kalaran..."

"Spare me." The dragon sighed. "Just go and fetch Spotty and we'll see what he has to say."

"At once, Lord Dragon."

The dwarf turned to go, then hesitated.

"Um...Lord Dragon?"

"Now what is it?"

"If I might suggest...in the interest of keeping this a peaceful meeting...it might be best if you refrained from calling him 'Spotty.' The nickname is due to the fact that he breaks out in pale blotches whenever danger threatens. It's a trait that has saved us on numerous occasions, but he's more than a little self-conscious about it."

"A sensitive human," the dragon muttered. "What will they think of next?"

"Excuse me?"

"Never mind. Just fetch him...and I'll try to remember your suggestion."

Despite his suspicions, Schmirnov studied the figure the dwarf led back into his cavern with genuine curiosity. It was rare that he had an opportunity to study a human, particularly a warrior, at leisure. Traditionally, his encounters with them were brief, and what was left could not be examined without extensive reassembling.

Stiller was an impressive specimen...medium height, stocky build with massive arms and legs, all topped by a shaggy head of bronze-red hair. Fierce blue eyes met the dragon's levelly and without fear, though, like his companion, the man's belt and harness were notably lacking in weapons.

Schmirnov observed that, despite reassurances given, Stiller's skin was, indeed, covered with the pale blotches of danger warning that gave the man his nickname.

Good. Maybe it would encourage Stiller to mind his manners during the interview.

Then, too, it raised an interesting point. Did the blotches forewarn actual danger, or only danger the man perceived? If the latter were the case, it didn't seem the trait would be particularly helpful. If the former, then there was something about this meeting which could prove dangerous to the man despite the guarantees of safety. The dragon resolved anew to be on his guard.

"Are you Schmirnov?" the man demanded.

The reptile regarded him for a long moment, then slowly craned his neck around to sweep the cavern with his gaze.

"Do you see any other dragons around?" he said at last.

"Well . . . no."

"Then it would be safe to assume that I am, indeed, Schmirnov, wouldn't you say? Really, Stiller, if you're going to indulge in redundant questions, this meeting could last through a change of seasons."

The man started visibly at the mention of his name.

"I told you so," Ibble murmured to him as an aside, which earned him a sharp elbow in the ribs.

"You know me?"

"Another redundant question." The dragon sighed. "As I told your little friend there, I know *of* you. You have a fairly sizable reputation . . . mostly from your habit of reducing the population, both human and non. You're supposed to be quite good at it...if you take pride in that sort of thing."

Stiller's blotches paled as the skin beneath them flushed.

"I take pride in the fact that I have never drawn blood from anyone or anything that did not first mean harm to others," he said angrily. "Unlike *some* here I could name."

"*Stiller!*" the dwarf hissed in warning, but the damage was already done.

"And what's *that* supposed to mean?"

"Warrior I may be," Gulick announced, shaking off Ibble's hand on his arm, "but I earned my reputation fighting against other arms bearers...aye, and a few creatures as well. It is not my way, however, to lay waste to entire villages or settlements, slaying fighter and noncombatant indiscriminately as is the habit of you and your kin. If it were, then I would not have the nerve to level accusations at those who set aside their normal prejudice to visit me in peace."

The dragon regarded him levelly for a moment.

"I can see," he said at last, "that if we are to have a civilized conversation, there will first have to be some air clearing between us. Consider this, warrior."

Schmirnov paused slightly to organize his thoughts.

"If you had a home, one with good hunting and clean water, where you had dwelt contentedly most of your life, and that home was invaded by a new species which completely disrupted the lifestyle to which you had become accustomed, how would you react?"

"It would depend on the nature of the invader," Stiller said stiffly.

"Fair enough." The dragon nodded. "For the moment, envision them as a colony of wasps. Few at first, and easily ignored. They nest, however, and begin to multiply at an alarming rate. What's worse, in their new numbers, they begin to drive out the game which is your normal livelihood. In fact, you often find yourself in direct competition with them for the same food sources. What would be your course of action?"

"I'd try to drive them out or eliminate them," the man said, averting his eyes with the admission.

"Kill as many as you can, and burn their colonies." Schmirnov smiled. "Probably killing both fighter wasps and noncombatant workers indiscriminately in the process. Right?"

Neither of his visitors replied.

"Now then, to continue our scenario," the dragon said, "let us assume that, in your own mistaken feeling of superiority, you have waited too long. There are too many of the invaders to deal with effectively. Not only that, you find that, once aroused, they are capable of harming you...even killing you if skillful enough or in great enough numbers. With that knowledge comes the realization that you have lost. You and all your kind will be replaced by this new species...one you might have squashed if you had taken it seriously enough when it first appeared."

Schmirnov's voice changed, becoming tinged in bitterness as memories played their scenes once more on the stage of his mind.

"All you can do then is retreat. Find some out-of-the-way place so desolate that no one will contest you for it and wait for the end as gracefully as you can. The trouble is these 'wasps' have memories. Memories and emotions. They recall the damage you have wreaked in the past, and begin to hunt you and the scattered remains of your kind...whether for vengeance or to eliminate a threat which no longer truly exists."

He shook his great head briefly.

"Some of my kind went mad from the pressure, launching fierce but hopeless attacks until they met the legend-inspiring deaths they sought. Others remain in hiding, and some, such as myself, have even reached a tenuous truce with small groups of humans. While I am genuinely grateful for the mutual tolerance, you'll forgive me if my view of you humans remains less than admiring."

The dragon lapsed into silence, which his visitors emulated, unable to think of anything to say.

Finally, Schmirnov heaved a great sigh and lowered his head in a slow bow.

"I fear, upon reflection, I owe you an apology. Both of you. You have come to me openly requesting a peaceful meeting and, after granting you safe passage, I have received you with thinly veiled insults and threats. If nothing else, this violates the very spirit of hospitality, and I must beg your forgiveness. My only excuse is ill temper caused by prolonged isolation. If anything, I should welcome company, not drive it away."

Gulick returned the bow.

"Your apology is accepted, but unnecessary, Lord Dragon," he said. "Having now heard your side of the human-dragon conflict, I'll confess that I am shamed by some of the things I have done or said in the past. However our meeting goes, you have given me much food for thought in the future. What's more, you have my promise that I will pass it along to others that they might also reflect on this long-standing injustice. As to our reception, I am only grateful that it was as nonviolent as you promised. I fear you would not have been received half as graciously had you chosen to visit us at our own homes."

"That much I can testify to." Schmirnov smiled. "As can my scars. But we've agreed to leave such memories to the past. Tell me now, what brings you to my lair on a mission of peace? It must be important, as I can't imagine it was an easy journey for you."

Stiller snorted.

"Indeed it was not. If you are interested, I could tell you tales of the dangers we braved to stand where we are now."

"Spare me," the dragon said.

"First, we were set upon by... Excuse me?"

Stiller paused in his oration as the reptile's words sank in.

"I said 'spare me,'" Schmirnov repeated. "Not to be rude, but I'll wager I've heard it all before. I have yet to hear of a quest, campaign, or simple trip undertaken by a warrior that didn't involve ambushes by bandits, attacks by various ferocious creatures, shortages of food and water, and at least one side trip to deal with a crisis that arose along the way. Did I overlook anything?"

Stiller and Ibble exchanged glances.

"Well... no."

"Tell me, has it ever occurred to you that peasants, peddlers, and merchants traverse these same lands virtually unarmed without encountering a fraction of the dangers you heroes seem to accept as daily fare?"

Again his visitors looked at each other, each waiting for the other to answer.

"You might discuss it at leisure once this meeting is over," the dragon said. "When you do, and if you discover I'm right, I suggest you consider two possible explanations. First, that the mere presence of a warrior or armed force will be perceived by whatever armed force or creature is in residence in the land you're traveling across as an attack, and will therefore provoke a response. That is, they will launch what they feel is a counterattack to your attack, which you in turn perceive as an attack and counter accordingly. What you see as a necessary defense only confirms their fears that you mean them harm, and the fight will continue to the death. A fight, I might add, that was not really necessary in the first place."

Stiller scowled thoughtfully.

"And the second possible explanation?" Ibble said.

"If your path is constantly barred by fights and challenges, you might consider your choice of routes." Schmirnov smiled. "If someone gave you a map or suggested such a dangerous path, they might actually be trying to engineer your deaths in the guise of assisting you. If, on the other hand, the route is of your own choosing, then there's a chance that you're letting your warrior's pride outweigh your common sense. That is, you try to bull your way through obstacles and dangers on the strength of you sword arm that others would simply walk around."

Stiller cleared his throat.

"Again, Lord Dragon, you give us food for thought. Might I point out, however, that it was you who raised the subject of our journey?"

"I did?"

"Yes. You said that you supposed it had not been

an easy journey for us, which I took as an invitation to tell you of our travels."

"Ah! I see the difficulty now. Actually, my reference to your doubtless hard trip was meant to imply that your mission would have to be important, or you wouldn't have undertaken it."

"Oh."

"Which brings us back to our original point. To wit, what mission is it that brings you to my cavern?"

Stiller blinked several times, then shook his head as if to clear it.

"My mission. Quite right," he said, almost to himself. "Simply put, Lord Dragon, I've been sent as a personal emissary from Prince Rango, to request a favor of you."

"That much your comrade here has explained to me," the dragon said patiently. "Tell me, just who is this Prince Rango?"

"He is the rightful ruler of these lands, both by bloodline and by right of conquest. He has recently succeeded in overthrowing the evil tyrant Kalaran, and will ascend the throne as King shortly at a combination marriage and coronation."

"This Kalaran you keep mentioning," Schmirnov said, "is he dead?"

"Why do you ask?"

"Before I start granting favors to any human or group of humans, it's nice to know who else might be popping up who might take offense at my taking sides."

"Kalaran is dead," Stiller said firmly. "I myself was present at the time of his demise."

"Why do I get the feeling it was not an easy death?" the dragon said wryly.

"Indeed it was not," the warrior confirmed. "Though evil, Kalaran was as powerful a foe as any I've faced or heard of. He had his followers, of course, and was no stranger to the Dark Arts. Much of our preparation for our assault involved locating and retrieving several powerful relics to assist us in our attack. As a warrior, I generally disdain the use of magick, but I must admit that in that final confrontation, I was glad we had taken the time to gather them. No lesser items than the scroll of Gwykander, the amulet called Anachron, and the ring Sombrisio had to be employed before Kalaran was weakened enough to be downed by a sword stoke. Without them, I fear our plans would have fallen to ruin."

"Impressive," Schmirnov said. "I'm not sure I understand, however. If this Kalaran has already been disposed of, then of what assistance can I be?"

"Well, it has to do with an artifact," Stiller said, uncomfortably.

"An artifact?"

Schmirnov's head soared up as he looked toward the rear of his cavern where his own treasures were stored. Determining at a glance they were undisturbed, he returned his attention to the warrior.

"While I appreciate the originality of asking for one of my treasures rather than trying to either steal it or kill me to gain possession, I'll admit to being bewildered by your request. Nothing in my trove approaches the power of those items already in your possession. Even if I did have something that might help, I thought you said the battle was already over."

"You misunderstand, Lord Dragon," Stiller said hastily. "We're not seeking any of your treasure. Quite the contrary. What we would ask is to *add* one of our items to your undoubtedly valuable collection."

"Now, why would you want to do that?" the dragon said suspiciously.

"Well ... so that you could guard it for us."

"You're trying to say that you think an artifact would be safer here in my cavern than in the kingdom capital surrounded by legions of royal guards?" Schmirnov's vice was tinged with incredulity. "Forgive me, but that seems to go against everything I've heard or learned of the arrogance of humans ... unless there's something you're omitting from your tale."

Stiller heaved a deep sigh.

"The truth is, Lord Dragon," he said, "we've been told that we *have* to scatter the artifacts again. Because of that, my old comrades and I have been assigned to find new hiding places for each of them. *That* is what has brought me to you this day."

"Perhaps the years are dulling my mind after all," the dragon said, "but I still don't understand. Could you explain further why it is that you have to scatter these items?"

"Strange things have been happening in these lands since the artifacts of power have been gathered together," Stiller said darkly. "Fish and other creatures rain from the heavens when there are no clouds. Unearthly sounds ... some call it music ... issue forth from thin air with no apparent source. Flying machines have appeared and disappeared in the sky over the capital. Most frightening, ungodly creatures unknown to science or legend have begun to appear at various places around the land. Perhaps you have observed some of these phenomena yourself?"

"Not really," Schmirnov said. "But then again, I haven't been watching very closely. Usually, when something strange or unexplainable occurs, I attribute it to the latest shenanigans of your kind, and do my best to ignore it."

"Well, they are happening nonetheless," Stiller said. "The learned men of the capital have reached the conclusion that the combined power of the artifacts we gathered has somehow created a rift in the fabric between our reality and others. What's more, they predict that it will grow worse. The only solution they can suggest is that the artifacts be scattered once more. This is the task Prince Rango has assigned to my comrades and I while he makes his preparations for ascending the throne . . . the task that has brought me to you today."

He drew himself and bowed slightly.

"Hmmm. Very interesting," the dragon said thoughtfully. "And what's the rest of it?"

"The rest of it?" The warrior frowned. "I don't understand."

"There must be more," Schmirnov insisted. "There are still questions unanswered by your tale. For example, why is the Prince scattering *all* of the artifacts? If a problem is created when they are all gathered together, then why doesn't he simply order that *one* be removed for hiding? At the very least, I think he would scatter all *but* one, keeping the most powerful close at hand to ensure his continued rule."

His visitors looked at each other and shrugged.

"I really don't know," Stiller said. "The Prince gave me my orders, and I'm following them."

"Commendable loyalty," the dragon said. "But that raises another point. Couldn't he have delegated this task to others? Why is it necessary to send forth those who are closest to him and know him best at a time when it would be most reasonable to have them at his side? After helping him to win a throne, it seems a strange reward to send you forth into danger once more rather than granting you rest and honors."

"I wondered about that myself," the dwarf growled.

"Shut up, Ibble," Stiller shot back. "As to your question, Lord Dragon, I can only assume that the Prince deemed our mission to be of such importance that it could only be trusted to his most proven friends and followers. I take my honor from being included in that number."

"Hmm. If you say so," Schmirnov said doubtfully. "Oh, well, if that's all you know, then there's little point in pressing you for more details. It doesn't really concern me, anyway. All that really matters is whether or not I will accept this artifact into my keeping."

"And what is your answer to that question, Lord Dragon?" Stiller pressed.

"I suppose it all depends," the dragon said. "What's in it for me?"

"I beg your pardon?"

"Come, now, Stiller. We're all supposed to be intelligent creatures here. You want something from me, which is to say a favor. What are you offering me in return?"

"Well . . ." the warrior said, looking at Ibble for support and receiving only another shrug in return, "I hadn't really been thinking in terms of payment. I suppose if we can agree on a figure, I can get clearance from the Prince to guarantee it."

"Of course, that would take time." Schmirnov sighed.

"Not really," Stiller said. "We have with us a wizard

who specializes in communication spells. Since he's been contacting the Prince's wizard on a regular basis to report our progress, I imagine we would have no difficulty obtaining approval on a payment."

"In all honesty, I hadn't been thinking in terms of payment," the dragon said. "Though I'll admit this new speedy method of communications intrigues me."

"But you said..."

"I inquired what you might be willing to offer me in return. I have sufficient treasure on hand already. It's actually rather easy to accumulate, since I have no place to spend it."

Schmirnov gestured negligently toward the back of his cavern with his tail.

"Well, if you aren't interested in gold or jewels, what would you like in exchange for the favor?" Stiller said, tearing his eyes away from the cavern's depths with some difficulty.

"I really hadn't given it much thought, beyond the basic instinct of not giving something for nothing. Remember, this is new to me, though you may have been thinking it for some time. Let me see..."

The great reptile stared thoughtfully at the cavern's ceiling for several moments.

"What I could really use," he said, almost to himself, "is something to relieve the boredom."

"What was that again?"

"Hmmm? Oh. Excuse me. I was thinking out loud. You see, the biggest problem with my current existence is that it's incredibly boring. Don't tell the villagers, but there are times when I've actually contemplated breaking my truce with them, just to have something to do."

"You know, that's something *we* might give some thought to, Stiller," Ibble said. "Once this mission is over and the kingdom is at peace, things could get uncommonly dull for us as well. For years, all we've done is travel and fight."

"There's an interesting question, warrior," the dragon said. "What do humans do to while away inactive time?"

"Different people do different things." Stiller shrugged. "Some garden, which I never cared for. Others take up hobbies."

"And what do *you* do?"

"Me? Well, whenever I get the opportunity, I like to play cards...poker, specifically."

"Poker?" Schmirnov said. "And what, pray tell, is poker?"

"*Stiller!*" The dwarf's voice had a new note of warning in it.

"Relax, Ibble," the warrior said, waving a hand at his comrade. "I'm just answering the Lord Dragon's questions. Poker is a card game...one of many, actually. You might say it's a time-consuming way to redistribute wealth through the study of mathematical probability."

"It's what?" The dragon frowned.

"It's gambling," Ibble said in a flat voice. "Two or more players are each dealt several cards, and they bet on who is holding the highest-ranked combination."

"That's oversimplifying it a bit." Stiller scowled.

"And your explanation was unnecessarily obtuse." The dwarf grimaced back.

"That sounds fascinating," Schmirnov said. "Could you teach me?"

"I would be honored to teach you the basics, Lord

Dragon," the warrior said. "It takes years of practice to master the game, however. Then, too, we *would* have to include wagering as part of the lesson. Much of the subtlety of the game is involved in the betting and bluffing."

"*Stiller!*"

"Will you relax, Ibble?" Stiller hissed. "Remember, this isn't *my* idea. It's a request of the Lord Dragon. If he wishes to make this a condition for his assistance, who am I to deny it? I *did* promise the Prince that I would let no danger sway me from completing the mission."

"Danger?" the dragon said. "Excuse me, but what danger could be involved in such a lesson?"

"Forgive me, Lord Dragon," the dwarf said, "but the danger I fear would be to Stiller here, and not you. You see, when we refer to betting . . . wagering gold or jewels on the turn of a card . . . such exchanges are permanent. That is to say, the wealth is not returned to the loser after the game is over. Often, players become upset after having lost large portions of their wealth, and attack the winners out of frustration. As Stiller is extremely skillful at this particular game, he has come under attack more often than I would care to remember from ill-tempered opponents. Consequently, when I see him about to become embroiled in a game with someone as obviously formidable as yourself, especially one who, like yourself, professes little if any knowledge of the game, I find myself growing more than a little anxious."

"You needn't fear, little man," Schmirnov said. "I have sufficient treasure that I will not become angry over giving up a portion of it in exchange for knowledge."

"Excellent," Stiller said, rubbing his hands together.

"That is, of course, unless I find the mathematical probabilities you mentioned are being artificially tampered with. That would be tantamount to stealing from me, which is something I will not tolerate."

"Oh." The warrior became a bit more subdued.

"Actually, there is only one thing which troubles me in this potential arrangement," the dragon said. "You mentioned that the game requires two or more players. While the game sounds fascinating, and the lessons enjoyable, what will I do with the knowledge once you depart?"

"I could make it part of the agreement that I would return occasionally . . . say two or three times a year . . . and we could continue the game."

Stiller only let his eyes wander toward the back of the cavern once as he made this selfless offer.

"That would be splendid!" Schmirnov exclaimed. "I believe we have a bargain. Go and fetch your little trinket."

A nod from Stiller sent Ibble scrambling out of the cavern.

"I must say, Lord Dragon," the warrior said as they waited, "this method of dealing with each other has much to recommend it over the way I used to approach your kind."

"As a member of the species all but wiped out by previous encounters with your kind, I can only concur," the dragon said. "There is a lot to be said for peaceful coexistence."

"Along with the gratitude of Prince Rango, I would like to extend my personal thanks for this favor," Stiller said. "I will rest much easier knowing the artifact is guarded by one who is not only fierce, but intelligent as well."

"You're too kind," Schmirnov responded. "By the way, you never got around to saying which of the artifacts you were intrusting to my care. I hope it isn't Sombrisio. That ring can be a real—"

He broke off suddenly as a glow lit up the cavern.

Ibble had reappeared, bearing with him a sword which radiated a soft but definite light.

"No need to worry about Sombrisio," Stiller said. "Jancy has the problem of dealing with—"

"That's Mothganger!!"

The dragon's voice rang with horror and accusation.

"Well . . . yes," the warrior said, taken a bit aback by his host's reaction.

"You didn't say anything about Mothganger," Schmirnov hissed. "You spoke only of the scroll of Gwykander, the amulet Anachron, and the ring Sombrisio."

"Didn't I?" Stiller frowned. "I know I said that Kalaran was finally felled by a sword stroke. I may have neglected to mention that the sword was Mothganger. I assure you, no deception was intended on my part."

"I'm sorry. The deal's off," the dragon said stiffly.

"Off?" the warrior cried. "But why? It was an innocent mistake on my part. I mean, an artifact is and artifact. Isn't it?"

"Are you mad, Stiller Gulick," the reptile said, "or simply stupid? Under no conditions will I allow that sword anywhere near me."

"But—"

"That weapon is one of the few items known to your kind that can actually do me great damage. Why I could be killed by a single blow from that accursed sword. You can't really expect me to keep the potential implement of my own doom in my cavern, can you? I thought we had agreed that we were both intelligent."

"But that's specifically why I thought of you for Mothganger's guardian," Stiller said, his voice edged with desperation. "If the sword were in your possession, then no one else could find it and bring it to use against you. Keeping Mothganger out of evil hands is a common goal between us."

"Hmm. An interesting point," Schmirnov said, mollified slightly. "Still, I couldn't relax, much less rest, with such a deadly threat residing in my cavern. I'm sorry, but it will have to go."

"Where would it be safer than right here?" the warrior argued. "If you won't take it, where should I go with it?"

"I really don't care," the dragon said. "Why not take it back to wherever it was you found it in the first place?"

"We can't. It's not a safe hiding place anymore."

"Why not? As I recall, Mothganger was supposed to be guarded by a rather ferocious ogre. What happened to him?"

"He . . . umm . . . we killed him," Stiller admitted uncomfortably.

"Really?" Schmirnov said. "Pity. Still, no great loss there. From what I heard, he was truly uncivilized."

"Do you have any suggestions at all as to where we could hide it?"

"Not a one," the great reptile said, shaking his head. "It's as I said earlier, you and your kind have been extremely efficient at eliminating creatures you felt were dangerous or threatening. Ironic, isn't it?

After devoting so much time and energy killing off creatures, you're now unable to find one when you really need one."

"Yeah. Ironic." Stiller growled. "Forgive me if my appreciation is less than enthusiastic, but I'm the one who's stuck with the sword in the meantime."

"Too bad you don't have one of the other artifacts instead," Schmirnov observed. "I wouldn't mind watching over the scroll or the amulet. I don't suppose there's any chance you could trade missions with one of the other comrades you mentioned?"

"I doubt it," the warrior said. "We were all riding in different directions...the idea *was* to separate the artifacts, you'll recall. I fear by the time I caught up with one of the others, they'd have already disposed of theirs."

"Well, sorry I can't help you...and I mean that sincerely," the dragon said. "I was really looking forward to learning about poker. I don't suppose you'd be willing to teach me anyway?"

"We'll have to see," Stiller said, remembering briefly the dragon's treasure trove. "Perhaps sometime in the future. At the moment, I have a mission to complete."

"Good luck with that," Schmirnov said. "If no solution presents itself, remember what I said before. If the others are successful, there should be no trouble keeping *one* of the artifacts at the capital."

The two friends were silent as they trudged down the slope from the mouth of Schmirnov's cavern.

"Well, *that* got us nowhere," Stiller said at last, his voice heavy with weariness.

"I really thought we were going to pull it off that time." Ibble sighed. "I mean, he had agreed and everything. Right up until he realized it was Moth-ganger we were asking him to guard."

"It's the end of the battle that counts," the warrior reminded him. "However close it was during the skirmishes, the final outcome is that he said 'no.'"

"Let's rest here a moment while we consider our next move," the dwarf suggested, drawing to a halt.

"Tired?" Stiller said, squatting down on his heels as was his habit when resting. "You must be getting old, Ibble. I can recall when an easy climb like this was nothing to you."

"It isn't that," Ibble said, waving off his friend's attempt at humor. "I'm just in no hurry to report our latest failure to the Prince's wizard. At the very least, it would be nice if we had our next destination in mind *before* passing the word to the Prince. It might sound a bit less hopeless and beaten if we had a positive plan to suggest at the same time as we admitted the negative results of our latest scheme."

Stiller grimaced, his earlier tight smile replaced by wrinkles of concern.

"I only hope that wizard is adding his own disappointment and scorn when he tells us of the Prince's reactions. I'd hate to think that Rango is really that upset with us, even allowing for our unbroken string of failures."

"Remember, it's *Prince* Rango now," Ibble said pointedly. "It wouldn't be the first time that a gold hat changed the personality of the one wearing it."

"You might be right," Stiller said. "He certainly hasn't been himself lately. I'm just hoping it's the pressure of his pending marriage and coronation that's doing it, and that he'll settle down again once all that is over."

"We can always hope." The dwarf shrugged. "In the meantime, what are we going to do with Mothganger?"

"I was hoping you'd have some ideas." The warrior sighed. "The dragon Schmirnov was my last card. I haven't even *heard* of another creature fierce enough to guard such a prize."

"If only you hadn't killed that manticore," Ibble said.

"You mean the ogre, don't you?"

"No, I mean the manticore," the dwarf insisted. "Remember, the one you chopped down *before* we could talk to it?"

"Hey. It surprised me. Okay?" Stiller said defensively. "I expected to find it on top of the hill and approach it slowly. When it burst out of the bushes right on top of us, I just swung out of reflex."

"I was there. Remember?" Ibble said. "That's most of why I thought it would be best if I made the first approach with Schmirnov."

"I've already apologized a hundred times for that. You want to hear it again? Okay. I'm sorry. I shouldn't have killed the manticore. There. Does that make things any better for us?"

"All I meant was, it left us with one less potential guardian for the sword . . . and we didn't have that big a list to start with."

"I know," the warrior said dejectedly. "Let's see, the original ogre guardian and the manticore are both dead, the merpeople refused the job, as did the dragon. Where does that leave us?"

"Sitting on a hillside talking to ourselves." Ibble sighed. "I still think we could just bury it or drop it down a ravine or something."

Stiller shook his head.

"We've been over that before," he said stubbornly. "The only way that would work is if we killed everyone in our party afterward...including the Prince's pet wizard and ourselves. Otherwise, someone's bound to talk and the word would get out that there was a powerful artifact just lying around waiting to be picked up. No, we need a guardian, a fierce one. Something nasty enough that even if someone finds out where Mothganger is hidden, they'll think twice about trying to fetch it."

"I don't supposed you'd consider just taking it back to the capital," the dwarf said. "As the dragon pointed out, there shouldn't be any danger if it's the only artifact there."

"That's assuming the others are successful," Stiller pointed out. "Besides, I don't like the idea of being the only one of the old fellowship that couldn't carry out my assignment."

"Then we're stuck," Ibble said, picking up a rock and throwing it at a bush. "I guess we could try talking to the merpeople again."

"They seemed pretty adamant in their refusal," the warrior said. "Besides, I'm not sure that it would do a sword any good to be kept under water."

"It's *supposed* to be indestructible," the dwarf observed dryly. "That's what makes it so valuable."

"Against wear and breakage, maybe. But it's still steel, and water and steel are old enemies."

As he spoke, Stiller drew the sword and studied its glowing blade.

"It looks ordinary enough, except for that glow," he said. "I wonder if that has anything to do with its indestructible nature."

"Naw. That's just a light spell." Ibble waved.

"Excuse me?"

"The glow. It's just an elven light spell," the dwarf said. "They're fairly easy to cast, and last a couple centuries. Whoever made the sword probably tossed it in as a bonus."

"You never said anything about that before."

"You never asked before. I assumed you already knew about it."

"I never heard of such a thing. How do you know about it?"

"There's an elven sword maker in the village where I grew up. He would add a light spell to anything if you asked him."

"How far away is your village?"

"A couple day's ride from here. If we have the time when we're done with this mission, maybe we could stop there and I'll introduce you to him."

"Let's go there now," Stiller said, rising to his feet.

"Now?"

"Yes. I think I have an idea."

The elven weaponsmith looked disdainfully at his two visitors.

"Young man," he said, "if it were not for the fact that little Ibble here says you're his friend and a hero, I'd say that you were either a fool or insane."

"I assure you, sir, I'm neither," Stiller said calmly.

"Well, it certainly couldn't be told from your request. Duplicate Mothganger?"

He gestured at the glowing sword they had placed on his workbench.

"If I could do that, I wouldn't be running my shop

out of a tiny village like this. Half the spells that went into the making of this sword have been lost in the march of time, and the ones that are still remembered would require years just to assemble the ingredients. You're wasting your time...and mine!"

"Please, Anken," Ibble said. "Hear us out."

"You misunderstand me, sir," the warrior said. "I'm not asking if you can produce a second Mothganger. As you say, that is well beyond the skills and knowledge of any weapons maker known today. What I require is a sword that *looks* like Mothganger. An ordinary weapon with a light spell cast on its blade."

Anken looked back and forth at the two comrades for a moment.

"A bogus Mothganger," he said at last. "I never heard of such a thing. You two wouldn't be thinking of trying to sell the phony as the real thing, would you? Or maybe give the fake to the rightful owner, while keeping the real one for yourselves?"

"I cannot disclose the reason for our request," Stiller said stiffly. "But I give you my word that our mission and need are honorable and aboveboard."

"You've known me all my life, Anken," the dwarf put in. "Have you ever known me to be anything other than honest?"

"That's true," the elf said thoughtfully. "The fact is you were always a bit dull that way."

"So can you do it?" Stiller urged. "More importantly, *will* you do it?"

In answer, Anken picked up Mothganger and began studying it closely.

"Really isn't much to look at, is it?" he said, almost to himself. "Have a seat, boys. I think I've got a couple old swords in storage that will give us just the parts we need. Might have to rework the pommel, but that shouldn't take long."

"Lord Dragon? Are you here? It's Stiller Gulick and Ibble."

The great reptile turned his head toward the source of the sound.

"Stiller?" he said. "Are you back so soon? Does this mean you're ready to start my poker lessons?"

"As a matter of fact, yes," the warrior said. "But first, I have a surprise for you."

He gestured to the dwarf, who reached into the gunnysack he was carrying and withdrew a sword with a glowing blade.

"*Stiller.*" Schmirnov's voice was heavy with warning and menace. "I thought I already made my feeling on the subject of that sword *very* clear."

Stiller seemed to ignore him completely.

"Set it there, Ibble," he said, pointing to a spot a mere three paces from the cavern's entrance.

"*STILLER!*"

"Now, then, Lord Dragon," Stiller said calmly. "As I understand it, your concern is that some misguided or overconfident person will take that weapon and attempt to use it on you. Is that correct?"

"I told you before, I won't have Mothganger in my cavern. It's too dangerous."

"But Schmirnov, if someone tried to use that sword against you, they would be in for a very rude surprise. You see, that isn't Mothganger."

"Nonsense," the dragon growled. "I'd know that accursed sword anywhere."

"That's what any interloper would think," the warrior agreed. "But they would be wrong."

He nodded again at Ibble, who withdrew a second glowing sword from the gunnysack.

"*This* is the real Mothganger," Stiller announced triumphantly. "It would be hidden safely in this sack in the depths of your cavern. The one by the door is a forgery . . . powerless except for a harmless light spell. Anyone who attempted to use *that* weapon against you would be committing suicide."

Schmirnov craned his neck forward, swaying his head first one way, then the other as he examined the two weapons.

"Very clever," he said at last. "Of course, your kind always excelled at treachery. I'll admit I can't tell the two swords apart. Are you sure the one by the door is the forgery?"

The dragon was so busy with his inspection, he missed the startled glance the two comrades exchanged.

"Trust me," Stiller said smoothly, signaling Ibble to return the second sword to the sack. "So, with this added refinement, do we have a deal?"

"Well," the dragon said, "you are very persuasive and I would very much like to learn poker, but I don't feel precisely safe about having the sword laying around in my hoard. Even stashed in a gunnysack, it is still Mothganger. I am not immune to the irony of being slain by a sword the wielder believes is second-rate."

Stiller and Ibble exchanged despairing glances. Then the dwarf perked up.

"Our visit to Anken reminded me that the elves are not the only masters of magic." He let his voice drop mysteriously. "Dwarves know how to make stone!"

"That's really nice, Ibble," Stiller said, "but what does that have to do with our finding a guardian for Mothganger?"

Ibble puffed up happily. "We imbed both swords in stone. Mothganger gets buried in a slab—I can wrap it beforehand so that it won't get gritty—and the false Mothganger gets imbedded partway in a showy pedestal."

Stiller picked up the thread of his comrade's thought. "Then you set the false Mothganger up as a sort of a decoration and lure. The real Mothganger gets stowed, one more block of stone in a stony cave! That's beautiful, Ibble!"

"Thank you," the dwarf said modestly.

The dragon's voice rumbled with appreciation. "What do you need to make your magic rock?"

"Oh, just some sand, gravel, lime, and clay," the dwarf said. "The ingredients are common. The real magic is in the combination. I'll needs some planks to make the form into which I'll pour the stone."

"Oh, can you make it into any form you choose?" Schmirnov asked.

"Pretty much," Ibble said proudly, hastening to add, "but making an elaborate form takes longer."

"I didn't want anything elaborate. I was just thinking that a slab of stone about this high," he gestured with a taloned foot, "would make a perfect card table."

"I can do it," Ibble promised.

"Now," Stiller said, hiding his eagerness, "with this new added refinement, do we have a deal?"

"We do indeed," Schmirnov said. "Now we can start our poker lessons."

"Excellent!" the warrior said, rubbing his hands together. "I thought we'd start with five card draw."

"Actually, I'd prefer it if you started with stud instead."

"Excuse me?" Stiller blinked.

"I think stud would be easier for me to learn because the cards are quite small for me, and hole cards would be easier to manipulate than an entire handful of cards. Five or seven would be satisfactory."

The warrior's eyes narrowed with suspicion.

"I though you said you didn't know how to play poker."

"Just because I don't know how to play doesn't mean I never *heard* of the game," Schmirnov explained.

"Hmmm," Stiller said thoughtfully.

"Trust me." The dragon smiled.

"It was only by the strangest sequence of coincidence that it came into my possession," Anken was saying. "But I won't bore you with that. All that's important is that it goes to a proper warrior who will put it to good use while keeping its location a secret."

His customer continued to study the glowing blade with a mixture of awe and skepticism.

"So this is really the legendary Mothganger," he said. "It's actually very ordinary looking, isn't it? You're sure there's no mistake?"

"Trust me." Anken smiled.

The elf waited for the warrior's first offer, trying to decide how hard he should haggle. He had three more copies he could sell to others, but that shouldn't affect the price of this one.

A Gift in Parting

ROBERT LYNN ASPRIN

The sun was a full two handspans above the horizon when Hort appeared on the Sanctuary docks; early in the day but late by fishermen's standards. The youth's eyes squinted painfully at the unaccustomed brightness of the morning sun. He fervently wished he were home in bed...or in someone else's bed...or anywhere but here. Still, he had promised his mother he would help the Old Man this morning. While his upbringing made it unthinkable to break that promise, his stubbornness required that he demonstrate his protest by being late.

Though he had roamed these docks since early childhood and knew them to be as scrupulously clean as possible, Hort still chose his path carefully to avoid brushing his clothes against anything. Of late he had been much more attentive to his personal appearance; this morning he had discovered he no longer had any old clothes suitable for the boat. While he realized the futility of trying to preserve his current garb through an entire day's work in the boat, newly acquired habits demanded he try to minimize the damage.

The Old Man was waiting for him, sitting on the overturned boat like some stately sea-bird sleeping off a full belly. The knife in his hand caressed the stray piece of wood he held with a slow, rhythmic cadence. With each pass of the blade a long curl of wood fell to join the pile at his feet. The size of the pile was mute testament to how long the Old Man had been waiting.

Strange, but Hort had always thought of him as the Old Man, never as Father. Even the men who had fished these waters with him since their shared boyhood called him Old Man rather than Panit. He wasn't really old, though his face was deceptive. Wrinkled and crisscrossed by weather lines, the Old Man's face looked like one of those red clay river beds one saw in the desert beyond Sanctuary: parched, cracked, waiting for rain that would never fall.

No, that was wrong. The Old Man didn't look like the desert. The Old Man would have nothing in common with such a large accumulation of dirt. He was a fisherman, a creature of the sea and as much a part of the sea as one of those weathered rocks that punctuated the harbor.

The Old Man looked up at his son's approach then let his attention settle back on the whittling.

"I'm here," Hort announced unnecessarily, adding, "sorry I'm late."

He cursed himself silently when that remark slipped out. He had been determined not to apologize, no matter what the Old Man said, but when the Old Man said nothing...

His father rose to his feet unhurriedly, replacing his knife in its sheath with a gesture made smooth and unconscious by years of repetition.

"Give me a hand with this," he said, bending to grasp one end of the boat.

Just that. No acceptance of the apology. No angry reproach. It was as if he had expected his reluctant assistant would be late.

Hort fumed about this as he grunted and heaved, helping to right the small boat and set it safely in the water. His annoyance with the whole situation was such that he was seated in the boat, accepting the oars as they were passed down from the dock, before he remembered that his father had been launching this craft for years without assistance. His son's inexpert hands could not have been a help, only a hindrance.

Spurred by this new irritation, Hort let the stern of the boat drift away from the dock as his father prepared to board. The petty gesture was in vain. The Old Man stepped into the boat, stretching his leg across the water with no more thought than a merchant gave his keys in their locks.

"Row that way," came the order to his son.

Gritting his teeth in frustration, Hort bent to the task.

The old rhythms returned to him in mercifully few strokes. Once he had been glad to row his father's boat. He had been proud when he had grown enough to handle the oars himself. No longer a young child to be guarded by his mother, he had basked in the status of the Old Man's boy. His playmates had envied his association with the only fisherman on the dock who could consistently trap the elusive nya—the small schooling fish whose sweet flesh brought top price each afternoon after the catch was brought in.

Of course, that had been a long time ago. He'd wanted to learn about the Nya then—he knew less now; his memories had faded.

As Hort had grown, so had his world. He learned

that away from the docks no one knew of the Old Man, nor did they care. To the normal citizens of Sanctuary, he was just another fisherman and fishermen did not stand high in the social structure of the town. Fishermen weren't rich, nor did they have the ear of the local aristocrats. Their clothes weren't colorful like the S'danzo's. They weren't feared like the soldiers or mercenaries.

And they smelled.

Hort had often disputed this latter point with the street urchins away from the docks until bloody noses, black eyes and bruises taught him that fishermen weren't good fighters, either. Besides, they did smell.

Retreating to the safety of the dock community, Hort found that he viewed the culture which had raised him with a blend of scorn and bitterness. The only people who respected fishermen were other fishermen. Many of his old friends were drifting away—finding new lives in the crowds and excitement of the city-proper. Those that remained were dull youths who found reassurance in the unchanging traditions of the fish-craft and who were already beginning to look like their fathers.

As his loneliness grew, it was natural that Hort used his money to buy new clothes which he bundled and hid away from the fish-tainted cottage they called home. He scrubbed himself vigorously with sand, dressed and tried to blend with the townsfolk.

He found the citizens remarkably pleasant once he had removed the mark of the fishing community. They were most helpful in teaching him what to do with his money. He acquired a circle of friends and spent more and more time away from home until...

"Your mother tells me you're leaving."

The Old Man's sudden statement startled Hort, jerking him rudely from his mental wanderings. In a flash he realized he had been caught in the trap his friends had warned him about. Alone in the boat with his father he would be a captive audience until the tide changed. Now he'd hear the anger, the accusations and finally the pleading.

Above all, Hort dreaded the pleading. While they had had their differences in the past, he still held a lingering respect for his father, a respect he knew would die if the Old Man were reduced to whining and begging.

"You've said it yourself a hundred times, Old Man," Hort pointed out with a shrug, "not everyone was meant to be a fisherman."

It came out harsher than he had intended, but Hort let it go without more explanations. Perhaps his father's anger would be stirred to a point where the conversation would be terminated prior to the litanies of his obligations to his family and tradition.

"Do you think you can earn a living in Sanctuary?" the Old Man asked, ignoring his son's baiting.

"We . . . I won't be in Sanctuary," Hort announced carefully. Even his mother hadn't possessed this last bit of knowledge. "There's a caravan forming in town. In four days it leaves for the capital. My friends and I have been invited to travel with it."

"The capital?" Panit nodded slowly. "And what will you do in Ranke?"

"I don't know yet," his son admitted, "but there are ten jobs in Ranke for every one in Sanctuary."

The Old Man digested this in silence. "What will you use for money on this trip?" he asked finally.

"I had hoped... There's supposed to be a tradition in our family, isn't there? When a son leaves home his father gives him a parting gift. I know you don't have much, but..." Hort stopped; the Old Man was shaking his head in slow negation.

"We have less than you think," he said sadly. "I said nothing before, but your fine clothes, there, have tapped our savings; the fishing's been bad."

"If you won't give me anything, just say so!" Hort exploded angrily. "You don't have to rationalize it with a long tale of woe."

"I'll give you a gift," the Old Man assured him. "I only wanted to warn you that it probably would not be money. More to the left."

"I don't need your money," the youth growled, adjusting his stroke. "My friends have offered to loan me the necessary funds. I just thought it would be better not to start my new life in debt."

"That's wise," Panit agreed. "Slow now."

Hort glanced over his shoulder for a bearing then straightened with surprise. His oars trailed loose in the water.

"There's only one float!" he announced in dumb surprise.

"That's right," the Old Man nodded. "It's nice to know you haven't forgotten your numbers."

"But one float means..."

"One trap," Panit agreed. "Right again. I told you fishing was bad. Still, having come all this way, I would like to see what is in my one trap."

The Old Man's dry sarcasm was lost on his son. Hort's mind was racing as he reflexively maneuvered the boat into position by the float.

One trap! The Old Man normally worked fifteen to twenty traps; the exact number always varied from day to day according to his instincts, but never had Hort known him to set less than ten traps. Of course the nya were an unpredictable fish whose movements confounded everyone save Panit. That is—they came readily to the trap if the trap happened to be near them in their random wanderings.

One trap! Perhaps the schools were feeding elsewhere; that sometimes happened with any fish. But then the fishermen would simply switch to a different catch until their mainstay returned. If the Old Man were less proud of his ability and reputation he could do the same...

"Old Man!" The exclamation burst from Hort's lips involuntarily as he scanned the horizon.

"What is it?" Panit asked, pausing as he hauled his trap from the depths.

"Where are the other boats?"

The Old Man returned his attention to the trap. "On the dock," he said brusquely. "You walked past them this morning."

Open-mouthed, Hort let his memory roam back over the docks. He had been preoccupied with his own problems, but...yes! there had been a lot of boats lying on the dock.

"All of them?" he asked, bewildered. "You mean we're the only boat out today?"

"That's right."

"But why?"

"Just a minute...here!" Panit secured a handhold on the trap and heaved it onto the boat. "Here's why."

The trap was ruined. Most of the wooden slats

which formed its sides were caved in and those that weren't dangled loose. If Hort hadn't been expecting to see a nya trap he wouldn't have recognized this as something other than a tangle of scrap wood.

"It's been like this for over a week!" the Old Man snarled with sudden ferocity. "Traps smashed, nets torn. That's why those who call themselves fishermen cower on the land instead of manning their boats!" He spat noisily over the side of the boat.

Was it also why his mother had insisted Hort give the Old Man a hand?

"Row for the docks, boy. Fishermen! They should fish in buckets where it's safe! Bah!"

Awed by the Old Man's anger, Hort turned the boat toward the shore. "What's doing it?" he asked.

There was silence as Panit stared off to the sea. For a moment Hort thought his question had gone unheard and was about to repeat it. Then he saw how deep the wrinkles on his father's face had become.

"I don't know," the Old Man murmured finally. "Two weeks ago I would have said I knew every creature that swam or crawled in these waters. Today . . . I just don't know."

"Have you reported this to the soldiers?"

"Soldiers? Is that what you've learned from your fancy friends? Run to the soldiers?" Panit fairly trembled with rage. "What do soldiers know of the sea? Eh? What do you want them to do? Stand on the shore and wave their swords at the water? Order the monster to go away? Collect a tax from it? Yes! That's it! If the soldiers declare a monster tax maybe it'll swim away to keep from being bled dry like the rest of us! Soldiers!"

The Old Man spat again and lapsed into a silence that Hort was loath to break. Instead he spent the balance of the return journey mentally speculating about the trap-crushing monster. In a way he knew it was futile; sharper minds than his, the Old Man's for example, had tried and failed to come up with an explanation. There wasn't much chance he'd stumble upon it. Still, it occupied his mind until they reached the dock. Only when the boat had been turned over in the late morning sun did Hort venture to reopen the conversation.

"Are we through for the day?" he asked. "Can I go now?"

"You can," the Old Man replied, turning a blank expression to his son. "Of course, if you do it might cause problems. The way it is now, if your mother asks me: 'Did you take the boat out today?' I can say yes. If you stay with me and she asks: 'Did you spend the day with the Old Man?' you can say yes. If, on the other hand, you wander off on your own, you'll have to say no when she asks and we'll both have to explain ourselves to her."

This startled Hort almost more than the discovery of an unknown monster loose in the fishing grounds. He had never suspected the Old Man was capable of hiding his activities from his wife with such a calculated web of half-truths, Close on the heels of his shock came a wave of intense curiosity regarding his father's plans for a large block of time about which he did not want to tell his wife.

"I'll stay," Hort said with forced casualness. "What do we do now?"

"First," the Old Man announced as he headed off down the dock, "we visit the *Wine Barrel*."

The *Wine Barrel* was a rickety wharf-side tavern favored by the fishermen and therefore shunned by everyone else. Knowing his father to be a nondrinker, Hort doubted the Old Man had ever before been inside the place, yet he led the way into the shadowed interior with a firm and confident step.

They were all there: Terci, Omat, Varies; all the fishermen Hort had known since childhood plus many he did not recognize. Even Haron, the only woman ever accepted by the fishermen, was there, though her round, fleshy and weathered face was scarcely different from the men's.

"Hey, Old Man? You finally given up?"

"There's an extra seat here."

"Some wine for the Old Man!"

"One more trap-wrecked fisherman!"

Panit ignored the cries which erupted from various spots in the shadowed room at his entrance. He held his stride until he reached the large table custom reserved for the eldest fisherfolk.

"I told you, you'd be here eventually," Omat greeted him, pushing the extra bench out with his long, thin leg. "Now, who's a coward?"

The Old Man acknowledged neither the jibe nor the bench, leaning on the table with both hands to address the veterans. "I only came to ask one question," he hissed. "Are all of you, or any of you, planning to do anything about whatever it is that's driven you from the sea?"

To a man, the fishermen moved their gazes elsewhere.

"What can we do?" Terci scowled. "We don't even know what's out there. Maybe it will move on..."

"... And maybe it won't," the Old Man concluded angrily. "I should have known. Scared men don't think; they hide. Well, I've never been one to sit around waiting for my problems to go away on their own. Not planning to change now."

He kicked the empty bench away and turned toward the door only to find Hort blocking his way.

"What are you going to do?" Terci called after him.

"I'm going to find an answer!" the Old Man announced, drilling the room with his scorn. "And I'll find it where I've always found answers—in the sea; not at the bottom of a wine cup."

With that he strode out the door. Hort started to follow when someone called his name and he turned back.

"I thought that was you under those city clothes," Omat said without rancor. "Watch over him, boy. He's a little crazy and crazy people sometimes get killed before they get sane."

There was a low murmur of assent from those around the table. Hort nodded and hurried after his father. The Old Man was waiting for him outside the door.

"Fools!" he raged. "No money for a week and they sit drinking what little they have left. Pah!"

"What do *we* do now, Old Man?"

Panit looked around then snatched up a nya trap from a stack on the dock. "We'll need this," he said, almost to himself.

"Isn't that one of Terci's traps?" Hort asked cautiously.

"He isn't using it, is he?" the Old Man shot back. "And besides, we're only borrowing it. Now, you're supposed to know this town, where's the nearest blacksmith?"

"The nearest? Well, there's a mender in the Bazaar, but the best ones are..."

The Old Man was off, striding purposefully down the street leaving Hort to hurry after him.

It wasn't a market-day; the bazaar was still sleepy with many stalls unopened. It was not necessary for Hort to lead the way as the sharp, ringing notes of hammer striking anvil were easily heard over the slow-moving shoppers. The dark giant plying the hammer glanced at them as they approached, but continued his work.

"Are you the smith?" Panit asked.

This earned them another, longer, look but no words. Hort realized the question had been ridiculous. A few more strikes and the giant set his hammer aside, turning his full attention to his new customers.

"I need a nya trap. One of these." The Old Man thrust the trap at the smith.

The smith glanced at the trap, then shook his head. "Smith; not carpenter," he proclaimed, already reaching for his hammer.

"I know that!" the Old Man barked. "I want this trap made out of metal."

The giant stopped and stared at his customers again, then he picked up the trap and examined it.

"And I'll need it today—by sundown."

The smithy set the trap down carefully. "Two silvers," he said firmly.

"Two!" the Old Man snorted. "Do you think you're dealing with the Kittycat himself? One."

"Two," the smithy insisted.

"Dubro!"

They all turned to face the small woman who had emerged from the enclosure behind the forge.

"Do it for one," she said quietly. "He needs it."

She and the smithy locked eyes in a battle of wills, then the giant nodded and turned away from his wife.

"S'danzo?" the Old Man asked before the woman disappeared into the darkness from which she'd come.

"Half."

"You've got the sight?"

"A bit," she admitted. "I see your plan is unselfish but dangerous. I do not see the outcome—except that you must have Dubro's help to succeed."

"You'll bless the trap?"

The S'danzo shook her head. "I'm a seer, not a priest. I'll make you a symbol—the Lance of Ships from our cards—to put on the trap. It marks good fortune in sea-battles; it might help you."

"Could I see the card?" the Old Man asked.

The woman disappeared and returned a few moments later bearing the card which she held for Panit. Looking over his father's shoulder, Hort saw a crudely drawn picture of a whale with a metal-sheathed horn proceeding from its head.

"A good card," the Old Man nodded. "For what you offer—I'll pay the two silvers." She smiled and returned to the darkness, Dubro stepped forward with his palm extended. "When I pick up the trap," Panit insisted. "You needn't fear. I won't leave it to gather dust."

The giant frowned, nodded and turned back to his work.

"What are you planning?" Hort demanded as his father started off again. "What's this about a sea-battle?"

"All fishing is sea-battle," the Old Man shrugged.

"But, two silvers? Where are you going to get that kind of money after what you said in the boat this morning?"

"We'll see to that now."

Hort realized they weren't returning to town but heading westward to the Downwinder's hovels. The Downwinders or ... "Jubal?" he exclaimed. "How're you going to get money from him? Are you going to sell him information about the monster?"

"I'm a fisherman, not a spy," the Old Man retorted, "and the problems of the fishermen are no concern of the land."

"But ..." Hort began then lapsed into silence. If his father was going to be closemouthed about his plans, no amount of browbeating was likely to budge him.

Upon reaching Jubal's estate, Hort was amazed at the ease with which the Old Man handled the slaver's underlings who routinely challenged his entry. Though it was well known that Jubal employed notorious cutthroats and murderers who hid their features behind blue-hawk masks, Panit was unawed by their arrogance or their arms.

"What do you two want here?" the grizzled gatekeeper barked.

"We came to talk to Jubal," the Old Man retorted.

"Is he expecting you?"

"I need an appointment to speak with the slaver?"

"What business could an old fisherman have with a slaver?"

"If you were to know, I'd tell you. I want to see Jubal."

"I can't just..."

"You ask too many questions. Does *he* know you ask so many questions?"

That final question of the Old Man's cowed the retainer, confirming Hort's town-refined suspicions that most of the slaver's business was covert rather than overt.

They were finally ushered into a large room dominated by a huge, almost throne-like, chair at one end. They had been waiting only a few moments when Jubal entered, belting a dressing gown over his muscular, ebony limbs.

"I should have known it was you, Old Man," the slaver said with a half-smile. "No other fisherman could bluff his way past my guards so easily."

"I know you prefer money to sleep," the Old Man shrugged. "Your men know it too."

"True enough," Jubal laughed. "So, what brings you this far from the docks so early in the day?"

"For some the day's over," Panit commented dryly. "I need money: six silver pieces. I'm offering my stall on the wharf."

Hort couldn't believe what he was hearing. He opened his mouth to speak, then caught himself. He had been raised to know better than to interrupt his father's business. His movement was not lost on Jubal, however.

"You intrigue me, Old Man," the slaver mused. "Why should I want to buy a fish-stall at any price?"

"Because the wharf's the only place your ears don't hear," Panit smiled tightly. "You send your spies in—but we don't talk to outsiders. To hear the wharf you must be on the wharf—I offer you a place on the wharf."

"True enough," Jubal agreed. "I hardly expected the opportunity to fall my way like ripe fruit..."

"Two conditions," the Old Man interrupted. "First: four weeks before you own my stall. If I repay the money—you don't own my stall..."

"All right," the slaver nodded, "but..."

"Second: anything happens to me these next four weeks you take care of my wife. It's not charity; she knows the wharf and the nya—she's worth a fair wage."

Jubal studied the Old Man a moment through hooded eyes. "Very well," he said finally, "but I sense there is much you are not telling me." He left the room and returned with the silver coins which rattled lightly in his immense palm. "Tell me this, Old Man," he asked suspiciously, "all these terms—why don't you just ask for a loan?"

"I've never borrowed in my life," Panit scowled, "and won't start now. I pay as I go—if I don't have enough I do without or I sell what I must."

"Suit yourself," the slaver shrugged, handing over the coins. "I'll be expecting to see you in thirty days."

"Or before."

The silence between father and son was almost habitual and lasted nearly until they had reached the town again. Strangely, it was the old man who broke the silence first.

"You're being quiet, boy," he said.

"Of course," Hort exploded. "There's nothing to say. You order things we can't pay for, sell your life-work to the biggest crook in Sanctuary and then wonder why I'm quiet. I know you don't confide in me—but Jubal! Of all the people in town...And that talk about conditions! What makes you think he'll stand by any of them? You don't trust soldiers but you trust Jubal!"

"*He* can be trusted," the Old Man answered softly.

"He's a hard one when he's got the upper hand—but he stands by his word."

"You've dealt with him before? Nothing can surprise me now," Hort grumbled.

"Good," his father nodded. "then you'll take me to the *Vulgar Unicorn*?"

"The *Vulgar Unicorn!*" He was surprised.

"That's right. Don't you know where it is?"

"I know it's in the Maze somewhere, but I've never been there."

"Let's go."

"Are you sure you want the *Vulgar Unicorn*, Old Man?" Hort pressed. "I don't think a fisherman's ever set foot in there. The people who drink at the *Unicorn* are mercenaries, cutthroats, and a few thieves thrown in for good measure."

"So they say," the Old Man nodded. "Wouldn't be going there if they weren't. Now, you leading or not?"

All conversation stopped as they entered that infamous tavern. As he struggled to see in the darkness, Hort could feel the eyes of the room on his, sizing them up, deciding if he was a challenge or a victim.

"Are you gentlemen looking for someone?" The bartender's tone implied he didn't think they should stay for a drink.

"I want some fighting men," the Old Man announced. "I've heard this is the place."

"You heard right," the bartender nodded, suddenly a bit more attentive. "If you don't know who you want, I'll be glad to serve as your agent—for a modest fee, of course."

Panit regarded him as he'd regarded his fellow fisherfolk. "I judge my own people—go back to your dishes."

The bartender clenched his fists in anger and retreated to the other end of the bar as the Old Man faced the room.

"I need two, maybe three men for a half-day's work," he called loudly. "A copper now and a silver when it's over. No swords or bowmen just axes or pole-arms. I'll be outside."

"Why are we going to talk to them outside?" Hort asked as he followed his father into the street.

"I want to know what I'm getting," the Old Man explained. "Couldn't see a thing in that place."

It took most of the afternoon but they finally sorted out three stalwarts from the small pack that had followed them. The sun was dipping toward the horizon as Panit gave his last man the advance coin and turned to his son.

"That's about all we can do today," he said. "You run along and see your friends. I'll take care of the trap."

"Aren't you going to tell me your plan?" Hort pleaded.

"Haven't got it all worked out yet," the Old Man admitted, "but if you want to see what happens, be on the dock at first light tomorrow. We'll see how smart this monster is."

Unlike the day before, Hort was at the dock well before the dawn. As the first tendrils of pre-dawn light began to dispel the night, he was pacing impatiently, hugging himself against the damp chill of the morning.

Mist hung deep over the water, giving it an eerie, supernatural appearance which did nothing to ease Hort's fears as he alternately cursed and worried about his absent father. Crazy old man! Why couldn't he be like the other fishermen? Why take it on himself to solve the mystery of the sea-monster? Knowing the best way to combat the chill was activity, he decided to launch the family's boat. For once, he would be ready when the Old Man got here.

He marched down the dock, then slowed, and finally retraced his steps. The boat was gone. Had Sanctuary's thieves finally decided to ply their trade on the wharf? Unlikely. Who would they sell a stolen boat to? The fishermen knew each other's equipment as well as they knew their own.

Could the Old Man have gone out already? Impossible—to be out of the harbor before Hort got there, the Old Man would have had to take the boat out at night—and in these waters with the monster. . . .

"You there!"

Hort turned to find the three hired mercenaries coming down the pier. They were a sullen crew by this light and the pole-arms two of them carried gave them the appearance of Death's own oarsmen.

"We're here," the leader of the trio announced, shifting his battle-axe to his shoulder, "though no civilized man fights at this hour. Where's the old man who hired us?"

"I don't know," Hort admitted, backing down from this fierce assemblage. "He told me to meet him here same as you."

"Good," the axe-man snarled. "We've appeared, as promised. The coppers are ours, small price for a practical joke. Tell that old man when you see him that we've gone back to bed."

"Not so fast," Hort surprised himself with his sudden outspoken courage as the men turned away. "I've known the Old Man all my life and he's no joker. If he paid you to be here, you'll be needed. Or don't you want the silver that goes with those coppers?"

The men hesitated, mumbling together darkly.

"Hort!" Terci was hurrying toward them. "What's going on? Why are there cut-throats on the dock?"

"The Old Man hired them," Hort explained. "Have you seen him?"

"Not since last night," the lanky fisherman replied. "He came by late and gave me this to pass to you." He dropped three silver coins into the youth's palm. "He said if he wasn't here by mid-day that you were to use this to pay the men."

"You see!" Hort called to the mercenaries as he held up the coins. "You'll be paid at midday and not before. You'll just have to wait with the rest of us." Turning back to Terci, he lowered his voice to a conspiratorial whisper. "What else did the Old Man say—anything?"

"Only that I should load my heaviest net this morning," Terci shrugged. "What's going on?"

"He's going to try to fish for the monster," Hort explained as the Old Man's plan came clear to him. "When I got here his boat was gone."

"The monster," Terci blinked. "The Old Man's gone out alone after the monster?"

"I don't think so. I've been here since before first light. Not even the Old Man would take a boat out in the dark—not after the monster. He must be..."

"Look there! There he is!"

The sun had finally appeared over the horizon and with its first rays the mist began to fade. A hundred yards offshore a small boat bobbed and dipped and in it they could see the Old Man pulling frantically at the oars.

As they watched, he suddenly shipped the oars, waiting expectantly. Then the boat was jerked around, as if by an unseen hand and the Old Man bent to the oars again.

"He's got it! He's got the monster!" Terci shrieked, dancing with delight or horror.

"No!" Hort disagreed firmly, staring at the distant boat. "He doesn't have it. He's leading it, baiting it into shallow water."

It was all clear to him now. The metal trap! The monster was used to raiding the Old Man's traps, so he fed it one that couldn't be crushed. Now he was teasing the unknown creature toward shore, dragging the trap like a child drags a string before a playful kitten. But this kitten was an unknown, deadly quantity that could easily attack the hand that held the string.

"Quick, Terci," Hort ordered, "get the net! It won't follow him onto the shore."

The lanky fisherman was gaping at the scene, his mind lost in his own thoughts. "Net the monster?" he mumbled. "I'll need help, yes, help . . . HELP!" He fled down the dock screaming at the still-dark, quiet huts.

This was not the Maze where cries for help went unheeded. Doors opened and bleary-eyed fishermen stumbled out to the wharf.

"What is it?"

"What's the noise?"

"Man your boats! The Old Man's got the monster!"

"The monster?"

"Hurry, Ilak!"

"The Old Man's got the monster." The cry was passed from hut to hut.

And they came, swarming over their boats like a nest of angry ants: Haron, her sagging breasts flopping beneath the nightdress she still wore; Omat, his deformed arm no hindrance as he wrestled his boat onto the water with one hand, and in the lead, Terci, first rowing, then standing, in the small boat to shout orders at the others.

Hort made no move to join them. They were fishermen and knew their trade far better than he. Instead he stood rooted on the dock, lost in awe of the Old Man's courage.

In his mind's eye Hort could see what his father saw: sitting in a small boat on an inky sea, waiting for the first tug on the rope—then the back-breaking haul on the oars to drag the metal trap landward. Always careful not to get too far ahead of the invisible creature below, yet keeping its interest. The dark was the Old Man's enemy as much as the monster was; it threatened him with disorientation—and the mist! A blinding cloud of white closing in from all sides. Yet the Old Man had done it and now the monster was within reach of its victims' nets.

The heavy net was spread now, forming a wall between the mystery beast as it followed the Old Man and the open sea behind them. As the boats at either end of the net began to pull for shore, the Old Man evened his stroke and began to move steadily through the water . . . but he was tired now; Hort could see that even if no one else could.

"There!" Hort called to the mercenaries, he pointed toward the shore-line. "That's where they'll beach it! Come on!"

He led their rush down the dock. He heard rather than saw the nets scoop up its prey; a cheer went up from the small boats. He was waiting waist-deep in the water when the Old Man's boat finally reached the shallows. Grabbing onto the cleats, Hort dragged the boat to the beach as if it were a toy while his father sagged wearily between the oars.

"The trap," the Old Man wheezed through ragged gasps, "pull it in before those fools get it tangled in their nets!"

The rope was cold and hard as cable, but Hort dragged the trap hand-over-hand away from the sea's grip. Not surprisingly, it was full of nya that shimmered and flopped in the morning sun. Without thinking, Hort reached behind his father and dumped the fish into the boat's live well.

All the boats were ashore now, and there was splashing and thrashing around the net in the shallows.

"What is it like?" the Old Man gasped; he could scarcely raise his head. "What's the monster like?"

"It looks to be a large crab," Hort announced, craning his neck. "The mercenaries have got to it."

And they had; waving the crowd back, they waded into the water to strike at the spidery giant even before the net was on the shore.

"I thought so," the Old Man nodded. "There weren't any teeth marks on the traps. Some damn sorcerer's pet run loose," he added.

Hort nodded. Now that he could see the monster, it fit the rumors he had heard from time to time in the town. The Purple Mage had kept large crabs to guard his home on the White Foal River. Rumor said he was dead now, killed by his own magic. The rumor was confirmed by the crab; it must have wandered downstream to the sea when its food no longer appeared.

"Whose catch is that?"

Hort turned to find two Hell Hounds standing close beside him. Simultaneously he noticed the crowd of townsfolk which had gathered on the streets.

"Everybody's," the Old Man declared, getting his strength back. "They caught it. Or anybody's. Maybe it's Terci's—it's mangled his net."

"No, Old Man," Terci declared, approaching them. "It's your catch. There's none on the wharf who'd deny that—least of all me. You caught it. We netted and gaffed it for you after the fight."

"It's yours then," the Hell Hound decided, facing the Old Man. "What do you plan to do with it?"

It flashed across Hort's mind that these soldiers might be going to fine his father for dragging the crab to the beach; they might call it a public nuisance or something. He tightened his grip on the Old Man's arm, but he'd never been able to hold his father.

"I don't know," Panit shrugged. "If the circus was still in town I'd try to sell it to them. Can't sell it for food—might be poisonous—wouldn't eat it myself."

"I'll buy it," the Hell Hound announced to their surprise. "The Prince has tasters and a taste for the unknown. If it's poisonous, it will still make table talk fit for an Emperor. I'll give you five silvers for it."

"Five? Ten—times're hard; I've got debts to Jubal for my fish-stall," the Old Man bargained, no more awed by the Hell Hounds than he had been by Jubal himself.

At the mention of the slaver's name, the tall Hell Hound scowled and his swarthy companion sucked air noisily through his teeth.

"Jubal?" the tall man mumbled as he reached for his pouch. "You'll have your ten silvers, fisherman—and a gold piece besides. A man should have more than a slaver's receipt for this day's work."

"Thankye," Panit nodded, accepting the coins. "Take your watch to the marshes and swamps; there's never one crab but there's ten. Corner 'em on dry land an' Kittycat'll eat crab for a month."

"Thanks for your information," the Hell Hound grimaced. "We'll have the garrison look into it."

"Not a bad day's catch," the Old Man chortled after the retreating soldiers, "and nya besides. I'll send two in luck-money to the blacksmith and the S'danzo and get new traps besides." He cocked his head at his son. "Well," he tossed the gold coin in the air and caught it again, "I've got this too, to add to your other gift."

"Other gift?" Hort frowned.

The smile fell from the Old Man's face like a mask. "Of course," he snarled. "Why do you think I went after that thing anyway?"

"For the other fishermen?" Hort offered. "To save the fishing ground?"

"Aye," Panit shook his head. "But in the main it was my gift to you; I wanted to teach you about pride."

"Pride?" Hort echoed blankly. "You risked your life to make me proud of you? I've always been proud of you! You're the best fisherman in Sanctuary!"

"Fool!" the Old Man exploded, rising to his feet. "Not what you think of me; what you think of yourself!"

"I don't understand," his son blurted. "You want me to be a fisherman like you?"

"No, no, no!" the Old Man leaped to the sand and started to march away, then returned to loom angrily

over the youth. "Said it before—not everyone can be
a fisherman. You're not—but be something, anything,
and have pride in it. Don't be a scavenger, drifting
from here to yon. Take a path and follow it. You've
always had a smooth tongue—be a minstrel, or even a
storyteller like Hakiem."

"Hakiem?" Hort bristled. "He's a beggar."

"He lives here. He's a good storyteller; his wealth's
his pride. Whatever you do, wherever you go—take your
pride. Be good with yourself and you'll be at home with
the best of 'em. Take my gift, son; it's only advice, but
you'll be the poorer without it." He tossed the gold coin
to the sand at Hort's feet and stalked off.

Hort retrieved the coin and stared at the Old Man's
back as he marched away.

"Excuse me, young sir?" Old Hakiem was scuttling
along the beach, waving his arms frantically. "Was that
the Old Man—the one who caught the monster?"

"That's him," Hort agreed, "but I don't think this
is a good time to be talking to him."

"Do you know him?" the storyteller asked, holding fast to Hort's arm. "Do you know what happened
here? I'll pay you five coppers for the story." He was
a beggar, but he didn't seem to starve.

"Keep your money, Hakiem," the youth murmured,
watching the now-empty beach. "I'll give you the story."

"Eh?"

"Yes," Hort smiled, tossing his gold coin in the air,
catching it and putting it in his pocket. "What's more,
I'll buy you a cup of wine to go with it—but only if
you'll teach me how to tell it."

To Guard the Guardians

ROBERT LYNN ASPRIN

The Hell Hounds were now a common sight in Sanctuary so the appearance of one in the bazaar created little stir, save for the concealment of a few smuggled wares and a price increase on everything else. However, when two appeared together, as they did today, it was enough to silence casual conversation and draw uneasy stares, though the more observant vendors noted that the pair were engrossed in their own argument and did not even glance at the stalls they were passing.

"But the man has offended me . . ." the darker of the pair snarled.

"He offends everyone," his companion countered, "it's his way. I tell you, Razkuli, I've heard him say things to the prince himself that would have other men flayed and blinded. You're a fool to take it personally."

"But, Zalbar . . ."

"I know, I know—he offends you; and Quag bores you and Arman is an arrogant braggart. Well this whole town offends me, but that doesn't give me the right to put it to the sword. Nothing Tempus has said to you warrants a blood feud."

"It is done." Razkuli thrust one fist against his other palm as they walked.

"It is *not* done until you act on your promise, and if you do *I'll* move to stop you. I won't have the men in my command killing each other."

The two men walked silently for several moments, each lost in his own dark thoughts.

"Look, my friend," Zalbar sighed, "I've already had one of my men killed under scandalous circumstances. I don't want to answer for another incident—particularly if it involves you. Can't you see Tempus is trying to goad you into a fight?—a fight you can't win."

"No one lives that I've seen over an arrow," Razkuli said ominously, his eyes narrowing on an imaginary target.

"Murder, Razkuli? I never thought I'd see the day you'd sink to being an assassin."

There was a sharp intake of breath and Razkuli faced his comrade with eyes that showed a glint of madness. Then the spark faded and the small man's shoulders relaxed. "You're right, my friend," he said, shaking his head, "I would never do that. Anger speeds my tongue ahead of reason."

"As it did when you vowed bloodfeud. You've survived countless foes who were mortal; don't try the favor of the gods by seeking an enemy who is not."

"Then the rumors about Tempus are true?" Razkuli asked, his eyes narrowing again.

"I don't know, there are things about him which are difficult to explain by any other logic. Did you see how rapidly his leg healed? We both know men whose soldiering career was ended after they were caught under a horse—yet he was standing duty again within the week."

"Such a man is an affront against Nature."

"Then let Nature take vengeance on him," Zalbar laughed, clapping a friendly hand on his comrade's shoulder, "and free us for more worthwhile pastimes. Come, I'll buy you lunch. It will be a pleasant change from barracks food."

Haakon, the sweetmeats vendor, brightened as the two soldiers approached him and waited patiently while they made their selections from his spiced-meat turnovers.

"That will be three coppers," he smiled through yellowed teeth.

"Three coppers?" Razkuli exclaimed angrily, but Zalbar silenced him with a nudge in the ribs.

"Here, fellow . . ." The Hell Hound commander dropped some coins into Haakon's outstretched hand. "Take four. Those of us from the Capitol are used to paying full value for quality goods—though I suppose that this far from civilization you have to adjust the prices to accommodate the poorer folk."

The barb went home and Zalbar was rewarded by a glare of pure hatred before he turned away, drawing Razkuli with him.

"Four coppers! You were being overcharged at three!"

"I know." Zalbar winked. "But I refuse to give them the satisfaction of haggling. I find it's worth the extra copper to see their faces when I imply that they're selling below value—it's one of the few pleasures available in this hell-hole."

"I never thought of it that way," Razkuli said with a laugh, "but you're right. My father would have been livid if someone deliberately overpaid him. Do me a favor and let me try it when we buy the wine."

Razkuli's refusal to bargain brought much the same reaction from the wineseller. The dark mood of their conversation as they had entered the bazaar had vanished and they were ready to eat with calm humor.

"You provided the food and drink, so I'll provide the setting," Razkuli declared, tucking the wine-flask into his belt. "I know a spot which is both pleasant and relaxing."

"It must be outside the city."

"It is, just outside the Common Gate. Come on, the city won't miss our presence for an hour or so."

Zalbar was easily persuaded though more from curiosity than belief. Except for occasional patrols along the Street of Red Lanterns he rarely got outside Sanctuary's North Wall and had never explored the area to the northwest where Razkuli was leading him.

It was a different world here, almost as if they had stepped through a magic portal into another land. The buildings were scattered, with large open spaces between them, in contrast to the cramped shops and narrow alleys of the city proper. The air was refreshingly free from the stench of unwashed bodies jostling each other in crowded streets. Zalbar relaxed in the peaceful surroundings. The pressures of patrolling the hateful town slipped away like a heavy cloak, allowing him to look forward to an uninterrupted meal in pleasant company.

"Perhaps you could speak to Tempus? We needn't like each other, but if he could find another target for his taunts, it would do much toward easing my hatred."

Zalbar shot a wary glance at his comrade but detected none of the blind anger which he had earlier expressed. The question seemed to be an honest attempt on

Razkuli's part to find a compromise solution to an intolerable situation.

"I would, if I thought it would help," he sighed reluctantly, "but I fear I have little influence on him. If anything, it would only make matters worse. He would redouble his attacks to prove he wasn't afraid of me either."

"But you're his superior officer," Razkuli argued.

"Officially, perhaps," his friend shrugged, "but we both know there are gaps between what is official and what is true. Tempus has the Prince's ear. He's a free agent here and follows my orders only when it suits him."

"You've kept him out of the Aphrodisia House. . . ."

"Only because I had convinced the prince of the necessity of maintaining the good will of that House before Tempus arrived," Zalbar countered, shaking his head. "I had to go to the prince to curb Tempus' ill-conduct and earned his hatred for it. You notice he still does what he pleases at the Lily Garden—and the prince looks the other way. No, I wouldn't count on my influence over Tempus. I don't think he would physically attack me because of my position in the prince's bodyguard. I also don't think he would come to my aid if I were hard-pressed in a fight."

Just then Zalbar noticed a small flower garden nestled beside a house not far from their path. A man was at work in the garden, watering and pruning. The sight created a sudden wave of nostalgia in the Hell Hound. How long had it been since he stood outside the Emperor's Palace in the Capitol, fighting boredom by watching the gardeners pampering the flowered grounds? It seemed like a lifetime. Despite the fact that he was a soldier by profession, or perhaps because he was a soldier, he had always admired the calm beauty of flowers.

"Let's eat there...under that tree," he suggested, indicating a spot with a view of the garden. "It's as good a place as any."

Razkuli hesitated, glancing at the gardened house and started to say something, then shrugged and veered toward the tree. Zalbar saw the mischievous smile flit briefly across his comrade's face, but ignored it, preferring to contemplate the peaceful garden instead.

The pair dined in the manner of hardened, but off-duty, campaigners. Rather than facing each other, or sitting side-by-side, the two assumed back-to-back positions in the shade of a spreading tree. The earthenware wine-flask was carefully placed to one side, but in easy reach of both. Not only did the arrangement give them a full circle of vision to insure that their meal would be uninterrupted, it also allowed a brief illusion of privacy for the individual—a rare commodity to those whose profession required that every moment be shared with at least a dozen colleagues. To further that illusion they ate in silence. Conversation would be neither attempted nor tolerated until both were finished with their meal. It was the stance of men who trusted each other completely.

Although his position allowed him a clear view of the flower garden, Zalbar found his thoughts wandering back to his earlier conversation with Razkuli. Part of his job was to maintain peace among the Hell Hounds, at least to a point where their personal differences did not interfere with the performance of their duties. To that end he had soothed his friend's ruffled feathers and forestalled any open fighting within the force ... for the time being, at least. With peace thus preserved, Zalbar could admit to himself that he agreed wholeheartedly with Razkuli.

Loudmouthed bullies were nothing new in the army, but Tempus was a breed apart. As a devout believer in discipline and law, Zalbar was disgusted and appalled by Tempus' attitudes and conduct. What was worse, Tempus did have the prince's ear, so Zalbar was powerless to move against him despite the growing rumors of immoral and illegal conduct.

The Hell Hound's brow furrowed as he reflected upon the things he had heard and seen. Tempus openly used *krrf*, both on duty and off. He was rapidly building a reputation for brutality and sadism among the not easily shocked citizens of Sanctuary. There were even rumors that he was methodically hunting and killing the blue-masked sell-swords employed by the ex-gladiator, Jubal.

Zalbar had no love for that crime-lord, who traded in slaves to mask his more illicit activities, but neither could he tolerate a Hell Hound taking it upon himself to be judge and executioner. But he had been ordered by the prince to allow Tempus free rein and was powerless to even investigate the rumors: a fine state of affairs when the law-enforcers became the lawbreakers and the lawgiver only moved to shelter them.

A scream rent the air, interrupting Zalbar's reverie and bringing him to his feet, sword in hand. As he cast about, searching for the source of the noise, he remembered he had heard screams like that before ... though not on any battlefield. It wasn't a scream of pain, hatred, or terror but the heartless, soulless sounds of one without hope and assaulted by horror too great for the mind to comprehend.

The silence was completely shattered by a second scream and this time Zalbar knew the source was the beautifully gardened house. He watched in growing disbelief as the gardener calmly continued his work, not even bothering to look up despite the now frequent screams. Either the man was deaf or Zalbar himself was going mad, reacting to imaginary noises from a best-forgotten past.

Turning to Razkuli for confirmation, Zalbar was outraged to find his friend not only still seated but grinning ear-to-ear.

"Now do you see why I was willing to pass this spot by?" the swarthy Hell Hound said with a laugh. "Perhaps the next time I offer to lead you won't be so quick to exert your rank."

"You were expecting this?" Zalbar demanded, unsoothed by Razkuli's humor.

"Of course, you should be thankful it didn't start until we were nearly finished with our meal."

Zalbar's retort was cut off by a drawn out piercing cry that rasped against ear and mind and defied human endurance with its length.

"Before you go charging to the rescue," Razkuli commented, ignoring the now fading outburst of pain, "you should know I've already looked into it. What you're hearing is a slave responding to its master's attentive care: a situation entirely within the law and therefore no concern of ours. It might interest you to know that the owner of that building is a..."

"Kurd!" Zalbar breathed through taut lips glaring at the house as if it were an archenemy.

"You know him?"

"We met once, back at the Capitol. That's why he's here . . . or at least why he's not still there."

"Then you know his business?" Razkuli scowled, a bit deflated that his revelations were no surprise. "I'll admit I find it distasteful, but there's nothing we can do about it."

"We'll see," Zalbar announced darkly, starting toward the house.

"Where're you going?"

"To pay Kurd a visit."

"Then I'll see you back at the barracks." Razkuli shuddered. "I've been inside that house once already, and I'll not enter again unless it's under orders."

Zalbar made no note of his friend's departure though he did sheathe his sword as he approached the house. The impending battle would not require conventional weapons.

"Ho there!" he hailed the gardener. "Tell your master I wish to speak with him."

"He's busy," the man snarled, "can't you hear?"

"Too busy to speak with one of the prince's personal guard?" Zalbar challenged, raising an eyebrow.

"He's spoken to them before and each time they've gone away and I've lost pay for allowing the interruption."

"Tell him it's Zalbar . . ." the Hell Hound ordered, ". . . your master will speak with me, or would you like to deal with me in his stead?"

Though he made no move toward his weapons, Zalbar's voice and stance convinced the gardener to waste no time. The gnome-like man abandoned his chores to disappear into the house.

As he waited, Zalbar surveyed the flowers again, but knowledge of Kurd's presence had ruined his appreciation of floral beauty. Instead of lifting his spirits, the bright blossoms seemed a horrifying incongruity, like viewing a gaily colored fungus growing on a rotting corpse.

As Zalbar turned away from the flowers, Kurd emerged into the daylight. Though it had been five years since they had seen each other, the older man was sufficiently unchanged that Zalbar recognized him instantly: the stained disheveled dress of one who sleeps in his clothes, the unwashed, unkempt hair and beard, as well as the cadaverously thin body with its long skeletal fingers and pasty complexion. Clearly, Kurd had not discontinued his habit of neglecting his own body in the pursuit of his work.

"Good day...citizen," the Hell Hound's smile did not disguise the sarcasm poisoning his greeting.

"It *is* you," Kurd declared, squinting to study the other's features. "I thought we were done with each other when I left Ranke."

"I think you shall continue to see me until you see fit to change your occupation."

"My work is totally within the limits of the law." The thin man bristled, betraying, for a moment, the strength of will hidden in his outwardly feeble body.

"So you said in Ranke. I still find it offensive, without redeeming merit."

"Without redeeming..." Kurd shrieked, then words failed him. His lips tightened, he seized Zalbar by the arm and began pulling him toward the house. "Come with me now," he instructed. "Let me show you my work and explain what I am doing. Perhaps then you will be able to grasp the importance of my studies."

In his career Zalbar had faced death in many guises, and done it unflinchingly. Now, however, he drew back in horror.

"I . . . That won't be necessary," he insisted.

"Then you continue to blindly condemn my actions without allowing me a fair hearing?" Kurd pointed a bent, bony finger at the Hell Hound, a note of triumph in his voice.

Trapped by his own convictions, Zalbar swallowed hard and steeled himself. "Very well, lead on. But, I warn you—my opinions are not easily swayed."

Zalbar's resolve wavered once they entered the building and he was assaulted by the smells of its interior. Then he caught sight of the gardener smirking at him from the doorway and set his face in an expressionless mask as he was led up the stairs to the second floor.

All that the Hell Hound had ever heard or imagined about Kurd's work failed to prepare him for the scene which greeted him when the pale man opened the door to his workshop. Half a dozen large, heavy tables lined the walls, each set at a strange angle so their surfaces were nearly upright. They were not unlike the wooden frames court artists used to hold their work while painting. All the tables were fitted with leather harnesses and straps. The wood and leather, both, showed dried and crusted bloodstains. Four of the tables were occupied.

"Most so-called medical men only repeat what has gone before . . ." Kurd was saying, ". . . the few who do attempt new techniques do so in a slipshod,

trial-and-error fashion borne of desperation and ignorance. If the patient dies, it is difficult to determine
if the cause was the original affliction, or the new
treatment itself. Here, under controlled conditions, I
actually increase our knowledge of the human body
and its frailties. Watch your step, please...."

Grooves had been cut in the floor, running along
beneath the tables and meeting in a shallow pit at
the room's far end. As he stepped over one, Zalbar
realized that the system was designed to guide the
flow of spilled blood. He shuddered.

There was a naked man on the first table and when
he saw them coming he began to writhe against his
bonds. One arm was gone from the elbow down and
he beat the stump against the tabletop. Gibberings
poured from his mouth. Zalbar noted with disgust
that the man's tongue had been cut out.

"Here," Kurd announced, pointing to a gaping wound
in the man's shoulder, "is an example of my studies."

The man had obviously lost control of his bodily
functions. Excretions stained his legs and the table.
Kurd paid no attention to this, gesturing Zalbar closer
to the table as he used his long fingers to spread
the edges of the shoulder wound. "I have identified
a point in the body which, if pressure like this..."

The man shrieked, his body arching against the
restraining straps.

"Stop!" Zalbar shouted, losing any pretense of
disinterest.

It was unlikely he could be heard over the tortured
sounds of the victim, but Kurd withdrew his bloody
finger and the man sagged back on the table.

"Well, did you see it?" the pale man asked eagerly.

"See what?" Zalbar blinked, still shaken by what he had witnessed.

"His stump, man! It stopped moving! Pressure, or damage to this point can rob a man of the use of his arm. Here, I'll show you again."

"No!" the Hell Hound ordered quickly, "I've seen enough."

"Then you see the value of my discovery?"

"Umm...where do you get your...subjects?" Zalbar evaded.

"From slavers, of course." Kurd frowned. "You can see the brands quite clearly. If I worked with anything but slaves...well, that would be against Rankan law."

"And how do you get them onto the tables? Slaves or not, I should think they would fight to the death rather than submit to your knives."

"There is a herbalist in town," the pale man explained. "He supplies me with a mild potion that renders them senseless. When they awaken, it's too late for effective resistance."

Zalbar started to ask another question, but Kurd held up a restraining hand. "You still haven't answered my question: do you now see the value of my work?"

The Hell Hound forced himself to look around the room again. "I see that you genuinely believe the knowledge you seek is worthwhile," he said carefully, "but I still feel subjecting men and women to this, even if they are slaves, is too high a price."

"But it's legal!" Kurd insisted. "What I do here breaks no Rankan laws."

"Ranke has many laws, you should remember that from our last meeting. Few live within all of them and while there is some discretion exercised between which laws are enforced and which are overlooked, I tell you now that I will be personally watching for anything which will allow me to move against you. It would be easier on both of us if you simply moved on now... for I won't rest while you are within my patrol range."

"I am a law-abiding citizen." The pale man glared, drawing himself up. "I won't be driven from my home like a common criminal."

"So you said before." The Hell Hound smiled as he turned to go. "But, you are no longer in Ranke— remember that."

"That's right," Kurd shouted after him, "we are no longer in Ranke. Remember that yourself, Hell Hound."

Four days later Zalbar's confidence had ebbed considerably. Finishing his night patrol of the city he turned down the Processional toward the wharves. This was becoming a habit with him now, a final off-duty stretch-of-the-legs to organize his thoughts in solitude before retiring to the crowded barracks. Though there was still activity back in the Maze, this portion of town had been long asleep and it was easy for the Hell Hound to lose himself in his ponderings as he paced slowly along the moon-shadowed street.

The prince had rejected his appeal, pointing out that harassing a relatively honest citizen was a poor use of time, particularly with the wave of killings sweeping Sanctuary. Zalbar could not argue with the prince's logic. Ever since that weapons shop had appeared, suddenly, in the Maze to dispense its deadly brand of magic, killings were not only more frequent but of an uglier nature than usual. Perhaps now that the shop had disappeared the madness would ease, but in the meantime he could ill afford the time to pursue Kurd with the vigor necessary to drive the vivisectionist from town.

For a moment Kurd's impassioned defense of his work flashed across Zalbar's mind, only to be quickly repressed. New medical knowledge was worth having, but slaves were still people. The systematic torture of another being in the name of knowledge was...

"Cover!"

Zalbar was prone on the ground before the cry had fully registered in his mind. Reflexes honed by years in service to the Empire had him rolling, crawling, scrabbling along the dirt in search of shelter without pausing to identify the source of the warning. Twice, before he reached the shadows of an alley, he heard the unmistakable *hisss-pock* of arrows striking nearby: ample proof that the danger was not imaginary.

Finally, in the alley's relative security, he snaked his sword from its scabbard and breathlessly scanned the rooftops for the bowman assassin. A flicker of movement atop a building across the street caught his eyes, but it failed to repeat itself. He strained to penetrate the darkness. There was a crying moan, ending in a cough; moments later, a poor imitation of a night bird's whistle.

Though he was sure someone had just died, Zalbar didn't twitch a muscle, holding his position like a hunting cat. Who had died? The assassin? Or the person whose call had warned him of danger? Even if it were the assassin there might still be an accomplice lurking nearby.

As if in answer to this last thought a figure detached itself from a darkened doorway and moved to the center of the street. It paused, placed hands on hips and hailed the alley wherein Zalbar had taken refuge.

"It's safe now, Hell Hound. We've rescued you from your own carelessness."

Regaining his feet Zalbar sheathed his sword and stepped into the open. Even before being hailed he had recognized the dark figure. A blue hawk-mask and cloak could not hide the size or coloring of his rescuer, and if they had, the Hell Hound would have known the smooth grace of those movements anywhere.

"What carelessness is that, Jubal?" he asked, hiding his own annoyance.

"You have used this route three nights in a row, now," the ex-gladiator announced. "That's all the pattern an assassin needs."

The Negro crime-lord did not seem surprised or annoyed that his disguise had been penetrated. If anything, Jubal gave an impression of being pleased with himself as he bantered with the Hell Hound.

Zalbar realized that Jubal was right: on duty or off, a predictable pattern was an invitation for ambush. He was spared the embarrassment of making this admission, however, as the unseen savior on the rooftops chose this moment to dump the assassin's body to the street. The two men studied it with disdain.

"Though I appreciate your intervention," the Hell Hound commented drily, "it would have been nice to take him alive. I'll admit a passing curiosity as to who sent him."

"I can tell you that." The hawk-masked figure smiled grimly. "It's Kurd's money that filled that assassin's purse, though it puzzles me why he would bear you such a grudge."

"You knew about this in advance?"

"One of my informants overheard the hiring in the

Vulgar Unicorn. It's amazing how many normally careful people forget that a man can hear as well as talk."

"Why didn't you send word to warn me in advance?"

"I had no proof." The black man shrugged. "It's doubtful my witness would be willing to testify in court. Besides, I still owed you a debt from our last meeting... or have you forgotten you saved my life once?"

"I haven't forgotten. As I told you then, I was only doing my duty. You owed me nothing."

"... And I was only doing my duty as a Rankan citizen in assisting you tonight." Jubal's teeth flashed in the moonlight.

"Well, whatever your motive, you have my thanks."

Jubal was silent a moment. "If you truly wish to express your gratitude," he said at last, "would you join me now for a drink? There's something I would like to discuss with you."

"I ... I'm afraid I can't. It's a long walk to your house and I have duties tomorrow."

"I was thinking of the Vulgar Unicorn."

"The Vulgar Unicorn?" Zalbar stammered, genuinely astonished. "Where my assassination was planned. I can't go in there."

"Why not?"

"Well ... if for no other reason that I am a Hell Hound. It would do neither of us any good to be seen together publicly, much less in the Vulgar Unicorn."

"You could wear my mask and cloak. That would hide your uniform and face. Then, to any onlooker it would only appear that I was having a drink with one of my men."

For a moment, Zalbar wavered in indecision, then the audacity of a Hell Hound in a blue hawk-mask seized his fancy and he laughed aloud. "Why not?" he agreed, reaching for the offered disguise. "I've always wondered what the inside of that place looked like."

Zalbar had not realized how bright the moonlight was until he stepped through the door of the Vulgar Unicorn. A few small oil lamps were the only illumination and those were shielded toward the wall leaving most of the interior in heavy shadow. Though he could see figures huddled at several tables as he followed Jubal into the main room, he could not make out any individual's features.

There was one, however, whose face he did not need to see, the unmistakably gaunt form of Hakiem the storyteller slouched at a central table. A small bowl of wine sat before him, apparently forgotten, as the tale-spinner nodded in near-slumber. Zalbar harbored a secret liking for the ancient character and would have passed the table quietly, but Jubal caught the Hell Hound's eye and winked broadly. Withdrawing a coin from his sword-belt, the slaver tossed it in an easy arch toward the storyteller's table.

Hakiem's hand moved like a flicker of light and the coin disappeared in mid-flight. His drowsy manner remained unchanged.

"That's payment enough for a hundred stories, old man," Jubal rumbled softly, "but tell them somewhere else ... and about someone else."

Moving with quiet dignity, the storyteller rose to his feet, bestowed a withering gaze on both of them, and stalked regally from the room. His bowl of wine had disappeared with his departure.

In the brief moment that their eyes met, Zalbar

had felt an intense intelligence and was certain that the old man had penetrated both mask and cloak to coldly observe his true identity. Hastily revising his opinion of the gaunt tale-spinner, the Hell Hound recalled Jubal's description of an informant whom people forgot could hear as well as see and knew whose spying had truly saved his life.

The slaver sank down at the recently vacated table and immediately received two unordered goblets of expensive qualis. Settling next to him, Zalbar noted that this table had a clear view of all entrances and exits of the tavern and his estimation of Hakiem went up yet another notch.

"If I had thought of it sooner, I would have suggested that your man on the rooftop join us," the Hell Hound commented. "I feel I owe him a drink of thanks."

"That man is a woman, Moria; she works the darkness better than I do . . . and without the benefits of protective coloration."

"Well, I'd still like to thank her."

"I'd advise against it." The slaver grinned. "She hates Rankans, and the Hell Hounds in particular. She only intervened at my orders."

"You remind me of several questions." Zalbar set his goblet down. "Why did you act on my behalf tonight? And how is it that you know the cry the army uses to warn of archers?"

"In good time. First you must answer a question of mine. I'm not used to giving out information for free, and since I told you the identity of your enemy, perhaps now you can tell me why Kurd would set an assassin on your trail?"

After taking a thoughtful sip of his drink, Zalbar began to explain the situation between himself and Kurd. As the story unfolded, the Hell Hound found he was saying more than was necessary, and was puzzled as to why he would reveal to Jubal the anger and bitterness he had kept secret even from his own force. Perhaps, it was because, unlike his comrades whom he respected, Zalbar saw the slaver as a man so corrupt that his own darkest thoughts and doubts would seem commonplace by comparison.

Jubal listened in silence until the Hell Hound was finished, then nodded, slowly. "Yes, that makes sense now," he murmured.

"The irony is that at the moment of attack, I was bemoaning my inability to do anything about Kurd. For a while, at least, an assassin is unnecessary. I am under orders to leave Kurd alone."

Instead of laughing, Jubal studied his opposite thoughtfully. "Strange you should say that." He spoke with measured care. "I also have a problem I am currently unable to deal with. Perhaps we can solve each other's problems."

"Is that what you wanted to talk to me about?" Zalbar asked, suddenly suspicious.

"In a way. Actually this is better. Now, in return for the favor I must ask, I can offer something you want. If you address yourself to my problem, I'll put an end to Kurd's practice for you."

"I assume that what you want is illegal. If you really think I'd . . ."

"It is not illegal!" Jubal spat with venom. "I don't need your help to break the law, that's easy enough to do despite the efforts of your so-called elite force.

No, Hell Hound, I find it necessary to offer you a bribe to do your job—to enforce the law."

"Any citizen can appeal to any Hell Hound for assistance." Zalbar felt his own anger grow. "If it is indeed within the law, you don't have to..."

"Fine!" the slaver interrupted. "Then, as a Rankan citizen I ask you to investigate and stop a wave of murders—someone is killing my people; hunting blue-masks through the streets as if they were diseased animals."

"I...I see."

"And I see that this comes as no surprise," Jubal snarled. "Well, Hell Hound, do your duty. I make no pretense about my people, but they are being executed without a trial or hearing. That's murder. Or do you hesitate because it's one of your own who's doing the killing?"

Zalbar's head came up with a snap and Jubal met his stare with a humorless smile.

"That's right, I know the murderer, not that it's been difficult to learn. Tempus has been open enough with his bragging."

"Actually," Zalbar mused drily, "I was wondering why you haven't dealt with him yourself if you know he's guilty. I've heard hawk-masks have killed transgressors when their offense was far less certain."

Now it was Jubal who averted his eyes in discomfort. "We've tried," he admitted, "Tempus seems exceptionally hard to down. Some of my men went against my orders and used magical weapons. The result was four more bloody masks to his credit."

The Hell Hound could hear the desperate appeal in the slaver's confession.

"I cannot allow him to continue his sport, but the price of stopping him grows fearfully high. I'm reduced to asking for your intervention. You more than the others have prided yourself in performing your duties in strict adherence to the codes of justice. Tell me, doesn't the law apply equally to everyone?"

A dozen excuses and explanations leapt to Zalbar's lips, then a cold wave of anger swept them away. "You're right, though I never thought you'd be the one to point out my duty to me. A killer in uniform is still a killer and should be punished for his crimes...all of them. If Tempus is your murderer, I'll personally see to it that he's dealt with."

"Very well." Jubal nodded. "And in return, I'll fill my end of the bargain—Kurd will no longer work in Sanctuary."

Zalbar opened his mouth to protest. The temptation was almost too great—if Jubal could make good his promise—but, no, "I'd have to insist that your actions remain within the law," he murmured reluctantly. "I can't ask you to do anything illegal."

"Not only is it legal, it's done! Kurd is out of business as of now."

"What do you mean?"

"Kurd can't work without subjects," the slaver smiled, "and I'm his supplier—or I was. Not only have I ended his supply of slaves, I'll spread the word to the other slavers that if they deal with him I'll undercut their prices in the other markets and drive them out of town as well."

Zalbar smiled with new distaste beneath his mask. "You knew what he was doing with the slaves and you dealt with him anyway?"

"Killing slaves for knowledge is no worse than having slaves kill each other in the arena for entertainment. Either is an unpleasant reality in our world."

Zalbar winced at the sarcasm in the slaver's voice, but was unwilling to abandon his position.

"We have different views of fighting. You were forced into the arena as a gladiator while I freely enlisted in the army. Still, we share a common experience: however terrible the battle, however frightful the odds, we had a chance. We could fight back and survive—or at least take our foemen with us as we fell. Being trussed up like a sacrificial animal, helpless to do anything but watch your enemy—no, not your enemy—your tormentor's weapon descend on you again and again . . . No being, slave or freedman, should be forced into that. I cannot think of an enemy I hate enough to condemn to such a fate."

"I can think of a few," Jubal murmured, "but then, I've never shared your ideals. Though we both believe in justice, we seek it in different ways."

"Justice?" the Hell Hound sneered, "that's the second time you've used that word tonight. I must admit it sounds strange coming from your lips."

"Does it?" the slaver asked. "I've always dealt fairly with my own or with those who do business with me. We both acknowledge the corruption in our world, Hell Hound. The difference is that, unlike yourself, I don't try to protect the world—I'm hard-pressed to protect myself and my own."

Zalbar set down his unfinished drink. "I'll leave your mask and cloak outside," he said levelly, "I fear that the difference is too great for us to enjoy a drink together."

Anger flashed in the slaver's eyes. "But you will investigate the murders?"

"I will," the Hell Hound promised, "and as the complaining citizen you'll be informed of the results of my investigation."

Tempus was working on his sword when Zalbar and Razkuli approached him. They had deliberately waited to confront him here in the barracks rather than at his favored haunt, the Lily Garden. Despite everything that had or might occur, they were all Army and what was to be said should not be heard by civilians outside their elite club.

Tempus favored them with a sullen glare, then brazenly returned his attention to his work. It was an unmistakable affront as he was only occupied with filing a series of saw-like teeth into one edge of his sword: a project that should run a poor second to speaking with the Hell Hound's captain.

"I would have a word with you, Tempus," Zalbar announced, swallowing his anger.

"It's your prerogative," the other replied without looking up.

Razkuli shifted his feet, but a look from his friend stilled him.

"I have had a complaint entered against you," Zalbar continued. "A complaint which has been confirmed by numerous witnesses. I felt it only fair to hear your side of the story before I went to Kadakithis with it."

At the mention of the prince's name, Tempus raised his head and ceased his filing. "And the nature of the complaint?" he asked darkly.

"It is said you're committing wanton murder during your off-duty hours."

"Oh, that. It's not wanton. I only hunt hawk-masks."

Zalbar had been prepared for many possible responses to his accusations: angry denial, a mad dash for freedom, a demand for proof or witnesses. This easy admission, however, caught him totally off-balance. "You . . . you admit your guilt?" he managed at last, surprise robbing him of his composure.

"Certainly. I'm only surprised anyone has bothered to complain. No one should miss the killers I've taken . . . least of all you."

"Well, it's true I hold no love for Jubal, or his sell-swords," Zalbar admitted, "but, there are still due processes of law to be followed. If you want to see them brought to justice you should have . . ."

"Justice?" Tempus laughed. "Justice has nothing to do with it."

"Then why hunt them?"

"For practice," Tempus informed them, studying his serrated sword once more. "An unexercised sword grows slow. I like to keep a hand in whenever possible and supposedly the sell-swords Jubal hires are the best in town—though, to tell the truth, if the ones I've faced are any example, he's being cheated."

"That's all?" Razkuli burst out, unable to contain himself any longer. "That's all the reason you need to disgrace your uniform?"

Zalbar held up a warning hand, but Tempus only laughed at the two of them.

"That's right, Zalbar, better keep a leash on your dog there. If you can't stop his yapping, I'll do it for you."

For a moment Zalbar thought he might have to

restrain his friend, but Razkuli had passed explosive rage. The swarthy Hell Hound glared at Tempus with a deep, glowering hatred which Zalbar knew could not be dimmed now, with reason or threats. Grappling with his own anger, Zalbar turned, at last, to Tempus.

"Will you be as arrogant when the prince asks you to explain your actions?" he demanded.

"I won't have to." Tempus grinned again. "Kittycat will never call me to task for anything. You got your way on the Street of Red Lanterns, but that was before the prince fully comprehended my position here. He'd even reverse that decision if he hadn't taken a public stance on it."

Zalbar was frozen by anger and frustration as he realized the truth of Tempus' words. "And just what is your position here?"

"If you have to ask," Tempus laughed, "I can't explain. But you must realize that you can't count on the prince to support your charges. Save yourselves a lot of grief by accepting me as someone outside the law's jurisdiction." He rose, sheathed his sword and started to leave, but Zalbar blocked his path.

"You may be right. You may indeed be above the law, but if there is a god—any god—watching, over us now, the time is not far off when your sword will miss and we'll be rid of you. Justice is a natural process. It can't be swayed for long by a prince's whims."

"Don't call upon the gods unless you're ready to accept their interference." Tempus grimaced. "You'd do well to heed that warning from one who knows."

Before Zalbar could react, Razkuli was lunging forward, his slim wrist-dagger darting for Tempus' throat. It was too late for the Hell Hound captain to intervene either physically or verbally, but then Tempus did not seem to require outside help.

Moving with lazy ease, Tempus slapped his left hand over the speeding point, his palm taking the full impact of Razkuli's vengeance. The blade emerged from the back of his hand and blood spurted freely for a moment, but Tempus seemed not to notice. A quick wrench with the already wounded hand and the knife was twisted from Razkuli's grip. Then Tempus' right hand closed like a vise on the throat of his dumbfounded attacker, lifting him, turning him, slamming him against a wall and pinning him there with his toes barely touching the floor.

"Tempus!" Zalbar barked, his friend's danger breaking through the momentary paralysis brought on by the sudden explosion of action.

"Don't worry, Captain," Tempus responded in a calm voice. "If you would be so kind?"

He extended his bloody hand toward Zalbar and the tall Hell Hound gingerly withdrew the dagger from the awful wound. As the knife came clear, the clotting ooze of blood erupted into a steady stream. Tempus studied the scarlet cascade with distaste, then thrust his hand against Razkuli's face.

"Lick it, dog," he ordered. "Lick it clean, and be thankful I don't make you lick the floor as well!"

Helpless and fighting for each breath, the pinned man hesitated only a moment before extending his tongue in a feeble effort to comply with the demand. Quickly impatient, Tempus wiped his hand in a bloody smear across Razkuli's face and mouth, then he examined his wound again.

As Zalbar watched, horrified, the seepage from the wound slowed from flow to trickle and finally to a slow ooze—all in the matter of seconds.

Apparently satisfied with the healing process, Tempus turned dark eyes to his captain. "Every dog gets one bite—but the next time your pet crosses me, I'll take him down and neither you nor the prince will be able to stop me."

With that he wrenched Razkuli from the wall and dashed him to the floor at Zalbar's feet. With both Hell Hounds held motionless by his brutality, he strode from the room without a backward glance.

The suddenness and intensity of the exchange had shocked even Zalbar's battlefield reflexes into immobility, but with Tempus' departure, control flooded back into his limbs as if he had been released from a spell. Kneeling beside his friend, he hoisted Razkuli into a sitting position to aid his labored breathing.

"Don't try to talk," he ordered, reaching to wipe the blood smear from Razkuli's face, but the grasping man jerked his head back and forth, refusing both the order and the help.

Gathering his legs under him, the short Hell Hound surged to his feet and retained the upright position, though he had to cling to the wall for support. For several moments, his head sagged weakly as he drew breath in long ragged gasps, then he lifted his gaze to meet Zalbar's.

"I must kill him. I cannot . . . live in the same world and . . . breathe the same air with one who . . . shamed me so . . . and still call myself a man."

For a moment, Razkuli swayed as if speaking had drained him of all energy, then he carefully lowered himself onto a bench, propping his back against the wall.

"I must kill him," he repeated, his voice steadying. "Even if it means fighting you."

"You won't have to fight me, my friend," Zalbar sat beside him. "Instead accept me as a partner. Tempus must be stopped, and I fear it will take both of us to do it. Even then we may not be enough."

The swarthy Hell Hound nodded in slow agreement. "Perhaps if we acquired one of those hellish weapons that have been causing so much trouble in the Maze?" he suggested.

"I'd rather bed a viper. From the reports I've heard, they cause more havoc for the wielder than for the victim. No, the plan I have in mind is of an entirely different nature."

The bright flowers danced gaily in the breeze as Zalbar finished his lunch. Razkuli was not guarding his back today: that individual was back at the barracks enjoying a much earned rest after their night's labors. Though he shared his friend's fatigue, Zalbar indulged himself with this last pleasure before retiring.

"You sent for me, Hell Hound?"

Zalbar didn't need to turn his head to identify his visitor. He had been watching him from the corner of his eyes throughout his dusty approach.

"Sit down, Jubal," he instructed. "I thought you'd like to hear about my investigations."

"It's about time," the slaver grumbled, sinking to the ground. "It's been a week—I was starting to doubt the seriousness of your pledge. Now, tell me why you couldn't find the killer."

The Hell Hound ignored the sneer in Jubal's voice. "Tempus is the killer, just as you said," he answered casually.

"You've confirmed it? When is he being brought to trial?"

Before Zalbar could answer a terrible scream broke the calm afternoon. The Hell Hound remained unmoved, but Jubal spun toward the sound. "What was that?" he demanded.

"That," Zalbar explained, "is the noise a man makes when Kurd goes looking for knowledge."

"But I thought . . . I swear to you, this is not my doing!"

"Don't worry about it, Jubal." The Hell Hound smiled and waited for the slaver to sit down again. "You were asking about Tempus' trial?"

"That's right," the black man agreed, though visibly shaken.

"He'll never come to trial."

"Because of that?" Jubal pointed to the house. "I can stop . . ."

"Will you be quiet and listen! The court will never see Tempus because the prince protects him. That's why I hadn't investigated him before your complaint!"

"Royal protection!" the slaver spat. "So he's free to hunt my people still."

"Not exactly." Zalbar indulged in an extravagant yawn.

"But you said . . ."

"I said I'd deal with him, and in your words 'it's done.' Tempus won't be reporting for duty today . . . or ever."

Jubal started to ask something, but another scream drowned out his words. Surging to his feet, he glared at Kurd's house. "I'm going to find out where that slave came from, and when I do..."

"It came from me, and if you value your people, you won't insist on his release."

The slaver turned to gape at the seated Hell Hound. "You mean..."

"Tempus," Zalbar nodded. "Kurd told me of a drug he used to subdue his slaves, so I got some from Stulwig and put it in my comrade's *krrf*. He almost woke up when we branded him... but Kurd was willing to accept my little peace offering with no questions asked. We even cut out his tongue as an extra measure of friendship."

Another scream came—a low animal moan which lingered in the air as the two men listened.

"I couldn't ask for a more fitting revenge," Jubal said at last, extending his hand. "He'll be a long time dying."

"If he dies at all," Zalbar commented, accepting the handshake. "He heals very fast, you know."

With that the two men parted company, mindless of the shrieks that followed them.

The Capture

ROBERT LYNN ASPRIN

to COMCON from AE449
    subject MISSOBJ priority III
        have arrived position System ST883-P4...as
        expected inhabitants have failed to quarantine

regular pick-up area...have detected surface
vessel...no detectable support or defense
in immediate area...request permission to
proceed with capture...ET

to AE449 from COMCON
proceed with mission as ordered...handle
with care...they are an easily excited
species...good luck...ET

to COMCON from AE449
subject MISSPROG priority III
target vessel in our possession...
no incident interference...SPECNOTE...
capture performed while vess-occ still awake
after delay...reported sleep patterns not
in evidence...no sign of alarm...request
permission to delay indoctrination until further
examination has been completed...ET

to COMCON from AE449
subject MISSPROG priority II
vess-occ not following anticipated behavior
patterns...repeat...not normal...request
permission to alter indoctrination...ET

to AE449 from COMCON
explain...ET

to COMCON from AE449
subject REQEXP priority II
prog of indoc...Q1 DO ANY OF YOU
READ SCIENCE FICTION?...

Expected answer... vague bewilderment...
Actual Answer... snickers and growls...
Q2 WOULD YOU BELIEVE YOU HAVE
BEEN CAPTURED BY AN ALIEN VESSEL?...
Expected... disbelief and terror... Actual...
cheers, hugging and kissing... indoc cancelled
pending further instruction from COMCON...
repeat... abnormal behavior... repeat...
request permission to alter indoctrination
procedure... ET

to AE449 from COMCON
permission granted... do not return COLLPT
until investigation complete... repeat...
hold position until normality is observed or
explanation for abnormality has been found...
advise COMCON of prog... ET

to COMCON from AE449
subject INVPROG priority III
vess-occ claim to be normal physically,
abnormal mentally... MEDREP confirms...
EXCEP... one MALESUBJ... claims to be a
Gremlin... other vess-occ concur... no rec on
Com Files of RELIG, SOC, NAT, or RACE
group known as Gremlins... please scan Mstr
File and inform... ET

to AE449 from COMCON
GREMLIN file under LEG... small, red-faced,
mischievous, non-existent beings... repeat...
non-existent... so inform MALESUBJ... ET

to COMCON from AE449
   subject GREMLIN priority III
       have informed MALESUBJ...claims he does
       not exist either...other vess-occ concur...
       please advise...ET

   to AE449 from COMCON
       Gremlins do not exist...therefore he does not
       exist...ignore him...ET

to COMCON from AE449
   subject INFOREQ priority II
       can Gremlins draw...ET

to AE449 from COMCON
  Gremlins do not exist...do not use Trans
  Gear for Unauth Messg...ET

to COMCON from AE449
  subject PROCREQ priority III
    Gremlin is drawing mural on wall of
    CAPRM...requests more Cobalt Blue...
    please advise...ET

  to AE449 from COMCON
    what is Gremlin drawing...ET

to COMCON from AE449
  subject REQUINFO priority III
    Gremlins do not exist...do not use Trans
    Gear for Unauth Messg...ET

  to AE449 from COMCON
    report INVPROG IMMEDIATELY...ET

to COMCON from AE449
  subject INVPROG prog III
    can't you take a joke...INVPROG is

    PRIORITY I PRIORITY I

    SECURITY HAS BEEN BREACHED

    MALESUBJ II HAS JUST ENTERED
    TRANS ROOM

    ET

to AE449 from COMCON
report at once...what is your condition...ET

to COMCON from AE449
subject CONDREP priority II
situation in hand...no apparent danger...
MALESUBJ II claims he was looking for more
Scotch...was informed adequate supplies of
same on hand in CAPRM for adjustment...
claims supplies were inadequate and have
been depleted...was informed to req another
bottle from the case if his first one was empty...
claims case is empty...repeats claim of
inadequate supplies...further claims we have
lousy security...please advise...ET

to AE449 from COMCON
confirm MALESUBJ II's claim of poor
security...investigate at once...ET

to COMCON from AE449
subject SECINV priority II
SecOff claims guards were seduced from post
by FEMSUBJS...will be disciplined as soon
as they are found...Gremlin is missing...
FEMSUBJ I claims this is normal...others
confirm...ET

to AE449 from COMCON
Gremlins do not exist...find him at once...
ET

to COMCON from AE449
  subject CLARF priority II
    please repeat . . . ET

  to AE449 from COMCON
    cancel last order . . . are any other SUBJS
    missing . . . ET

to COMCON from AE449
  subject SUBJCNT priority II
    yes and not . . . ET

  to AE449 from COMCÓN
    clarify . . . repeat . . . clarify . . . ET

to COMCON from AE449
  subject SUBJCNT priority II
    SUBJS are not in CAPRM . . . they are all
    over the ship . . . locations are known . . . except
    gremlin . . . ET

  to AE449 from COMCON
    Gremlins do not exist . . . how are locations
    known . . . do you expect unified escape
    attempt . . . request further info-bkgnd on
    SUBJS . . . they are displaying abnormal
    behavior . . . ET

to COMCON from AE449
  subject SUBJINFO priority III
    do not anticipated unified escape attempt . . .
    location of SUBJS known because they are

driving the crew nuts...may encounter morale
problem with crew...SUBJS are deluging
them with questions about ship equip...many
are laughing openly at the answers...claim
that we are very inferior as superior beings
go...SUBJBKGND...it seems that all vess-
occ are Science Fiction writers, editors, artists,
or fans...ET

to AE449 from COMCON
WHY WAS THIS INFORMATION NOT
FORWARDED AT ONCE...VESS-OCC MAY
BE EXTREMELY VALUABLE...ARTISANS
AND SCHOLARS ARE A RARE CATCH...
ALL FURTHER COMMUNICATIONS
ARE TO BE HELD DIRECTLY WITH
CENTCOM...ET

to CENTCOM from AE449
subject SUPTRANS priority II
SUBJS exhibit extreme willingness to
cooperate...supply list follows...TWO
CASES SCOTCH...SIX LBS COFFEE...
EIGHTEEN CARTONS OF CIGARETTES...
ONE TIN OF ASPIRIN...TWENTY REAMS
OF PAPER...ANY AND ALL TECH
MANUALS OF OUR SPACECRAFT...
also we would request a tube of Cobalt
Blue to use as bait in our attempts to locate
Gremlin...ET

to AE449 from CENTCOM

> Gremlins do not exist...therefore no need
> for Cobalt Blue...also reject request for
> Tech Manuals...let's not be stupid about our
> cooperation...all other requests granted...
> order is being assembled...ET

to CENTCOM from AE449

> subject SUBJCO-OP priority II
>
> > MALESUBJ II has offered to re-organize
> > our Military System...requests we return
> > HMPLNT to pick up friend of his to assist
> > in project...ET

to AE449 from CENTCOM
  clarification requested...if friends are regular
  military suspect plot...ET

to CENTCOM from AE449
  subject CLARIF priority II
    have inquired MALESUBJ II as to nature
    of his friends...gives assurance they are as
    irregular as they come...ET

  to AE449 from CENTCOM
    we have heard of the Irregulars...request
    denied...repeat...request denied...if he
    insists shoot him...ET

to CENTCOM from AE449
  subject INFOREQ priority II
    MALESUBJ III discovered in Captain's
    Quart reading ship's log...claims it lacks
    both originality and characterization...
    INFOREQ...what is a neo-alien...ET

  to AE449 from CENTCOM
    term neo-alien not in evidence on MstrFile...
    am forwarding INFOREQ to EMPSTFF...ET

  to AE449 from EMPSTFF
    WHAT IS THIS NONSENSE...RETURN
    SHIP TO MILITARY STATUS AT ONCE...
    SUBJS ARE CAPTORS...YOU ARE IN
    COMMAND OF SHIP...CONDUCT ALL

FURTHER COMMUNICATIONS IN A
MANNER FITTING TO YOUR RANK OR
IT WILL BE REDUCED...ET

to EMPSTFF from AE449
   subject EMPSTFF priority I
      BLOW IT OUT YOUR EARS...ET

   to AE449 from EMPSTFF
      CLARIFY LAST TRANS...ET

to EMPSTFF from AE449
   we have located Gremlin...ET

to AE449 from EMPSTFF
  Gremlins do not exist...still awaiting
  clarification...it had better be good...ET

to EMPSTFF from AE449
  subject FNLTRANS priority I
    WE HAVE CRASHED ON P-4 SYSTEM
    ST 883...THE MISSING GREMLIN HAS
    BEEN FOUND...HE HAD BEEN USING
    HIS TIME TO PAINT SPACESCAPES ON
    THE NAVIGATION VIEWSCREENS...
    THE STAR WE HAVE BEEN FOLLOWING
    LANDED US IN LAKE MICHIGAN...
    VESS-OCC HAVE OFFERED POLITICAL
    ASYLUM FOR CREW FROM BOTH YOU
    AND P-4 PLANETARY OFFICIALS...SO
    LONG TURKEY...
    PS is there any chance you can still send
    those two cases of Scotch...
    PPS Gremlins do too exist you Do-Do...ET

The Ultimate Weapon

ROBERT LYNN ASPRIN

*Tableau: Office—man in suit (Weston) is sitting at
desk—girl (Lori) in conservative office suit is perched
on edge of desk holding shotgun on him—youth in
white canvas coveralls (Sammy) is speaking on the
phone—as he is speaking, a second youth (George)
is stripping off blazer, tie and white shirt to show
a T-shirt.*

Sammy:	That's right, we've got Weston ... What do you mean who are we? The PFA, the Peoples Freedom Alliance ... Well you've heard of us now....
Weston:	May I compliment you? You were most convincing as a reporter.

*(Lori shrugs indifferently without moving the shot-
gun.)*

Sammy:	...Right here in his office...Just tell whoever you have to tell we'll kill him if you don't meet our demands....

(George dons a shoulder holster and pistol, surveys scene, guns, picks up camera from desk and takes pictures of Lori and Weston.)

George: Smile, Weston. We'll use this as the cover shot for our story.

Lori: Quit clowning, George.

(George snaps another picture of her.)

Lori: Sammy!

Sammy: George! Fix the door, huh?

(George snaps picture of him, but starts moving toward the door.)

Sammy: I'm sorry—what? Okay, all we want is this: first you stop the tests; second, you release full details of the weapon to the public; and third, we need a guarantee that it won't be tested until it has been thoroughly checked for . . . What? Don't give me that! . . . Just tell him!

(Slams phone down angrily.)

Lori: What did they say?

Sammy: Some doubletalk about not being authorized to act.

(George is pantomiming booby-trapping the door—carefully wiring detonator in place and setting charges around the room.)

Weston: Who did you call?

Sammy: The Pentagon. Who did you think we'd call, the Boy Scouts?

Weston: You'd probably get better results calling the police. The boys at the Pentagon are pretty secretive.

Sammy: What do the police have to do with it? They can't stop the tests.

Weston: But they're more inclined to talk to the media. You are doing this for publicity, aren't you?

Lori: Maybe you don't listen so good, mister. We want 'em stopped.

Sammy: Nothing. Just what's on the news—and that's nothing. That's why we want 'em stopped.

Weston: But if you don't know anything, how can you object to—?

Sammy: An Ultimate Weapon! An Ultimate Weapon nobody will talk about. The aliens want sanctuary on this planet and offer up an ultimate weapon that will guarantee world peace, and we're all supposed to sit back and not ask questions until it's tested? No way, mister.

Weston: Is that what's got you upset? Hell, kid, it was the press that gave it the Ultimate Weapon tag, not us.

George: No such thing.

Weston: What's that?

George: There's no such thing as an Ultimate Weapon. I mean, they've been inventing Ultimate Weapons since the crossbow. Each one is going to end all wars. Well, there's always something bigger, or nastier, or more powerful. There's no such thing as an Ultimate Weapon.

Weston: But then, why are you worried?

Sammy: Just because it isn't Ultimate doesn't mean it isn't dangerous. An A-bomb isn't ultimate, but I wouldn't want 'em to set one off in my backyard.

Lori: What do you know about this Ultimate Weapon, Weston?

Weston: Me? Nothing. I just handle the press
            releases. I don't know anything more
            about it than you do.

Sammy: Then why aren't you worried?

Weston: Why? Well...I guess I trust the Armed
            Forces' judgment.

Sammy: Why?

Weston: Why not? They haven't mishandled any
            of the other Ultimate Weapons at the
            control. If they were going to blow up
            the world, they would have done it by
            now.

Lori: The other weapons are public knowl-
            edge—at least, what they're supposed
            to do. Why are they being so secretive
            about this one?

Weston: Now, that's not right. Most of the weap-
            ons were secret until after they were
            tested. If anything is puzzling, it's why
            they even announced this one prior to
            testing it.

Sammy: Yeah, well what if they're wrong? What if
            all your experts have been flimflammed
            and it isn't safe? What happens then?

Weston: I'll admit I hadn't given it much thought.
            I guess they'd just abandon the project.

George: Can't be done.

Weston: Oh, really now. Why would the aliens
            bring in a weapon to destroy the planet
            if they want to settle here?

George: I mean, you can't abandon a weapon.
            Disarmament is an illusion. You can't
            un-invent a weapon once it's been intro-
            duced. It'd be used by somebody, until
            something better comes along to take
            its place. The only way you could stop,
            much less reverse the process, would be
            to retard or reduce Man's intelligence.
            That's why there's no such thing as an
            Ultimate Weapon.

Sammy: Spare us the lecture, George.

Lori: (*to Weston*) George is our pet violence
            expert.

Weston: I see. Where did you pick up all these
            gems of wisdom, George? In the Army?

George: Nah. I tried to enlist, but the combat
            units were full up. This is just a hobby
            for me, just like (*holds up the wires
            he's working on*) explosives.

Weston: Is he actually booby-trapping the door?

Sammy: That's right.

Weston: Why?

Lori: So if the police try to bust down the door, we'll all go up.

George: It's a deterrent so they won't try to rush us.

Weston: Have you told anybody yet? I don't remember hearing anything when you were talking on the phone.

Lori: Hey, he's right. You'd better call the police, Sammy.

Sammy: Right. *(Starts for phone)*

Weston: If you don't mind my saying so, you seem kind of new to this Terrorist game.

Lori: You're right. We just got together after the announcement about—

Sammy: *(phone in hand)* Hey! Lori! What's the phone number for the police?

Lori: I thought you had it memorized.

Sammy: *(puzzled)* I did. Well, I've forgotten... Never mind. I'll look it up.

George: *(standing up)* All done, Sammy.

Weston: *(craning his neck to see)* It doesn't look very complicated.

George: It isn't. *(points)* If they open the door, these two wires make contact—

Lori: Don't show him, you idiot.

George: Big deal. Anybody could figure it out just by looking at it.

Weston: You know, George, what you were saying about retarding Man's intelligence—if that happened, wouldn't everybody be the same? I mean, if we could have stopped our intellectual evolution in the Middle Ages, all that would mean is that we'd all be fighting with cross-bows instead of guns.

George: You're right. To be totally successful, it would have to be an unequal process. Let a select populace—the police or whoever—evolve normally and retard everybody else so they couldn't think of weapons to top what the police have. Better still, if you could drain their memory so they couldn't even use existing weapons. *(smiles suddenly)* You know, if you could do that, you'd have the Ultimate Weapon.

Weston: But I thought you said there was no such thing as an Ultimate Weapon.

George: *(frowns)* I did? Yeah, I guess I did.

Lori: Haven't you found that number yet, Sammy?

Sammy: *(flipping through phone book)* I'm having trouble finding it. What letter does 'police' start with?

Weston: What?

(Phone rings)

Sammy: *(answering phone)* Hello...Who?...Oh, yeah. That's us...I mean, speaking... Our demands?...Well, we want... um...*(hesitates, frowns as he drops the phone from ear and shakes his head. Finally speaks into receiver again)* Don't try to stall us, you know what they are...that's right.

Weston: *(to Lori)* Can't he remember the demands?

Lori: Of course he can...*(suddenly frowns thoughtfully and looks absently at floor)*

George: *(approaching Lori with camera)* Say, Lori, how do you set the shutter speed on this thing?

Lori: Not now, George.

Sammy: Okay...Yes, that will do...No, that's all we want...Fine...Thank you. *(hangs up phone)* Well, that's that. Okay, Weston, you can go now.

Weston: What?

Sammy: That's right. We've won!

Lori: *(leans shotgun against desk and runs to Sammy)* Oh, Sammy! We did it! *(They hug—Sammy frees an arm to shake hands with George)*

Weston: *(bewilderment)* Wait a minute! What happened?

Sammy: They gave in. They won't test the weapon. We've won.

Weston: Just like that? What guarantees did they give you?

Sammy: *(frowns)* Guarantees? They gave us their word.

Weston: That's all?

Lori: What more do we need? If we don't trust our country's leaders, who can we trust?

Weston: But this whole thing was because you didn't trust them.

Lori: No, it wasn't!

Sammy: Of course not. It was because ... *(frowns and looks at the other two)*

Weston: My God!

George: What is it?

Weston: My God! It's happened. Just like you said, George. The Ultimate Weapon! Intelligence drain!

George: What?

Weston: Don't you see? That's the weapon. And they've already tested it! They've tested on you! All of you!

George: What are you talking about?

Weston: Your theory. You sat right there and said the Ultimate Weapon would have to be an Intelligence Drain. Don't you remember?

(George frowns, then shrugs hopelessly)

Weston: Think, damn you! *(Weston shakes him)*

Sammy: Hey, ease up, Weston. What's your gripe? It's all over.

Weston: No, it isn't! It's just the beginning. Look. Get them back on the phone and tell them—

Sammy: Get who back on the phone?

Weston: Never mind, I'll do it myself. *(picks up phone angrily)*

George: Hey! If you're busy, we'll just clear out and let you work.

Sammy: Right. C'mon Lori.

Weston: Wait!

George: What?

Weston: The bomb! Don't you remember the bomb?

George: *(squints at door)* Is that what it is? How can we get past it?

Weston: But you . . . wait, just stand there. Don't move. Any of you. *(dials phone)* Preswell? . . . Weston here . . . Yes, I'm fine . . . No, listen . . . No! Dammit! You listen to me . . . it's an Intelligence Drain, isn't it . . . the new weapon . . . no, I don't think it's great! Who the hell decided to use it . . . Who made him God? . . . You're damn straight I'm mad. So will everybody else be . . . That's right, I'm going to the press . . . Bullshit! . . . You're crazier than they are! . . . Oh, go to hell! *(slams phone down)* The bastards! You kids were right.

Lori: About what?

Weston: About everything. Country leaders . . . a bunch of megalo-maniacs, that's what they are!

Sammy: What are you talking about?

Weston: *(picking up phone)* You'll see. When I tell the press—*(freezes with look of horror on face)* I can't remember! I can't remember a single news service. It's happening! *(drops phone and starts for door)* They're using it on me now.

We've got to get out of here—*(stops and stares at door)* The bomb! Got to disarm it. *(kneels down and reaches forward hesitantly)* Simple. Anyone can understand it. *(the others gather behind him)* The bastards! *(licks his lips and reaches forward)*

(Flood stage with red light. All freeze)

(Radio announcer's voice from PA system)

Radio: Press Secretary Weston was killed in his office today in an abortive terrorist attempt. The President will attend funeral services tomorrow—Elsewhere in the news, Air Force officials again deny reports of UFOs sighted over the country. Citizens are advised to remain calm until investigations are complete.

(CURTAIN)

The Saga of the Dark Horde

As Told by
Yang the Nauseating

Many and long are the tales told of the Dark Horde. As they are told and retold around the council fires, the heroic exploits of their ancestors grow until it is often difficult to distinguish fact from fantasy. Yet, it cannot be denied that during the reign of Ogati, son of Genghis Khan, a group did leave the Golden Horde and, under the title of the Dark Horde, begin to roam the continent. Thirteen generations later, they still exist in the bodies and spirits of the descendents and, again, the mystic power of the Mongol Hordes is being felt. Who are these people? From whence came their power? Their pride? Their codes? To know the men of the present, we must know their ancestors, the forces that shaped their destiny, and the threats they have survived.

This is the story of the Dark Horde from its beginning. In the last episode was chronicled the arrival of he who was to be known as the Warlord of Darkness and the Dark Horde. Bork of the Mountains had sought to removing the embarrassing (to Bork) Yang of the Silver Tongue from his place of influence as the councilor of the Ka-Khan. He approached Zalbar, a wizard and practitioner of the Black Arts, and gained his promise of a curse to be laid upon the Silver-tongued One: that at the time he should feel the most pressure, the most pressure, the greatest fear, at that time his nimble tongue would desert him, as well as his other poised airs, and in their stead should come the most brutish, vicious savage to ever gain access to the Ka-Khan's yurt.

This should have effectively destroyed Yang of the Silver Tongue, but the curse backfired. At the moment of Yang's greatest fear, his personality vanished, and in his stead was born Basta, a savage and ruthless warrior. Basta slaughtered the evil wizard, Zalbar, and would have turned on Bork, had not the mountain man declared that he had no further quarrel with Yang, and therefore no quarrel with Basta. The two (or was it three?) became fast friends and allies in the struggle against the ill-rule of Ogati, Ka-Khan of the Golden Horde....

Bork of the Mountains was clearly in a hurry. His powerful steed plunged headlong through the camp, scattering cooking fires and people before it, as he leaned forward along its neck, urging it to still greater speed. Finally, he ceased the frothing animal's mad progress, throwing it back on its haunches so violently that it almost fell, and in the same move, was off its back and sprinting through the door of a yurt.

"Basta!" his voice boomed. "We are finished! Our plans are undone!"

The purring voice that answered him did little to settle his mind. "Must you always explode noisily onto the scene, Bork? It would seem that is you, and not our plans, that have become undone."

Anger flared in Bork as the slender figure of Yang of the Silver Tongue stepped into the candlelight. Though the two were fast friends, Yang could still irritate him by remaining superficially calm in the most trying of situations. In his present stormy mood, Bork was in no condition for Yang's verbal fencing. Eyes blazing, he snatched his sword from its scabbard.

"None of your pretty word games! I tell you, we are in trouble! Now, summon Basta, or by the Gods I'll—"

He began to advance the sword in a threatening gesture, but suddenly found the movement restricted. Glancing down, he saw that his sleeve was pinned to the top of the low, lacquered table by a small, quivering throwing knife.

"A threat from you, my friend? After all these years?" The resounding voice of Basta of the Red Fist filled the tent, chilling in its controlled menace.

Bork's anger died as quickly as it had risen. "Forgive me, Basta, but my spirit cries for action before this crisis." As he spoke, he returned his weapon to its sheath; taking care to move slowly, he grasped the sword by the blade with his left hand, and eased it into the scabbard without gripping its handle, *before* removing the dart that imprisoned his left hand. Once before, under similar circumstances, he had made the mistake of switching the weapon rapidly to his left hand. The results were near-disastrous and, even though Yang himself had helped to bind the wound, he still wore the scar of that encounter. Bork had learned his lesson well.

"My concern was so great that, for a moment, I

forgot that, by your curse, it was Yang that I was addressing when I entered."

"Strange, that *you* would forget." Basta's voice was heavy with irony.

Bork winced. All too well he remembered that it was he who, in a moment of rage, had hired the late Zalbar to place a curse on Yang and his descendants, a curse that had backfired by changing a quick-witted court non-combatant into a cold, savage killer whenever danger threatened. While Bork was now friend to both Yang and Basta, the Tongue and the Fist, there were times when he felt a twinge of regret at the complications arising from his rash act.

"Ogati has found us out! His spies have armed with enough information to move against us at last. I told you he would not stand idly by while we stole the Golden Horde out from under him. We're finished, I tell you!"

"You mean the Ka-Khan is actually using force against us? Ogati sends his guards to cut us down? I did not think he would risk dividing the Horde by moving so openly against his own tar-khans."

Bork shook his head. "Worse than that. While his mind may not be as quick as Yang's, it is no duller. What faces us is thinly disguised exile. He is singling out the leaders of our movement and sending them forth on missions to the far corners of the known world. Using the excuse of seeking new campgrounds, he scatters our forces, dividing our unity in one fell swoop. To refuse a mission openly is to risk a charge of open treason. One at a time we are being beaten. Yaccus, Morbis, all the clan leaders we have won so hard to our cause. I myself just came from the

Ka-Khan's yurt. It is my belief he will summon you on the morrow. He holds the totem of the serpent in high enough regard that he'll wait until as many of your supporters as possible have beeen stripped from you before risking a confrontation."

Basta of the Red Fist remained silent long after Bork had finished his report. His features were immobile and expressionless as he stared into the fire, but Bork knew this only masked the stormy inner turmoil which was this man's trademark. At length he spoke, not taking his eyes from the flame.

"All the clan leaders are scattered, then? We are alone?"

"Not yet. Though Ogati's move caught them by surprise, they react with reflexive caginess. Most are stalling for time, claiming difficulty in preparations for their journey. Those that have left, have done so with a casual laziness that never marked their battle marches. It is my guess they will make first camp within a few hours' ride of the Horde proper. They accept their defeat reluctantly, seeking desperately some counter move to turn the tide."

Slowly now, Basta approached his friend. Standing before him, Bork saw the glitter in his eyes of the coiled Serpent. But coiled to what purpose? To pitilessly strike down a weak victim? Or to lash out angrily and defensively, spitefully killing the Enemy even while life was being crushed out of its frame?

"Summon the others, Bork. Whatever our fate, let us face it together. Ogati can do us no greater harm, and the decision of every man affects that of his Brother. Go at once, before what little time is left us for free choice is gone."

With a gentle push, he sped his friend along his way.

Pausing outside the yurt's door to readjust his sword belt, Bork's attention was arrested by the sound of voices emanating from within. Had he not just emerged from that dwelling, he would swear that there were two people within locked in heated argument. His scalp prickled as he realized that, for the first time, Yang of the Silver Tongue and Basta of the Red Fist were meeting. The problem of being threatened mentally without being threatened physically was creating a tug-of-war between the two persons housed in one body.

"Well, violent one, at last you're met with a situation you cannot conquer with a sword! I knew your brash boasting would tip our hand before we were ready."

"What do you mean, Yang? Never have I seen a situation which calls for bloodshed more. You think we will stand idle while the Ka-Khan scatters us like sheep? Ready or not, the time for fighting is upon us."

"Our half-formed forces against the might of Ogati's loyal guard? The outcome is both sure and disastrous. And even if he were overthrown, he need only call on his brothers to rally their own Hordes in the family name. The full might of the old Khan's Golden Horde descending on us from all points of the compass. Surely not even you would waste good fighting men on a lost cause like that."

"Perhaps not a full meeting of armies then. But Ogati is just a man. He can die like any other man. No one knows the Darkness like Basta. Tonight I'll creep through the shadows and put an end to his career, and with it his orders to ride. With this hand that dripped bloody at my birth I'll save our cause."

"You think his brothers will not know the engineer

of so timely an assassination? Besides, Ogati, too, knows you favor the Night. The ground for a hundred paces around his yurt will be lit to day-brightness with torches, and for every torch five guardsmen. And for all his precautions he'll sleep lightly and armed, if he sleeps at all."

"Demons take your logic!! How can you remain cool? My blood burns for action!!"

Bork shuddered as he finally hastened on his way. If he knew the two minds at work in that yurt, there would be a solution proposed when the clan leaders gathered, no matter how painful. The only question was, what?

Ogati was in a foul mood as he awaited his guards' return. A restless night full of false alarms did little toward brightening his disposition. More than anything he wanted this confrontation to be over with. Perhaps that is why he had sent an armed guard to the yurt of the Coiled Serpent. To insure it would be Basta he faced, if not to spark an incident that would justify wiping out his rival once and for all.

A murmur ran through the assemblage which packed the yurt and Ogati knew the party had returned. *Carrion Birds*, he thought, *Gathered to watch a battle without caring who wins*.

Now a lone figure approached him and dropped to the ground in a groveling bow. Ogati frowned. Where was Basta?

"Well?" he rumbled at the trembling figure.

"Gone!" was the reply. "All gone. Only empty yurts and smoldering campfires mark the place where the conspirators dwelt."

"Impossible! I had spies watching their every move. I would have heard if they tried such a move."

"It would seem your spies are dead or have chosen to ride with the conspirators."

Ogati staggered back, his head reeling. This he had not anticipated. Instead of a few scattered exiles living a life of terror in enemy lands, a fully mobilized strike force prowling the continents! A fanged, living animal hungry for conquest and revenge. He was suddenly aware of the silence hanging heavy over the assemblage. It would not do to have the Ka-Khan appear outmaneuvered in front of such an audience. Groping desperately for something, he fell back on old patterns.

"Yang, perhaps you have a few comments on the situation."

He turned to his ever-present spokesman, only to find himself addressing thin air. He had forgotten that he had also lost the Silver Tongue when Basta departed.

A titter broke the silence, followed by an avalanche of laughter, pelting the Ka-Khan in his embarrassment until his anger blazed and he silenced them with a roar.

"Laugh at your Ka-Khan, will you!?! You dare to laugh at the great Ogati!?!"

The crowd shrank back before his rage.

"Mark my words and mark them well. This desertion under the cloak of night may have caught me unawares. For now Basta of the Red Fist may be Warlord of Darkness and the Dark Horde! But the day will come when he or his descendants return to the Golden Horde. On that day there will be a reckoning such as the world has never witnessed. Then we shall see who laughs!"

Cold Cash War

ROBERT LYNN ASPRIN

*Military strategies and tactics change constantly.
But when the nature of the combatants changes,
the nature of war itself is altered.*

The sound of automatic weapons fire was clearly
audible in the Brazilian night as Major Tidwell silently
crawled the length of the shadow, taking pains to
keep his elbows close to his body. He probed ahead
with his left hand until he found the fist-sized rock
with the three sharp corners which he had gauged
as his landmark.

Once it was located, he sprang the straps on the
Jump Pad he had been carrying over his shoulder and
eased it into position. With the care of a professional,
he double-checked its alignment: front edge touching
the rock and lying at a 45° angle to an imaginary line
running from the rock to the large tree on his left,
flat on the ground, no wrinkles or lumps.

Check.

This done, he allowed himself the luxury of taking
a moment to try to see the Scanner Fence. Nothing.
He shook his head with grudging admiration. If it

317

hadn't been scouted and confirmed in advance, he would never have known there was a "fence" in front of him. The Set Posts were camouflaged to the point where he couldn't spot them even knowing what he was looking for, and there were no tell-tale light beams penetrating the dark of the night. Yet he knew that just in front of him was a maze of relay beams which, if interrupted, would trigger over a dozen automount weapons and direct their fire into a ten-meter square area centering on the point the beams were interrupted. An extremely effective trap as well as a foolproof security system, but it was only five meters high.

He smiled to himself. Those cost accountants will do it to you every time. Why build a fence eight meters high if you can get by with one five meters high? The question was, could they get by with a five-meter fence?

Well, now was as good a time as any to find out. He checked the straps of his small back pack to be sure there was no slack. Satisfied there was no play to throw him off balance, his hand moved to his throat mike.

"Lieutenant Decker!"

"Here, Sir!" The voice of his first lieutenant was soft in the earphone. It would be easy to forget that he was actually over 500 meters away leading the attack on the south side of the compound. Nice about fighting for the Itt-iots, your communications were second to none.

"I'm in position now. Start the diversion."

"Yes, sir!"

He rose slowly to a low crouch and backed away from the pad several steps in a duck walk. The tiny luminous dots on the corners of the Jump Pad marked its location for him exactly.

Suddenly, the distant firing doubled in intensity as the diversionary frontal attack began. He waited several heartbeats for any guard's attention to be drawn to the distant fight, then rose to his full height, took one long stride and jumped on the pad hard with both feet.

The pad recoiled from the impact of his weight, kicking him silently upward. As he reached the apex of his flight, he tucked and somersaulted like a diver, extending his legs again to drop feet first, but it was still a long way down. His forward momentum was lost by the time he hit the ground and the impact forced him to his knees as he tried to absorb the shock. He fought for a moment to keep his balance, lost it and fell heavily on his back.

"Damn!" He quickly rolled over onto all fours and scuttled crabwise forward to crouch in the deep shadow next to the Auto-Gun turret. Silently he waited, not moving a muscle, eyes probing the darkness.

He had cleared the "fence." If he hadn't, he would be dead by now. But if there were any guards left the sound of his fall would have alerted them. There hadn't been much noise, but it didn't take much. These Oil Slickers were good. Then again there were the explosives in his pack.

Tidwell grimaced as he scanned the shadows. He didn't like explosives no matter how much he worked with them. Even though he knew they were insensitive to impact and could only be detonated by the radio control unit carried by his lieutenant, he didn't relish the possibility of having to duplicate that fall if challenged.

Finally his diligence was rewarded...a small flicker of movement by the third hut. Moving slowly, the major loosened the strap on his pistol. His gamble of carrying the extra bulk of a silenced weapon was about to pay off. Drawing the weapon, he eased it forward and settled the luminous sights in the vicinity of the movement, waiting for a second tip-off to fix the guard's location.

Suddenly, he holstered the weapon and drew his knife instead. If there was one, there would be two, and the sound of his shot, however muffled, would tip the second guard to sound the alarm. He'd just have to do this the hard way.

He had the guard spotted now, moving silently from hut to hut. There was a pattern in his search, and that pattern would kill him. Squat and check shadows beside the hut, move, check window, move, check window, move, hesitate, step into alley between the huts with rifle at ready, hesitate three beats to check shadows in alley, move, squat and check shadows, move...

Apparently the guard thought the intruder, if he existed, would be moving deeper into the compound and was hoping to come to him silently from behind. The only trouble was the intruder was behind him.

Tidwell smiled. Come on, sonny! Just a few more steps. Silently he drew his legs under him and waited. The guard had reached the hut even with the turret he was crouched behind. Squat, move, check window, move, check window, move hesitate, step into alley...

He moved forward in a soft glide. For three heartbeats the guard was stationary, peering into the shadows in the alley between the huts. In those three heartbeats Tidwell closed the distance between them in for long strides, knife held low and poised. His left arm snaked forward and snapped his forearm across the guard's windpipe ending any possibility of an outcry as the knife darted home under the left shoulder blade.

The guard's reflexes were good. As the knife blade retracted into its handle, the man managed to flinch with surprise before his body went into the forced, suit-induced limpness ordered by his belt computer. Either the man had incredible reflexes or his suit was malfunctioning.

Tidwell eased the "dead" body to the ground, then swiftly removed the ID bracelet. As he rose to go, he glanced at the man's face and hesitated involuntarily. Even in the dark he knew him—Clancy! He should have recognized him from his style. Clancy smiled and winked to acknowledge mutual recognition. You couldn't do much else in a "dead" combat suit.

Tidwell paused long enough to smile and tap his fallen rival on the forehead with the point of his knife. Clancy rolled his eyes in silent acknowledgement. He was going to have a rough time continuing his argument that knives were inefficient after tonight.

Then the major was moving again. Friendship was fine, but he had a job to do and he was running behind schedule. A diversion can only last so long. Quickly he backtracked Clancy's route, resheathing his knife and drawing his pistol as he went. A figure materialized out of the shadows ahead.

"I told you there wouldn't be anything there!" came the whispered comment.

Tidwell shot him in the chest, his weapon making a muffled "pfut," and the figure crumpled. Almost disdainfully, the major relieved him of his ID bracelet.

Obviously this man wouldn't last long. In one night he had made two major mistakes: ignoring a sound in the night, and talking on Silent Guard. It was men like this that gave mercenaries a bad name.

He paused to orient himself. Up two more huts and over three. Abandoning much of his earlier stealth, he moved swiftly onward in a low crouch, pausing only at intersections to check for hostile movement. He had a momentary advantage with the two Quadrant Guards out of action, but it would soon some to an abrupt halt when the Roaming Guards made their rounds.

Then he was at his target, a hut indistinguishable from any of the other barracks or duty huts in the compound. The difference was that Intelligence confirmed and cross-confirmed that this was the Command Post of the compound.

No light could be seen from within and there were no guards posted outside to tip its position to the Enemy, but inside this hut was the nerve center of the Defense, all Tactical Officers as well as the communication equipment necessary to coordinate the trop movements in the area.

Tidwell unslung his pack and eased it to the ground next to him. Opening the flap, he withdrew four charges, checking the clock on each to ensure synchronization. He had seen beautiful missions ruled invalid because time of explosion (TOE) could not be verified, and it wasn't going to happen to him. He double-checked the clocks. He didn't know about the Communications or Oil Companies, but Timex should be making a hefty profit out of this war.

Tucking two charges under his arm and grasping one in each hand he made a quick circuit of the building, pausing at each corner just long enough to plant a charge on the wall. The fourth charge he set left-handed, the silenced pistol back in his right hand, eyes probing the dark. It was taking too long! The Roaming Guards would be around any minute now.

Rising to his feet he darted away, running at high speed now, stealth being completely abandoned to speed. Two huts away he slid to a stop, dropping prone and flattening against the wall of the hut. Without pausing to catch his breath, his left hand went to his throat mike.

"Decker! They're set! Blow it!"

Nothing happened.

"Decker! Can you read me? Blow it!" He tapped the mike with his fingernail.

Still nothing.

"Blow it, damn you..."

POW.

Tidwell rolled to his feet and darted around the corner. Even though it sounded loud in the stillness of night, that was no explosion. Someone was shooting, probably at him.

"Decker! Blow it!"

POW. POW.

No mistaking it now. He was drawing fire. Cursing, he snapped off a round in the general direction of the shots, but it was a lost cause and he knew it. Already he could hear shouts as more men took up the pursuit. If he could only lead them away from the charges. Ducking around a corner, he flattened against the wall and tried to catch his breath. Again he tried the mike.

"Decker!"

The door of the hut across the alley burst open, flooding the scene with light. As if in a nightmare he snapped off a shot at the figure silhouetted in the door as he scrambled backward around the corner.

POW.

He was dead... There was no impact of the "bullet," but his suit collapsed taking him with it as it crumpled to the ground. Even if he could move now, which he couldn't, it would do him no good. The same quartz light beam that scored the fatal hit on his suit deactivated his weapons. He could do nothing but lie there helplessly as his killer approached to relieve him of his ID bracelet. The man bending over him raised his eyebrows in silent surprise when he saw the rank of his victim, but he didn't comment on it. You didn't talk to a corpse.

As the man moved on, Tidwell sighed and settled back to wait. No one would reactivate his suit until thirty minutes after the last shot was fired. His only hope would be if Decker would detonate the charges, but he knew that wouldn't happen. It was another foul-up.

Damn radios! Another mission blown to hell!

The major sighed again. Lying there in a dead suit was preferable to actually being dead, but that might be opened to debate when he reported in. Someone's head would roll over tonight's failure, and as the planner he was the logical choice.

The bar was clearly military, high-class military, but military none the less. One of the most apparent indications of this was that it offered live waitresses as an option. Of course, having a live waitress meant your drinks cost more, but the military men were one of the last groups of holdouts who were willing to pay extra rather than be served the impersonal hydrolift of a Serv-O-Matic.

Steve Tidwell, former major, and his friend Clancy were well entrenched at their favorite corner table, a compromise reached early in their friendship as a solution to the problem of how they could both sit with their backs to the wall.

"Let me get this round, Steve," ordered Clancy dipping into his pocket. "That severance pay of yours may have to last you a long time."

"Hi Clancy, Steve," their waitress smiled delivering the next round of drinks. "Flo's tied up out back, so I thought I'd better get these to you before you got ugly and started tearing up the place."

"There's a love," purred Clancy, tucking a folded bill into her cleavage. She ignored him.

"Steve, what's this I hear about you getting cashiered?"

Tidwell took a sudden interest in the opposite wall. Clancy caught the waitress's eye and gave a minute shake of his head. She nodded knowingly and departed.

"Seriously, Steve, what *are* you going to do now?"

Tidwell shrugged.

"I don't know. Go back to earning my money in the live ammo set, I guess."

"Working for who? In case you haven't figured it out, you're blacklisted. The only real fighting left is in the Middle East, and the Oil Combine won't touch you."

"Don't be so sure of that. They were trying pretty hard to buy me away from the Itt-iots a couple months ago."

Clancy snorted contemptuously.

"A couple of months. Hell, I don't care if it was a

couple days. That was before they gave you your walking papers. I'm telling you they won't give you the time of day now. 'If you're not good enough for Communications, you're not good enough for Oil.' That'll be their attitude. You can bet on it."

Tidwell studied his drink in silence for a while, then took a hefty swallow.

"You're right, Clancy," he said softly. "But do you mind if I kid myself long enough to get good and drunk?"

"Sorry, Steve," apologized his friend. "It's just that for a minute there I thought you really believed what you were saying."

Tidwell lifted his glass in a mock toast.

"Well, here's to inferior superiors and inferior inferiors, the stuff armies are made of!"

He drained the glass and signaled for another.

"Really, Steve. You've got to admit the troops didn't let you down this time."

"True enough. But only because I gave them an assignment worthy of their talents: cannon fodder! 'Rush those machine guns and keep rushing until I say different!' Is it my imagination or is the quality of our troops actually getting worse? And speaking of that, who was that clown on guard with you?"

Clancy sighed.

"Maxwell. Would you believe he's one of our best?"

"That's what I mean! Ever since the corporations started building their own armies all we get are superstars who can't follow orders and freeze up when they're shot at. Hell, give me some of the old-timers like you and Hassan. If we could build our own force with the corporations' bankroll, if we could get our choice of the crop and pay them eighteen to forty grand a year, we could take over the world in a month."

"Then what would you do with it?"

"Hell, I don't know. I'm a soldier, not a politician. But dammit, I'm proud of my work and if nothing else it offends my sense of aesthetics to see some of the slipshod methods and tactics that seem to abound in any war. So much could be done with just a few really good men."

"Well, we're supposed to be working with the best available men now. You should see the regular armies the governments field!"

"Regular armies! Wash your mouth out with Irish. And speaking of that..."

The next round of drinks was arriving.

"Say, Flo, love. Tell Bonnie I'm sorry if I was so short with her last round. If she comes by again I'll try to make it up to her."

He made a casual pass at slipping his arm around her waist, but she sidestepped automatically without really noticing it.

"I'll tell her, Steve, but don't hold your breath about her coming back. I think you're safer when you're sulking!"

She turned to go and received a loud whack on her backside from Clancy. She squealed, then grinned and did an exaggerated burlesque walk away while the two men roared with laughter.

"Well, at least it's good to see you're loosening up a little," commented Clancy as their laughter subsided. "For a while there you had me worried."

"You know me. Pour enough Irish into me and I'll laugh through a holocaust! But you know, you're right, Clancy...about the men not letting me down, I mean. I think that's what's really irritating me about this whole thing."

He leaned back and rested his head against the wall.

"If the men had fallen down on the job, or if the plan had been faulty in its logic, or if I had tripped the fence beams, or any one of a dozen other possibilities, I could take it quite calmly. Hazards of the trade and all that. But to get canned over something that wasn't my fault really grates."

"They couldn't find any malfunction with the Throat-Mikes?"

"Just like the other two times. I personally supervised the technicians when they dismantled it, checked every part and connection, and nothing! Even I couldn't find anything wrong and believe me, I was looking hard. Take away the equipment failure excuse, and the only possibility is an unreliable commander, and Stevey boy gets his pink slip."

"Say, could you describe the internal circuitry of those things to me?"

In a flash the atmosphere changed. Tidwell was still leaning against the wall in a drunken pose, but his body was suddenly poised and his eyes were clear and wary—watchful.

"Come on, Clancy. What is this? You know I can't breach confidence with an employer, even an ex-employer. If I did I'd never work again."

Clancy sipped his drink unruffled by his friend's challenge.

"You know it, and I know it, but my fellow Oil Slickers don't know it. I just thought I'd toss the question to make my pass legit. You know the routine.

'We're old buddies and he's just been canned. If you'll just give me a pass tonight I might be able to pour a few drinks into him and get him talking.' You know the bit."

"Well, you're at least partially successful." Tidwell hoisted his glass again, sipped, and set it down with a clink. "So much for frivolity! Do you have any winning ideas for my future?"

Clancy tasted his drink cautiously.

"I dunno Steve. The last really big blow I was in was the Russo-Chinese War."

"Well, how about that one? I know they shut down their borders and went incommunicado after it was over, but that's a big hunk of land and a lot of people. There must be some skirmishes internally."

"I got out under the wire, but if you don't mind working for another ideology there might be something."

"Ideology, schmideology. Like I said before, I'm a soldier, not a politician. Have you really got a line of communication inside the Block?"

"Well..."

"Excuse us, gentlemen."

The two mercenaries looked up to find a trio of men standing close to their table. One was Oriental, the other two Caucasian. All were in business suits and carried attaché cases.

"If you would be so good as to join us in a private room, I believe it would be to our mutual advantage."

"The pleasure is ours," replied Tidwell formally rising to follow. He caught Clancy's eye and raised an eyebrow. Clancy winked back in agreement. This had contract written all over it.

As they passed the bar, Flo flashed them an old aviator's "thumbs-up" sign signifying that she had noticed what was going on and their table would still be waiting for them when they returned.

To further their hopes, the room they were led to was one of the most expensive available at the bar. That is, one the management guaranteed for its lack of listening or interruptions.

There were drinks already waiting on the conference table, and the Oriental gestured for them to be seated.

"Allow me to introduce myself. I am Mr. Yamada."

His failure to introduce his companions identified them as bodyguards. Almost as a reflex, the two mercenaries swept them with a cold, appraising glance, then returned their attention to Yamada.

"Am I correct in assuming I am address Stephen Tidwell..." his eyes shifted, "Michael Clancy?"

The two men nodded silently. For the time being they were content to let him do the talking.

"Am I further correct in my information that you have recently been dismissed by the Communications Combine, Mr. Tidwell?"

Again Steve nodded. Although he tried not to show it, inwardly he was irritated. What had they done? Gone though town posting notices?

Yamada reached into his pocket and withdrew two envelopes. Placing them on the table, he slid one to each of the two men.

"Each of these envelopes contains $1,000 American. With them, I am purchasing your time for the duration of the conversation. Regardless of its outcome, I am relying on your professional integrity to keep the existence of this meeting, as well as the context of the discussion itself in strictest confidence."

Again the two men nodded silently. This was the standard opening of a negotiating session, protecting both the mercenary and the person approaching him.

"Very well. Mr. Tidwell, we would like to contract your services for $60,000 a year plus benefits."

Clancy choked on his drink. Tidwell straightened in his chair.

"Sixty thousand . . ."

"And Mr. Clancy, we would further like to contract your services for $45,000 a year. This would of course not include the $18,500 we would have to provide for you to enable you to terminate your contract with the Oil Coalition."

By this time both men were gaping at him in undisguised astonishment. Clancy was the first to regain his composure.

"Mister, you don't beat around the bush, do you?"

"Excuse my asking," interrupted Steve, "but isn't that a rather large sum to offer without checking our records?"

"Believe me, Mr. Tidwell, we have checked your records. Both your records." Yamada smiled. "Let me assure you, gentlemen, this is not a casual offer. Rather, it is the climax of several months of exhaustive study and planning."

"Just what are we expected to do for this money?" asked Clancy cagily, sipping his drink without taking his eyes off the Oriental.

"You, Mr. Clancy, are to serve as aide and advisor to Mr. Tidwell. You, Mr. Tidwell, are to take command of the final training phases of, and lead into battle, a select force of men. You are to have final say as to qualifications of the troops as well as the tactics to be employed."

"Whose troops and in what battle are they to be employed?"

"I represent the Zaibatsu, a community of Japanese-based corporations, and the focus of our attention is the Oil vs. Communications War currently in process."

"You want us to lead troops against those idiots? Our pick of men and our tactics?" Clancy smiled. "Mister, you've got yourself a mercenary!"

Tidwell ignored his friend.

"I'd like a chance to view the force before I give you my final decision."

"Certainly, Mr. Tidwell," Yamada nodded. "We agree to this condition willingly because we are sure you will find the men at your disposal more that satisfactory."

"In that case, I think we are in agreement. Shall we start now?"

Tidwell started to rise, closely followed by Clancy, but Yamada waved them back into their seats.

"One last detail, gentlemen. The Zaibatsu believes in complete honesty with its employees, and there is something I feel you should be aware of before accepting our offer. The difficulties you have been encountering recently, Mr. Tidwell with your equipment and Mr. Clancy with your assignments, have been engineered by the Zaibatsu to weaken your current employers and ensure your availability for our offer."

Again both men gaped at him.

"But . . . how?" blurted Tidwell finally.

"Mr. Clancy's commanding officer who showed such poor judgment in giving him his team assignments is in our employment and acting on our orders. And as for Mr. Tidwell's equipment failure..." he turned a bland stare toward Steve, "...let us merely say that even though Communications holds the patent on the Throat-Mikes, the actual production was subcontracted to a Zaibatsu member. Something to do with the high cost of domestic labor. We took the liberty of making certain 'modifications' in their design, all quite undetectable, with the result that we now have the capacity to cut off or override their command communications at will."

By this time the two mercenaries were beyond astonishment. Any anger they might have felt at being manipulated was swept away by the vast military implications of what they had just been told.

"You mean we can shut down their communications any time we want? And you have infiltrators at the command level of the Oiler forces?"

"In both forces, actually. Nor are those our only advantages. As I said earlier, this is not a casual effort. I trust you will be able to find some way to maximize the effect of our entry?"

With a forced calmness, Tidwell finished his drink, then rose and extended his hand across the table.

"Mr. Yamada, it's going to be a pleasure working for you!"

A few scrawny weeds dotted the cliff's face, outlining the outcroppings and crevices there. It would be a real obstacle, but there wasn't time to look for another route down.

The man at the top of the cliff didn't even break stride as he sprinted up to the edge of the precipice.

He simply stepped off the cliff into nothingness, as did the three men following closely at his heels. For two long heartbeats they fell. By the second beat, their swords were drawn, the world famous Katanas, samurai swords unrivaled for centuries for their beauty, their craftsmanship and their razor edges. On the third heartbeat, they smashed onto a rock slide, the impact driving one man to his knees, forcing him to recover with a catlike forward roll. By the time he had regained his feet, the others were gone darting and weaving through the straw dummies, swords flashing in the sunlight. He raced to join them, a flick of his sword decapitating the dummy nearest him.

The straw figures, twenty of them, were identical, save for a one-inch square of brightly colored cloth pinned to them, marking five red, five yellow, five white, and five green. As they moved, each man struck only at the dummies marked with his color, forcing them to learn target identification at a dead run. Some were marked in the center of the forehead, some in the small of the back. It was considered a cardinal sin to strike a target that was not yours. A man who did not identify his target before he struck could as easily kill friend as foe in a firefight.

The leader of the band dispatched his last target and returned his sword to its scabbard in a blur of motion as he turned. He sprinted back toward the cliff through the dummies, apparently oblivious to the deadly blades still flashing around him. The others followed him, sheathing their swords as they ran. The man who had fallen was lagging noticeably behind.

Scrambling up the rock slide they threw themselves at the sheer cliff face and began climbing at a smooth effortless pace, finding handholds and toeholds where none could be seen. It was a long climb, and the distance between the men began to increase. Suddenly the second man in the formation dislodged a fist-sized rock that clattered down the cliffside. The third man rippled his body to one side and it missed him narrowly. The fourth man was not so lucky. The rock smashed into his right forearm and careened away. He lost his grip and dropped the fifteen feet back onto the rock slide.

He landed lightly in a three-point stance, straightened, and gazed ruefully at his arm. A jagged piece of bone protruded from the skin. Shaking his head slightly, he tucked the injured arm into the front of his uniform and began to climb again.

As he climbed, a small group of men appeared below him. They hurriedly cut down the remains of the straw dummies and began lashing new ones to the supporting poles. None of them looked up at the man struggling up the cliffside.

They had finished their job and disappeared by the time the lone man reached the top of the cliff. He did not pause or look back, but simply rolled to his feet and sprinted off again. As he did, five more men brushed past him, ignoring him completely, and flung themselves off the cliff. Tidwell hit the hold button on the videotape machine and the figures froze in midair. He stared at the screen for several moments, then rose from his chair and paced slowly across the thick carpet of his apartment. Clancy was snoring softly on the sofa, half buried in a sea of personnel folders. Tidwell ignored him and walked to the picture window where he stood and stared at the darkened training fields.

The door behind him opened and a young Japanese girl glided into the room. She was clad in traditional Japanese robes and was carrying a small tray of lacquered bamboo. She approached him quietly and stood waiting until he noticed her presence.

"Thanks, Yamiko," he said, taking a fresh drink from her tray.

She gave a short bow, and remained in place, looking at him. He tasted his drink, then realized she was still there.

"I'll be along shortly, Love. There's just a few things I've got to think out."

He blew a kiss at her and she giggled and retired from the room. As soon as she was gone, the smile dropped from his face like a mask. He slowly returned to his chair, leaned over and hit the rewind button. When the desired point had been reached, he hit the slow motion button and stared at the screen.

The four figures floated softly to earth. As they touched down, Tidwell leaned forward to watch their feet and legs. They were landing on uneven ground covered with rocks and small boulders, treacherous footing at best, but they handled it in stride. Their legs were spread and relaxed, molding to the contour of their landing point, then those incredible thigh muscles bunched and flexed, acting like shock absorbers. Their rumps nearly touched the rocks before the momentum was halted.

Tidwell centered his attention on the man who was going to fall. His left foot touched down on a head-sized boulder that rolled away as his weight came to bear. He began to fall to his left, but twisted his torso back to the centerline while deliberately buckling his right leg. Just as the awful physics of the situation seemed ready to smash him clumsily into the rocks, he tucked like a diver, curling around the glittering sword, and somersaulted forward rolling to his feet and continuing as if nothing had happened.

Tidwell shook his head in amazement. Less than a twentieth of a second. And he thought his reflexes were good.

The swordplay he had given up trying to follow. The blades seemed to have a life of their own, thirstily dragging the men from one target to the next. Then the leader turned. He twirled his sword in his left hand and stabbed the point toward his hip. An inch error in any direction would either lose the sword or run the owner through. It snaked into the scabbard like it had eyes.

Tidwell hit the hold button and stared at the figure on the screen. The face was that of an old Oriental, age drawing the skin tight across the face making it appear almost skull-like—Kumo. The old sensei who had been in command before Tidwell and Clancy were hired.

In the entire week they had been reviewing the troops they had not seen Kumo show any kind of emotion. Not anger, not joy—nothing. But he was a demanding instructor and personally led the men in their training. The cliff was only the third station in a fifteen-station obstacle course Kumo had laid out. The troops ran the obstacle course every morning to loosen up for the rest of the day's training. To loosen up.

Tidwell advanced the tape to the sequence in which the man's arm was broken. As the incident unfolded, he recalled the balance of that episode. The man had finished the obstacle course, broken arm and all. But his speed suffered, and Kumo sent him back to run the course again *before* he reported to the infirmary to have his arm treated.

Kumo ran a rough school. No one could argue with his results, though. Tidwell had seen things in this last week that he had not previously believed physically possible.

Ejecting the tape cassette, he re-filed it, selected another, and fed it into the viewer.

The man on the screen was the physical opposite of Kumo, who knelt in the background. Where Kumo was thin to the point of looking frail, this man looked like you could hit him with a truck without doing significant damage. He was short, but wide and muscular, looking for all the world like a miniature fullback, complete with shoulder pads.

He stood blindfolded on the field of hard-packed earth. His poise was relaxed and serene. Suddenly another man appeared at the edge of the screen, sprinting forward with upraised sword. As he neared his stationary target, the sword flashed out in a horizontal cut aimed to decapitate the luckless man. At the last instant before the sword struck, the blindfolded man ducked under the glittering blade and lashed out with a kick that took the running swordsman full in the stomach. The man dropped to the ground, doubled over in agony as the blindfolded man resumed his original stance.

Another man crept onto the field, apparently trying to drag his fallen comrade back to the sidelines. When he reached the writhing figure however, instead of attempting to assist him, the new man sprang over him high into the air launching a flying kick at the man with the blindfold. Again the blinded man countered, this time raising a forearm which caught the attacker's leg and flipped it in the air dumping him on his head.

At this point, the swordsman, who apparently was not as injured as he had seemed, rolled over and aimed a vicious cut at the defender's legs. The blindfolded man took to the air, leaping over the sword, and drove a heel down into the swordsman's face. The man fell back and lay motionless, bleeding from both nostrils.

Without taking his eyes from the screen, Tidwell raised his voice.

"Hey, Clancy."

His friend sat up on the sofa, scattering folders onto the floor and blinking his eyes in disorientation.

"Yeah, Steve?"

"How do they do that?"

Clancy craned his neck around and peered at the screen. Three men were attacking simultaneously, one with an axe, two with their hands and feet. The blindfolded man parried, blocked and countered, unruffled by death narrowly missing him at each turn.

"Oh, that's an old martial artist's drill—blindfolded workouts. The theory is that if you lost one of your five senses, such as sight, the other four would be heightened to compensate. By working out blindfolded, you heighten the other senses without actually losing one."

"Have you done this drill before?"

Clancy shook his head. He was starting to come into focus again.

"Not personally. I've seen it done a couple of times, but nothing like this. These guys are good, and I mean really good."

"Who is that one, the powerhouse with the blindfold?"

Clancy pawed through his folders.

"Here it is. His name's Aki. I won't read off all the black belts he holds, I can't pronounce half of them. He's one of the originals. One of the founding members of the martial arts cults that formed up after that one author tried to get the Army to return to the ancient ways, then killed himself when they laughed at him."

Tidwell shook his head.

"How many of the force came out of those cults?"

"About 95%. It's still incredible to me that the Zaibatsu had the foresight to start sponsoring those groups. That was over twenty years ago."

"Just goes to show what twenty years of training six days a week will do for you. Did you know some of the troops were raised into it by their parents? That they've been training with unarmed and armed combat since they could walk?"

"Yeah, I caught that. Incidentally, did I show you the results from the firing range today?"

"Spare me."

But Clancy was on his way to the case.

"They were firing Springfields today," he called back over his shoulder. "Those old bolt-action jobs. Range at 500 meters."

Tidwell sighed. These firing range reports were monotonous, but Clancy was a big firearms freak.

"Here we go. These are the worst ten." He waved a stack of photos at Tidwell. On each photo was a man-shaped silhouette target with a small irregular-shaped hole in the center of the chest.

"There isn't a single shot grouping in there you couldn't cover with a nickel, and these are the worst."

"I assume they're still shooting five-shot groups."

Clancy snorted.

"I don't think Kumo has let them hear of any other kind."

"Firing position?"

"Prone unsupported. Pencil scopes battlefield zeroed at 400 meters."

Tidwell shook his head.

"I'll tell you, Clancy, man for man I've never seen anything like these guys. It's my studied and considered opinion that any one of them could take both of us one-handed. Even..."

He jerked a thumb at the figures on the screen behind them.

"...even blindfolded."

On the screen, a man tried to stand at a distance and stab the blindfolded Aki with a spear, with disastrous results.

Clancy borrowed Tidwell's drink and took a sip.

"And you're still standing by your decision? About extending our entry date to the war by two months?"

"Now look Clancy..."

"I'm not arguing. Just checking."

"They aren't ready yet. They're still a pack of individuals. A highly trained mob is still a mob."

"What's Kumo's reaction? That's his established entry date you're extending."

"He was only thinking about the new 'superweapons' when he set that date. He's been trained from birth to think of combat as an individual venture."

"Hey, those new weapons are really something, aren't they?"

"Superweapons or not, those men have to learn

to function as a team before they'll be ready for the
war. They said I would have free rein in choosing
men and tactics and by God this time I'm not going
into battle until they're ready. I don't care if it takes
two months or two years."

"But Kumo . . ."

"Kumo and I work for the same employer and
they put *me* in charge. We'll move when *I* say we're
ready," Tidwell said.

Clancy shrugged his shoulders.

"Just asking, Steve. No need to . . . Whoa. Could
you back that up?"

He pointed excitedly at the screen. Tidwell obligingly
hit the hold button. On the screen, two men were in
the process of attacking simultaneously from both sides
with swords. Images of Clancy and Tidwell were also
on the screen standing on either side of Kumo.

"How far do you want it backed?"

"Back it up to where you interrupt the demonstration."

Tidwell obliged.

The scene began anew. There was an attacker on
the screen cautiously circling Aki with a knife. Suddenly Tidwell appeared on the screen, closely followed
by Clancy. Until this point they had been standing off
camera watching the proceedings. Finally Tidwell could
contain his feelings of skepticism no longer and stepped
forward, silently holding his hand up to halt the action.
He signaled the man with the knife to retire from the
field then turned and beckoned two specific men to
approach him. With a series of quick flowing motions
he began to explain what he wanted.

"This is the part I want to see. Damn. You know
you're really good, Steve. You know how long it would

take me to explain that using gestures? You'll have to coach me on it sometime. You used to fool around with the old Indian sign language a lot didn't you? Steve?"

No reply came. Clancy tore his eyes away from the screen and shot a glance at Tidwell. Tidwell was sitting and staring at the screen. Every muscle in his body was suddenly tense, not rigid, but poised as if he was about to fight.

"What is it, Steve? Did you see something?"

Without answering, Tidwell stopped the film, reversed it, then started it again.

Again the knifeman circled. Again the two mercenaries appeared on the screen. Tidwell punched the hold button and the action froze.

He rose form his chair and slowly approached the screen. Then he thoughtfully sipped his drink and stared at a point away from the main action. He stared at Kumo.

Kumo, the old sensei who never showed emotion. In the split second frozen by the camera, at the instant the two men stepped past him and interrupted the demonstration, in that fleeting moment, as he looked at Tidwell's back, Kumo's face was contorted into an expression of raw, naked hatred.

The men and women of the force were kneeling in the traditional student's position, backs straight, hands open and resting palms down on their thighs. To all appearances, they were at ease listening to the morning instruction.

This morning, however, the assembly was different. This morning the raised instructor's platform held a dozen chairs filled by various Corporation dignitaries.

More importantly, the subject at hand was not instruction, but rather the formal transfer of command from Kumo to Tidwell.

Tidwell was both nervous and bored. He was bored because he was always bored by long speeches, particularly if he was one of the main subjects under discussion. Yet there was still the nervousness born from the anticipation of directly addressing the troops for the first time as their commander.

The speech was in English, as were all the speeches and instructions. One of the prerequisites for the force was a fluent knowledge of English. That didn't make it any the less boring.

He grimaced about the platform again. The Corporation officials were sitting in Tweedle-dee and Tweedle-dum similarity, blank-faced and attentive. If nothing else in this stint of duty, he was going to try to learn some of the Oriental inscrutability. Depending on the Oriental, they viewed Westerners with distaste or amusement because of the ease with which their emotions could be read in their expressions and actions. The keynote of the Orient was control, and it started with control of oneself.

Craning his neck slightly, he snuck a glance at Clancy, standing in an easy parade rest behind him. There was the Western equivalent to the Oriental inscrutability: the military man. Back straight, eyes straight ahead, face expressionless. Behind the mask, Clancy's mind would be as busy and opinionated as ever, but from viewing him, Tidwell did not have the faintest idea what he was thinking.

In fact, Tidwell realized, he himself was currently the most animated figure on the platform. Suddenly self-conscious, he started to face front again when his eyes fell on Kumo.

Kumo was resplendent in his ceremonial robes. Protruding from his sash at an unlikely angle to the Western eyes, was a samurai sword. Tidwell had heard that the sword had been in Kumo's family for over fifteen generations.

He held the weapon in almost a religious awe. Its history was longer than Tidwell's family tree, and it seemed to radiate a blood aura of its own. Anyone who didn't believe that a weapon absorbed something from the men who used it, from the men it killed, anyone who didn't believe that a weapon could have an identity and personality of its own had never held a weapon with a past.

He suddenly snapped back into focus. The speaker was stepping away from the microphone, looking at him expectantly, as were the others on the platform. Apparently he had missed his introduction and was "on."

He rose slowly, using the delay to collect his scattered thoughts, and stepped to the edge of the platform, ignoring the microphone to address the force directly. A brief gust of wind rippled the uniforms of his audience, but aside from that, there was no movement or reaction.

"Traditionally Japan has produced the finest fighting men in the world. The Samurai, the Ninjas, are all legendary for the prowess in battle."

There was no reaction from the force. Mentally he braced himself. Here we go!

"Also, traditionally, they have had the worst armies!"

The force stiffened without moving. Their faces remained immobile.

"The armies were unsuccessful because they fought as individuals, not as a team. As martial artists, you train the muscles of your body, the limbs of your body to work together, to support each other. It would be unthinkable to attempt to fight if your arms and legs were allowed to move in uncontrolled random motions."

They were with him, grudgingly, seeing where his logic was going.

"Similarly, an army can only be effective if the men and women in it work in cooperation and coordination with each other."

He had made his point. Time to back off a little.

"Different cultures yield different fighting styles. I am not here to argue which style is better, for each style has its time and place. What must be decided is what style is necessary in which situation. In this case, that decision has been made by the executives of the Zaibatsu. As a result of that decision, I have been hired to train and lead you."

Now came the real crunch.

"You are about to enter a highly specialized war. To successfully fight in this war, you must abandon any ideas you may have of nationalism or glory. You are mercenaries as I am a mercenary in the employment of the Zaibatsu complex. As such you must learn to fight, to think in a way which may be completely foreign to what you have learned in the past. To allow time for this training, the date for our entry into the war has been moved back by two months."

"I disagree, Mr. Tidwell."

The words were soft and quiet, but they carried to every corner of the assemblage. In an instant the air was electric. Kumo!

"I disagree with everything you have said."

There it was. The challenge. The gauntlet. Tidwell turned slowly to face his attacker. Kumo's words were polite and soft as a caress, but the act of interrupting, let alone disagreeing, carried as much emotional impact in the Orient as a Western drill sergeant screaming his head off.

"In combat, the action is too fast for conscious thought. If one had to pause and think about coordination of one's limbs, the battle would be lost before a decision was made. It is for this reason that martial artists train, so that each limb develops eyes of its own, a mind of its own. This enables a fighter to strike like lightening when an opening presents itself. Similarly, we train each man to be a self-contained unit, capable of making decisions and acting as the situation presents itself. This means he will never be hamstrung by slow decisions or a break in communications with his superior. As to your 'specialized war,' a trained fighting man should be able to adapt and function in any situation. Your failure to recognize this betrays your ignorance of warfare."

Tidwell shot a glance at the Corporate officials. No one moved to interfere or defend. He was on his own. They were going to let the two of them settle it.

"Am I to understand that you are questioning the qualifications of Mr. Clancy and myself?" He tried to keep his voice as calm as Kumo's.

"There is nothing to question. After two weeks here you presume to be an expert on our force and seek to change it. You expect the force to follow you because the Corporation tells them to. This is childish. The only way one may lead fighting men is if he holds their respect. That respect must be earned. It cannot be ordered. So far, all we have for proof is words. If your knowledge of battle is so vastly superior to ours, perhaps you could demonstrate it by defeating one of the force that we might see with our own eyes you are fit to lead us."

Tidwell was thunderstruck. This was unheard of. In paperback novels leaders would issue blanket challenges to their force to "any man who thinks he can lick me." In life it was never done. Leaders were chosen for their knowledge of strategy and tactics, not their individual fighting prowess. It was doubtful that either Patton or Rommel, or Genghis Khan for that matter, could beat any man in their command in a fistfight. No commander in his right mind would jeopardize his authority status by entering into a brawl.

It crossed his mind to refuse the challenge. He had already acknowledged the superior ability of the Japanese in individual combat, contesting only their group tactics. Just as quickly he rejected the thought.

No matter how insane it was, he could not refuse this challenge. He was in the Orient. To refuse would be to indicate cowardice, to lose face. He would have to fight this battle and win it.

"Sensei, I have publicly stated that the people of Japan have produced the greatest fighters in history. I will elaborate and say that I have no doubts that the men and women under your instruction equal or surpass those warriors of old in skill. Moreover, I must bow to your superior knowledge of their abilities and attitudes."

Kumo bowed his head slightly, acknowledging the compliment, but his eyes were still wary.

"However, what you tell me is that they must be convinced with action, not words. It has been always a characteristic of man that he can settle differences, pass his experiences from one generation to the next, and develop new ideas and concepts through the use of words. If you are correct in your appraisal of your students, if they are unable to be swayed by words, if the only way their respect can be earned is by action, then they are not men, they are animals."

Kumo's back stiffened.

"This is not surprising because you have trained them like animals."

There was an angry stirring in the ranks.

"Normally I would stand aside for men and women of such training, for they could defeat me with ease. But you tell me they are animals. As such I will accept your challenge, Kumo. I will stand and defeat the man or woman of your choice anytime, anyplace, with any weapon, for I am a man, and a man does not fear an animal."

There were scattered angry cries from the ranks. First singly, then as a group, the force rose and stood at the ready position, wordlessly volunteering to champion the force by facing Tidwell. Tidwell suppressed an impulse to smile at the sensei's predicament. Kumo had obviously planned to face Tidwell himself. In slanting his retort toward the force, Tidwell had successfully forced Kumo into choosing a member from the ranks. A teacher cannot defend his students without implying a lack of confidence in their prowess. If the abilities of a student are challenged, the student must answer the challenge. Terrific. Would you like to face a tiger or a gorilla?

"Mr. Tidwell, your answer is eloquent if unwise. You aware that such a contest would be fought to the death?"

Tidwell nodded. He hadn't been, but he was now. Inwardly he gritted his teeth. Kumo wasn't leaving him any outs.

"Very well. The time will be now, the place here. For weapons, you may have your choice."

Clever bastard! He's waiting to see weapons choice before he picks my opponent.

"I'll fight as I stand."

"I will also allow you to choose your opponent. I have faith in each of my students."

Damn! He'd reversed it. Now if Tidwell didn't choose Kumo for an opponent, it would appear he was probing for a weaker foe.

Tidwell scanned the force slowly, while he pondered the problem. Finally he made his decision.

Finishing his survey, he turned to Kumo once more.

"I will face Aki."

There was a quiet murmur of surprise as Aki rose and approached the platform. Obviously Tidwell was not trying to pick a weak opponent.

The powerhouse bounded onto the platform and bowed to Kumo. Kumo addressed him in rapid Japanese, then much to everyone's astonishment, removed his sword and offered it to his student. Aki's glanced flickered over Tidwell, then he gave a short bow, shaking his head in refusal. Raising his head in calm pride, he rattled off a quick statement in Japanese, then turned to face Tidwell. Kumo inclined his head, then returned the sword to his sash. He barked a few quick commands, and several men sprang to clear the platform, relocating the dignitaries and their chairs to positions in front of and facing the scene of the upcoming duel.

Tidwell shrugged out of his jacket and Clancy stepped forward to take it.

"Are you out of your bloody mind, Steve?" he murmured under his breath.

"Do you see any options?"

"You could have let me fight him. If Kumo can have a champion, you should be able to have one, too."

"Thanks, but I'd rather handle this one myself. Nothing personal."

"Just remember the option next time, if there is a next time."

"Come on Clancy, what could you do I can't in a spot like this?"

"For openers, I could blow him away while he's bowing in."

Clancy opened his hand slightly to reveal the derringer he was palming. Tidwell recognized at once as Clancy's favorite holdout weapon, two shots, loads exploding on impact, accurate to 50 feet in the hands of an expert and Clancy was an expert.

"Tempting, but it wouldn't impress the troops much."

"But it would keep you alive!"

"Academic. We're committed now."

"Right. Win it."

"Win it!" The mercenaries' send-off. Tidwell focused his mind on that expression as he took his place facing Aki. At times like this when the chips were down it meant a lot more than all the "good luck's" in the world.

Suddenly the solution to the problem occurred to him. Chancy, but worth a try.

"Clancy, give me a pad and pencil."

They appeared magically. No aide is complete without those tools. Tidwell scribbled something quickly on the top sheet, ripped it from the pad, and folded it twice.

"Give this to Mr. Yamada."

Clancy nodded and took the note, stashing the pad and pencil as he went.

Everything was ready now. With relatively few adaptations a lecture assembly had been converted into an arena. As he was talking to Clancy, Tidwell had been testing the platform surface. It was smooth sanded wood, unvarnished and solid. He considered taking off his boots for better traction, but discarded the idea. He'd rather have the extra weight on his feet for the fight, increased impact and all that.

Kumo sat at the rear center of the platform, overseeing the proceedings as always. Then Clancy vaulted back onto the platform, his errand complete. Deliberately he strode across the platform and took a position beside Kumo on the side closest Tidwell. Kumo glared, but did not challenge the move.

Tidwell suppressed a smile. Score one for Clancy. This was not a class exercise and Kumo was not an impartial instructor. It was a duel, and the seconds were now in position. One thing was sure, if he ever took a contract to take on the devil, he wanted Clancy guarding his flanks.

But now there was work to be done. For the first time he focused his attention on Aki, meeting his enemy's gaze directly. Aki was standing at the far end of the platform, relaxed and poised, eyes dead. The eyes showed neither fear nor anger. They simply watched, appraised, analyzed, and gave nothing in return. Tidwell realized that he was looking into a mirror, into the eyes of a killer. He realized it, accepted, and put it out of his mind. He was ready.

He raised an eyebrow in question, Aki saw and gave a fractional nod of his head, more an acknowledgement than a bow, and the duel began.

Tidwell took one slow step forward and stopped, watching; Aki moved with leisurely grace into a wide, straddle-legged stance, and waited, watching.

Check! Aki was going to force Tidwell into making the opening move. He was putting his faith in his defense, in his ability to weather any attack Tidwell could throw at him and survive to finish the bout before his opponent could recover. However the duel went, it would be over quickly. Once Tidwell committed himself to an attack, it would either succeed or he would be dead.

Tidwell broke the tableau, sauntering diagonally to his right. As he approached the edge of the platform he stopped, studied his opponent, then repeated the process, moving diagonally to the left. Aki stood unmoving, watching.

To an unschooled eye, it would appear almost as if Tidwell were an art connoisseur, viewing a statue from various angles. To the people watching, it was Aki's challenge. He was saying "Pick your attack, pick your angle. I will stop you and kill you."

Finally Tidwell heaved a visible sigh. The decision was made. He moved slowly to the center of the platform, paused considering Aki, then placed his hands behind his back and began moving toward him head-on. Theatrically he came, step-by-step, a study in slow motion. The question now was how close? How close would Aki let him come before launching a counterattack? Could he bait Aki into striking first? Committing first?

Ten feet separated them. Step. Seven feet. Step.

Tidwell's right fist flashed out, whipping wide for a back-knuckle strike to Aki's temple, a killing blow. In the same instant Aki exploded into action, left arm coming up to block the strike, right fist driving out for a smashing punch to Tidwell's solar plexus. Then in mid-heartbeat the pattern changed. Tidwell's left hand flashed out and the sun glinted off the blade of a stiletto lancing for the center of Aki's chest. Aki's counterpunch changed and his right arm snapped down to parry the knife thrust.

Instead of catching Tidwell's forearm, the block came down on the raised knife point as the weapon was pivoted in mid-thrust to meet the counter. The point plunged into the forearm, hitting bone and Tidwell ripped the arm open drawing the knife back toward him.

As his arm came back, Tidwell jerked his knee up, slamming it into the wounded arm, then straightened his leg, snapping the toe of his boot into the wound for a third hit as Aki jerked backward, splintering the bone and sending his opponent off balance.

Aki reeled back in agony, then caught his balance and tried to take a good position, even though his right arm would no longer respond to his will. His eyes glinted hard—a tiger at bay.

Tidwell bounded backward, away from his injured foe and backpedaled to the far end of the platform. As Aki moved to follow, the mercenary pegged the knife into the platform at his feet, dropped to one knee, and held his arms out from his body at shoulder height.

"Aki! Stop!"

Aki paused, puzzled.

"Stop and listen!"

Suspicious, Aki retreated slowly to the far end of the platform, but he listened.

"Mr. Yamada! Will you read aloud the note I passed you before the fight began."

Mr. Yamada rose slowly from his seat, unfolded the note, and read:

"I will strike Aki's right forearm two to four times, then try to stop the fight."

He sat down and a murmur rippled through the force.

"The point of the fight was to determine if I was qualified to lead this force in battle. At this point I have shown that not only can I strike your champion repeatedly, but that I can predict his moves in advance. This will be my function as your commander, to guide you against an enemy I know and can predict, giving maximum effectiveness to your skills. Having demonstrated this ability, I wish to end this duel if my opponent agrees. I only hope he embraces the same philosophy I do, that if given a choice he will not waste lives. I will not kill or sacrifice my men needlessly. That is the way of the martial arts, and the way of the mercenary. Aki! Do you agree with me that the duel is over?"

Their eyes met for a long moment. Then slowly Aki drew himself up and bowed.

Kumo sprang to his feet, his face livid. He barked an order at Aki. Still in the bow, Aki raised his head and looked at Kumo, then at Tidwell, then back at Kumo and shook his head.

Clancy tensed, his hand going to his waistband. Tidwell caught his eye and shook his head in a firm negative.

Kumo screamed a phrase in Japanese at Aki, then snatched the sword from his sash and started across the platform at Tidwell.

Tidwell watched coldly as the sensei took three steps toward him, then stood up. As he did, the leg he had been kneeling on flashed forward and kicked the knife like a placekicker going for an extra point. The point snapped off and the knife somersaulted forward, plunging hilt-deep into the chest of the charging swordsman. Kumo stopped, went to one knee, tried to rise, then the sword slipped from his grasp and he fell.

For several minutes there was silence. Then Tidwell turned to address his force.

"A great man has died here today. Training is cancelled for the rest of the day that we might honor his memory. Assembly will be at 0600 hours tomorrow to receive your new orders. Dismissed."

In silence, the force rose and began to disperse. Tidwell turned to view the body again. Aki was kneeling before his fallen sensei. In silence, Tidwell picked up the sword, removed the scabbard from Kumo's sash and re-sheathed the weapon. He stared at the body for another moment, then turned and handed the sword to Aki. Their eyes met, then Tidwell bowed and turned away.

"Jesus Christ, Steve. Have you ever used that placekick stunt before? In combat?"

"Three times before. This is the second time it worked."

"I saw it but I still don't believe it. If I ever mouth off about your knives again you can use one of them on me."

"Yeah, right. Say, can you be sure someone takes care of Aki's arm? I just want to go off and get drunk right now."

"Sure thing, Steve. Oh, someone wants to talk to you."

"Later, huh? I'm not up to it right now."

"It's the straw bosses."

Clancy jerked a thumb toward the row of Company officials.

"Oh."

Tidwell turned and started wearily toward the men, because they were his employers and he was a mercenary.

The straw dummies waited passively at the base of the cliff. Tidwell's interest was at a peak as he sat waiting with Clancy for the next group to appear. The two mercenaries were perched on the lip of the cliff about five meters to the left of the trail.

They came, five of them darting silently from tree to tree like spirits. As they approached the cliff, the leader, a swarthy man in his thirties, held up his hand in a signal. The group froze, and he signaled one of the team forward. Tidwell smiled as a girl in her mid-twenties slung her rifle and dropped to her stomach, sliding forward to peer over the cliff. The leader knew damn well what was down there because he had run the course hundreds of times before, but he was playing it by the book and officially it was a new situation to be scouted.

The girl completed her survey, then slid backward

for several meters before she rose to a half crouch. Her hands flashed in a quick series of signals to the leader. Clancy nudged Tidwell, who smiled again, this time from flattered pleasure. Since he had taken over, the entire force had begun using his habit of sign language. It was a high compliment. The only trouble was that they had become so proficient with it and had elaborated on his basic vocabulary to a point that now he sometimes had trouble following the signals as they flashed back and forth.

The leader made his decision. With a few abrupt gestures from him, the other three of the team, two men and a woman, slung their rifles and darted forward, diving full speed off the cliff to confront their luckless "victims" below. The leader and the scout remained topside.

The two observing mercenaries straightened unconsciously. This was something new. The leader apparently had a new trick up his sleeve.

As his teammates sprinted forward, the leader reached over his shoulder and fished a coil of rope out of his pack. It was black, lightweight silk line, with heavy knots tied in it every two feet for climbing. He located and grasped one end, tossing the coil to the scout. She caught it and flipped it over the cliff, while the leader secured his end around a small tree with a quick-release knot. This done, he faded back along the trail about ten meters to cover the rear, while the scout unslung her rifle and eased up to the edge of the cliff ready to cover her teammates below.

Clancy punched Tidwell's shoulder delightedly and flashed him a thumbs-up signal. Tidwell nodded in agreement. It was a sweet move. Now the three attackers below had an easy, secure route back out as well as cover fire if anything went wrong.

Tidwell felt like crowing. The reorganization of the force was working better than he would have dared hope. The whole thing had been a ridiculously simple three-step process. First had been a questionnaire asking eight questions: Which four people in the force would you most like to team with? Why? Who would you be least willing to team with? Why? Who would you be least willing to follow as a leader? Why?

The next step was to pass the data through the computers a few times and two jobs were done simultaneously. First, the five-man teams were established along the lines of preference stated by the individuals; second, the deadwood and misfits were weeded out to be sent back to other jobs in the Corporate structure.

The final step was to pull various members of the teams for special accelerated training in the more specialized skills necessary in a fighting unit. He had had to argue with Clancy a little on this point, but had finally won. Clancy had felt the existing specialists should be seeded through the teams to round out the requirements regardless of preference lines, but Tidwell's inescapable logic was that in combat you're better off with a mediocre machine gunner you trust and can work with than an expert machine gunner you wouldn't turn your back on.

From then on, the teams were inseparable. They bunked together, trained together, went on leave together; in short, they became a family. In fact, several of the teams had formed along family lines with mother, father, and offspring all in the same team, though frequently the leadership went to one of the offspring.

It was a weird, unorthodox way to organize an army, but it was bearing fruit. The teams were tight-knit and smooth-running and highly prone to coming up with their own solutions to the tactical problems Tidwell was constantly inventing for them. It was beyond a doubt the finest fighting force Tidwell had ever been associated with.

The attackers were regaining the top of the cliff now. Suddenly, a mischievous idea hit Tidwell. He stood up and wigwagged the team leader. With a few brief gestures he sketched out his orders. The team leader nodded, and began signaling his team. The scout re-coiled the rope and tossed it to the team leader. He caught it, stowed it in his pack, surveyed the terrain, and faded back into a bush. Tidwell checked the terrain and nodded to himself. It was a good ambush. He couldn't see any of the team even though he had seen four of them take cover. He hadn't seen where the scout went after she tossed the rope.

Clancy was smiling at him.

"Steve, you're a real son-of-a-bitch."

Tidwell shrugged modestly, and they settled back to wait.

They didn't have to wait long. The next team came into sight, jogging along the trail in a loose group. The leader, a girl in her late teens that Clancy was spending most of his off-hours with, spotted the two sitting on the edge of the cliff. She smiled and waved at them. They smiled and waved back at her. They were still smiling when the ambush opened up.

The girl and the two men flanking her went down to

the first burst of fire. The remaining two members dove smoothly under cover and started returning their fire.

Tidwell stood up.

"All right! Break it up!"

There was an abrupt cease-fire.

"Everybody over here!"

The two teams emerged from their hiding places and sprinted over to the two mercenaries. Tidwell tossed his "activator key" to one of the survivors of the second team who ducked off to "revive" his teammates.

"Okay. First off, ambushers. There's no point in laying an ambush if you're going to spring it too soon. Let 'em come all the way into the trap before you spring it. The way you did it, you're left with two survivors who've got you pinned down with your backs to a cliff!"

The "revived" members of the second team joined the group.

"Now then, victims! Those kill suits are spoiling you rotten. You're supposed to be moving through disputed terrain. Don't bunch up where one burst can wipe out your whole team."

They were listening intently, soaking up everything he said.

"Okay, we've held up training enough. Report to the firing range after dinner for an extra hour's penalty tour."

The teams laughed as they resumed their training. Sending them to the firing range for a penalty tour was like sending a kid to Disneyland. Ever since the new weapons had arrived the teams had to be driven away from the ranges. They had even had to take head count at meals to be sure teams didn't skip eating to sneak out to the range for extra practice.

The girl leading the second team shot a black look at Clancy as she herded her team off the cliff.

"Now who's the son of a bitch, Clancy old friend? Unless I miss my guess, she's going to have a few words for you tonight."

"Let her scream." Clancy's voice was chilly. "I'd rather see her gunned down here than when we're in live action. I wouldn't be doing her any favors to flash her warning in training. Let her learn the hard way. Then she'll remember."

Tidwell smiled to himself. Underneath that easygoing, nice guy exterior was as cold and hard-nosed a mercenary as he was. Maybe colder.

"Nit-picking aside, Clancy, what do you think?"

"Think? I'll tell you, Steve. I think they're the meanest, most versatile fighting force the world has ever seen, bar none. Like you say, we're nit-picking. They're as ready now as they're ever going to be."

"How do you think they'd stack up against regular government troops?"

Clancy snorted.

"No contest—our team would eat them alive. It's the difference between a professional and an amateur. To us, war is a livelihood, not a hobby. I'd like nothing better than taking on some of the governmental boy scouts. It'd be a damn sight easier than moving in on the Oilers or the Itt-iots."

Tidwell felt a tightening in his gut, but he kept it out of his voice.

"I'm glad our opinions agree, Clancy. I just received new orders from Yamada this morning. The jump-off date has been changed. We're moving out next week."

❖   ❖   ❖

"Spare change? Hey, man . . . any spare change?"

The youthful panhandlers were inevitable, even in a Brazilian airport. Tidwell strode on, ignoring the boy, but Clancy stopped and started digging in his pocket.

"Come on, Clancy! We've got to beat that mob through Customs."

"Yeah, ain't it a bitch?" the youth joined in. "Do you believe this? It's been like this for almost a week."

Curiosity made Tidwell continue the conversation.

"Any word as to what they're doing?"

"Big tour program. Some Jap company is giving free tours instead of raises this year." He spat on the floor. "Damn cheap bastards. Haven't gotten a dime out of one of them yet."

"Here." Tidwell handed him a dollar. "This'll make up for some of it."

"Hey man, thanks. Say, take your bags to that skinny guy on the end and slip him ten, no hassle!"

The youth drifted off, looking for fresh game.

"Hypocrite!" accused Clancy under his breath. "Since when were you suddenly so generous."

"Since I could write it off on an expense account. That item is going in as a ten-dollar payment for an informant. Come on, I'll buy you a drink out of the profits."

"Actually, I'd rather loiter around out here and make sure everything goes okay."

"Relax." Tidwell shot a glance down the terminal. "They're doing fine. Damnedest invasion I've ever seen."

At the other end of the terminal, the rest of their infiltration group was gathered, taking pictures and chattering together excitedly. Clancy and Tidwell had arrived by commercial flight half an hour after the charter plane, but the group was still fluttering around getting organized. They were perfect, right down to the overloaded camera bags and the clipboards. Even with his practiced eye, Tidwell could not have distinguished his own crew of cold killers from a hundred other groups of Orientals which frequent the tourist routes of the world.

"Hey! There you are!"

Both men winced. The irritating voice of Harry Beckington was unmistakable. After seven hours of his company on the plane, the mercenaries had not even had to confer before dodging him as they got off the plane. He would have made nice camouflage, but...

"Thought I lost you guys with all the slant-eyes in here!"

Their smiles were harder than usual to force.

"Sure are a lot of them," volunteered Clancy gamely.

"You know how they are, first a few, then you're hip deep in 'em."

"That's the way it is all right," smiled Tidwell.

"Come on. Let me buy you boys a..."

As he spoke, he gestured toward the bar and collided with one of the "tour group." He collided with Aki.

There was no reason for Aki to be passing so close, except that there was no reason for him not to. He was returning from the souvenir stand and the group of three men happened to be in his path. One of the forces' instructions for the invasion was to not avoid each other. Nothing is as noticeable to a watchful eye as a group of people studiously ignoring each other. It would have been unnatural for Aki to alter his path, so he simply tried to walk past them, only to run into Beckington's wildly flailing arm.

Aki's arm was still in a sling from his duel with

Tidwell, and it suffered the full brunt of the impact. He instinctively bounced back, and stumbled over Beckington's briefcase.

"Watch it! Look what you did!"

Aki was the picture of politeness. He bobbed his head, smiling broadly.

"Please excuse. Most clumsy!"

"Excuse, Hell. You're going to pick all that stuff up."

Beckington seized his injured arm angrily, pointing to the scattered papers on the floor.

"For Christsake, Beckington," interrupted Tidwell, "the man's got a bad arm."

"Injured, my ass. He's probably smuggling something. How 'bout it? What are you smuggling?"

He shook the injured arm. Small beads of sweat appeared on Aki's forehead, but he kept smiling.

"No smuggle. Please...will pick up paper."

Beckington released him with a shove.

"Well, hurry up!"

"Careful, Beckington, he might know karate," cautioned Clancy.

"Shit! They don't scare me with that chop-chop crap!" snarled Beckington, but he stepped back anyway.

"Here are papers. Please excuse. Very clumsy."

Beckington gestured angrily. Aki set the papers down and retreated toward the other end of the terminal.

"Boy, that really frosts me. I mean, some people think just 'cause they're in another country they can get away with murder."

"Yeah, people like that really burn me, too," said Tidwell dryly. The sarcasm was lost.

"Where were we? Oh yeah...I was going to buy you boys a drink. You ready?"

"Actually, we can't."

"Can't? Why not?"

"Actually, we're with Alcoholics Anonymous. We're here to open a new branch," interrupted Clancy.

"Alcoholics Anonymous?"

"Yes," said Tidwell blandly. "On the National Board, actually."

"But I thought you were drinking on the plane."

"Oh, that," interrupted Clancy. "Actually it was iced tea. We've found that lecturing people while we're traveling just alienates them, so we try to blend with the crowd until we have time to do some real work."

"Have you ever stopped to think what alcohol does to your nervous system? If you can hold on a second we've got some pamphlets here you could read."

Tidwell started rummaging energetically in his flight bag.

"Ah . . . actually I've got to run now. Nice talking with you boys."

He edged backward, started away toward the bar, then turned, smiled, and made a beeline for the Men's Room.

Tidwell collapsed in laughter.

"Alcoholics . . . Oh Christ, Clancy, where do you come up with those?"

"Huh? Oh, just a quickie. It got rid of him, didn't it?"

"I'll say. Well, let's go before he comes back."

"Um, can we stall here for a few minutes, Steve?"

Tidwell stopped laughing in mid-breath.

"What is it? Trouble?"

"Nothing definite. Don't want to worry you if it's nothing. Just talk about something for a few minutes."

"Terrific. Remind me to fire you for insubordination.

How about that Aki? Do you believe he managed to keep his cool through all that crap?"

"Uh-huh."

"That Beckington is a real shit. If we weren't under contract, I'd like nothing better than realigning his face a little."

"Uh-huh."

"Dammit that's enough! If you don't tell me what's up, I'll cut your liquor allotment!"

"Well...we might have a little problem."

"Come on Clancy!"

"You saw where Beckington went?"

"Yeah, into the Men's Room. So?"

"So, Aki's in there."

"What?"

"Doubled back and ducked in while we were doing the A.A. bit with Beckington. Probably needed to take a pain killer."

"Who else is in there?"

"Just the two of them."

"Christ! You don't think Aki..."

"Not out here in the open, but it must be awfully tempting in there."

The two men studied the ceiling in silence for several moments. Still no one emerged from the Men's Room. Finally Tidwell heaved a sigh and started for the door. Clancy held up a hand.

"Come on Steve. Why not let him do..."

"Because we can't afford any attention. None at all. All we need is to have them detain all the Orientals in the airport for a police investigation. Now let's go!"

The mercenaries started for the door. Tidwell raised his hand to push his way in, and the door opened.

"Oh, hi boys. How's the 'dry' business? Just do me a favor and don't close down the bars until after I've left the country, know what I mean?"

"Um . . . Sure, Harry. Just for you—anything you say."

"Well, see you around."

He brushed past them and strode toward the bar.

Almost mechanically, the two mercenaries pushed open the door and entered the washroom. Aki looked up inquiringly as he dried his hand on a blo-jet.

"Um . . . are you okay Aki?"

"Certainly, Mr. Tidwell, why do you ask?"

The two men shifted uncomfortably.

"We . . . ah . . . we just thought that after what happened outside . . ."

Aki frowned for a moment, then suddenly smiled with realization.

"Ah! I see. You feared that I might . . . Mr. Tidwell, I am a mercenary under contract. Rest assured I would do nothing to draw needless attention to our force or myself."

"Tell the driver to slow up. It should be right along here somewhere."

"I still haven't seen the buses." Clancy scowled through the dust and bug-caked windshield of the truck.

"Don't worry they'll be . . . there they are!"

The buses were rounding the curve ahead bearing down on them with the leisurely pace characteristic of this country. Tidwell watched the vehicle occupants as they passed, craning his neck to see around the driver. The bus passengers smiled and waved joyously, but Tidwell noticed none of them had their cameras out.

The mercenaries smiled and waved back.

"The fix is in!" chortled Clancy.

"Did you see any empty seats?"

"One or two. Nothing noticeable."

"Good. Look, there it is up ahead."

Beside the road there was a small soft shoulder, one of the few along this hilly, jungled route. Without being told, the driver pulled off the road and stopped. They sat motionless for several long moments, then Aki stepped out of the brush and waved. At the signal, the driver cut the engine and got out of the car. The two mercenaries also piled out of the car, but unlike the driver who leisurely began taking off his shirt, strode around to the back of the truck and opened the twin doors. Two men in the back, men of approximately the same description and dressed identically to Tidwell and Clancy. They didn't say anything, but strode to the front of the truck and took the mercenaries' places in the cab. Like the driver, they had been briefed.

The two mercenaries turned their attention to the crates in the back. Aki joined them.

"Are the lookouts in place?"

"Yes, sir."

"You worry too much, Steve," chided Clancy. "We haven't seen another car on this road all day."

"I don't want this messed up by a bunch of gawking tourists."

"So we stop 'em. We've done it before and we've got the team to do it."

"And lose two hours covering up? No thanks."

"I'm going to check the teams. I'll send a couple back to give you a hand here."

He hopped out of the truck and strode down the road, entering the brush at the point where Aki had emerged.

Fifteen feet into the overgrowth was a clearing where the teams were undergoing their metamorphosis. Nine in the clearing, and one in the truck made ten. Two full teams, and the buses had looked full.

The team members were in various stages of dress and undress. One of the first things lost when the teams were formed was any vague vestige of modesty. The clothes had been cunningly designed and tailored. Linings were ripped from jackets and pants, false hems were removed, and the familiar kill-suits began to come into view.

Clancy arrived carrying the first case. He jerked his head and two already-clothed team members darted back toward the road. Clancy slit open the sealing tape with his pocket knife. He folded the flaps back, revealing a case of toy robots.

Easing them out onto the ground, he opened the false bottom where the swamp boots were kept. These were not new boots. They were the members' own broken-in boots. Clancy grabbed his pair and returned to a corner of the clearing to convert his clothes. One by one, the members claimed their boots and a robot and stooped to finish dressing.

Tidwell had worn his boots to speed the changing process. He whistled low and gestured, and a team member tossed him a robot. He caught it and opened the lid on its head in a practiced motion. Reaching in carefully, he removed the activator unit for his kill-suit and checked it carefully. Satisfied, he plugged it into his suit and rose to check the rest of the progress, resealing the lid on the robot and stacking it by the carton as he went.

Conversion was in full swing as more cartons arrived. The shoulder straps came off the camera gadget bags, separated, and were reinserted to form the backpacks. Fashionable belts with gaudy tooling were reversed to reveal a uniform black with accessory loops for weapons and ammunition.

Tidwell particularly wanted to check the weapons assembly. Packing material from the toy cartons was scooped into plastic bags, moistened with a fluid from the bottles in the camera bags, and the resulting paste pressed into molds previously covered by the boots to form rifle stocks. The camera tripods were dismounted, the telescoping legs separating for various purposes. First, the rounds of live ammo were emptied out and distributed. Tidwell smiled grimly at this. All the forces' weapons were "convertibles." That is, they were basically quartz crystal weapons, but were also rigged to fire live ammo if the other forces tried to disclaim their entry into the corporate wars.

The larger section of the legs separated into three parts, to form the barrels for both the flare pistols and the short double-barreled shotguns so deadly in close fighting. The middle sections were fitted with handles and a firing mechanism to serve as launchers for the minigrenades, which up to now had been carried in the 35mm film canisters hung from the pack straps.

The smallest diameter section was used for the rifle barrel, fitted with a fountain-pen telescopic sight. The firing mechanisms were cannibalized from the cameras and various toys which emerged and were reinserted into the cartons.

One carton only was not refilled with its original contents. This carton was filled with rubber daggers and swords, samurai swords. These were disbursed to the members, who used their fingernails to slice through and peel back the rubber coating to reveal the actual weapons, glittering in the sun. These were not rigged for use on the kill-suits.

The label on the empty box was pulled back to reveal another label declaring the contents camera parts, and the skeletons of the cannibalized cameras were loaded in, packed by the shreds of the outer clothing now torn to unrecognizable pieces.

The cartons were resealed and reloaded, and the truck was again sent along its way with a driver, two passengers, and a load of working toys and camera gear.

Tidwell watched it depart and smiled grimly. They were ready.

"Call in the lookouts, Clancy. We've got a long hike ahead of us."

"What's with Aki?"

The Oriental was running toward them waving excitedly.

"Sir! Mr. Yamada is on the radio."

"Yamada!"

"This could be trouble, Steve."

They returned hurriedly to the clearing where the team was gathered around the radio operator.

Tidwell grabbed the mike.

"Mr. Tidwell." Yamada's voice came through without static. "You are to proceed to the rendezvous point to meet with the other teams at all haste. Once there, do not, I repeat, do not carry out any action against the enemy until you have received further word from me."

Tidwell frowned, but kept his voice respectful.

"Message received. Might I ask why?"

"You are not to move against the enemy until we have determined who the enemy is."

"What the hell..."

"Shut up, Clancy. Please clarify, Mr. Yamada."

"At the moment, there is a cease-fire in effect on the war. The government of the United States has chosen to intervene."

CORPORATION WARS CHARGED

A federal grand jury was appointed today to investigate alleged involvement of several major corporations in open warfare with each other. The Corporations have refused to comment on charges that they have been maintaining armies of mercenaries on their payrolls for the express purpose of waging war on each other. Included on the list of corporations charged were several major oil conglomerates as well as communications and fishing concerns. The repercussions may be international as some of the corporations involved (continued on pg. 28)

CORPORATIONS DEFY ORDERS

In a joint press release issued this afternoon, the corporations under investigation for involvement in the alleged Corporate Wars flatly refused to comply with government directives to cease all hostilities toward each other of a warlike nature and refrain from any future activities. They openly challenge the government's authority to intervene in these conflicts, pointing out that the wars are not currently being conducted within the boundaries of the US or its territories.

They have asked the media to relay to the American people their counter-charges that the government is trying to pressure them into submission by threatening to move against the corporations' US holdings. They refer to those threats as "blatant extortion" being carried on in the name of justice, pointing out the widespread chaos which would be caused if their services to the nation were interrupted. (continued pg. 18)

AFRICANS JOIN
CORPORATE OPPOSITION

The League of African Nations added their support to the rapidly growing list of countries seeking to control the multinational corporations. With the addition of these new allies, virtually all major nations of the Free World are united in their opposition to the combined corporate powers. Plans are currently being formulated for a united armed intervention if the corporations continue to defy (continued pg. 12)

WORLDWIDE PROTESTS
SCHEDULED

Protest demonstrations are scheduled for noon tomorrow in every major city across the globe as citizen groups from all walks of life band together to voice their displeasure of the proposed governmental armed forces intervention in the Corporate Wars. War is perhaps the least popular endeavor governments embark on, and it is usually sold to the populace as a step necessary to ensure national security, a reason which many feel does not apply in this situation. Groups not usually prone to voicing protest have joined the movement, including several policemen's unions and civil service organizations. Government officials (cont. pg. 8)

COURT MARTIALS THREATENED

Armed Forces officials announced today that any military personnel taking part in the planned demonstrations will be arrested and tried for taking part in a political rally whether or not they are in uniform.

GOVERNMENT–CORPORATE TALKS SUSPENDED

Negotiation sessions seeking peaceful settlement between the Combined Corporations and the United Free World Governments came to an abrupt halt today when several government negotiators walked out of the sessions. Informed sources say that the eruption occurred as a result of an appeal on the part of the corporations to the governments to "call off a situation involving needless bloodshed which the government troops could not hope to win." It is believed that what they were alluding to were their alleged "superweapons," which the governments continue to discount. "A weapon is only as good as the man behind it" a

high-ranked US Army officer is quoted as
saying. "And we have the best troops in the
world." With scant hours remaining before
the deadline (continued pg. 7)

Lieutenant Worthington, US Army, was relieved
as the convoy pulled into the outskirts of town. He
only wished his shoulders would relax. They were still
tense to the point of aching.

He tried to listen to the voices of the enlisted men
riding in the back of the truck as they joked and sang,
but shrugged it off in irritation.

The bloody fools. Didn't they know they had been
in danger for the last hour? They were here to fight
mercenaries, hardened professional killers. There had
been at least a dozen places along the road through
the jungle that seemed to be designed for an ambush,
but the men chatted and laughed, seemingly oblivious
to the fact the rifles on their laps were empty.

The lieutenant shook his head. That was one
Army policy to which he took violent exception. He
knew that issuing ammunition only when the troops
were moving into a combat zone reduced accidents
and fatal arguments, but damn it for all intents and
purposed the whole country was a combat zone. It
was fine and dandy to make policies when you're
sitting safe and secure at the Pentagon desk looking
at charts and statistics, but it wasn't reassuring when
you're riding through potential ambush country with
an empty weapon.

He shot a guilty sidelong glance at the driver. He
wondered if the driver had noticed Worthington had a
live clip in his pistol—probably not. He had smuggled

it along and switched the clips in the john before they got on the trucks. Hell, even if he had noticed he probably wouldn't report him. He was probably glad that someone in the truck had a loaded weapon along.

They were in town now. The soldiers in back were whooping and shouting crude comments at the women on the sidewalk. Worthington glanced out the window, idly studying the buildings as they rolled past. Suddenly he stiffened.

There, at a table of a sidewalk café, were two mercenaries in the now-famous kill-suits, leisurely sipping drinks and chatting with two other men in civilian dress. The lieutenant reacted instantly.

"Stop the truck!"

"But sir..."

"Stop the truck, damn it!"

Worthington was out of the truck even before it screeched to a halt, fumbling his pistol from its holster. He ignored the angry shouts behind him as the men in back were tossed about by the sudden braking action and leveled his pistol at the mercenaries.

"Don't move, either of you!"

Still they ignored him. Worthington was starting to feel foolish, aware of the driver peering out the door behind him. He was about to repeat himself when one of the mercenaries noticed him. He tapped the other one on the arm, and the whole table craned their necks to look at the figure by the truck.

"You are to consider yourselves my prisoners. Put your hands on your head and face the wall!"

They listened to him, heads cocked in alert interest. When he was done, one of the mercenaries replied with a rude gesture of international significance. The others at the table rocked with laughter, then they returned to their conversation.

Worthington suddenly found himself ignored again. Reason vanished in a wave of anger and humiliation. Those bastards!

The gun barked and roared in his hand, startling him back to his senses. He had not intended to fire. His hand must have tightened nervously and...

Wait a minute! Where were the mercenaries? He shot a nervous glance around. The table was deserted, but he could see the two men in civilian clothes lying on the floor covering their heads with their arms. Neither seemed to be injured. Thank God for that! There would have been hell to pay if he shot a civilian. But where were the mercenaries?

The men were starting to pile out of the truck behind him, clamoring to know what was going on. One thing was sure, he couldn't go hunting mercenaries with a platoon of men with empty rifles. Suddenly a voice rang out from the far side of the street.

"Anybody hurt over there?"

"Clean miss!" rang out another voice from the darkened depths of the café.

The lieutenant squinted, but couldn't make out anyone.

"Are they wearing kill-suits?" came a third voice from further down the street.

"As a matter of fact, they aren't!" shouted another voice from the alley along side the café.

"That was live ammo?"

"I believe it was."

The men by the truck were milling about craning

their necks at the unseen voices. Worthington suddenly realized he was sweating.

"You hear that, boys? Live ammo!"

"Fine by us!"

The lieutenant opened his mouth, shouted something, anything, but it was too late. His voice was drowned out by the first ragged barrage. He had time to register with horror that it was not even a solid hail of bullets that swept their convoy. It was a vicious barrage of snipers, massed marksmen. One bullet, one soldier. Then a grenade went off under the truck next to him and he stopped registering things.

There was no doubt in anyone's mind as to the unfortunate nature of the incident. For one thing, one of the men in civilian clothes sharing a drink with the mercenaries was an Italian officer with the Combined Government Troops who corroborated the Corporation's claim the action was in response to an unprovoked attack by the convoy.

The fourth man was a civilian, a reporter with an international news service. His syndicated account of the affair heaped more fuel on an already raging fire of protest on the home fronts against the troops' intervention in the Corporate Wars.

Even so, the Corporations issued a formal note of apology to the Government Forces for the massacre. They further suggested that the government troops be more carefully instructed as to the niceties of off-hours behavior to avoid similar incidents in the future.

An angry flurry of memos did the rounds of the Government Forces trying vainly to find someone responsible for issuing the live ammo.

The mayor of the town was more direct and to the point. He withdrew the permission for the American troops to be quartered in the town, forcing them to bivouac outside the city limits. Further, he signed into law an ordinance forbidding the Americans from coming into town with any form of firearm, loaded or not, on their person.

This ordinance was rigidly enforced, and American soldiers in town were constantly subject to being stopped and searched by the local constables, to the delight of the mercenaries who frequently swaggered about with loaded firearms worn openly on their hips.

Had Lieutenant Worthington not been killed in the original incident, he would have doubtlessly been done in by the troops under him, then definitely by his superiors.

The sniper raised his head a moment to check the scene below before settling in behind the sights of his rifle.

The layout was as it had been described to him. The speaker stood at a microphone on a raised wooden platform in the square below him. The building behind him was a perfect backdrop. With the soft hollow-point bullets he was using there would be no ricochets to endanger innocent bystanders in the small crowd which had assembled.

Again he lowered his head behind the scope and prepared for his shot. Suddenly, there was the sound of a "tunggg" and he felt the rifle vibrate slightly. He snapped his head upright and blinked in disbelief at what he saw. The barrel of his rifle was gone, seared cleanly by some unseen force.

He rolled over to look behind him and froze. Three men stood on the roof behind him. He hadn't heard them approach. Two were ordinary looking, perhaps in better shape than the average person. The third was Oriental. It was the last man who commanded the sniper's attention. This was because of the long sword, bright in the sun, which the man was holding an inch in front of the sniper's throat.

The man behind the Oriental spoke.

"Hi guy! We've been expecting you."

The speaker was becoming redundant. The crowd was getting a little restless. Why did the man insist on repeating himself for the third and fourth time, not even bother to change his phrasing much?

Suddenly there was a stir at the outer edge of the crowd. Four men were approaching the podium with a purposeful stride, three men shoving the fourth as they came.

They bounded onto the platform, one taking the microphone over the speaker's protests.

"Sorry, Senator, but part of the political tradition is allowing equal time to opposing points of view."

He turned to the crowd.

"Good afternoon ladies and gentlemen. You've been very patient with the last speaker, so I'll try to keep this brief. I represent the Corporations the Senator here has been attacking so vehemently."

The crowd stirred slightly, but remained in place, their curiosity piqued.

"Now, you may be impressed with the senator's courage, attacking us so often publicly as he has been doing lately when it's known we have teams of assassins roaming the streets. We were impressed, too. We were also a bit curious. It seemed to us he was almost inviting an assassination attempt. However, we ignored him, trusting the judgment of the general public to see him as the loudmouthed slanderer he is."

The senator started forward angrily, but the man at the mike froze him with a glare.

"Then he changed. He switched from his pattern of half-truths and distortions that are a politician's stock and trade and moved into the realm of outright lies."

"This worried us a bit. It occurred to us that if someone did take a shot at him, that it would be blamed on us and give credence to all his lies. Because of this, we've been keeping a force of men on hand to guard him whenever he speaks to make sure nothing happened to him."

He paused and nodded to one of his colleagues. The man put his fingers in his mouth and whistled shrilly.

Immediately on the rooftops and in the windows of the buildings surrounding the square, groups of men and women stepped into view. They were all dressed in civilian clothes, but the timeliness of their appearance, as well as the uniform coldness with which they stared down at the crowd left no doubt that they were all part of the same team.

The man whistled again, and the figures disappeared. The man at the mike continued.

"So we kept watching the senator, and finally today we caught something. This gentleman has a rather interesting story to tell."

The sniper was suddenly thrust forward.

"What were you doing here today?"

"I want a lawyer. You can't..."

The Oriental twitched. His fist was a blur as it

flashed forward to strike the sniper's arm. The man screamed, but through it the crowd heard the bone break.

"What were you doing here today?" The questioner's voice was calm, as if nothing had happened.

"I..."

"Louder!"

"I was supposed to shoot at the senator."

"Were you supposed to hit him?"

"No," the man was swaying slightly from the pain in his arm.

"Who hired you?"

The man shook his head. The Oriental's fist lashed out again.

"The senator!" The man screamed.

A murmur ran through the crowd. The senator stepped hurriedly to the front of the platform.

"It's a lie!" he screamed. "They're trying to discredit me. They're faking it. That's one of their own men they're hitting. It's a fake."

The man with the microphone ignored him. Instead he pointed to a policeman in the crowd.

"Officer! There's usually a standing order about guarding political candidates. Why wasn't there anyone from the police watching those rooftops?"

The officer cupped his hands to shout back. "The senator insisted on minimum guards. He pulled rank on the chief."

The crowd stared at the senator who shrank back before their gaze. The man with the mike continued.

"One of the senator's claims is that the Corporations would do away with free speech. I feel we have proved this afternoon that that statement is a lie. However, our business, like any business, depends on public support, and we will move to protect it. As you all know, there's a war on."

He turned to glare at the senator.

"It is my personal opinion that we should make war on the warmakers. Our targets should be the people who send others out to fight. However, that is only my personal opinion. The only targets in my jurisdiction are front-line soldiers."

He looked out over the crowd again.

"Are there any reporters here? Good. When this man took money to discredit the Corporations, he became a mercenary, the same as us. As such, he falls under the rules of war. I would appreciate it if you would print this story as a warning to any other two-bit punks who think it would be a good idea to pose as a Corporate mercenary."

He nodded to his colleagues on the platform. One of the men gave the sniper a violent shove that sent him sprawling off the platform, drew a pistol from under his jacket, and shot him.

The policeman was suspended for allowing the mercenaries to leave unchallenged, a suspension that caused a major walk-off on the police force.

The senator was defeated in the next election.

The young Oriental couple ceased their conversation abruptly when they saw the group of soldiers, at least a dozen, on the sidewalk ahead of them. Without even consulting each other, they crossed the street to avoid the potential trouble. Unfortunately, the soldiers had also spotted them and also crossed the street to block their progress. The couple turned to retrace their steps, but the soldiers, shouting now, ran to catch them.

Viewed up close, it was clear the men had been drinking. They pinned the couple in a half circle, backing them against a wall, where the two politely inquired as to what the soldiers wanted.

The soldiers admitted it was the lady who was the reason for their attention and invited her to accompany them as they continued on their spree.

The lady politely declined, pointing out that she already had an escort.

The soldiers waxed eloquent, pointing out the numerous and obvious shortcomings of the lady's escort, physically and probably financially. They allowed as how the fourteen of them would be better able to protect the lady from the numerous gentlemen of dubious intent she was bound to encounter on the street. Furthermore, they pointed out that even though their finances were admittedly depleted by their drinking, that by pooling their money they could doubtless top any price her current escort had offered for her favors.

At this, her escort started forward to lodge a protest, but she laid a gentle restraining hand on his arm and stepped forward smiling. She pointed out that the soldiers were perhaps mistaken in several of their assumptions about the situation at hand.

First, they were apparently under the impression that she was a call girl, when in truth, she was gainfully employed by the Corporate forces.

Second, her escort for the evening was not a paying date, but rather her brother. Finally, she pointed out that while she thanked them for their concern and their offer, she was more than capable of taking care of herself.

By the time she was done explaining this last point, the soldiers had become rearranged. Their formation was no longer in a half circle, but rather scattered loosely for several yards along the street. Also, their position in that formation was horizontal rather than vertical.

Her explanation complete, the lady took her brother's arm and they continued on their way.

As they walked, one of the soldiers groaned and tried to rise. She drove the high heel of her shoe into his forehead without breaking stride.

Julian rolled down his window as the service station attendant came around to the side of his car.

"Fill it up with premium."

The attendant peered into the back seat of the car. "Who do you work for, sir?"

"Salesman for a tool and die company."

"Got any company ID?"

"No, it's a small outfit. Could you fill it up, I'm in a hurry."

"Could you let me see a business card or your samples? If you're a salesman..."

"All right, all right. I'll admit it. I work for the government. But..."

The attendant's face froze into a mask.

"Sorry, sir." He started to turn away.

"Hey, wait a minute!" Julian sprang out of the car and hurried to catch up with the retreating figure. "Come on, give me a break. I'm a crummy clerk. It's not like I had any say in the decisions."

"Sorry, sir, but..."

"It's not like I'm on official business. I'm trying to get to my sister's wedding."

The attendant hesitated.

"Look, I'd like to help you, but if the home office found out we sold gas to a government employee, they'd pull our franchise."

"Nobody would have to know. Just look the other way for a few minutes and I'll pump it myself."

The man shook his head.

"Sorry, I can't risk it."

"I'll give you $50 for half a tank of..."

But the attendant was gone.

Julian heaved a sigh and got back into his car. Once he left the station, though, his hangdog mask slipped away.

Things were going well with the fuel boycott. It had been three weeks since he had had to report a station for breaking the rules. He checked his list for the location of the next station to check out.

The mercenary was wearing a jungle camouflage kill-suit. The hammock he was sprawled in was also jungle camouflage as was the floppy brimmed hat currently obscuring his face as a sunscreen. He was snoring softly, seemingly oblivious to the insects buzzing around him.

"Hey Sarge!"

The slumbering figure didn't move.

"Hey Sarge!" The young private repeated without coming closer. Even though he was new, he wasn't dumb enough to try to wake the sleeping mercenary by shaking him.

"What is it, Turner?" his voice had the tolerant tone of one dealing with a whining child.

"The tank. You know, the one the detectors have been tracking for the last five hours? You said to wake you if it got within 500 meters. Well, it's here."

"Okay, you woke me up. Now let me go back to sleep. I'm still a little rocky from going into town last night."

The private fidgeted.

"But aren't we going to do anything?"

"Why should we? They'll never find us. Believe in your infrared screens, my son, believe."

He was starting to drift off to sleep again. The private persisted.

"But Sarge! I . . . uh . . . well I thought we might . . . well, my performance review's coming up next week."

"Qualifying, huh? Well, don't worry. I'll give you my recommendation."

"I know, but I thought . . . well . . . you know how much more they notice your record if you've seen combat."

The sergeant sighed.

"All right. Is it rigged for quartz beams?"

"The scanners say no."

"Is Betsy tracking it?"

"Seems to be. Shall I . . ."

"Don't bother, I'll get it."

Without raising his hat to look, the sergeant extended a leg off the hammock. The far end of his hammock was anchored on a complex mass of machinery, also covered with camouflaging. His questing toe found the firing button, which he prodded firmly. The machine hummed to life and from its depths a beam darted out to be answered by the chill *whimp* of an explosion in the distance.

The private was impressed.

"Wow, hey, thanks Sarge."

"Don't mention it, kid."

"Say, uh, Sarge?"

"What is it, Turner?"

"Shouldn't we do something about the infantry support?"

"Are they coming this way?"

"No, it looks like they're headed back to camp, but shouldn't we..."

"Look, kid," the sergeant was drifting off again. "Lemme give you a little advice about those performance reviews. You don't want to load too much stuff onto 'em. The personnel folk might get the idea it's too easy."

That evening the news on the Corporate Wars was the news itself. It seemed some underling at the FCC had appeared on a talk show and criticized the lack of impartiality shown by the media in their reporting on the Corporate Wars.

News commentators all across the globe pounced on that item as if they had never had anything to talk about before. They talked about freedom of speech. They talked about attempted government control of the media. They talked about how even public service corporations like the media were not safe from the clumsy iron fist of government intervention.

But one and all, they angrily defended their coverage of the Corporate Wars. The reason, they said, that there were so few reports viewing the Government troop efforts in a favorable light was that there was little if anything favorable to be said for their unbroken record of failures.

This was followed by a capsule summary of the Wars since the government stepped in. Some television channels did a half-hour special on the ineptitude of the Government efforts. Some newspapers ran an entire supplement, some bitter, some sarcastic, but all pointing out the dismal incompetence displayed by the governments.

The man from the FCC was dismissed from his post.

The blood-warm waters of the Brazilian river were a welcome change from the deadly iciness of the Atlantic. The two frogmen, nearly invisible in their camouflage kill-suits and bubbleless rebreather units, were extremely happy with the new loan labor program between the Corporate mercenaries.

One of the men spotted a turtle and tapped the other's arm, gesturing for him to circle around and assist in its capture. His partner shook his head. This might have the trappings of a vacation, but they were still working. They were here on assignment and they had a job to do. The two men settled back in the weeds on the river bottom and waited.

It was oven-hot in the armor-encased boat. The Greek officer in command mopped his brow and spoke in angry undertones to the men with him in the craft. It was hot, but this time there would be no mistakes. He peered out of the gun slit at the passing shore as the boat whispered soundlessly upstream.

This time they had the bastards cold. He had the best men and the latest equipment on this mission, and a confirmed target to work with. This time it would be the laughing mercenaries who fell.

"Hello the boats?"

The men froze and looked at each other as the amplified voice echoed over the river.

"Yoo-hoo! We know you're in there."

The officer signaled frantically. One of his men took over the controls of the automount machine gun and peered into the periscope. The officer put his mouth near the gun slit, taking care to stand to one side of the view.

"What do you want?"

"Before you guys start blasting away, you should know we have some people from the World Press out here with us."

The officer clenched his fist in frustration. He shot a glance at his infrared sonar man who shrugged helplessly; there was no way he could sort out which blips were soldiers and which were reporters.

"We were just wondering," the voice continued, "if you were willing to be captured or if we're going to have to kill you?"

The officer could see it all now. The lead on the target had been bait for a trap. The mercenaries were going to win again. Well, not this time. This boat had the latest armor and weaponry. They weren't going to surrender without a fight.

"You go to hell!" he screamed and shut the gun slit.

The mercenary on shore turned to the reporters and shrugged.

"You'd better get your heads down."

With that, he triggered the remote control detonator switch on his control box, and the frogmen-planted charges removed the three boats from the scene.

✧   ✧   ✧

The mercenary doubled over, gasping from the agony of his wounds. The dark African sky growled a response as lightning danced in the distance. He glanced up at it through a pink veil of pain.

Damn Africa! He should have never agreed to this transfer.

He gripped his knife again and resumed his task. Moving with the exaggerated precision of a drunk, he cut another square of sod from the ground and set it neatly next to the others.

Stupid! Okay, so he had gotten lost. It happens. But damn it, it wasn't his kind of terrain.

He sank the knife viciously into the ground and paused as a wave of pain washed over him from the sudden effort.

Walking into an enemy patrol—that was unforgivably careless but he had been so relieved to hear voices.

He glanced at the sky again. He was running out of time. He picked up his rifle and started scraping up handfuls of dirt from the cleared area.

Well, at least he got 'em. He was still one of the best in the world at close, fast pistol work, but there had been so many.

He sagged forward again as pain flooded his mind. He was wounded in at least four places. Badly wounded. He hadn't looked to see how badly for fear he would simply give up and stop moving.

He eased himself forward until he was sitting in the shallow depression, legs straight in front of him. Laying his rifle down beside him, he began lifting the pieces of sod and placing them on his feet and legs, forming a solid carpet again.

He head swam with pain. When he had gotten

lost, his chances of survival had been low. Now they were zero.

But he had gotten them all. He clung to that as he worked, lying now and covering his bloody chest.

And by God, they weren't going to have the satisfaction of finding his body. The coming rain would wash away his trail of blood and weld the sod together again.

If they ever claimed a mercenary kill, it was going to be because they earned it and not because he had been stupid enough to get lost.

The rain was starting to fall as he lifted the last piece of sod in place over his face and shoulders.

Tidwell frowned as he scanned the bar. Damn! Where was Clancy? This was the fourth bar he had been in looking for his drinking partner. It wasn't like Clancy to be this elusive.

He started to leave, then a figure caught his eye. Was it...it was! Clancy! Tidwell wondered why he hadn't seen his friend in his earlier scan, then realized with a start that this was the first time he had ever seen Clancy's back.

"Good news, Clancy!" he announced dropping into a vacant seat at the table.

"Oh, hi Steve!"

"It's been finalized! A fat percent increase for fighting the government's boy scouts! Is that a gift?"

Clancy mumbled something.

"How's that again?"

"I said that's terrific."

Tidwell cocked a sharp eye at his friend.

"You all right, Clancy?"

"Me? Sure, why?"

"I dunno. You seem to be taking the news pretty calmly. The only times I've seen you act calm if there was any other option was when you were drunk, thinking deep thoughts, negotiating a contract, or all three."

His gentle prodding was rewarded by a wry smile from his friend.

"Guilty as charged, Steve."

"Which?"

"Well, I haven't been offered another contract if that's what's bothering you. As for the other two, I've been drinking a little and thinking a lot."

Tidwell signaled for a round of drinks.

"That can be a dangerous combination, Clancy. Do you want to talk it out?"

Clancy leaned back, sipping at the remnants of his drink.

"How would you say the war's going, Steve?"

"Well..." Tidwell scowled in mock consideration. "It's my studied and learned opinion that we're kicking the hell out of them."

"And you think that's good?"

"What do you mean, 'do I think that's good?' That's what we're getting paid to do isn't it?"

"Let me put it differently. Do you think we'll win?"

"You said it yourself, there's no contest! They can't even find us unless we want 'em to, and we only want 'em to when we're sure we'll win. We may not be able to win the war, but we can run 'em in circles until they quit. The worst we could get out of it is a draw."

"Then what?"

"Huh?"

"I said then what? What happens when the governments back down?"

Tidwell lapsed into thought, only to be interrupted by the arrival of their drinks.

"I really don't know, Clancy," Tidwell resumed after the waitress retreated. "I've never really thought that far ahead."

"Well maybe you'd better start. First off, it won't be a draw from the government's viewpoint. Either they win it, or they've lost. They've issued orders, made laws, whatever, that the corporations have refused to obey. Right now, their armies are trying to enforce those orders. If they can't enforce it, they're dead. Any governing body that can't enforce its orders loses the ability to issue orders."

"Then who would..."

"The corporations, that's who. They're the ones with the power now, military as well as economic."

"So what? We've picked the right side."

"Have we? Steve, would you really want to live in a world controlled by the corporations?"

Tidwell shrugged and sipped his drink. He was getting a bit annoyed.

"Frankly, I don't see that it would be much different than the world we're in right now."

"Controls, Steve!" Clancy was leaning forward now.

"If the governments lose the war, there will only be the corporations, one power with no counter balance, no court of appeals. If you get blacklisted by the corporations, you don't work, period!"

Tidwell shook his head.

"That's too heavy for me, Clancy. Like I told you before, I'm just a soldier, and I don't..."

"Bullshit!" Clancy was looming over Tidwell in his anger. "I'm just a soldier... I'm just a housewife...

I'm just an executive . . . I'm just a kid . . . Bullshit! Nobody's responsible for anything. Everybody's just earning a living, just following orders, just looking out for themselves. I'm telling you, Steve, unless people stop taking the easy route, unless we start thinking instead of letting other people think for us, unless we do it now, we may not ever get a chance to think!"

"If you are quite through, Mister Clancy . . ." their eyes glared into each other. "It's too late for all that crap. Too late. The governments are finished. The corporations are going to get a chance at running the world."

"I don't think it's going to be all that great a world, Steve."

"We'll see, buddy," Tidwell said. Then he smiled, slowly. "If we don't like it . . ."

"Yeah?"

"We're soldiers, aren't we? There'll be work for us to do."

You Never Call

ROBERT LYNN ASPRIN

The two fleets maneuvered subtly as they drew ominously closer. The crowd would have held its breath in anticipation ... if there had been a crowd to witness the spectacle ... or if there were breath for it to hold in the vacuum of outer space.

On the bridge of the Terran flagship, the crew waited in nervous silence. Steely-eyed, with his jaw set in stern determination, the human commander's authoritative pose would have sent any artist scrambling for his or her sketch pad. Without unclenching his teeth, he nodded to his communications officer to open the hailing frequency.

An annoying shrill whistle sounded as the enemy's image swam into focus on the main view screen. While to the untutored human eye, it might look like just another huge reptile in a uniform, the commander was a seasoned space veteran and could readily recognize the individual differences of several alien races.

"Well, Zoltron?" he said harshly. "Have you reconsidered your position? This is your last chance to avoid needless bloodshed. Will you relinquish your claim on this sector and withdraw your forces?"

His rival's response was a sharp bark of laughter.

"Really, Raymond. I thought you knew us better, or at least that you knew me. Did you really expect me to back down from a threat?"

"That's 'Commander Stone,' under the circumstances," the commander spat back. "And I thought you knew us better, Zoltron. Did you think I was bluffing? You have five minutes to begin your withdrawal. Then we open fire."

On the screen, Zoltron stared back for several seconds in silence before speaking.

"We've been friends for a long time, Raymond," he said softly, his voice heavy with regret.

The Terran commander hesitated as years of memories flashed through his mind. Memories of happier days before the alliance fell apart... of shared holidays and family outings... of how he was first surprised, the friendship with this non-human counterpart.

Then the moment passed.

"Times change, Zoltron," he said firmly. "We aren't the first friends that politics have set against each other, nor will we be the last. We used to kid about what would happen if someday we found ourselves on opposite sides. Well, it would seem that day has come. You have five minutes."

Another curt nod and the screen reverted to its original display showing the opposing fleet hanging motionless in space.

"Well, that's that," the commander said, almost to himself. Then he hardened his tones to the firm voice of command.

"Pass the word! Battle stations!"

"Battle stations aye, sir!"

"Sir!" It was his communications officer again. "There's a call coming in on subspace."

A frown flashed across the commander's face as he both felt and hid his irritation at this unexpected interruption.

What in heaven's name could that be? A late change in orders from Command Central?

"Patch it through," he said, trying to sound calm and unruffled.

Again came the annoying whistle.

"Commander Stone here," he said, knowing that subspace communications did not allow visual exchanges.

There was a moment's silence, then a tentative voice came from the speakers.

"Raymie? Is that you?"

The crew exchanged startled glances, then looked at their commander who was staring at the speakers in what could only be described as frozen horror.

"Mom?" he said, at last.

"There you are, Raymie." The unseen voice was now confident. "I was just calling to see if everything was all right with you."

"Mom, what are you doing calling me here?" The commander shot an uncomfortable look at his crew, who were now steadfastly ignoring the exchange. "It must be costing you a fortune to call me direct."

"It's not cheap, but I'll manage." The vast void of space was not sufficient to mask the martyrdom in his mother's tones. "It's worth it just to hear from you."

"What do you want, Mom? I'm kind of busy right now."

"I know, I know. My son, the big-shot fleet commander. I could grow old and die before you found time to call me on your own."

"That's right. I'm busy," the commander grumbled. "And right now is a very bad time for me. So if you can just tell me what it is you want?"

"I just wanted to check to see if you were all right," his mother said. "I mean, it's Mother's Day and I hadn't heard from you. So I thought there might be something wrong."

"Nothing's wrong, Mom. I'm fine. Really. It's just been a very busy day...and it's about to get busier in a few minutes."

"I knew it had to be something important. I mean, after you didn't call on my birthday...and couldn't find time to come home for Christmas, I knew that you wouldn't let Mother's Day go by without calling unless something life or death came up."

"As a matter of fact, it is a matter of life or death, Mom," the commander said. "We're about to go into battle in a few minutes, and I have a lot to do before we start. So if there's nothing else..."

"You're what? Going into battle?"

"That's right, Mom. So..."

"On Mother's Day??"

"Come on, Mom. It's not like I planned it this way. It's just how it happened. Okay?"

"NO, it's not okay! And don't take that tone with me, Raymond!"

"But Mom..."

"'But Mom' nothing! You listen to me, Raymond. I've accepted that you're working in the fleet now, and that on any day you could get blown up or shot down or whatever it is that you do to each other. I haven't liked it, but I've accepted it. A mother has to let her children make their own choices, however painful it may be."

"Mom . . ."

"Now you tell me that you're going into battle, maybe get yourself killed, on the one day of the year set aside for mothers? I've never heard of anything so inconsiderate or heartless. You want me to spend the rest of my life remembering Mother's Day as the day my son got himself killed? I won't hear of it!"

"So what am I supposed to do? Call it off? Because it would make my mother unhappy?"

"Is that so much to ask? Oh, I suppose if making your mother happy isn't enough of a reason, you can say that you ran out of fuel or something. Just promise me that you'll postpone this war or whatever of yours until tomorrow or next week."

"But Mom . . ."

"I don't ask you for much, Raymie, but I'm asking for this. I want your solemn promise . . . and I'll sit right here on this communicator until I get it."

"I . . . I'll see what I can do."

"PROMISE!"

"ALL RIGHT, ALL RIGHT. I PROMISE!"

"There. Now that wasn't so hard, was it? Well, I've got to go now myself. Wish your mother a happy Mother's Day!"

"Happy Mother's Day, Mom."

The commander's voice and face were expressionless for this salutation, and remained so after the shrill whistle signaled the end of the exchange.

After a long silence, he turned to his communications officer.

"Get me Zoltron on the hailing frequency."

Again, the enemy commander's face swam into focus on the main screen.

"Commander Zoltron. I don't know how to say this, but..."

"Let me help you, Commander Stone," Zoltron said. "Your mother has made you promise to postpone our engagement for a least one day."

Raymond joined his crew in staring at the screen in shock.

"How...how did you know that?" he managed at last.

"Simple, commander. I just received a similar call from my mother. It seems your mother called her to find out your ship code so that she could call you. To further shorten our exchange, allow me to inform you that my own mother exacted a similar promise from me."

"Really? I didn't know your empire celebrated Mother's Day at all, much less that the days were identical."

"We don't," Zoltron grimaced. "Apparently after your mother explained to my mother the reason for her call, my mother thought it was such a good idea that she's adopting the holiday personally."

"Gee. I'm sorry about that."

"It could be worse. I'm only afraid that she'll pass it along to other mothers in the Empire. By this time next year, it could be a legitimate Empire holiday. In case you didn't know it, our mothers hold no less sway than yours do."

"Hmmm. Tell you what, Zollie. Did you and your ships have anything planned for the rest of the day... except this battle, I mean?"

"Not really. We had kind of figured this would be it. In fact, we left our schedules open in case it ran long."

"Tell you what. There's a neutral refueling station not far form here, and I know the bar never closes. What say you and your crews join us in hoisting a few?"

"Sounds good to me. Just be sure everyone on your side joins you in swearing to the Mother's Day truce, and I'll do the same with mine."

"No problem...but why?"

"Well, I figure if nothing else, it will eliminate the chance of interservice brawls once the drinking gets serious. It will be hard enough to explain to our respective superiors why we don't fight today without also having to explain to our mothers if we did end up squaring off."

"Amen to that!"

Con Job

ROBERT LYNN ASPRIN

The hotel room was American generic. Perhaps a bit larger and better decorated than most, but after all, this was the Hyatt in downtown Atlanta. Not so much better, though, as to justify the inflated room, room service, and drink prices the hotel charged. Especially at times like now when they were hosting a large convention.

Max spent most of his time on the road, and often wondered exactly why it was that his fellow travelers, businessmen and vacationers, would be willing to pay such high prices for impersonal rooms, short pour drinks, and mediocre food. The only answer he had come up with was that the situation was pretty much the same all across the country, so people became blind to how much they were paying for how little. Either that or they were willing to pay premium prices just to get away from wherever it was they called home.

Max knew exactly why he was willing to eat the expense. He was planning to make it all back, and then some, by the end of the long Labor Day weekend. He wasn't a businessman or a vacationer. Max was a professional thief and scam artist.

To be more exact, he was part of a team that toured the country, following the crowds and the money they brought to sports events, conventions, and festivals. While they had never worked a science fiction/fantasy media convention before, how different could it be? A crowd was a crowd, and the people that make up a crowd are notoriously careless with their money when away from home.

This DragonCon was supposed to draw somewhere between thirty and thirty-five thousand people. While they had worked bigger events before, they should be able to turn a tidy profit here.

He started to reach for the phone, then changed his mind. It would be better to get in the habit of using the cell phones. While today's computerized switchboards made it harder to listen in on conversations, there was no sense in getting careless. Reminding himself to keep his unit recharged, he flipped open his cell phone and cued up a number from his memory file.

"HELLO?" came the shouted response.

"Yeah, Doc. It's me, Max. Pass the word around the team that I've got Briar Patch established. It'll be room 912."

"WHAT ROOM?"

"Nine twelve."

"FIVE TWELVE?"

"Negative. That's NINE twelve."

"NINE TWELVE. GOT IT."

"Where are you, anyway? It sounds noisy at your end."

"I'M IN THE PARASOL. THAT'S THE LOBBY BAR AT THE HYATT. IT'S KIND OF A MADHOUSE DOWN HERE."

"What are you doing there?"

"JUST THOUGHT I'D SCOUT THE LAY OF THE LAND A LITTLE. YOU SHOULD SEE IT DOWN HERE."

"I thought the convention didn't start until tomorrow."

"IT DOESN'T. A LOT OF THE ATTENDEES HAVE ROLLED IN EARLY. WHY DON'T YOU COME DOWN AND I'LL BUY YOU A DRINK."

"No thanks. I think I'll turn in early so I'm rested tomorrow. Besides, I thought we agreed we shouldn't be seen together too much."

"BELIEVE ME, MAX, NO ONE WOULD NOTICE."

"Yeah, well, don't forget to get some sleep yourself. Oh, and while you're down there, see if you can pick up a program schedule for me. Top priority."

Max stared at the phone for several moments after ending the call.

Doc had sounded a bit strange, even for Doc. Of course, Doc had been the one to question this job when it was first proposed.

"DragonCon?" he had said. "That's one of the biggest multimedia cons in the country, if not *the* biggest."

"What? You've been to it before?" someone had asked.

"No, but I've heard of it. It's big."

"C'mon, Doc. We've worked Superbowls before. Weekend-long partying crowds are our bread and butter."

Doc had shaken his head.

"Yeah, but these are fans," he said.

"Overaged Trekkies in homemade costumes. So what? They can't be any worse than sports jocks."

"If you say so." Doc had shrugged, and they had moved on with their plans.

Maybe Doc was more familiar with these events than he had let on. Maybe that's why he seemed to be "going native." They'd just have to keep an eye on him and remind him to stay focused.

Check in _had_ taken a bit longer than normal, but Max had shrugged it off as being the regular early rush at a big convention. In some ways, he had been lucky to even get a room at one of the main hotels. That's why they were resorting to the "briar patch" system.

One of the crew's usual tactics was to hire someone locally to infiltrate the hotel staff a few weeks before the event, preferably in reservations or on front desk. That would get them a master key to the rooms and access to room bookings.

This time, however, it turned out that all the rooms had been booked solid months in advance. Fortunately, with their man in place, they had managed to highjack a cancellation and put it in Max's name. Or, at least, the name he was using this weekend. Unfortunately, they could only manage one room, so they would be using this as their base of operations, their "briar patch" for the weekend.

The rest of the crew would be using it to change outfits and to stash various things it would be wisest not to carry with them constantly—like large amounts of cash or identifiable items that fell into their possession during the course of the job.

That also meant that someone would have to be in the room at all times, both to let people in and out, and to keep housekeeping from coming in and finding the very things they wanted to keep quiet. Max had been elected as room sitter and coordinator for the crew, though he expected to be relieved from time to time.

It was a system that had worked for them in the past, and there was no reason not to expect it to work now.

The next day, Max was roused by a knock on his door. It was Doc bearing, among other things, a Styrofoam takeout food box and a cardboard beverage cup.

"Morning, Max," he said gaily. "Wanted to drop off that program schedule you wanted and swung through the food court on the way to pick you up some breakfast. Wasn't sure if they had in-room coffee makers here, so I brought you some wake-up juice as well."

"'Preciate it, Doc," Max said, seizing the coffee. "What does the event schedule look like?"

"Big," Doc said, with a shrug. "It's like I told you coming into this thing. What do you want a schedule for, anyway?"

Max frowned at him.

"I thought we went over this in the planning sessions," he said. "If we're going to hit some of the guest rooms, we need to know when they'll be out. The professional guests are most likely to be traveling with extra money and valuables, and the schedule tells us when they're slated for appearances, so we know they won't be in their rooms. All we need to do now is pass a list of their names to our plant at the front desk, and he can tell us what rooms they're in."

"Well, you'd better start on that fast, then," Doc said, shaking his head. "Registration is up to their eyebrows with check-ins, and someone is bound to notice if he tries to take an hour off to look up specific room bookings. He'll have to work it in a bit at a time."

"You think it will take him an hour?" Max frowned.

"Easy," Doc said. "There are something like eight hundred professional guests at this thing. You'll see when you try to sort out the schedule. There are fourteen or fifteen separate lines of programming running hourly starting at nine in the morning and going on until midnight or later. I don't envy you the job of sorting out who's going to be where and when."

Max rubbed a hand across his mouth and scowled.

"Maybe we'd be better off focusing on the attendees," he said. "I'm sure there are some major events that most of them will be attending. That might be a good time to hit the rooms."

"I don' know," Doc said. "The costume competition is probably the best attended, but not everyone goes to that. I heard they cover it with closed-circuit television, so people can watch it in their rooms or in the bar."

"This just gets better and better," Max said, shaking his head.

"Well, here's another little goodie to try planning around," Doc said. "After today, maybe even as soon as tonight, security will only let people into the various main hotels if they have convention membership badges."

"What? They can't do that!" Max said. "What about someone like me who's a paid, registered guest of the hotel but not registered for the convention?"

"You'll probably have to work something with hotel security," Doc said. "Of course, that will draw attention to yourself as someone who's wandering through the hotel who isn't a member of the convention . . ."

". . . and we don't want that," Max finished for him. "We'll just have to get convention badges for everyone."

"I was afraid you were going to say that." Doc sighed.

"What's wrong?"

"Well, there's about a three-hour wait in line to register for the convention," Doc said, "plus it costs something like a hundred dollars apiece. That'll run our overhead for this job right through the ceiling."

Max stared at him.

"Doc, we're thieves," he said carefully. "I didn't say 'buy us all memberships.' *Steal* us some badges. Got it?"

"Got it," Doc said with a nod,

"I can't believe how tight a lid they're trying to keep on this thing," Max grumbled. "Who are they expecting, anyway? The Pope?"

"No. He was a guest two years ago," Doc said.

Max stared at him.

"I told you it was a big convention." Doc shrugged.

"You're kidding. Right?" Max said at last.

"As a matter of fact, I am." Doc grinned. "But it's still a big convention."

Max heaved a sigh.

"Okay. You got me, that time."

"Sure," Doc said. "If you bothered to check their website, you'd know the Pope canceled two months ago."

"Website?" Max said. "This thing has a website?"

Doc gave him a hard look.

"Max, my nephew has his own website. You might try living in this decade sometime."

"Yeah, well, they teach kids all kinds of stuff in college these days." Max grimaced.

"That's true enough," Doc said. "But my nephew's still in junior high. Well, I'd better start working on getting us those badges."

He headed for the door.

"The Pope canceled two months ago?" Max said, the comment finally sinking in. But Doc was already gone.

But Max's day was just beginning.

The next ones to check in at Briar Patch were Allen and Alexis, the brother/sister team of pickpockets. They both seemed a bit down at the mouth, which was surprising—particularly for Alexis. She was petite and curvaceous and always seemed to glow with sunny innocence. It was part of what made her the perfect distracter and let her brother do his work unnoticed.

"What's the trouble?" Max said. "You two look as if they just made petty theft a capital crime."

"It's this job," Allen said. "I'll tell you, Max, I'm about ready to throw in the towel. Pack it in and write the whole thing off as a bad caper."

"Is it the badges?" Max said. "They can't be *that* hard to liberate."

"No. In fact, that was easy. Here, we even got an extra for you in case you decide to wander around a little," Allen said, handing over a laminated rectangle on a lanyard. "We didn't even have to steal them. Doc figured out an angle. You see, if someone loses their badge, they go back to registration and report it, show some identification, and are issued a new badge for a token penalty fee. All we had to do is buy some badges from attendees for twenty bucks over the penalty fee. We get badges and they get replacement badges and a profit."

"Isn't that kind of crooked?" Max said.

"Well, duh. We are supposed to be thieves, aren't we?"

"I meant for the attendees."

"So?" Allen shrugged. "It's not like we have an exclusive on being crooked."

"Then what *is* the problem?" Max pressed. "I think that with crowds like this, the two of you would make out like bandits, if you'll excuse the expression."

"You haven't seen the crowds," Allen said. "There are a lot of costumes out there—and I mean a *lot*. It's hard to pick a pocket when all they're wearing is a spangled G-string and some glitter. If nothing else, it kills Little Sister's bit as a distraction. With so much flesh parading around, she barely rates a glance."

Max suddenly realized why Alexis seemed depressed.

"And that's not the worst of it," Allen continued. "Right along with the costumes everywhere, there are the photographers."

"Photographers?" Max said.

"So many of them that sometimes it's hard to move across the lobby," Allen confirmed. "They're mostly focusing on the costumers, but they're bound to get some of the crowd in the pictures as well. All we need is to have some sharp-eyed bunko expert spot us in a bunch of pictures and the balloon will go up big time."

"Well, if you two haven't been working, then what's all this?" Max said, waving a hand at the shopping bags the two had brought in with them.

"Alexis decided we should hit the Dealers' Room," Allen said.

"Dealers' Room?"

"It's kind of like a huge flea market," Allen explained. "There are three ballroom-sized rooms full of tables and booths selling just about anything. They've got T-shirts, DVDs, swords, capes, jewelry, posters, games, and masks. It's really quite impressive."

"If you can't beat 'em, join 'em," Alexis put in.

"I'm not going to let a bunch of bimbos in wings and bondage rigs make me look like a wallflower. I picked up a few items that will put them in their place and put me back in position as the team's distracter."

"A few items?" Max said, eyeing the bags and trying not to picture Alexis in a spangled G-string. "Say, wait a minute. How many of those dealers are taking plastic and how many are only accepting cash?"

"I haven't the foggiest," Allen said. "To be honest, I wasn't paying attention. Why?"

"I just thought of a new angle for getting some money out of this job." Max smiled. "Hang on a second."

He grabbed his cell phone and called Doc.

"Hey, Doc," he said when the other answered, "I've got an assignment for you."

"Can it wait a half hour to an hour?" Doc said. "I'm in the autograph line right now."

"Autograph line?" Max said.

"Yeah. They've got a whole Hall of Fame here full of actors and actresses from the movies and television series," Doc explained. "Some of my favorite Scream Queens from the B-films are here signing pictures of themselves and I want to meet them and pick up a couple souvenirs."

Max rubbed his forehead between his eyes.

"Well, when you get done there, I want you to scout the Dealers' Room," he said. "Watch to see which ones are only taking cash, and try to get their names. If we can find out what rooms they're in, it might be a better score than trying to go after the professional guests. Okay?"

There was only silence.

"Doc?"

"Yeah, I'm here, Max," came the reply. "I just got distracted for a moment. There's a Klingon and an Imperial Storm Trooper squaring off for duel."

"Did you hear what I said?"

"Sure. Dealers' Room. Look for cash only. Get names," Doc recited. "I'm on it."

"Check in with me when you're done," Max said, and broke the connection.

Staring at the phone, he shook his head.

"Autograph line," he muttered under his breath.

The day didn't get any better.

Several members of the team never checked in and weren't answering their phones. Max wasn't sure if that was because they had been picked up by the authorities, quit the job in disgust, or had been lured off by the various attractions of the convention.

The members that did check in were mostly discouraged by their lack of success, though nearly all admitted to being distracted by the convention attendees.

It was nearly eight o'clock when Doc knocked on the door again. Max was not smiling as he let him in.

"It's been over six hours," he said coldly.

"Yeah, well, it's worth your life to catch an elevator," Doc said, putting down his bags and packages.

"Elevators," Max said flatly.

"It's a mob scene what with everyone trying to get somewhere else," Doc said. "It must have taken me half an hour to get up here. Anyway, I brought you some dinner."

"That's half an hour," Max said, accepting the bag of food. "I want to hear about the other five and a half hours."

"Well, it took me another two hours to finish up in the Hall of Fame," Doc said, flopping down in a chair. "Then I hit the Dealers' Room like you told me. Man, that Dealers' Room is really something."

"I notice you made a few purchases," Max said, gesturing at the collection of stuff piled on the floor.

"Okay, I'll admit. I got sucked in a little," Doc said. "But really, you should see the stuff they have down there. I figure I'm all set for Christmas. I picked up some T-shirts and a couple Anime DVDs for my nephew. I even scored the complete run of some of the old television shows my Mom and Dad like. I don't know who I'll give the jewelry to, but it's nice enough to keep until the right person or occasion comes along."

"Of course, none of this is for you," Max said drily.

"Some of it is, sure," Doc said. "They've got stuff down there that I haven't seen for sale anywhere else."

"Did you manage to get any of the information I sent you after?" Max said.

"Sure I did," Doc said, acting slightly injured. "I'm not sure how much good it will do you, though. First of all, a lot of them go by nicknames like Big Buddha or the Dark Prince, which probably aren't the names they're registered under. I thought of trying to follow them back to their rooms, but with the crowds and the elevator situation, tailing them won't be all that easy."

"Did you even try?"

"I tried a couple times, but both times they headed for the bar and not their rooms," Doc said. "What's more, from what I overheard of their conversations, most of them have a pack of people staying in their rooms to run down extra inventory as needed, so I'm not sure that we'd ever find a time when the rooms were empty that we could crack them."

"Okay. That's it," Max said, getting to his feet. "I want you to man the Patch for me for a while."

"Where are you going?" Doc said.

"I'm going to check out this convention myself," Max said, gathering up the badge that Allen and Alexis had given him.

"But I think the Dealers' Room is closed now," Doc protested.

"I'm not thinking about the Dealers' Room," Max said. "I want to take a cruise through the whole convention and see exactly what's going on. I still think there's a way to make money of this damn event, and I'm going to try to figure out what it is."

It was early afternoon the next day before Max let himself back in the Briar Patch.

Dropping a couple bags of purchases on the floor, he flopped down on the bed and heaved a deep sigh.

"That," he said, "is one hell of a convention going on out there."

"You'll notice I'm not giving you the 'Where have you been' greeting that I got," Doc said, looking up from the book he was reading.

"Yeah, well a couple of those bimbos Alexis was complaining about invited me to a room party," Max said. "One thing led to another, and it took a while."

"I see you found the Dealers' Room," Doc said, glancing at the bags.

"Yes, and you were right. They have some incredible things down there," Max said. "Some of it is flat out irresistible."

"Well, for your information, while you were out

the team had a little pow-wow," Doc said, putting his book aside. "The consensus seems to be that we should call it quits. There's no real score here worth our time, and we seem to be spending more than we're making. We'll write it off to experience and know not to come back next year."

Max sat up on the bed and gave him a grin.

"I wouldn't be too sure of that if I were you," he said.

"Why not?"

"I told you I'd find an angle, and I did," Max said.

"What've you got?" Doc said.

"Well, at that room party I mentioned, I got to chatting with a couple of the convention organizers," Max said, lying back down. "We'll be back next year, all right, but working for the convention as Security Consultants. That gets us free memberships and rooms, as well as a hefty fee. It'll be a different kind of con job for us, but it gives us an excuse to come back."

editor's note: There is a sad aspect to this amusing story. It first appeared in August 2008 in Here Be Dragons, *a collection of stories set at one of Bob's favorite conventions, DragonCon in Atlanta. The day after he emailed it Bob died peacefully, but very unexpectedly at his home in New Orleans.*